The Rebel Guardian

Other Books by Lexi Blake

ROMANTIC SUSPENSE

Masters and Mercenaries
The Dom Who Loved Me
The Men With The Golden Cuffs
A Dom is Forever
On Her Master's Secret Service
Sanctum: A Masters and Mercenaries Novella
Love and Let Die
Unconditional: A Masters and Mercenaries Novella
Dungeon Royale
Dungeon Games: A Masters and Mercenaries Novella
A View to a Thrill
Cherished: A Masters and Mercenaries Novella
You Only Love Twice
Luscious: Masters and Mercenaries~Topped
Adored: A Masters and Mercenaries Novella
Master No
Just One Taste: Masters and Mercenaries~Topped 2
From Sanctum with Love
Devoted: A Masters and Mercenaries Novella
Dominance Never Dies
Submission is Not Enough
Master Bits and Mercenary Bites~The Secret Recipes of Topped
Perfectly Paired: Masters and Mercenaries~Topped 3
For His Eyes Only
Arranged: A Masters and Mercenaries Novella
Love Another Day
At Your Service: Masters and Mercenaries~Topped 4
Master Bits and Mercenary Bites~Girls Night
Nobody Does It Better
Close Cover
Protected: A Masters and Mercenaries Novella
Enchanted: A Masters and Mercenaries Novella
Charmed: A Masters and Mercenaries Novella
Taggart Family Values

Treasured: A Masters and Mercenaries Novella
Delighted: A Masters and Mercenaries Novella

Masters and Mercenaries: The Forgotten
Lost Hearts (Memento Mori)
Lost and Found
Lost in You
Long Lost
No Love Lost

Masters and Mercenaries: Reloaded
Submission Impossible
The Dom Identity
The Man from Sanctum
No Time to Lie
The Dom Who Came in from the Cold, Coming February 21, 2023

Butterfly Bayou
Butterfly Bayou
Bayou Baby
Bayou Dreaming
Bayou Beauty
Bayou Sweetheart
Bayou Beloved, Coming March 28, 2023

Lawless
Ruthless
Satisfaction
Revenge

Courting Justice
Order of Protection
Evidence of Desire

Masters Of Ménage (by Shayla Black and Lexi Blake)
Their Virgin Captive
Their Virgin's Secret
Their Virgin Concubine
Their Virgin Princess
Their Virgin Hostage
Their Virgin Secretary
Their Virgin Mistress

The Perfect Gentlemen (by Shayla Black and Lexi Blake)
Scandal Never Sleeps
Seduction in Session
Big Easy Temptation
Smoke and Sin
At the Pleasure of the President

URBAN FANTASY

Thieves
Steal the Light
Steal the Day
Steal the Moon
Steal the Sun
Steal the Night
Ripper
Addict
Sleeper
Outcast
Stealing Summer
The Rebel Queen
The Rebel Guardian

LEXI BLAKE WRITING AS SOPHIE OAK

Texas Sirens
Small Town Siren
Siren in the City
Siren Enslaved
Siren Beloved
Siren in Waiting
Siren in Bloom
Siren Unleashed
Siren Reborn

Nights in Bliss, Colorado
Three to Ride
Two to Love
One to Keep
Lost in Bliss

The Rebel Guardian

Outlaw: A Thieves Series, Book 2

Lexi Blake

The Rebel Guardian
Outlaw: A Thieves Novel, Book 2
Lexi Blake

Published by DLZ Entertainment LLC
Copyright 2022 DLZ Entertainment LLC
Edited by Chloe Vale
ISBN: 978-1-942297-81-9

This is a work of fiction. Names, places, characters and incidents are the product of the author's imagination and are fictitious. Any resemblance to actual persons, living or dead, events or establishments is solely coincidental.

Acknowledgments

The Rebel Queen had a deep grounding in the idea of losing time, of the world seeming to tip on its axis and the heroine finds she's been left behind. Kelsey seems to handle things well in that book, but you'll discover as you read her story that no mother handles this well. Some just hide it better. As with all books, I start out thinking these are just stories and somehow they reveal my soul. While I'd meant to write the twist of the royals losing twelve years for a very long time, actually getting into the ins and outs of the story meant confronting some of my own feelings. I don't think I would have written these books the same way had I been in my twenties or thirties. I think it took a fifty-year-old version of me to truly understand how time is so precious, how it seems to slip away. My work over the course of the last few years seems to revolve around time and memory. My kids are adults now, and it seemed to happen so quickly. I look back and wish I'd understood how much those years would mean, how amazing it was to be in those moments with them. This year I was forced to deal with my own mortality and the fact that the world can change very quickly and we're left trying to navigate without a map. But what we do have are the people we love, the ones who love us. They can reach out a hand and pull us up and though we might not know where we are going, we do not have to go alone. Time will keep marching forward. We cannot stop it. But we can make memories, hold hands, ride this wave to the end—always with the ones we love.

To those I still have time with
To those I still have memories of
I love you all

Acknowledgments

Sign up for Lexi Blake's newsletter
and be entered to win a $25 gift certificate
to the bookseller of your choice.

Join us for news, fun and exclusive content
including free Thieves short stories.

There's a new contest every month!

Go to www.LexiBlake.net to subscribe.

Chapter One

"Hey, Mom. You ready? Eddie's packed up all our sh…stuff, and he says he feels better and is ready to work his magic." Fenrir strode into my room, a backpack on one broad shoulder.

Five days ago he'd been nine and Eddie—our butler/all-around keeper—would run behind him in the magnificent apartment we lived in, trying to make sure the kiddo kept his pants on.

And now he stood before me, a young man. Technically an adult, though I thought it would take me a while to process that hard truth.

I had to force a smile on my face because if I didn't, Fen would see the depths of my pain, and he didn't need that. He needed a mom who loved him, who was happy to see him as he was today. Not one who longed desperately to turn back time and never have gone into that painting. "Almost good to go. I'm not taking much. Your dad promised he'll take me shopping when we get to Atlanta."

I needed that shopping trip since I didn't have much. I hadn't exactly packed for the excursion to the outer planes, and my condo full of clothes and shoes was now occupied by a bunch of witches who'd taken over the supernatural world, including the building I'd planned to raise my kids in.

I'd had to shut out every emotion that flooded my system the minute we'd come back through the painting and we'd realized that twelve years had passed here on the Earth plane. In our time, it had been mere days. Not even a week. We'd expected to return to a familiar world, to hold our children close and be happy to be home.

Instead, we'd found our world utterly changed and our places in it dangerous.

It had been less than twenty-four hours from the time we'd found ourselves in that basement staring down at the wanted posters to walking into the city of Frelsi, located deep inside a mountain on the northernmost part of Iceland. But it felt like I'd aged years.

My wolf, the one I'd finally properly integrated with, was rattling around inside me. She was not handling the situation as well as my human self was, and it was getting harder and harder to keep her in check.

I needed to see Trent.

Fenrir—the little wolf I'd adopted years before—was twenty-one years old. He looked more like his wolf now. Big, predatory, dangerous. But I could still see the little boy who'd just wanted someone to love him.

"I doubt you'll need a parka where we're going. The primals keep it pretty warm in their nest." Fen leaned against the dresser as I checked over my pack one last time. "Did you talk to Lee?"

Oh, I'd definitely talked to Lee Donovan-Quinn. Lee had changed, too. He'd been one of my favorite people as a kid, one of the first people I'd really connected with and for some of the strangest reasons. "I'm still processing the fact that he's a latent vampire. Is the king sure? How did he not know? It's not like he didn't live with Lee for eleven years."

I'd been hit with so much change in the course of a few days that I was still trying to keep up. The kids were adults and warriors, and they'd spent the majority of the last decade off plane training to fight. Fenrir was in love with the queen's daughter, Evangeline, and apparently he was also at war with a whole bunch of wolves who were either pissed with him because he wouldn't assume their throne or afraid that he would.

And Lee—little Lee, whose small body housed my father's soul—was now big Lee, and he loved a lot of people because he didn't discriminate when it came to sex. He would turn into a vampire when he died, which could be any day now, from what I'd heard. He was every bit as reckless an adult as he'd been a child.

I'd asked him if he wanted to come with me to Atlanta. Beyond Fenrir, I was most concerned with Lee. He'd turned me down and said he was needed here.

Fen ran a hand over his shaggy hair, shoving it back. "Apparently puberty has something to do with it, though I got the feeling the king has always had his suspicions. Lee is being perfectly annoying about it. He's going to be an obnoxious vampire. I hope he's an academic and his primary skill turns out to be math or something. A supercharged Lee will be unbearable. I wonder how many years it will be before he stops whining about food. He hasn't even turned and he's already worried about missing pizza."

Fen and Lee had a whole deep, familial relationship I hadn't been a part of. They bickered like brothers. It was the relationship I'd wanted them to have, but the fact that I hadn't seen it bloom made my heart ache.

I had to stay calm.

"When we get there, will you be able to cry, Mom?" Fen asked quietly. When I looked up at him, his expression had turned serious. "When you see Dad, will it be safe enough for you?"

I stopped, closing my eyes and forcing myself to be still. This was one of the reasons why I'd skipped breakfast this morning. I hadn't been certain I could sit down with the royals and the kids and not lose my shit. I'd finally found the one thing that could squash my often never-ending appetite. Sorrow. Deep and aching loss. Well, I'd also had a little morning sickness, but I couldn't think about the fact that I was pregnant right this second. It was all too much. "I can't do this right now, Fen."

If I let the emotion out, the wolf would come, too. It had been a while since I'd felt this deep need—to either fight or fuck—and I wasn't doing either here.

"It's okay to be upset. I think the queen's already lost it a couple of times. Lee's worried about her." Fen moved over to sit on the bed I'd slept in the night before. "He thinks she might try to fix things."

That sounded like the queen. Zoey Donovan-Quinn wasn't the type to simply accept bad things happening to the people around her. I knew better. Also, Zoey didn't lose her mind from time to time and threaten to wipe out the people around her because she had no control. "There's no fixing this. Your papa saw it coming a long time ago. The queen probably thinks she's in the wrong timeline or something, but I know now we were always going to end up here."

"It would have been nice if Gray had found a way to give us a heads-up." There was no mistaking the hint of bitterness in Fen's tone.

"It doesn't work that way. Please tell me what he's done to hurt you." I set the pack down and faced my son.

I had twelve years of family drama to catch up on. The apparent rift between my demon prophet husband, Grayson Sloane, and Fenrir was one thing I couldn't afford to avoid dealing with.

I wanted to know why Gray hadn't contacted me yet, where he was and if he'd missed me or if he'd moved on.

Because this was his baby I was carrying.

I'd been transported to the outer planes a few days ago, and that act along with the royals falling in as well had fulfilled one of the prophecies that my life seemed to revolve around. I'd fallen into Myrddin's trap—the trap my dark prophet husband had been warning me about for years.

It turned out the trap was a painting, and now I understood why I'd never been a big art fan. Somewhere in the back of my head I'd always known fine art would fuck up my life.

When we'd returned to our plane, we discovered twelve years had passed. The pain was so overwhelming I wasn't sure I would be able to breathe if I let it wash over me. I worried that pain was a tidal wave that would drown me in it, the fury of the water stripping me of my every defense.

I'd walked into a time where Myrddin had taken over the supernatural world and turned my best friend into something twisted and evil, where my son was an adult who'd grown up without me and he didn't call Grayson Sloane Dad, where everything had flipped and I was reeling. I needed my defenses.

"It's nothing he did. He hasn't been around a lot in the last couple of years." Fen's shoulders shrugged. "I will certainly call him Papa if that's what you want."

"Why won't anyone talk to me about this?" I asked the question quietly because I was worried about the answer. Fenrir had been upbeat the whole time we'd been here. When I'd briefly talked to Trent on the phone, he'd been cagey with me. When I'd asked Lee Donovan-Quinn, he'd changed the subject.

Of course he'd changed the subject by telling me he was a latent vampire. As diversions went, it was a good play.

"It's complicated," Fen replied quietly. "Honestly, I don't understand everything that happened. It wasn't one thing. After Papa started descending, he changed. He's not cruel or mean. He's simply distant, and he's gone for long periods of time. Trent is my dad. Christopher and Gray have become…helpful male role models."

Christopher was Fen's biological father. He'd been accidentally killed when Fen was very young, and no one had suspected he was a latent vampire. When he'd turned, he hadn't had the king around. Fen's family had been on the run, and they'd hidden behind wards that stopped Daniel Donovan from sensing the vampire's rising. So Christopher had turned, and he'd done what almost all vampires did in the first days of a turn. He'd killed. He'd killed his wife and would likely have killed Fenrir if Fen hadn't run. "He's still with the primals? You see him from time to time?"

"I didn't for many years," Fen admitted. "When we were on the run, we didn't get back to the Earth plane a lot. When we did, the primals often gave us sanctuary. My biological father is doing well. He's even taken a companion, and she's wonderful. I think she's helped him find some peace with what happened."

There was a knock and before I could call out, Fen had the door open and Casey was walking through. "I am ready to get back to civilization, my brother." He slapped Fen's hand in some familiar greeting before glancing my way. "The primals have the best Internet. It's hard here. Because we're in a mountain. Behind twelve million wards. Also, not a lot of Internet connections on the coast of Iceland."

Casey Lane was a vampire, a young academic who'd become part of my team over the last few years. He'd also been my BFF's boyfriend when I'd left. My BFF who'd gone Dark Willow on me and seemed to be happily sitting at Myrddin's side. As a vampire, his appearance hadn't changed at all.

So why did he look older to me?

"Kelsey, it's so freaking good to have you back." He walked right up to me and wrapped his arms around me. "I know I've said it a million times in the last twenty-four hours, but it's true."

I held myself apart because if I gave up a single brick of my wall, it would crumble to the ground.

Casey stepped back, his expression turning blank as though he knew I couldn't handle anything else right now.

But then Casey was an academic like my first mentor, Marcus Vorenus, who could always sense my emotional state.

Casey had matured in the years I'd been gone, and it seemed he'd truly come into his power.

"Eddie is almost ready for us to go. You don't have long to wait." Casey said the words evenly, and I realized he could feel how close to the edge I was. He wouldn't have twelve years before. He'd honed his powers in the years I'd been gone. I had to wonder what else had happened to him during that time. "We need to have a long talk. I worried that I wouldn't see you again, but that doesn't mean I haven't kept meticulous records for you. I've got a report on pretty much everything that has happened in the last twelve years here on the Earth plane. When we get to Atlanta, I'll get you a laptop and send them to you so you can read the details, but there's some stuff that's personal and you need to hear it from me."

I nodded, grateful that Casey had been on top of things. We'd already had one debrief, and I was sure we would spend a lot of time talking about what had happened over the last few years. He'd told me that my assistant, Justin, had been killed in the initial attack, but Henri and Hugo had survived. I'd been able to see them the night before.

Henri Jacobs and Hugo Wells were academics who, along with Casey, formed the vampire portion of my team. Justin had been my assistant and I felt bad for him. He'd been young for a vampire. He should have had hundreds of years of life, but Myrddin had taken that from him.

Casey had given me the updates on my mom and brothers, too.

The one thing Casey had avoided talking about was the situation with Liv. I'd let it go the night before because I'd still been reeling, but we had to face the fact that Liv had tried to take the royal group prisoner, and she'd been willing to play dirty to get the job done. But when we got to Atlanta, I intended to have a long discussion about what was going on with my bestie.

Casey glanced over at the backpack I'd set on the bed. "Is it in there?"

Casey was talking about the book, the one I'd brought back from the outer planes. The one I'd nearly died for. I nodded his way.

Fen took a deep breath, filling his nose. "Some of it's written in blood. And the binding is animal skin, but I don't recognize the species. It's not from this plane at all. I suspect it's never been here. It reeks of witch, but not Earth plane witches."

I pulled it out of the pack and offered it up to Fen. I knew a bit about the book I'd risked my life for, but I was curious what Fen could ascertain. "It originated on one of the outer planes. A witch plane called Arete."

Many of the outer planes held incredible supernatural civilizations, places where creatures who hid in shadows on the Earth plane rose up and dominated. On Arete, there were very few humans. It's a matriarchal society and witches rule.

They also like to collect prophecies, and that was what the book was all about. I hoped that one of the prophecies would lead us to the weapon that could take Myrddin down and place the proper king back on the throne.

And it would be good to not allow Myrddin to open the door to the Hell plane and let demons run wild here on Earth. That was pretty much what we thought he was going to do, and I intended to stop him.

Fen frowned down at the book. "I don't like it."

I sighed. "Yeah, it's got a lot of wards."

"It doesn't want me to even look at it," Casey said, putting a hand to his stomach. "I'm feeling some nausea. I didn't think I could feel that anymore. How are you touching it?"

I ran a hand over the thick cover, and the book sent out a pulse of warmth. The book liked me. The book wanted to stay with me. "According to experts, the book has something of a mind, or rather a will, of its own. It knows what it's supposed to do. It also isn't into dudes. That's a whole witches of Arete thing. They wrote it and they don't think much of males."

Men couldn't read the words.

Fen took a step back. "Then why do we think the primals will know anything about it? They're all male and all from this plane."

"Because the primals protect the Council's library." Casey got his academic on. He was so much more serious than the awkward man boy I'd known a few days before. He'd matured in a way that only came about from trauma. "The primals have spent millennia curating knowledge. They have access to the world's most arcane information, and that includes some volumes we've collected from other planes."

"I thought the academics kept those records." History tended to be the academics' realm.

"Records, yes," Casey replied. "But the arcane library has always been kept in a primal nest. This is for several reasons, one being the Council sometimes finds itself involved in wars, and we all know what that did to the humans." He waited as though he wanted us to acknowledge his level of smarty pantsness. "Come on, guys. The Library of Alexandria?"

He should remember he was dealing with wolves. I'm going to be honest. I love my people. Wolves are all kinds of awesome, but we do not tend to rank high on the intellectual scale. That's not to say we're not smart. I've solved many a mystery using logic. But ask me to search my brain for some piece of ancient history and you're going to be waiting for a long time.

I was betting my son was pretty much the same.

"Uh, it was a library that got destroyed in a war?" Fen tried.

I probably should have felt guilty about that. He hadn't had a proper education, but honestly, he also wouldn't have had that with me around. Fen was never going to discuss human history around a dinner table.

Casey sighed. "Yes. It got destroyed in a war and set humanity back centuries. We don't want to do that in our world, so the primals protect the knowledge vampires have accrued over time. We'll be meeting with Rufus. He's the leader of the primals."

"And they live in Atlanta?" It seemed like an odd place to stash a big group of scary, mostly ancient vampires.

"They relocated the nest when the Council moved to Dallas," Casey explained. "The primals originally had a couple of nests in Europe, but after the king took down the old Council, they chose to move to be closer. They have two nests in the States—New York City and Atlanta. Both have extensive underground spaces the colonies use. They're, of course, far larger spaces than the human world acknowledges exists. The nest is protected with the usual wards, though the primals have other ways of protecting themselves. The library is kept in Atlanta. The New York underground floods too often and far too many people know about it. Atlanta was deemed the safest place."

"So we're hoping one of these scary-looking dudes is going to be able to point us in the right direction when it comes to a prophecy from another plane." I wasn't convinced, but I was willing to try. Mostly I wanted to see Trent. I wanted my husband's arms around me. I wanted to look him in the eyes and tell him how sorry I was to have left him alone with our son.

I wanted him to tell me what had gone wrong with Gray.

My wolf wanted to smell him, to touch him, to know he was safe and still ours.

"They're smart, Mom. Super smart, and I know they look scary but they're cool," my son assured me. "I spent a lot of time with them the last couple of years, especially when we had to hide out from the fuc...from some vampires who were after Evan. Trent stashed her with the primals while Rhys, Lee, and I took down a whole group of vamps who were selling companions."

One of the repercussions of the king being gone for twelve years and Myrddin taking over his throne had been him throwing out all the rules Daniel had put in place when it came to vampires taking companions. Daniel had stopped the enslavement of the class of supernatural creatures known as companions. As superpowers go, the companions got the short end of the stick. Oh, sure once they'd been known as the warrior women Amazons and their DNA shared angelic properties, but the vampires mostly used them as convenient, pretty blood banks. Companion blood makes a vampire stronger and faster than a vampire drinking regular old human blood. It also turns the vamp into an addict who gets awfully sick if he can't get his fix, but those vamps keep coming back for more.

And many of them didn't give a crap about consent.

I was curious about how the companions were being treated in that nest. I wanted to make sure they weren't being forced to trade their bodies and blood for protection.

"How many did you kill?" I asked my son, who happened to be in love with a companion.

Fen shrugged. "My fair share."

"How many, Fenrir?" I needed him to understand he didn't have to hide from me. "And I know you kept count. Your father would have taught you that."

Trent understood the need for revenge and for marking the

occasion. I was sure beers had been handed out long before any human law would have allowed. But then we didn't live by those.

"Fourteen, though I think I should count the one who ran from me right onto Lee's stake. I was going to rip his throat out. Lee got lucky." Fen's eyes went dark.

I put a hand on his arm. "Good. I don't care if they're using persuasion and the companions seem happy. If the companion didn't agree to the relationship, it's rape, and the vampire deserves to die."

"There she is." Casey looked to Fen. "I told you. She won't judge you for anything. She'll always be on your side, and when you fuck up, she'll help you with that, too. Also, I know Trent's given you this rosy picture of how delicate your mom is, but she can and will cuss up a storm."

"Trent did what?" No one knew better how not delicate I was than my werewolf husband. While Gray always tried to treat me like I was breakable, Trent would toss me onto the front lines with him because he wouldn't want anyone else watching his back.

Of the two approaches to marriage with me, there was definitely one I preferred, though Gray had been coming around to my way of thinking.

I was worried I'd taken one step forward and twelve years back with my demon husband.

Fen's lips curled up. "Dad said I might want to watch my language around my mother. Out of respect."

"Huh. I should think about that. I'm worried about this one's first words." I put a hand on my belly and then realized it might be weird for Fen.

"Dad's going to be so excited." Fen got down on one knee, his face lit with joy. "Hey, little bro. We're all waiting for you. Stop making Mom sick. We need her to kick some ass."

Or it wouldn't be weird at all.

"I'm hoping I don't have to kick ass for a while." In my defense, when I'd gotten pregnant the world had seemed pretty sweet to me. The Council had been rock solid, and we'd made some real inroads to get the king to meet with the demons and renew our contracts. The day I'd married my superhot guys and asked Dev Quinn to perform a fertility ritual on our wedding night, I'd deemed it as perfect a time as I would get.

Now I had to face the fact that the world had changed, was infinitely more dangerous, and I couldn't sit this one out because I was pregnant.

I was the *Nex Apparatus*, the Council's death machine, and it was my job to find a way to put the world to rights, and it started with that book.

There was a brief knock and then Eddie was walking through the door. Our demon butler still wore a suit even in the wilds of Iceland. He carried a small tray with a mug and a Danish on it.

"My mistress, I've brought you some ginger tea. I was hoping you were feeling better," Eddie said, looking me over. "Perhaps we should put this trip off. I can go to Atlanta and bring Master Trent back here for you. Frelsi is safe, and there is a midwife. His Grace is also here."

I was sure having a fertility god around who could put a hand on me and tell me if my baby was okay would be comforting to all of us, but like I said, I had a job to do. Skipping breakfast this morning because I had my head in the toilet had obviously worried Eddie. He wasn't used to me passing on food. Luckily my gut was calmer now, and though I didn't deeply want a pastry, I could eat one.

I took the Danish and had a big bite. I knew it should taste delicious, but it was sawdust in my mouth. Still, I forced myself to eat. "I'm good, Eddie. I want to go. I need to talk to the primals, and Casey assures me we'll be safe down there." I had to wonder how comfy this nest thing would be, but it didn't truly matter. It was underground, so I wasn't expecting luxury. "I'm ready to go."

Fen gave me a thumbs-up. "I'll go get Evan."

"Fen, are you sure? Her mom just got back. Maybe you should stay here with her." I didn't want to leave him. I wanted to grab him with both hands and never let him out of my sight again, but honestly, I was feeling guilty for asking Lee to come with us. I hadn't thought about it at the time. I'd only thought about how much I wanted to get to know this Lee.

I was sure Zoey did, too. I was sure the idea of not being with her daughter would make her ache, and she'd ached enough.

"No." Fen was back to frowning and looking worried. "I want to go with you. I was planning on joining Dad no matter what. And Evan comes with me."

The wolf was back in the house. Jealous and possessive. I would have to talk to Trent about that, too. However, I knew better than to try to talk down crazy wolf hormones. "All right. Then it's time to head out."

Eddie nodded. "I shall gather our things. We'll be in Atlanta in no time."

And then I would start looking for answers.

Chapter Two

The world shimmered around me, and the sunshine we'd been in turned to a deep gloom. Where my skin had been warm, a delicious cool wave caressed me and I could smell both wet stone and burning wood.

We were in some kind of cave.

Yep. This was pretty much what I'd expected. Dark, dank, a bit tight.

Fen turned my way, his hand already in Evangeline's. "You and Dad take whatever time you need. We'll be here."

I was confused. Somehow I'd expected Trent to be standing here waiting for me, but we were alone in this alcove, the world eerily quiet around us. Evan had a small flashlight in her hands, and she pointed it at the stony ground beneath us. She was the only one who would likely need it. My eyes were already adjusting, and I could see a hint of light in the distance. Casey had already taken a few steps away from us, and I could see he stood on what appeared to be the top of steps that went even further down.

"Where is your dad?" I ignored the hurt that nestled in my chest. No one knew where Gray was, but I'd talked to Trent and I'd expected him to be waiting here for me.

Eddie's hand was in mine again, the feel of his callused fingers comforting against my palm. "Mistress, Master Trent requested privacy for your reunion. I'm taking you to him now, and I'll leave you there. He knows how to contact me when it's time to bring you both back here. I promise I shall have your rooms in all readiness. You'll find the primals are good hosts and look forward to meeting with you."

"Don't do anything I wouldn't," Fen said with a grin. "Or at least don't tell me about it."

"Yes, don't be like Fen. Trent would be disappointed. Fen won't do anything," Evan complained. "So don't listen to him."

The fact that they hadn't hit the sheets yet seemed to bug the queen's daughter. I was happy about it because that purity seemed to be the only reason Dev Quinn hadn't lost his damn mind when he found out about my son's relationship with his daughter.

"Someday, baby," Fen promised as the world shifted around me again.

I didn't need to hear that, but I should get used to it. Trent didn't have any issues talking about sex. It was a wolf thing. Of course I'd been raised by uptight humans, so it was an adjustment. Over the last few years I'd gotten totally used to talking about my own sex life, but I'd thought I'd had years before I would have to talk to Fen about sex. I'd been planning to ease into it. No such luck.

Warmth hit me and a shocking bright light. We weren't in the caves anymore. Sunlight flooded my world and a sweet wind moved over my skin.

"I will see you soon, my mistress. It is a joy to have you back," Eddie said, and he squeezed my hand before he was gone again.

I blinked in the bright light and allowed my eyes to adjust yet again. I'd gone from Frelsi, where magic kept the city warm, to the chilly depths of an underground nest to… I wasn't sure where I was, but it was warm and there was water nearby and a small cabin. Trees rose around me, and I realized the water was more like a bayou.

That was the moment I knew someone was watching me.

The world went watery because Trent stood near the cabin. His beard had grown out and his hair was longer. He looked far more like the wolf he was than the soldier he'd presented to the world twelve years before.

I stood there, our gazes locked.

Twelve years. He'd taken in Fenrir because we were going to

make a family together, and I'd left him alone. He'd had to raise not only Fen, but Lee and Rhys and Evan. He'd gone from single and free one day to raising a pack on the run, protecting and sheltering them.

From what I could tell the only person he'd been able to rely on had been Sasha Federov, a vampire. While Sasha had no doubt been an amazing general for their little army, he would also be dead at least half the day.

Years will pass. Your wolf will howl but he will remain steadfast.

Gray's prophecy had told me that we would be standing here, Trent and I. We would be standing here with the years between us, my wolf's steadfast faith still binding us.

I knew that because I could feel him. Even with yards between us, I could feel Trent's love.

I had never seen my wolf cry, but there were tears rolling down that face I loved.

That was when my walls broke down. Trent was here, and we'd lost so much. We'd lost all that time, and he was still here with me. I recognized somewhere in the background that the old me would have wondered if he'd brought me out here so he could explain that he'd moved on.

But I'd meshed my soul with his, and I trusted and believed in him completely.

He was my mate.

The wall crumbled because he was here.

The world went watery, and I heard someone scream. Me. I let the pain out.

Twelve years. Twelve years. Myrddin had taken twelve fucking years. My son's childhood. Twelve years of my marriage, of love between us. Gray was gone because I'd been trapped.

Olivia. He'd taken my best friend.

He'd killed people I knew, people who had lives and loves and should have had more of both. All gone because one wizard wanted power.

He'd scattered our families to the winds without a care for any of us.

I started to fall but Trent was there before I could hit the ground. His big arms went around me and through my wracking sobs, I could smell him. That woodsy, wolfy smell that felt safe, that brought me home, hit my soul, and I wrapped myself around him.

"I'm so sorry." I was sorry I'd gone into that painting, sorry I'd spent the four days I'd been on the outer planes not thinking much about him. That was the worst. I'd practically viewed it as nothing more than a job. I'd felt inconvenienced, while his world had been turned upside down and he'd lost everything.

He squeezed me so tight. "I missed you. I missed you every second of every day for twelve years, Kelsey. But you're here now. Fuck it all, you're here. It's okay now, baby. You howl all you need to. We're alone. No one else can see you. Let it all out."

He understood that I couldn't lose it in front of our son. I couldn't let my pain out because it might drown me, and I was a creature who could take the whole world down with her. I'd needed to stay calm until he was here with me, until my mate could hold me and ease me.

I screamed my pain. I shouted and sobbed and let my wolf howl.

At some point, Trent picked me up and carried me back to the cabin, cradling me to his strong chest while I shuddered with an odd relief.

I could breathe again because he was here and whole, and we could make things right. We could do so much as long as we were together, this man and I.

He carried me across the yard, up the steps and into the small cabin. When he set me on my feet, he kissed my forehead. "I'll get you a beer."

I shook my head. It was a good bet that I would want something to drink, but that would have to wait. "I can't."

I hadn't told him, had asked Fenrir and the others not to tell him. This was a moment between the two of us.

It should have been between the three of us.

His expression shuttered as though he was trying to figure out how the world had shifted and I didn't want a beer. Then his hands came up to my shoulders. "Holy shit, it worked. Baby, are you pregnant? Did Quinn verify it?"

I nodded and those tears were back in my eyes. I wasn't used to crying this much, and not for such complex reasons. Those tears were both anger and sorrow and relief and joy. Even in this horror, I found some joy. "Yes, and it's a boy. Trent, you know…"

He shook his head. "He's ours. Yours and mine and Gray's.

Come here. I wanted to give you time, but I have to…I have to kiss you, Kelsey. I have to hold you."

He needed to do more than that. "I'm not a delicate princess, Wilcox. I'm a wolf, and I need my mate. I was told you managed to turn down a couple of good shots. I need to show you why you waited."

His eyes immediately went dark, and a low growl came from the back of his throat. "That sounds like Lee. Fenrir would understand there were no fucking shots to be taken. There is one woman in all the planes for me. One."

His mouth came down on mine, and the world seemed to melt away.

There was no horror in this place. Nothing but him.

Somehow he found his way to a bed. I dropped my backpack close. Even in this intimate moment I didn't want the book too far away.

My clothes came off, some of them in a way that would be hard to wear them again unless Trent was handy with a needle. He kind of ripped them off, as though he couldn't stand to wait even a second to bring us skin to skin again.

He managed to get my bra off and then his mouth was on me, licking, sucking, and nipping in that way that sent my arousal right through the roof. Not that it already hadn't been there. It was mixed up with all the other emotions this wolf brought out in me.

I helped Trent get me out of the rest of my clothes, each of us desperate. Tugging and pulling and tossing the needless items away. Before I knew it, I was on my back and that wolf was naked and on top of me. Pure connection sizzled over my skin. Everywhere we touched seemed to come alive, crackling like electricity between us.

He didn't play around, didn't wait. He'd already waited far too long, and I didn't want him to. I was ready for him, ready for the hard thrust of his cock, for the bite of discomfort that came from him pushing his full length in without a pause.

His hands were in my hair, twisting slightly so I had to look him in the eyes. "I dreamed of this every fucking night."

I let my hands find his back, nails scoring him lightly. This was what I adored about fucking my wolf. My demon was always so careful with me, but Trent knew I needed to be a little out of control. I could handle it, wanted it so badly. The wolf inside me needed the tiniest bit of brutal passion, and Trent gave it to us.

His fangs were out slightly as he pulled back and thrust in again, moving the bed with the power of those hips. I couldn't help the moan that came from the back of my throat as Trent's cock glided over my sweet spot.

He fucked into me over and over, my legs going around his waist and holding him close.

Then every muscle in my body tightened as he sent me over the edge. I called out my mate's name and felt him spill himself inside me, the pleasure making my sight go fuzzy while the world became a softer, warmer place.

This was what I'd needed since the moment I found myself in a world I didn't understand.

Trent fell on top of me, holding not an ounce of his weight up. He pressed me into the bed, surrounding me with the feel of him, the smell of him.

I held my werewolf and proved to him I was finally home.

* * * *

"And he's happy?"

A few hours later, my head lay against Trent's chest, and I felt truly calm for the first time in days. "Yes. He's in love with Summer."

A chuckle went through my wolf. "I wish I'd been there to see how Quinn handled that. I would think he might be relieved because he was always worried Marcus would come after Evan, but I would also bet that he was still freaked out by it. I take it Summer was fully grown."

"She was, and she's gorgeous," I replied. "She looks like the queen's twin almost. And you're one hundred percent right. Quinn got all kinds of pissy about it, but Donovan was cool."

"The king has always been a more practical man when it came to the children."

I gasped and sat up, not bothering with the sheet that covered the comfy bed. "I forgot. I actually know something about the kids that you don't."

"Lee's a latent vamp?" Trent's lips curled up slightly, and he was the sexiest wolf in the world.

"How did you know that? I just found out."

"I do have a cell phone, baby." That grin did funny things to my heart. "Fen texted me, and then I got the news from Lee himself. I suspect Fen practically ran to the portal to send me the news. There's no cell service in Frelsi. We have mirrors we can use, but Fen claims they are... What's the word he uses? Sus. Mirrors are sus. So when he wants to talk, he uses the portal to Reykjavík. There's a bookstore that serves as a front for the portal. They check in quite regularly when I'm on assignment. We're used to being in contact."

Because they had formed a tight unit. They'd been forced to rely on each other.

In the hours since he'd brought me inside the cabin, I'd told him everything that had happened on the outer planes, but we hadn't gotten to the heart of what I wanted to know.

Now that it was here, I was scared of the answers.

Although I wasn't sure where *here* was. "Where are we? Eddie didn't tell me where we were going. Just said you would be here."

"We're in Southern Louisiana. This is a cabin Gray bought a long time ago. Don't worry. It's a safe house. We're absolutely secure here." Trent's hand brushed over my thigh as he shifted so he was on his side, his head held up on his other hand like he was a deliciously hot centerfold. "We're in an unincorporated part of Papillon Parish. There's a small town not far from here with a truly excellent restaurant. I go there and I sit out on this big porch they have, and I think of you while I eat gumbo and jambalaya and drink a beer. Though I haven't been here in a while because a few years ago Fenrir scared the crap out of some locals, and now they think there's this weird Cajun werewolf thing running around. I couldn't exactly tell them that he was a regular old normal werewolf."

"He's not." I smiled because I could see Fen running around the bayou in that massive body of his and not knowing how to properly hide from the humans. He'd been that way when he was a little boy, a tiny human body that contained a massive wolf.

"No, he's not," Trent conceded with a sigh. "None of them are normal, so I'm not surprised it turns out Lee is a latent vampire. Honestly, it explains a lot. He's the single most reckless kid I've ever met. Keeping him alive has been the hardest thing I've ever done." Trent went quiet for a moment. "That's a lie. Being without you was the hardest thing. Damn, you're gorgeous, baby. You have no idea how hard it was to not get on a plane last night. Only logic saved me. Rufus pointed out that it would take longer to fly than it would to simply wait for Eddie to bring you to me."

Rufus was the leader of the Atlanta primal nest and apparently a fan of logic.

"I know. I sat up most of last night wishing I could be with you. And then I finally managed to sleep and when I woke up, I yakked for a long time." I'd talked to Quinn a bit before we'd left. He'd explained that because my pregnancy was facilitated with a pretty heavy fertility ritual, I should look forward to rapid onset of all the fun, you're-carrying-another-life-inside-you symptoms.

Trent's hand went to my belly. "How are you feeling right now?"

It was time to get to the rough part of this reunion. I'd been told the good stuff. My mom was okay. She was still in Dallas with my brothers. Jamie still worked for the Rangers and Nate had joined him. Jamie had married his forensic expert and they had two young children who were also protected by his status with the Rangers. Nate had married a shifter named Jeanie and he was about to become a dad.

I had a niece and a nephew I'd never met and one more on the way. My brothers were moving through their lives without me.

"Lost. A little broken." I took a long breath and got to what I'd needed to ask since the moment Fen had called his papa Gray. "What happened to Gray?"

Trent's eyes closed and he laid back. "Nothing at first. He was our best shield. He ran a lot of interference for us those first few years. Gray dealt with Myrddin. He played the game well."

"He should have been with you. He shouldn't have been playing the game at all."

"No, baby. We needed him. Gray saved our asses many times. His position was important. As the dark prophet, Myrddin can't touch him."

"Then he should have walked in and cut the fucker's head off."

"Yeah, I don't think it works that way. Gray has some very specific rules surrounding him now. The same as Jacob, the Heaven plane's prophet. He isn't allowed to use his knowledge to specifically change things. All he can do is move pieces into place, and he's done that for us. He's the one who negotiated to get your brothers and mom protected status."

"But not the children. Not you."

"I wouldn't have taken it," Trent admitted. "Not that it would have been offered. No one would believe for a second that I would accept Myrddin taking the crown. You know that."

Like my father. Lee Owens had been the queen's guard when he'd been alive. When the old Council had taken the queen and Quinn into custody, they'd killed my father because he wouldn't stop attempting to protect her. They'd known Lee Owens wouldn't make the practical choice to allow their atrocities. He would fight and fight and fight.

Like Trent.

"I was always going to be on the rebel side of this war."

But I would bet he hadn't thought he would end up being dad to a whole group of kids. "Why didn't you hand the kids over to Neil Roberts? You and Sasha could have led an army. Albert and Eddie would have taken care of the kids, and Neil would have watched over them. He's practically their uncle."

Trent's brows came together. "Leave my son? Leave the children I've guarded since the day they were born? I was there when Lee and Rhys came into this world. The same for Evan, and I'd taken Fenrir into my home and my heart by that time. Leave them to someone else? Even someone I trusted? Never."

Well, Gray had gotten it right when he'd described that unnamed wolf in his prophecy. Steadfast. "I was just wondering how the war went in those first days."

"What you're doing is questioning my decisions and why I didn't murder Myrddin and install an academic at the head of the Council until the king got back."

I wasn't. But I kind of was. "Maybe."

He growled, a sound that went straight to my pussy even though he'd satisfied me thoroughly mere moments before. "There are times I sat up and wondered what a pain in my ass you would have been had you been here with me. At least as bad as Lee." He reached for my hand, his thumb tracing the lines of my palm. "It was pure chaos when Myrddin first took control. Gray insisted that we flee as quickly as possible. That was why Neil wasn't with us. Or Sarah, for that matter. Gray basically shoved me into the penthouse along with Eddie and we took the kids and Albert and ran. He made it clear that the children could not fall into Myrddin's hands. Not even for a second. He was particularly concerned with Lee. At the time I thought it was because Lee was human. Now I wonder."

I could answer that question. "Lee is one of two beings in all the planes who can wield the weapon that can kill Myrddin. So no, I wasn't truly asking you why you didn't try to assassinate him. It wouldn't have worked. I'm glad you didn't."

"You explained some of this last night, but I'm not sure I understand. I thought Lee was one of two who could kill him. What's this about a weapon?"

I glanced over to where my backpack sat. I was sure Trent had thought it was weird that I wouldn't be separated from the damn thing even when my mind should have been on sex. I'd made sure we hadn't left that pack in the other room.

Never leave The Path.

It was another of Gray's edicts, though I hadn't understood it was a book at the time.

"I told you I brought a book back," I began.

"Yes, the one with all the prophecies the witches have collected."

I'd told him about the book during our call the night before, but I hadn't gone into detail about what I'd found. "It contains the prophecies of the witches of Arete. That's a whole plane where witches dominate."

"We did not end up there," Trent replied. "Though we did manage to find a wolf plane. Very cold. Harsh. They have a hard pack organization I found distasteful, but we stayed for a bit and allowed Fen to learn some of their fighting techniques. I suspect the witch plane would be more comfortable."

"Not for you." I hadn't stepped onto the witch plane, but I'd heard enough about it. "It's a matriarchal society. Men are viewed as labor and sperm, from what I can tell. Even the book doesn't like men."

Trent sat up. "So why do you think this prophecy you read has anything to do with Myrddin? If it's like an Earth plane prophecy, I would assume it doesn't make itself plain."

It didn't. Prophecy is the same everywhere, it seems to me. It's overly pretentious and likes to fuck with a person's mind. But I had my reasons. "I told you about Dean Malone."

"Briefly." His hand moved over my skin like he was petting me, like he couldn't stand to not touch me.

I wanted that connection, too. I moved closer to him. I'd only had four days without his touch. He'd been starved for years. Wolves need touch, and the touch of a mate most of all. He'd been without, which was likely why he was thinner than he'd been. I intended to give him what he needed. Food and fucking. He would get a lot of both from me. "His mother was kidnapped and taken off plane by a Planeswalker demon."

"Yes. We were told to stay away from them," Trent explained. "When we decided to leave the Earth plane, Gray told us to avoid the Planeswalkers. Apparently if you ask them for a ride, your soul is the payment."

"Yeah, well, they don't mind kidnapping people either. They kidnapped Dean's mom and dragged her to a vampire plane. She was pregnant at the time, and that child grew up and studied witchcraft. He's quite good at it. The prophecy is about Dean, but I think it also refers to Lee and Myrddin. Myrddin believes that Lee and one other—a baby he sent off plane, according to Stewart—are the only beings in the universe who can kill him."

"I assure you if I get close enough, I can kill him," Trent replied.

"Don't even try. I'm not joking. I lived through a prophecy, and there was no getting around it. I firmly believe Myrddin's wrong about his interpretation. Probably because he used that fucker Stewart as his focal point." The magic Myrddin had worked wasn't so much prophecy as seeing into the future. It was a form of clairvoyance that became prophecy once it was spoken aloud. And Myrddin was interpreting what he'd seen all kinds of wrong. "The prophecy concerning Dean and Lee talks about a weapon."

"That's what you want the primals to help with," Trent deduced.

"I've already given the prophecy to Henri and Hugo." I'd met with the academics the night before, and we'd talked about Marcus and everything that had happened. They would give me their thoughts when I returned to Frelsi. "I need the primals to look at it and see if they can figure out what this weapon is and where I should look for it.

Now tell me what's wrong with Gray."

Trent growled but he turned toward me, laying his head down on my lap. He took a long breath through his nose as though surrounding himself with my scent, our mingled scents. They would form a blanket of comfort around him. "After we ran, he needed to stay away in order to avoid leading Myrddin's forces to us. Like I said, he could protect your brothers. Both Nate and Jamie were willing to state they would stay out of the war."

"We should bring them to Frelsi. Once Myrddin knows for sure we're here, he'll use my brothers as a way to draw me out."

"No, he won't. He can't use them against you at all," Trent said, his tone going grave.

"Why wouldn't he..." The answer became crystal clear. "Tell me they didn't sign a contract."

"They didn't." The "they" portion was emphasized heavily.

The enormity of what had happened hit me. "Gray did."

"It was already signed by the time I spoke to him again. Sasha had moved us to New Zealand, and we'd been there a couple of months before Gray returned to us. We had a pretty big fight, and one that I regret now. I didn't realize how long it would be, how much this war would cost us. Deep down he did, though I understand he can't see everything. He was playing a bit fast and loose by protecting your family, but I suppose putting himself on the line made it acceptable to whoever judges these things."

Heaven. I was pretty sure it was Heaven who decided what a prophet—dark or light—got to do. No matter how much Hell likes to think of itself as this mighty, independent thing, I often wonder if they're not merely a recalcitrant child who serves their father's purpose. I wonder if Hell isn't a necessary thing because all beings must find a balance between their light and dark, and sometimes that means punishment.

I often think if Heaven chose, Hell would cease to be.

Unless someone took that choice away. Unless someone wanted to cut out the dominant plane. To tell Mommy and Daddy we're on our own now. That's what Myrddin was attempting to do. He planned to close off the Earth and Hell planes from the Heavenly planes, and then no interference could harm his plans.

I wasn't so sure about that, but I wasn't about to test the theory.

I got the feeling I hadn't heard the worst of it. I needed to know everything. "What all was part of this contract?"

Trent sighed and hugged me closer.

"Who is he working for?" I knew when one of my men didn't want to talk about a specific thing, it was probably bad news.

The grim look on Trent's face had me bracing myself for whatever he said next. "In order to protect your family, he has to descend at least once a month for a week of Earth plane time, and he must work as a focal point for Lucifer Morningstar. Sometimes it's more than once a month, but never for more than a week."

"I'm sorry, what?" Yep. It was bad.

"Don't get upset with me. I didn't sign that contract, Kelsey."

"No, Gray did, and now he's fucking working for Lucifer? Who thought that would go well?" I rolled out of bed and started looking for whatever clothes I had left.

Trent sat up, his gaze going stony. "Nicole was pregnant. Jamie had gotten her pregnant, and they'd just found out."

"Well then Jamie should have protected her. He should have wrapped Nicole up and figured out where you were and hidden with you." All I could think about was how nice and safe and happy Frelsi seemed to be.

"Kelsey, I couldn't have handled them. And I wouldn't even have known what to do with a bunch of humans on some of those planes we found ourselves on. Keeping Lee alive was hard enough. We didn't have a home most of the time. I have no idea what we would have done with a human infant. Gray did the best he could. I know we think he knows everything, but he was as lost as I was when you were gone. He was trying to protect your family the best he could. And me. He knew if Myrddin put Jamie or Nate up for public execution, I would have come running. I would have done it for you. Gray made sure that didn't happen. He made sure I could do the job I needed to do without worrying that I was letting you down."

I shook my head because this whole situation was fucked up. "He's working with Lucifer. With the literal devil himself, and you think I'm not let down?"

Trent's eyes went steely. "I didn't have a fucking say in that, Kelsey. Gray does what he thinks is right, and most of the time he doesn't ask for my input. Do you think I wasn't upset? He didn't consult me or I would have told him we would find another way. But quite frankly, at the time I was dealing with traumatized children and the fact that I had no idea if my mate was alive or dead, and I was holding on by a fucking thread."

I was handling this all wrong. I was losing my shit when Trent needed me to totally keep track of it. I took a long breath. "That is not a being I want in our lives. Lucifer Morningstar is as bad as it gets. I didn't want Gray working for his father, much less for Lucifer. How much damage is already done? Fen won't call him Papa."

Trent stood, and I knew he was upset with me because he started to look for his clothes. "Fen sees the world in black and white. He doesn't understand that Gray was trying to protect us all."

I had to point out some truths to my mate. "There are bounties on the kids' heads, so he didn't do a good job of it."

"He made certain Myrddin didn't send demons chasing us across the planes. As long as we were off plane, we were safe."

I stared at him because I didn't need to say a thing. Why the fuck hadn't they stayed off plane, then?

He shoved his legs into jeans, every movement a testament to how much I was annoying him. "You try to deal with a Green Man, a wolf king, a latent vampire, and Zoey Donovan-Quinn's daughter and see how long you can keep them from coming back to fight for their home and their people. I had to raise those kids. Me and Sasha. We're not sit-on-the-sidelines types. We had to teach them how to fight, and we always knew we would have to come back. Do you understand what's been going on here? What he's done to the other supernatural creatures? How many of us he's killed? He wiped out packs who wouldn't submit to him. Both here and across the globe. You know that pack in Italy you used to run with? It's gone. He wiped them out with a snap of his hand once he had some real power. You would have me cower and hide while my people—your people—are dying? While the great packs that my son should be leading are suffering? Well, my mate, I guess you don't know me as well as you should, and this reunion doesn't mean what I thought it did."

I was fucking up and hard. I'd been so careful around Fen, but I wasn't giving Trent any of the same consideration. He was my safe space and I let him have my every unfiltered opinion, and maybe that worked when I was there with him all the time. But there were years and years between us, years where he'd changed and I hadn't.

Years for him to idealize me.

I could prove him wrong about that in a few seconds.

Insecurity came down like the gates of a cage snapping into place. He'd waited for me, and I suddenly wasn't sure I was worth it.

"I'm sorry. I'm not handling this well." I didn't want to be so angry. He didn't deserve my anger. Honestly, until I talked to Gray and got his perspective, he didn't deserve my anger either.

"I should have known." He reached for his shirt, pulling it over his head. "I should have known you would come back and find flaws with every single thing I've done. I should have known this would go the way everything seems to fucking go lately."

Something was wrong. This wasn't Trent. Trent was the guy who calmed me down.

Of course, that had been Trent before I left him.

He stopped and closed his eyes as though trying to reset himself. When he opened them, he was calmer than before, but the disappointment was right there. "I'll call Eddie."

"We can stay for a while."

He was reaching for his cell. "I don't think that's a good idea. I think we should get to the point of your visit."

Guilt twisted through me. "It's not a visit, Trent. I'm home. I'm here and I'm not going anywhere. I'm sorry I'm not adjusting as quickly as I should and that I'm being a bitch. I was with you four days ago and you would have rolled your eyes at me and handed me a beer and told me to deal with it."

"Yeah, well, it's been longer for me, and having my mate tell me what a shitty father I've been hurts."

"That's not what I said." I moved toward him.

He shook his head. "It's what I heard. My ears changed. I could have handled that criticism twelve years ago, Kelsey, and hopefully I'll be able to handle it again someday when we're on stable ground, but for now it hurts."

I hadn't meant to hurt him. Not at all. I'd missed him. Even the short time we'd been apart from my perspective had been far too much. "I'm sorry. I'm pushing you when I should give you space. I love you. I love you so much and I hate that I made you feel like you've done a bad job. Babe, I've been here five minutes and I shouldn't have an opinion. If you were Gray, I would have treated you with kid gloves. I'm not used to this. Please forgive me."

He sighed and moved into my space, his arms going around me and pulling me close to him. "Forgive me. I'm being touchy because I saw Gray yesterday. Being near him…it's unsettling when he's been in Lucifer's presence. It's getting worse, and I don't know what to do."

"Because he was an angel." I hugged Trent close. "Lucifer was an angel. Being in his presence must rub off on Gray and affect those around him. What happened to your talisman?"

He stepped back, his shoulders dropping in an expression I recognized as frustration from him. "Damn it. I didn't think of that. I lost that talisman years ago when we were off plane. I haven't thought about it in a long time. I've got the demonic one, but I'll be honest, I don't wear it unless I'm out in the field."

We'd dealt with angels years before. When they were unbalanced, they could infect those around them with their instability. I couldn't think of anyone more unbalanced than Lucifer Morningstar. Despite the fact that he ruled over the Hell plane, he was still angelic in nature. But we'd found ways to deal with it. The main one being a tattoo to counter the influence.

Unfortunately—unlike me—my man actually changed his whole form. I was a weird hybrid wolf and the only actual change I could make was my arm. And even that didn't turn to a wolf claw. Instead I got a handy demon arm due to having some royal demonic blood in my system the first time it changed. I found it helpful and way tougher than a wolf claw. Let's face some facts. Wolf claws are more useful when the person who has one is running around on four legs. The demon arm is way easier to use on two feet.

But I digress. The point is, any tat on Trent would disappear once he changed. He could sit on that chair for hours and the next full moon his skin would be pure as a baby's butt.

"We need to get you another one before you meet with Gray again." I let my hand slip under his shirt, connecting us skin to skin.

I felt him relax.

I had to remember to treat him like a wolf who'd been separated from his pack for a long time. Sometimes they could be touchy, unsure of their place no matter how many words were said. Especially if they had fucking Lucifer influencing them.

"I really am sorry, babe." I needed him to understand that I wasn't going to make more problems for him. "The kids are alive and they're good. I can't ask for more. You're alive. Gray's alive. I'm so sorry I left you."

The grief of those lost years rose again, wild and overwhelming.

He turned and he was the one holding me. "Don't fight it. Let it out, baby. If you do, maybe I can, too. I'm not…"

He wasn't supposed to cry, wasn't supposed to show his pain. I'd held it in for a day. He'd had to do it for twelve years so his pain didn't worry the children he'd never thought he'd have to raise alone.

He'd been raised in a harsh pack, one where no wolf was allowed emotion.

But we were emotion. It ran wild through us, drawing us together, holding our packs so much more securely than fear. Our love was our strength, and there was no room for walls between us.

I let it out again and Trent joined me, holding me tight as we rode the storm out.

Together.

Chapter Three

"So how bad is this place?" I stood on the yard of the cabin Gray had bought years before and settled my pack on my back. My jeans had survived the werewolf lovefest, but I wore what I'd been told had been Fen's T-shirt when he was thirteen. It was way too big on me.

"Bad? It's not at all. I mean, we're pretty far out of town, but there's a Jeep in the garage over there." Trent looked deliciously rumpled. No matter how he tried to comb that hair of his it managed to look like he'd just rolled out of bed, and not alone, if you know what I mean. It was likely why he'd kept it so high and tight all those years.

We'd called Eddie half an hour before and told him we would be ready to go soon. Then we'd gotten dressed and I'd kind of made the bed up. After we'd cried some more, we'd made love again, slower this time and without all that tension between us. For me it had been proof that he'd survived. For him it seemed like a long, luxurious reacquaintance with my body. My wolf was humming with satisfaction. The human part of me was a little worried about the next couple of days we would spend in a cave. "I wasn't talking about here. I meant where we're going. I've never been in a primal nest before. I've only met the one, and he lived in that creepy cave. Christopher was not concerned with comfort."

"Well, he'd died and hadn't been through a proper turn at that point. He was more concerned with blood at the time," Trent explained.

He was right about that. I'd met Fenrir's biological father before the king had been brought in to take him through his turn. Vampires don't do well when they first rise. It tends to be all fangs and blood and murder until an older vamp feeds the young dude some blood and gives him the whole orientation meeting. Lucky for Lee, his father would likely be standing right there for his turn. He wouldn't have more than a few moments of confusion and uncontrolled blood lust. Christopher hadn't been so lucky. "I know, but I also know that the primals have a lot in common with bats, hence the caves. Casey said something about a library. How do they keep the books dry?"

Trent's eyes rolled. "Yeah, just wai…"

The world seemed to stop on a dime. Like someone had pressed the pause button. Everything went completely silent, and the wind that had been brushing over my skin went still. There had been crickets chirping seconds before and the sound of water moving in the distance.

And then there was a horrible nothingness.

"Trent?"

He stood there, his expression frozen in what I like to think of as his dumbass face. Someone else was the dumbass. Not Trent. Usually me.

Everything was still, and yet I knew I wasn't alone.

"He can't hear you."

I turned because I knew that voice, and the woman attached to it had tried to capture me twenty-four hours before. "Olivia. What have you done to him?"

Olivia Carey had been my best friend since we were in high school. I never thought that would change. Liv was a constant in my life, one of the only constants I could absolutely count on. I knew she'd gone through a lot lately. Well, back then. Liv was a witch. She'd come into her powers as an adolescent and quickly found her place in the supernatural world. She'd been dedicated to her coven and to the light magic they'd used to help others.

Then we'd gotten into some trouble and a group of dark magic witches had stripped her of her power and she'd changed. She'd turned in on herself in a way Liv never had before. Liv was thoughtful. She was the friend who remembered birthdays and always asked how you were.

Then she'd cared about one thing and one thing only—getting her power back.

"He's fine. He'll barely notice what's happened."

I seriously doubted that. Trent's instincts are good. "I take it this is a new power."

Her lips curled up, but the smile wasn't Liv's. I didn't know this person. "I have many new powers since Myrddin blessed me."

My stomach turned at the satisfaction in her tone. "What happened to you, Liv?"

"I woke up and realized I'd been a stupid sheep for years," Liv replied, flipping back her long dark hair. It used to be a warm brown, like she carried all the best things of autumn around with her. Now it was a pitch black without a hint of warmth or anything else. I've seen some gorgeous raven-haired women, the color so dark there were hints of blue and purple.

This was black with nothing to lighten it. Liv's hair was like an abyss no color could counter.

And that didn't even begin to touch the darkness I saw in her eyes.

"Why are you here? If you try to hurt him, we're going to have a problem." I needed to see how changed she was. She was the first person we'd met when we'd gotten back from the outer planes yesterday, and she'd promptly announced she was hauling us all in so Myrddin could pronounce sentence on us. We were enemies of the state, it seemed.

Liv glanced to where Trent stood. "I wouldn't bother with him. He's fairly useless. Now if you'd like to tell me where that big vampire spy is, I'd love a crack at him."

I was sure she would love to get inside Sasha's head and uncover what I believed would be a vast network of spies who helped the resistance. Apparently she didn't know Trent was the only other person in all the planes who knew exactly what Sasha was doing. I was cool with that. "Don't know who you're talking about, friend. I just got here yesterday. Still getting settled in."

She snorted. "Sure you don't. I suspect the king and queen and Quinn are already nestled into wherever little rebels go to hide. I hope it's shitty. They're used to opulence, that trio. I should know. I live in their penthouse. It's too bad the queen's feet are so small. I would have loved taking over her wardrobe. I would bet they're having a blast roughing it in…" She stared at me for a moment, and I could feel the fine tendrils of her magic trying to reach deep inside my mind. "Europe?"

I'd shoved far better mind readers out of my head. I didn't this time, though, merely sent her a vision of a place she could go looking for the rebels in.

She frowned. "Is that seriously the Small World ride at Disney World? Fuck you, Kelsey. Now that song is in my head."

I couldn't match her magical powers, but my powers of annoyance were unparalleled. "I'm not telling you where they are."

"I could make you."

Marcus Vorenus hadn't been able to get through my mental shields. Liv couldn't. I didn't care how much power she'd built up. I was born this way. I was born to counter demonic influence, and I would bet a whole lot of her new powers were demonic in nature.

We'd become natural enemies, she and I. It broke my heart, but I could actually feel the demonic power coming off her.

"You could try. Don't, Liv. I've been told it hurts, and I don't think you'll handle it well. I would rather talk to you than fight." I felt her retreat, though she was still there. I was starting to wonder if this magic of hers wasn't all in my head. I felt safe enough to allow it to continue. I'd sensed the minute she'd tried to access my memory.

"I believe you when you say that. I hope you'll believe me when I tell you talking is exactly why I'm here." She looked around. "Not that I know where here is, exactly. Somewhere on the coast. It's got a swampy vibe."

I wasn't going to tell her that either. "So talk, bestie. What's been going on for the twelve years your master stole from me?"

"I would love to lie and say you weren't meant to fall into that trap, but it was built for you and Vorenus," she said, crossing her arms over her chest. I had to hope that was a push-up bra or my bestie'd had some serious augmentation. And she liked the leather now. "He had too much influence on the king, and you couldn't be dealt with. You would never have given my master a fair chance. He knew whose daughter you were. The truth is you were lucky he didn't kill you outright."

I kind of wished he'd given it a shot. Then I might not have lost twelve years. I'd managed to kill a duke of Hell and an actual angel from Heaven. I was willing to go *mano y mano* with Myrddin. But I was playing this cool with my bestie. She was here for a reason, and I didn't think it was to try to take me out. There was also the question of whether she was actually here or not. I couldn't smell her. I couldn't sense her being physically here, so I had to assume this was magic and she was showing off.

And I couldn't forget what Dean had said when he'd stood in front of Olivia in the Council headquarters.

There's still a spark of love in your heart, and it has to do with her. And one other. Casey. You still feel for Kelsey and Casey.

At the time I'd held on to it as proof she wasn't so far gone. This was another. She hadn't stormed in raining down hell on me. She'd come to talk. I could still feel her in my head. I rather thought that's where we were right now, in some space where she could talk to me.

I could also shove her out whenever I liked.

"Remind me to thank him."

She stared at me for a moment and then her lips curled ever so slightly. "You are such a bitch."

I shrugged. "Four days didn't change me. Twelve years does seem to have changed you."

The smile faded and arrogance was back on her face. "For the better."

I gestured up and down that outfit she was wearing. "Girl, we make fun of people who try to cosplay superheroes. What the hell is this? And please tell me how you are breathing in that corset thing. Your boobs are damn near to your ears. And the heels. How are you going to fight in those? What did I teach you?"

Her eyes narrowed. "Nothing of value. You taught me to hide behind you, to dim my light for you."

She'd obviously learned to rewrite history. "Yes, I needed to always be the center of attention. That's me. I had to always be the prettiest girl at the fucking ball. I know what happened in Wyoming hurt, but this isn't you, Liv. This is Myrddin. You got too close to him. I think he influences the people around him." I couldn't come right out and ask her the question I wanted to.

Hey, bestie, did that mean old wizard maybe shove a thrall stone in your old noggin and that's how you got the goth makeover you never needed?

I had to pretend to not know what a thrall stone was in case we had a shot at fooling Myrddin. We'd taken out the ones he'd placed in the king and Quinn's heads years and years before. It was how he'd maintained such influence over them both.

The corners of her lips ticked up again, her "I know something you don't know and now I'm evil" look. "*Influence* is a good word to use. You should tell Donovan and Quinn that they're welcome to come to the Coven House. Donovan left his kingdom behind. Myrddin merely had to step in or war could have happened."

"Yeah, he fell into the trap Myrddin placed, but sure, he abandoned his post."

One slim shoulder shrugged. "He didn't have to follow the queen. Like I said—it wasn't meant for him."

"Just me and Marcus. I wonder why Myrddin didn't remove the painting after he had us." We'd talked about this and decided that after Quinn mistakenly fell in, the wizard had known Donovan wouldn't let it pass. Quinn's disappearance had been the one that truly fucked over Myrddin's plan.

Or hey, maybe it had been the mistake that helped him along since he'd gotten to put the crown on his own head this time around.

"I don't question the Great One," Liv said in a big old kiss-ass voice.

"Which is funny because I thought I was the sheep." She'd obviously forgotten the definition of the word hypocrisy.

She frowned. "I never called you that, Kelsey. I was talking about my fellow witches who do not understand what true power feels like. I honestly didn't come here to fight with you. I want to try reason before things get nasty. This is Myrddin's time. The vampires have ruled for too long. The witches own the supernatural world now."

"Own?" I didn't like the wording she was using. It told me way too much about Myrddin's true political ambitions. "Are the rest of us slaves? Is that what you are, Liv? His slave?"

"I am his good right hand. I am his enforcer," Liv announced. "I'm in a position of great power, and I have more magic than I could have dreamed to have. I'm no slave. Myrddin has provided me with everything I need."

She was forgetting a few things she'd previously required. "What about Casey?"

Dark eyes rolled. "Casey is ridiculous. He's a child."

"He doesn't seem to be anymore. He seems to have matured, and even when he was young, he had a bravery that came out when he needed it to." I had to find a way to get to her. "Who loves you now, Liv? Who loves the Olivia Carey who doesn't have power? Because there will come a time when it's stripped from you again and all you'll have to rely on is who you are down deep inside and the people who love and adore you. Me and Casey. Who loves you in that coven house of yours?"

She was still for a moment and for a second I thought she would soften. But her shoulders went back, eyes going steely again. "If there is one thing I've learned from you it's to stay away from love. It's all a lie. It's a biological impulse that controls us, nothing more. Feelings and emotions are useless things. They're useful for manipulation and trade. Logic is better. You understand logic. Kelsey, Donovan can't win this war. We've had twelve years to fortify ourselves against him. Twelve years to put our plans in place."

"Your plans to give the Earth plane to Hell?" It was what Sasha had told me they'd learned. He'd gone over all the hows and whys, but it boiled down to Myrddin couldn't hold the plane without the demons, and the demons were sick of Heavenly interference. They sought to close the doors to the Heaven plane and allow demons to rule the lower planes.

Unfortunately, to do that Myrddin needed his grimoire and my sword, and that sneaky queen had managed to steal and hide both before she got thrown to the outer planes. She was planning on stealing them back, and I couldn't wait to get Gladys in my hands again. She's the sword the *Nex Apparatus* carries. She came from the Heaven plane, and the people smarter than me theorized she might be used to close the door. After all, one of Gladys's most formidable talents is to store the unique energy of the creatures she kills. Is used to kill. I don't know. I only know it works and the last thing I killed with Gladys had been an angel from the Heaven plane, and that meant there was an enormous amount of Heavenly power stored in that sword.

Olivia shook her head. "Do you honestly believe I want to live in a hellscape where demons run everything? Of course not. Is that what the rebels believe? Well, I suppose that's what happens when the majority of your army is barely able to drink."

"Oh, I assure you Lee can drink and do lots of other way too adult things." The sweet kid I'd known had turned into a horny man who did not discriminate when it came to the…people, creatures…in his bed. The queen had her hands full with that one. At least I only had to worry about Fen sneaking into Evan's bed.

I was a bit more practical about that than Quinn was. They were young and in love. They had adult responsibilities and had been forced to mature long before they should have. If they were safe, I said go for it. This was war. They should find comfort where they could.

"Yes. I don't think any of us thought he would turn into such a little manwhore. Or that his brother would be an uptight prick. That poor Green Man. He must be dying. One day he's going to explode and then we'll be able to find him and put him out of his misery. Don't think we're not looking for Fae magic. He'll light up like a firefly on our locator maps."

I stared at the woman who'd been my best friend, nausea rolling through me. "You taught those children. You babysat them. You held them in your arms and they trusted you."

That seemed to stop her for a moment. "They aren't the same. I'm not the same either."

That was where she was wrong. "They are. I assure you those are the same babies you used to make grilled cheeses for and watch Disney movies with. You were the teacher they all wanted when they got to high school. Liv, you were part of the reason they never made it to high school. You had a hand in this. You stole my son's childhood."

"And you left." Liv shouted the words, one finger pointing my way. "You were stupid and blind, and you couldn't help yourself. You had to go and try to find that vampire. Your arrogance made you fall into that trap. You left me alone, and I couldn't even protect myself. What the fuck should I have done? I was alone and I had no power without Myrddin. I had nothing. I was as weak as any human, and you were supposed to protect me. I lost my power for you,

Kelsey. So you could save that kid and your men. I was there to help you, but you left me behind. You want to talk about me teaching kids? That was my job. I was good at it until you dragged me into yours and cost me everything."

I hadn't meant to leave her behind, but she didn't want to hear that rationale. I went with another. "You had Casey. Even after I disappeared, he would have been there for you. You could have told the king what was happening."

"Do you think I knew then? Do you think I had any power with Myrddin when I could barely shape a spell with these useless hands?" She held them up and I was shocked to see the heavy veins running up and down the back of her hands only to disappear in that shield she wore. I knew what that costume was. It was a shield.

And unfortunately I knew what those veins meant.

Liv had been taking demon blood.

"Myrddin only cared about me because you cared about me. He didn't tell me anything back then. I was trapped and scared." For a moment she sounded like my Liv. "Casey couldn't help me. Casey barely managed to get out on his own. He didn't think to look for me. I was alone. But then I realized what an opportunity I'd been given. The Dark One offered me power, and I took it. I realized it didn't matter what I had to give up. It didn't matter. I felt better without it."

"Without what?" I didn't like the suspicion that was creeping across my mind. "What did you give up? How long have you been taking demon blood? Do you have any idea what that's going to do to your soul?"

"Who needs a soul when you can have power?"

A cold chill moved over my skin. "Liv, what have you done?"

Her jaw tightened, eyes boring into me. "What I had to. What you made me do. Now I'll ask the question I came here to ask. It's more of a bargain. Stay out of this fight. I've talked to Myrddin and he's agreed that if you go to your mother and brothers and live a human life, he'll stay away from you. I'll even throw in Trent if you can get that wolf to keep his nose out of our business."

"Stay out of this war? So we can have a couple of months before demons take over?"

"I told you that's not what's happening," Liv insisted.

"Because Myrddin wouldn't do that?" I sensed a way to start

shoving a wedge between Liv and her beloved maniac wizard.

"Because he would tell me if he was."

"You're still on the outside," I said with a shrug. "He's taken your soul and infected you with evil and he still doesn't trust you. He's lying to you. He's planning on using the Sword of Light along with a spell from his grimoire to close the door to the Heaven plane and then he'll open the one to Hell and they will rule."

Her chin came up. "If he is, then he's planning to take his rightful place as the leader of this whole plane. The humans have done nothing but fuck things up."

I was getting to her. If I could just get her to see reason, I had a chance to save her. "Lucifer won't cede the Earth plane. Not when he could take it. Do you honestly believe Myrddin can beat Lucifer Morningstar? The demons will make slaves of us all if you close the door to the Heaven plane. No souls will be able to move on. It will be Hell on Earth. Is that what you want? Do you want us all to die because you lost your power?"

Her eyes suddenly flashed fire. "I got it all back and more. It's obvious you're going to be stubborn. So I'll simply take what my master needs."

The tendrils in the outer chambers of my brain suddenly became talons, and she began her assault.

I slammed my mental shields down.

"Fuck," Liv shouted in obvious pain as the world shifted around me and she was gone.

Like I said. I've bested far better mind readers, and that was before Marcus taught me how to truly control it. In my case, the demon blood in her system made her more susceptible to my power.

If only she was susceptible to my reason.

"Kelsey? Kelsey, baby?"

I blinked and Trent stood in front of me, worry plain on his handsome face. "So you weren't the one who was stuck."

He breathed a major sigh of relief and dragged me into his arms. "I was trying to tell you that we'll be perfectly comfortable in the primal nest and you stopped. Like someone turned you off. You didn't blink or respond."

"Mistress, we were most worried. I arrived here and Master Trent couldn't bring you out of it. I was about to transport back to Frelsi to bring a doctor." Eddie put a hand to his chest as though trying to slow his heart.

My own heart felt heavy. Liv was so far from me, and the words she'd said had done their job. I felt guilty. I had brought her into this dangerous part of our world. Oh, I know on an intellectual level in many ways it had been the other way around. She and my brother, Nate, had helped the king bring me in, but I understood why now. That was something I'd forgiven long ago. Now I was left with the worry that she wouldn't be here had I not brought her into my investigations, put her on the team. She'd been a happy teacher with a fiancé. I think what happened with Scott would have happened no matter what, but she was right about what had happened to her. It was my fault. I should never have involved her in such a dangerous case.

And then I'd disappeared. When we started this journey of ours, she'd been the happy one. I'd been the sad sack with no connections other than her. She'd been the one with all the power.

When I'd disappeared she'd had no one, and I'd become one of the most important people in the supernatural world. I could see where she might think I'd had something to do with her fall.

"It was Liv."

Trent's whole body went on alert. "She's here?"

That told me everything I needed to know. Trent genuinely believed Olivia was a threat. He believed she would hurt him, hurt me, hurt our family.

I shook my head. "No. She was in my mind somehow. I kicked her out."

"She attempted to get into your mind?" Eddie asked. "She was looking for clues to where the king is?"

"Well the only thing she got out of me was a mad earworm and probably a hell of a headache," I replied. "How long has she been taking demon blood?"

"I don't know. She was like this when I got back from the outer planes," Trent replied. "It had been years, and she was one of the first witches who tried to catch the kids. They were barely in their teens the first time. Rhys recognized her, and she almost had him when Fenrir caught a scent he didn't like and attacked. It took a long time for Rhys and Lee to believe she'd been trying to harm them."

"None of us wanted to believe it." The fact that Eddie's tail was out and swishing like an upset cat's was proof he was unnerved. While Eddie almost never changed his demonic form around his family, he did typically keep his tail in check. "Olivia used to be the kindest soul."

Fuck. Eddie was the most formal of demons. He always called friends of the family by Miss or Mister and always Sir or Ma'am. Not calling her Miss Olivia or Mistress Olivia meant she wasn't part of our clan. She was an outsider and not a trusted one to Eddie. My butler tended to give the people around him the benefit of the doubt. If he'd pushed Liv out of his trust circle, she'd done something to deserve it.

"No one tried to help her?" I couldn't forget how lost she'd looked when she'd talked about those first few hours. She might not have even known I was gone. "Did Gray reach out to her? Did you?"

"You should talk to Casey about that. He knows more than I do. I was busy trying to save the kids. She'd forgotten them by then." Trent's bitterness was a palpable thing. He took a deep breath and seemed to banish it, his expression softening. "Are you sure she didn't hurt you?"

Tears pulsed behind my eyes. She didn't even know I was pregnant. Probably shouldn't know. I'd dreamed about this, dreamed about Liv and I starting families around the same time and our kids being best friends, too. I knew when she fell for Casey that part wouldn't happen, but I certainly never thought I would have to protect my child from the woman who should have been his godmother. I couldn't respond to him. Emotion was running hard through me. I simply nodded.

She hadn't physically hurt me.

But she'd shredded my heart.

Trent's arms came around me. "It's going to be okay, baby. I love you. Let's go and have dinner with our son and then I'll show you around the nest and take you back to bed. I'm going to show you how happy I am you're here. I'm going to take care of you and this new son of ours."

"And I have a magnificent feast planned for you, my beautiful mistress," Eddie promised. "It's all of your favorite things. Please come and see the home I've put together for our stay with the primals. I think you will find it comforting."

I found him comforting. And Trent. I nodded. "Let's go. I don't think she can follow. I got the feeling she slipped in because I wasn't guarding against her."

I'd wanted to talk to her. It had been in my head all day. I wouldn't make that mistake again.

Eddie put a hand on me and the sun blinked away, and I was surrounded by darkness.

Chapter Four

I found myself in the same place I had before—a dank, dark cave alit only with a few torches.

"We welcome the *Nex Apparatus*," a deep voice said.

It seemed twelve years hadn't taken my title away. I turned, my eyes adjusting to the gloom, and a shadow stepped away from the wall and into the light, his scarred face becoming visible. "Hey. Nice to meet you. Please call me Kelsey. *Nex Apparatus* is a lot."

I'm used to meeting crazy-looking creatures. I've shaken hands with some creatures who didn't actually have hands. More like talons or weird appendages. Despite what the new more demonic Liv would have you believe, I'm pretty low maintenance. I'm not a person who judges based on appearance.

So it didn't bother me at all to reach out a hand to the primal I found in front of me.

"And you must call me Rufus." He was a good foot and a half taller than me and wore what seemed to be some kind of formal robe. It was dark and would likely help him blend into the stone walls around him. The hood was back, draped around what seemed to be slender shoulders.

I often wonder if the dudes who did Voldemort's makeup for the movies had encountered a primal before. It's the no nose thing that's the weirdest. The bald head and slightly pointed ears can be shrugged off, but the lack of a nose draws one's attention. He took my hand gently and bowed in a courtly gesture. Most vampires look perfectly human until the need to do any of the three Fs—feed, fight, or fuck. Then the claws and fangs come out. But the primals always have theirs. They don't recede into the body, protecting the vampire from human freak-outs. Hence the staying completely away from humans' thing.

"We welcome you to the Atlanta nest, and we're so pleased to have the king on the plane with us once again." Rufus's fangs gleamed in the low light, but he didn't seem to have any trouble speaking around them. "It has been a hard twelve years, but we are proud to do our service to our culture."

"And a great service you have done," Trent replied.

Rufus let go of my hand, stepping back. "Please allow me to show you to the proper entrance of the nest. For obvious reasons, we guard it zealously."

Eddie had a flashlight out. "Be careful, my mistress. It can be slippery down here, and I would not have you fall."

I'd missed that little guy. I have to admit I've become far too used to having Eddie around. I hadn't started out thinking I would get this cool butler person who organized my life and also happened to genuinely give a crap about me and my family.

Of course, if you'd asked me years ago if I'd have a family, I would have laughed. Before my time as the *Nex Apparatus* began, I didn't think I would be alive at this point, much less surrounded by people who loved me. I reached out a hand. "You can guide me, my friend."

Eddie squeezed my hand. "It would be my greatest pleasure."

"Casey is already meeting with one of the chief librarians, and Fen and Evan are inside somewhere." Trent took a position behind us, guarding our back. "Likely with Christopher and Rose."

"Rose?" I asked and then remembered something Fen had told me earlier. "Is she the companion he married?"

"Yes." Rufus took the lead, starting down a series of stairs. "Rose Beasley sought safety here when Myrddin the Pretender first took the crown. You must understand that the primals have always offered refuge to supernatural creatures who need it. Primal vampires are not the only beings you will encounter in the Under. In the past we have remained neutral when it comes to Council infighting. We have no deep ties to most of the classes of vampire, though we do much work with the academics."

If anyone was comfortable in libraries, it was the academics. And I was comfortable around academics. That particular class of vampire has always had a strong relationship with the women of the supernatural world known as Hunters. Women like me. There was a reason Casey had been able to sense I needed space earlier today. He'd grown into his powers, and he'd been able to find a certain synch with me. Of course, I'd likely been broadcasting my need for emotional control quite loudly at the time. "So when Myrddin took the leash off the vampires the companions ran here? How did they know to come? Primals aren't well known in the supernatural world. Very few vampires have even met a primal."

I wouldn't have if I hadn't been sent to put one down. Of course I hadn't known at the time Christopher Miller was a primal.

"We have friends in the human world," Rufus explained. "Mostly scientists who know of our world and are trusted. When we learned of Myrddin's attack on the Council, we sent word to those with protected status that they were welcome here and would receive safe passage."

"Did the academics contact you?" I was curious how everything had gone down.

"Yes. Almost immediately." Even though he was a few steps down from me, Rufus was still taller. "We have a network of mirrors that work here in the Under. Our nest is well protected, but we do need contact with the outside world. The academics set up a Fae mirror network for us long ago. Hugo Wells sent word that we should lock down our nest and be prepared to smuggle in refugees when we could. That was when we sent out the bat signal."

Trent chuckled, but the words made me stop since up until this point Rufus seemed like a very old-school, refined vampire type. "I'm sorry? You have a bat signal?"

Rufus stopped and turned, an oddly sweet grin on his hollowed-out face. "It is a joke among us. Bats are close to our hearts and our physical beings." His voice went low. "I am Batman."

I had to laugh. "Now a sense of humor that includes pop culture references is not something I expected. You guys watch superhero movies?"

He returned to his long descent. "Of course. We enjoy entertainments of all kinds. I think you'll find us quite accommodating. We live underground, but we try to keep up with the world. As I said, there are many non-primals living in the nest now, and they bring us vitality and a diversity I find invigorating. Our lives are long, and so much of before was spent in the darkness. It is good to surround ourselves with light. Welcome to our nest, Kelsey Owens."

Ahead of me a set of doors swung open and warm light spilled over the stairs I stood on. Rufus walked inside, his taloned hand gracefully sweeping out to gesture to the grand foyer I found myself in front of.

"Like I would take you to sleep in a cave." Trent snorted as he walked past me. He stopped on the last step. "You've spent far too much time with Devinshea. He spoiled you, baby."

I had gotten used to a certain level of opulence and comfort. He was right about that. It didn't look like I would be in a sleeping bag. The lobby of this nest of the primals looked like something out of *Architectural Digest*, with gleaming wood floors and a stunning chandelier overhead. There were flowers covering one of the walls, thick green vines and blooming purple flowers.

"How do you get them to grow down here?" I was fascinated with this place already. I let go of Eddie's hand and entered the nest.

"We have several helpful gnomes who aid in the gardens. Because we are in the Under, we have had to adapt our techniques. The gnomes have lived on this plane for centuries and chose not to leave when the other Fae did. When we immigrated from Europe, they chose to come with us," Rufus explained. "They do good work, though these spectacular blooms come from another creature."

"My brother was here a couple of weeks ago," a familiar voice said.

"Rhys's sexual frustration totally helps plants grow," another finished. "They bloom because he can't."

Evangeline Donovan-Quinn leaned against a wall that likely led farther into the nest, and my son was right beside her. Naturally he was the one who'd thrown his friend under the bus, but I suspected that was all a part of this group's love language.

"The Green Man has been kind to us," Rufus acknowledged. "He has helped grow the crops that feed our guests. He gives us the beauty that nature usually reserves for those who live above. We are so grateful to him."

"You have been more than kind to us, Rufus. The primals have shown us hospitality we could not have expected from anyone, and we are so grateful and humbled by your compassion," the queen's daughter said.

Rufus's head bowed. "We are honored to do you service, bright one."

Evan was a companion, and I'd heard that she glowed as brightly as her mother did now that she was almost an adult by human standards. The way she presented herself was more mature than most almost eighteen-year-olds I knew. I had a few questions, though. I was going to follow Evan's lead and be as polite as I possibly could when I asked questions that might be sensitive. "Rufus, I hope you will forgive my ignorance about your culture, and please take anything I ask as a genuine request for knowledge."

"Of course. You should feel free to ask anything you like. I assure you we are an open society," Rufus replied. "We have to be. I assume you are going to ask the obvious question. Why are companions safe here when we are vampires who are known for being closer to our savage selves than others?"

"There is nothing savage about the primals," Evan insisted.

"Ah, but that is where you are wrong, Princess," Rufus countered. "Our outer appearance is but a hint at our inner selves. They call us primal for a reason. When a primal first rises, we change in a way other vampires do not. We regress to our earliest form, a combination of demon, human, and bat. Our instincts are primal as well, but we are gifted with intelligence, and through discipline and knowledge and faith, we can tame the inner beast and become our truest self. The companions are safe because we honor them. We honor the light they bring, the uniqueness in each one. As we honor the life brought by all creatures."

"Is it true you don't drink the blood of humans?" I'd heard they were considered vegetarians by other vampires.

"We feed off our animal brethren, but even there we honor the sacrifice all creatures make for the world to keep moving." Rufus began to walk toward Evangeline and Fen. "You found your rooms satisfactory?"

Fen's nose wrinkled. "No. I usually get the big room, but apparently my mother and father require privacy." He grinned our way. "I'm joking. Please, please remember the privacy part. I'm young and do not need to know why Mom is so calm right now." He turned back to Rufus. "Yes, our rooms are perfect, as always."

I frowned my son's way. "Our?"

Evan huffed. "It's okay. We have a wing and our own bedrooms. You can tell my papa my virginity is intact and will remain so while we're here. Fenrir is referring to the fact that the boys usually stay in the largest and most luxurious of the guest rooms. It has one large bed, but Fen, Rhys, and Lee have shared a bed many times."

"I usually change into wolf form and sleep at the end," Fen explained as though it was a totally normal thing to do. "But I have to make Lee take a long shower before bed because he's got the stinkiest feet. I don't know why. Rhys's are perfectly normal. Lee hit fifteen and yuck. Rhys always smells like flowers and nice shit, and Lee smells like dea… Huh. I should have known, shouldn't I?"

A short, low growl came from Trent, an obvious warning.

Fen went a bit pink. "Should have known that those human hormones kick in and make a dude smell nasty."

Evan sent Fen a pointed look and a shake of her head. "Because you always smell so nice. Come along. I think your mom needs to call mine and let her know I'm alive and well and perfectly virginal."

Evan and her papa were already clashing, but I didn't think she should bring her mom into that. I knew the queen. "I doubt your mother cares, but you're right. I need to let her know we made it okay and that we've already had an unwelcome visitor. Rufus, how does security work down here because I have a friend who seems to be having trouble with boundaries, and by friend I mean one of Myrddin's leather-clad enforcers."

Rufus straightened to his full height, and his shoulders went back as though prepared for a threat. "One of the Profane?"

"It's what they call Myrddin's three enforcers," Trent explained. "The Profane are the three witches Myrddin shares his power with. Liv, Calliope, and Shera. Casey will update you on all three and yes, Rufus, it was Olivia Carey. She has a former connection with Kelsey, but we believe the contact was purely mental and allowed by the *Nex Apparatus*. When Liv attempted to probe deeper, Kelsey shoved her out. She's likely nursing a headache right now."

Rufus seemed to relax. "We are warded against magic in the Under. Obviously there are Council records of us, but one of our protections is the very nature of the Under. Long ago we embedded wards in the earth around us. There are only two routes in and out, so sending in an army would only allow us to quickly disperse of the invading force at the bottleneck they would find. We're near a ley line and physical entrances to both the Hell plane and a secret route to the Unseelie plane. Both are heavily warded, which offers us more protection. Anyone attempting to transport directly into the nest risks being detected by many wards, and some of them tend to eradicate whatever is being transported, though there are exceptions to that. There are some beings who are immune to such wards. The prophets, for example."

So Gray could get in and out. That was good to know. I had to hope he would hear the news I was home and come for a visit. If he wasn't hanging with Lucifer, of course.

"I am allowed to teleport in and out, but only with people who are acknowledged by the wards, which is why I brought you to closest place outside the nest," Eddie explained. "Now that you are here and Rufus is satisfied we have verified your identity, the security team will give you clearance and I will be able to teleport you should the need arise."

So we were safe here. "How about someone show me to a mirror, I catch the queen up, and then we can get to work." My stomach growled. "I mean, you know, after some food."

"We are prepared for you," Rufus assured me. "After all, we've been feeding Fenrir since he was but a boy. Even then he was a walking, talking gut."

At least they were used to wolves.

* * * *

It was long past midnight when I settled into the great room of the library. I'd called the queen and updated her about her salty female child and let her know Liv had been in contact. Then I'd sat down with Fen, the previously mentioned salty princess, and Trent and we'd eaten Eddie's fabulous tenderloin with mashed potatoes, mac and cheese, asparagus, and big puffy, buttery rolls. And I'd eaten most of a chocolate pie on my own.

After the days I'd spent eating nothing but sandwiches without all the condiments I usually put on them, the diversity of food choices was welcome. And by choice, I don't mean I actually chose. I ate all of it. Even the veggies because I was supposed to be thinking about nutrition.

Casey sank down to the seat across from me at the big conference table. He was carrying his laptop and a couple of books. His former T-shirts were gone, and in their place were button-downs and khakis. His emo hair had been tamed, and all he was missing was a pair of glasses to complete his academic wardrobe.

This was a far more serious Casey than the goofball I'd left behind, and that made my heart ache.

"You seem much more comfortable." Casey sent me a smile. "I would say Trent is as well. He's missed you. You should know Gray's missed you, too, but it's hard for him to show it. Emotionally, he's had to shut down in order to do what he's had to do."

At this point it was only me and Casey. Trent had shown me to the library and then went off to find Fenrir and Evan, who'd disappeared after dinner. Rufus was bringing in his top off-plane specialist, a vampire named Alvis. The library was quiet, though I'd seen some primals working in the stacks.

The fact that there was a magnificent library so far underground was proof that the primals had control of some serious magic. I'd been told it was both Fae and Earth-centered witch magic. Part of the magic included the way the lights worked. In our bedroom there were almost human-looking lights that turned off and on, but there were spaces in the nest where the light came from above, as though from a gentle sun. Even the ceiling in some spaces looked like the sky at night, and I'd been told it would change to a vibrant blue with puffy white clouds.

The primals had found a way to bring light to their darkness, to enjoy a semblance of the outside world even in the safety of their caves.

I wondered if Gray ever saw the sun in Hell.

"You're talking about being a focal point for Lucifer." Casey would be a good source of information. I worried Trent was holding back on how bad things were.

"Yes. I'm going to be honest. I haven't spent much time with Gray," Casey admitted. "When I fled the Council building, I was forced underground for a few years. I was brought here and not allowed to leave."

"What? Why?"

"Because Henri thought I was being unreasonable. This nest was the first refuge for the academics, and you should understand that all academics were declared enemies of the state whether or not we offered to remain neutral. On several occasions academics were lured out of hiding with promises of protection in exchange for neutrality. They disappeared."

I was glad Henri took a hard line with Casey's safety. Henri was Casey's sponsor. It was part mentor with a pinch of dad thrown in. "You wanted to try to get protection from Myrddin?"

He hesitated for a moment and then his reply came in a soft, almost aching tone. "I wanted to find Liv."

Well, there was the answer to one question. I didn't think he would have fled with no thought for her. "She thinks you abandoned her."

His jaw tightened. "That's ridiculous. I had to be carried out of the Council building because I wouldn't leave without her. Henri and Hugo dragged me out. Myrddin's forces were actively killing vampires, and they wouldn't allow me to stay. I fought but... It took me months to forgive them. Now I understand. Liv has had many chances to leave. We've seen each other. I've pled my case."

Liv hadn't mentioned that to me. She'd made it sound like he'd forgotten her. I had to wonder if that was manipulation or if she had another point of view. "When did you see her?"

"When she offered me protection in exchange for a promise of staying out of the war," he said with the saddest smile. "I would have done it, too, if it had been real. I would have done it so I could be close to her, so I could have tried to save her. I only survived that day because Gray saved me. I don't even know why he was there, but he showed up and gave Henri and Hugo time to get me away and bring me back here. I didn't try to leave them again. I didn't realize what had truly happened, what she'd done."

My heart ached for him. "What had she done? Trent mentioned a word for her. Profane."

Casey nodded. "Yes. The Profane are Myrddin's elite witches. There are three of them, and they live in the upper levels of the Council building, from what we can tell. They are the only ones allowed into the penthouse where Myrddin lives with his familiars. It's possible they're his concubines."

My stomach clenched at the thought, and this time my nausea had nothing to do with the baby growing inside me. "She's sleeping with him?"

"I don't know, but I wouldn't be shocked."

"She said something about what she gave up. Did she give up her soul?"

"Yes, though not wholly, and not in the way you are familiar with." Casey seemed to go into an almost professorial mode, shutting down the emotions that had played on his face. "Myrddin keeps a piece of Olivia's soul in a jar somewhere. I'm not sure where, but it's not the Council building. I know because we have spies who have confirmed it. We believe if we can find those jars, we could potentially turn the Profane back to our side."

I'd known it was coming, but having it confirmed that Liv had given up a piece of her soul still hit me hard. I needed some kind of a plan, and that meant getting as much information as I could. "Potentially? I would rather deal in certainty, but I would probably take any shot I had."

"One aspect of the spell is a willingness on the part of the person giving up the soul," Casey explained. "You need to understand that Liv doesn't have a thrall stone in her head. She wasn't coerced. She chose this path. I know that sounds harsh, but it's the reality of it. I still love her, but I've had to step back and realize I'm not sure I can save her."

"You're just pissy because she tried to kill you," I replied with sympathy. "I get it. She apparently tried to trap my son and the royal kids. But I'm not willing to give up on her. I say we catch her and torture her. She'll either break and become our Liv again or I'll feel fine because I get to torture her for being an asshole. Either way, we win."

"Goddess, I've missed you. You have no idea how uptight I've become without you...or her. Losing Liv and you being missing, it's been harder than anything I've gone through, including death and the turn." He went still for a moment as though he needed to find some control. "My family before my turn wasn't the most loving. My parents divorced when I graduated from high school, and they were both done with the family thing by then. They paid for college but made excuses to why I shouldn't come home for holidays. Even when they were together, they didn't pay much attention to me. Henri is the closest thing I have to a father. Hell, that's not even right. He's more of a father to me than I've ever had. You were more of a sister. Henri wouldn't let... I thought about walking into the light. I mean that in a non-literal sense, of course, given my status as an academic. It's not that easy for us, but it's a nicer phrase than walking onto a stake."

"Casey," I began, my heart aching at what this world had done to my friends and family.

"It was so fucked up. I watched them stake Justin." His eyes closed, tears pooling there. They ran down his cheeks when he opened them again. "One minute it was okay, you know. One minute the world made sense, and I was happy. Liv had trouble, but I knew all I had to do was love her enough and I could fix it. And then it was blood and death, and I never saw it coming. I didn't even know what to do. When they started to come at me, I froze. All I knew was the woman who joked with me when I would buy Liv's lattes still had Justin's ashes all over her when she came for me. She said some spell and then I was frozen for real. I still wonder if they think I killed her."

"Who did?" I asked.

"Lily Tucker. Sarah Day's sister. She was looking for Sarah, but she found me instead. I'd gone to find Justin to see if he knew where Liv was. I'd already tried her apartment. Isn't that the stupidest thing? That's how chaotic it was in that moment. I knew it was still light outside, but I went looking for a vampire to talk to. He was my friend."

I reached a hand out and vowed to thank Lily Tucker when we all returned to Frelsi. "You'd never been through a war before. Any case we worked on, you knew what you were getting into. That day all you were supposed to do was work on figuring out where I'd gone."

"For a while I thought they'd killed you, too. It took Henri, Hugo, and I a while to make it to here. I looked for Liv. I tried to go back and find her. I tried to reach her any way I could, but until that day when she sent for me, I got nothing. I heard rumors but I didn't believe them. Even when she tried to capture me, I didn't believe it. I fought the people who love me. Hugo knocked my ass out and dragged me back here. I didn't believe it until she tried to catch the kids. She tried to catch your son, Kelsey. I don't know if she was going to kill him then and there or present him to her master, but she was going to take him by force. She's not Liv anymore."

But I'd seen little pieces that were still Liv. "Yes, because she's missing a piece of her soul, and until that piece is back in place, I will not believe our Liv is completely gone."

"You would pick her over Fen?" Casey asked, his eyes flaring in obvious surprise.

"She's not." Fenrir strode into the room, Evan's hand in his as she walked by his side. "She would never do that. What my mother is doing is being the loyal, stubborn bitch she is. Her loyalty is legendary, and I only use the word loyalty because she would get grossed out if I used the right word."

"Love," Evan said. "The word is love. And given all the things the wolves say about Fenrir being the one who will one day break the world, I'm all for Kelsey being the loyal, don't-just-kill-a-person-because-they-might-be-evil guardian she is."

Trent stood in the doorway, his gaze warm on me. "She's that kind of a woman. She would never choose Liv over her children or me or you, Casey. She's saying that if Liv isn't whole and she has a chance to fix her, she'll take it. Fenrir and Evan, you should understand if you see Liv, you don't play around. You take her out if you have to."

Trent always had my back, and that wolf understood me. "But if I see a chance to help her, I will take it. Pain does funny things to a person. Liv lost a part of herself, and she wasn't used to feeling that kind of grief. I played a part in this. While she was suffering, I was planning a wedding."

"And she was selling her soul to Myrddin Emrys," Casey countered.

"I don't think it started that way." I remembered those days because they'd literally been last week. "She was working with

Nimue to try to find her power again. Do we know if Nimue had anything to do with convincing Liv to part with a piece of her soul?"

I was sure at some point Sasha had gone over what part the legendary Lady of the Lake had played in all of this, but I hadn't been in that meeting and I hadn't gone over the notes yet. The queen believed Nim could have a thrall stone, one forced on her at the same time stones had been placed in the king and Devinshea.

"No one has seen Nimue in years." Casey sounded tired as though even thinking of the past caused him pain. "I don't know if she's dead or if Myrddin got rid of her the way he did you and the royals. I seriously doubt she was the one who convinced Liv. I do remember her being seemingly kind to Liv. Liv believed she was starting to feel a bit of her old power when she was working with Nim."

I didn't like the idea that Nim hadn't been seen in years, but I had to leave that to the royals. I had other problems. "That's my point. She wasn't trying to go bad. She was trying to get something back, something important to her, and none of us understood. None of us knows exactly how it felt to be tied down on that altar and to have something essential ripped from her soul. Do what you have to when it comes to Liv, and I'll do the same."

"Do you honestly believe she can come back from this?" Casey asked.

"I hope so." I couldn't stand the thought of losing her. "Even if it's only for a moment. Even if it's only to say good-bye."

"My mother once ran a job on the Hell plane to save her friend. The one who shot her, who tried to trick her into giving up Summer to a demon," Evan said quietly. "She could have left Sarah there to rot. No one would have blamed her. Instead she saved her, and Sarah became instrumental to my mother surviving many a battle. From what we can tell, Sarah likely saved the world when she risked her life to steal the bag of holding from where Mom had hidden it. If Myrddin had gotten his hands on the grimoire and the Sword of Light, the door would already be closed and there would have been nothing for her to come home to. It's one of the things Albert always taught us. The grace we show others can become the ground upon which we stand. It can be cold and shifting or warm and solid. That doesn't mean everyone is worthy of a second chance, only that we shouldn't write someone off immediately. I agree with Kelsey. She's not Olivia Carey without her whole soul."

I might have to ask the queen for a favor. No one was as good at thievery as Queen Zoey. "Do we have any idea where one might keep a soul?"

"I'll study up on it," Evan promised. "There are a couple of witches down here I can talk to. Don't worry. They're all Sasha approved."

I'd been told some witches had gone into hiding once Myrddin took over. There were several in Frelsi, including Lily Tucker and her light magic coven. "Good. Now does anyone know the primal Rufus wants us to meet tonight? What's this guy like?"

I liked to go into any meeting with at least some info on who I was going to be talking to.

"Alvis is an elder in the community," Evan explained. "He's an expert on witchcraft and prophecy."

"He's super old. Like Marcus old," Fen added.

"Not quite." Trent shifted in his chair. "Marcus has a couple hundred years on him, but Alvis is one of the oldest vampires walking the Earth plane. Perhaps the oldest since Marcus is no longer here."

"And good riddance," Fen said with a grin.

I was not having that. "Fenrir."

Fen grimaced. "Wow. She has the mom voice down. Look, you can't expect me to be unhappy that the old dude stayed behind. All of my life I've been told someday this vampire is going to show up, and he'll either try to get it on with my mom or the girl I'm in love with."

I turned to Trent. "Who told him that?"

Trent sighed. "Who do you think, baby?"

Of course I knew. "I'm having a talk with Lee when we get back."

"Well, I'm also happy I don't have to deal with some vamp creeping on me," Evan announced.

"He wouldn't have creeped on you." I felt the need to defend my former mentor. And, yes, lover. He'd been an excellent lover, by the way, but I wasn't going to point that out in front of my son and husband. "He thought you might be his fated mate."

"Nope. She's *my* fated mate," Fenrir said, possessively reaching for her hand.

Evan sighed. "Then you should be happy I like you because if you were an asshole, fate wouldn't mean a thing to me, wolf. I know you cared for Marcus, Kelsey, but he's kind of been the boogeyman in my life. Since I was a kid, I heard whispers of this prophecy. Discovering it was never me at all but my big sis is a huge relief. Especially if she's happy with the old guy."

"She is," I assured her.

"Well, good for Summer, and now Mom's having a new baby and it's a girl, so I don't even have to worry about being the only girl anymore." Something about the tight set to Evan's jaw belied the casualness of her words. "I just have to worry about all the wolves in the world wanting me dead. I have to say, at least Marcus wanted me alive."

Fen moved closer to her. "Hey, like I'm going to let that happen."

"Wait, the queen's pregnant again?" Casey asked, looking more animated than he'd been.

"Hah, I knew something before Casey." Trent looked pleased with himself.

"You always know things before I do," Casey shot back.

"Not gossip stuff," Trent countered. "No one ever tells me anything gossipy."

This was rapidly getting out of control. "Hey, someone tell me more about this Alvis person."

"He's dead."

All heads turned as Rufus entered the library. I stood up, facing the slender primal. "I'm sorry, what?"

Rufus's gaze was grave as he moved my way. "Alvis has been murdered. I must ask for your professional services, Ms. Owens."

I sighed. Not even two days back on the plane and I had a dead body to deal with.

Some things never changed.

Chapter Five

"Someone doesn't want you here," Casey said as we stood in the former librarian's rooms.

I would bet at one point in time they had been neatly kept, but it looked like a tornado had come through the book-lined apartment and torn through all of Alvis's things. Including his body.

Which was pretty much everywhere.

When a vampire dies it can go one of two ways. The first is the classic dust to dust method of death. The vampire takes a stake to the heart or gets separated from his noggin and suddenly there's a big old pile of ashes where he'd previously been standing.

Way number two is my least favorite. One of said methods of death occurs and the vampire in question sort of explodes, like a bomb that was filled with blood and guts and bone fragments.

I don't know why some vamps dust their way to whatever afterlife awaits them and others leave a massive mess behind, but I know which one I prefer. However, dust doesn't leave a mega-shit-ton of DNA to investigate.

"Why do you think this is about me?" I wasn't really questioning Casey's thinking, merely wanted to know the logic behind his reasoning.

"Well, he wasn't dead yesterday. I talked to him before you got here. He was alive after sunset, and he was looking forward to meeting with you. Sometime between talking to him and Rufus coming to collect him for the meeting, he was murdered." Casey was way calmer around a dead body than I'd ever remembered him being. Casey was the kid who hadn't liked to be around blood when he'd first turned.

Yeah, we'd made a lot of fun of him in the beginning.

"We need to figure out how many people know about your mission." Trent stood in the foyer of Alvis's apartment, a bit outside the big living room. It was done in dark wood, an elegant, masculine space.

Before all the blood and guts.

I had left the book with Fenrir and Evan, who had explicit instructions to murder anyone who tried to get their hands on it. From the gleam in Evan's eyes, I got the feeling she wouldn't hate having that opportunity.

The queen's daughter was sexually frustrated and ready to take it out on her enemies.

Fen had merely nodded and promised he would protect it before taking Evan's hand and walking back to our rooms.

I wasn't sure if he was worried about the assignment or upset I wasn't taking him with me. If he'd been Lee, I would have expected him to show up at the most inopportune time, but Trent had assured me Fen would follow orders.

"Everyone," Rufus replied. The leader of the primals stood in the foyer with Trent, his mouth turned down in a frown. "Our council of elders was informed of the happenings outside the nest, that the King of all Vampire and his group had returned. We put it to a vote whether we should aid you in your endeavors. I was hoping I wouldn't have to tell you that, but we are a democratic society, and working directly with the *Nex Apparatus* could have consequences."

"Of course." I understood the need to have everyone on board, but the whole *everyone* thing doesn't usually happen in a democracy. What Rufus didn't want to tell me was that there had been members of his society who either wanted to remain neutral or wanted to take their chances with Myrddin. Unfortunately, that was knowledge I needed. "Was Alvis on this council?"

"Oh, yes," Rufus replied. "And he was quite vocal that we should do everything we can to aid the true king."

"Even using that phrase could cause problems for the primals," Trent pointed out. "On the surface you're supposed to remain neutral."

Rufus's head shook slightly, a gentle denial. "We've sheltered too many of Myrddin's enemies to believe the witches think we're truly neutral."

"Yet they've left you alone?" I asked.

"You have to understand that Myrddin's hold on the plane is tenuous at best," Rufus began. "He doesn't have a good grip on the werecreatures, and only a quarter of the vampires have pledged their loyalty to him."

"All of them warriors?" I knew the academics were on our side, but I needed to know how many warrior vamps should be considered enemies.

"Yes." Trent took that one. "Sasha and I keep a list. They're all warriors. The academics are either with us or in safe houses across Europe and Asia. We keep in contact."

Warriors are the most common type of vampire, and also the most physically strong, but don't count out the other vampire classes. We would still have plenty of physical strength on our side. "So Myrddin doesn't attack the primals because he needs to keep the peace while he works on his plans."

"That's a good way to describe the situation. In some ways, we've all been biding time." Rufus had a hand against his chest as though he was struggling to keep his emotions in check. "Myrddin hasn't made good on his deals with the demons, so he needs the plane to stay calm. We have been waiting for the king. We've always known if it came to it, we would be on the side of the Council of Supernatural Creatures. It's the government that formed after the king went missing, an attempt to keep the idea of democracy alive in our world. It's taken a battering over the last few years, but I have hopes the king can bring it back to life."

"How many of your own group didn't want me here?" I was going to have to investigate and potentially win over hearts and minds with my sparkling personality. While we talked, I gingerly made my way around the living space, careful to avoid all of Alvis's parts.

"Of the council of nine, only three voted against allowing you into the nest," Rufus explained. "Their reasoning was to keep the peace with the witches."

"So appeasement, in a sense." I could tell him that hadn't worked out during World War II, but I suspected the primals knew their history. Fear and an unwillingness to start a war that would doubtless come anyway would be the reasons for their hesitancy.

"I assure you that word has been used and argued over," Rufus conceded. "However, I cannot believe any of our elders would do this, but some of our elders have non-vampires attached to their houses. These are beings who are under primal protection. We have a variety of Fae creatures like the gnomes and trolls along with witches, companions, and some werecreatures, including a few orphaned children. I will, of course, give you a list of all our elders and let them know you will need a bit of their time. We've already met concerning Alvis's murder and this investigation, and there were no dissenters this time. We all voted to place the investigation into the hands of the *Nex Apparatus*."

So at least someone was happy the sheriff was back. I hoped they didn't mind my methods, which would include some high-tech fun if Eddie was successful in the errand I'd sent him on.

Less than a full day back on the plane and I was already dragging people I love into murder investigations. It was kind of a thing with me.

"I have asked everyone to stay in their assigned rooms until you sign off on cleaning up in here," Rufus continued. "We have rituals to perform, but we understand how important it is that you have time with the scene of the crime and that we mustn't interfere."

It was actually quite refreshing. Too often people who want my professional services also want power over how I investigate. I usually find these people are the ones who often actually did the crime. Or worse, they think they've watched enough *Law & Order* to really help me out.

Those *Law & Order* cops didn't have to deal with magic and victims who went boom and would decay real fucking fast. I needed our version of *CSI*. *CSI: Supernatural*. I would be the one ripping off my sunglasses and making sarcastic quips.

"I promise I'll get everything I need as quickly as I can when it comes to the forensics." I needed to process the mess of a scene, and there was only one person I knew who could get the job done properly. Unfortunately, she lived a couple of states over, and I wasn't sure her husband would be happy with my request. Though I was certain he would show up.

"Kelsey Jean," a deep voice said.

I closed my eyes and let that sound wash over me. It had been mere days for me, but if there was one thing I'd learned in the hours since I'd returned home, it was that I would feel those years whether I lived them or not. Those twelve years would be between us. I turned and my brothers were standing there.

Jamie and Nate.

"Well, at least she still remembers how to make an entrance," Nate said with a shake of his head.

I moved toward them and held out my arms, taking these men who I'd shared a childhood with into them and holding them close. "Hey, guys. I'm sorry I'm late."

I felt a shudder go through Nate, and Jamie held me so tight.

"We thought we lost you," Jamie admitted quietly.

"Thank god you're back. I was almost going to name my daughter after you," Nate admitted. "Now she can have a good name."

"Asshole," I whispered.

"It's good to have you back," Nate returned.

"It's good to be back. I'm sorry I was away so long." I wasn't sure why I kept apologizing, but it seemed like the thing to do. After hearing everything Casey had told me, sensing all the things Fenrir wasn't telling me, I knew my absence had been felt deeply. It didn't matter that it wasn't my fault. I still wished I'd been here to fight with them, to fight for them.

Jamie stepped back, and I could see the sprinkling of gray in his dark hair. He looked me over, a smile on his face. "Damn, you look exactly the same. I mean I understand it's only been a couple of days for you, but in my mind I guess I always saw you aging with us. Mom…you have to come and see her when it's safe or let us come to whatever crazy base Donovan and Quinn will set up."

"Tell Dan that I'm not staying out of this war forever," Nate agreed. "Gray convinced us to stay out of it until the Council was ready to move, but we're going to be there. I married a shifter. She's pregnant. This is my war, too."

Nate had been friends with Donovan since he was a kid. They'd been in a game group for years together, and I'd played with them. When we were kids, Nate had been the brother who played with me, and Jamie had watched out for us both. Our dad—their biological father—had been an abusive prick, and sometimes I only thought I survived my childhood because of my brothers.

And Olivia.

I wasn't about to get into a fight with my brothers over staying out of a war I would have to fight. But that didn't mean I wouldn't do everything in my power to make sure they were safe. "Let's worry about that another day. I'll talk to Donovan. As for the war, well, there's a lot to do. I have to figure out this whole mystical weapon that can kill Myrddin thing. Which recently got harder since our subject matter expert is…well, he's all over the place. Where's Nicole? I thought Eddie was bringing her back?"

"That's what I'm here for," Nate said. "I assure you I've learned all of Nicole's ways. She's on maternity leave."

"She had David three weeks ago, Kels," Jamie explained. "She wanted to be here but she's not allowed to do anything more than feed the baby. It was a rough birth. C-section. She needs her rest, and Nate is nowhere near as good as my wife, but he's getting there."

Nate's eyes rolled. "I'm excellent, and you wouldn't know what to do without me."

I never imagined my brothers, who had been raised by an actual hunter, would end up being law enforcement's liaisons to the supernatural world. "We're sure I'm not breaking the contract by bringing you in? I don't want to bring Myrddin down on your head. Trent said this would be an exception."

"We're allowed to investigate crimes," Jamie assured me. "We've even worked two jobs at different coven houses. One in Massachusetts and one in Idaho. It's in our contract that we can investigate. We can protect ourselves if attacked. We can't interfere beyond that. We're good. The primals will put in the paperwork, though they'll leave you out of it, of course."

At least they were safe. "Well, then we should get to work."

I stood back and let my brothers do their jobs.

* * * *

"Here's what I can tell you," Nate began, looking up from his microscope. My brother had taken business classes in college, but he was all about the science now. "The DNA is definitely from a vamp, and he's totally dead."

I rolled my eyes. We were out of Alvis's murder rooms and into a set of what Rufus described as the laboratories/medical facilities. Not that vamps tended to need doctors, but as he'd explained, there were other creatures in the Under, and the primals attempted to be accommodating. In this case that meant a couple of high-tech, ultra-modern rooms where all the scientific stuff Nate had brought looked at home.

I was rapidly discovering the primals' nest was an intricate circuit of fantasy rooms. I hadn't seen a space yet that wasn't the ultimate expression of what that room should be. Like the "bedroom" we'd been assigned that looked like a suite at the Ritz in Paris. I only knew what that looked like because Marcus had taken me once.

They were almost like Hollywood sets, except these were all functional spaces.

"Tell me something I don't know, Nathan."

We'd spent a couple of hours going over every inch of Alvis's apartment and the hallway outside before surrendering the remains to Rufus and his group of official mourners. The service for Alvis would take place sometime before dawn, though I'd been told the mourning would last several days.

"All right." Nate turned to the team, clapping his hands together. "I'll tell you something I find interesting. There's Atropa belladonna in the toxicology report on the soup."

I hated the term, but there wasn't a lot of other words for what a vampire who didn't turn to dust left behind. Soup. Nate and Jamie had carefully collected as much of Alvis as they could, and they'd processed the remains. Jamie had taken a ton of photographs while Casey followed me and took notes. Trent was still out in the nest tracking scents. Fenrir had followed him while Evan had joined us in the lab, the backpack and book in tow.

"Deadly Nightshade?" Evan's mahogany-colored hair was in a long braid, and she wore jeans and boots with a dark tunic that she'd belted. There was a knife in a holster around her waist, though I'd learned that wasn't her preferred weapon. She was a bow and arrow girl. "That's a poison, but it certainly wouldn't kill a primal."

"Belladonna?" I'd heard the term but didn't know what kind of poison we were talking about.

"It's a plant mostly grown in Europe," Evan replied. "Though you can certainly find it in the States. It's used medicinally to treat any number of human ailments. But it's also known as a deadly poison if the berries are orally ingested, though you should know the whole plant is considered dangerous. The berries contain atropine, which can stop the heart."

"Is it possible it's grown down here?" I asked.

Evan shook her head. "They have gardens in the Under, but I've never seen them grow belladonna. The gnomes would know. They pretty much rule the gardens."

"Dare I ask how there are gardens with no sun?" I was fairly certain I knew the answer, but it's good to make sure.

"Magic, of course." Evan leaned against the counter. "And Rhys. He can imbue these globes with his power, and the gnomes use them to grow the plants they need. There's a magical sun in the gardens, but it's for show. No UV light allowed in the Under. The primals are super sensitive to it. I know the gnomes grow food for the companions who live here, along with the Fae creatures. There are definitely some medicinal plants, but I worked in the gardens many times, and no one ever pointed out belladonna to me. I don't think our healers use it, but I can ask."

"It's also historically been used as a hallucinogen," Jamie pointed out.

Evan nodded. "Witches' ointment. As far back as the fifteenth century, witches discovered that if they combined belladonna with fats or oils, they could topically apply it and avoid the deadly effects of oral ingestion."

"And they would do this, why?" I asked.

"Applied in that fashion it's a powerful hallucinogen." Nate joined the parade of smarty pants I found myself in.

I wasn't a smarty pants, but that's why I surrounded myself with them. Normally the witch knowledge came from Liv, but she was busy going through some things, so I was happy Evan and my brothers were serious about keeping up with arcane knowledge.

"Would it work on a vamp?"

Evan shrugged. "No idea. Nate, did you turn up any other herbs? Like henbane or mandragora?"

Nate held up the report. "Got trace amounts of both. Are you thinking a ritual or a party?"

"Could be either. Though I'm not sure why Alvis would be involved." Evan turned my way, not requiring me to ask. "So historically witches would use the witches' ointment combined with other herbs they either put in the mixture, or they would burn the herbs—henbane specifically—and that along with a spell would send the witch into an altered state. And by witch, I really mean anyone. It would totally work on humans, very likely Fae and werecreatures as well. The Fae are not immune to hallucinogens, and neither are wolves, though you should know Fen just mostly wants belly rubs and to eat. It was only the once, and I was smart enough to not eat the damn things. But in this case the henbane could also potentially be a way to contact the Hell plane. Since it's a virtual call and not physical, I don't know that the wards here in the Under would work to shut it down. I also have no idea how a vampire would react."

"First off, the vampire wouldn't simply down a couple of berries." I knew quite a bit about vampire dietary habits since I'd lived with one for a while. Vampires don't eat solid food, and they don't drink the way the rest of us did. It's pretty much all blood all the time for those guys. But there were ways around it. "However, if he fed off someone who had belladonna in their system, it might affect him. I know some vampires can get drunk if their feeding partner for the night has had enough liquor."

"You're talking about my dads." Evan made a gagging sound. "Aren't you?"

"I could be talking about any number of vampires." I didn't want to put Donovan and Quinn in an awkward position.

"She's totally talking about your dads." Nate did not have the same problem. "Your dad—the faery one—used to drink an entire bottle of Scotch. Like he would down that sucker in minutes and it wouldn't affect him at all, but then Dan would feed and he would be so drunk."

"Dude, you're talking about her dads." Jamie stared at our brother. "You know you're about to be one. Do you want me to tell your daughter how you used to miss the toilet when you had a little too much?"

Nate went a nice shade of red. "Well, I mean, it's not like they did anything weird after or anything."

"Weird like what?" Evan's brows had risen, a queenly expression.

"You know. Weird." Nate knew how to throw a friend under a bus but not how to deal with said friend's baby girl calling him on it.

"Like sex? You think I don't know my dads have sex? Or do you think the fact that they're married and in a loving relationship means sex between two men is still wrong?" Evan asked pointedly. "Is it weird for people who love each other to have sex, Nathan?"

Nate looked my way. Like I was going to save him.

"Yeah, Nathan, do you have a problem with two men having sex?" I happily threw my brother under a lot of busses. It was fun to watch him squirm.

A low chuckle came from behind me, and I turned around to see Trent walking in, Fenrir behind him. Trent winked my way. "Are you giving your brother hell, baby?"

"I would like to point out that I don't have any problem with consensual sex of any kind," Nate began. "And obviously I'm thrilled that my sister is in a healthy relationship with a werewolf, and also Gray gets worked in there, too. Like I don't know when I became the bad guy."

Evan's whole face lit up, and even though I couldn't see that girl's glow, there was no question when she wanted to, she could light up a room. "I'm giving you shit, Nathan. I know all about Dad's and Papa's weird drinking experiments. And to answer Kelsey's question, it would be possible to infect a vampire's blood supply with belladonna, though again, I'm not sure how it would affect the vamp. Since the atropine affects the heart, it potentially could slow down a vampire's heart function, and that might make the vamp easier to kill."

"Oh, you know I love it when you talk all smart and stuff." Fenrir got into Evan's space, his arm going around her waist and pulling her back against his body.

"I always talk smart," Evan protested, though she had a grin on her face.

"She's mean," Nate complained. "Aren't you supposed to protect me, sis?"

"Not from yourself." I turned to my husband, who was smoking hot. Even after everything he'd done to me earlier, I was still thinking about getting my hands on him. "Anything interesting?"

"Well, the weird thing is there's not a discernable scent in the apartment beyond Alvis himself," Trent replied with a frown. "Even around his apartment there's like a dead zone. We're the only ones I can smell, along with Rufus. It's like no one had walked up to his apartment for days, but that would be surprising."

"Alvis is a very social guy." Fen relaxed as Evan leaned back against him. "He's always having people over."

"He counsels the younger primals," Evan explained. "I would be shocked if he hadn't had a party or meeting of some kind in the last few days. The last time we were here, he was holding regular counseling meetings every other day with Christopher. I think he had a few other regulars. And while primals are extremely tidy here in the nest, they don't use anything that would get rid of scents so thoroughly Trent couldn't follow it."

"There are some herbs and spells that would, however," Evan pointed out. "We might need to talk to a witch."

"He definitely had people come to his door today. I picked up some scents about halfway down the hall. I believe those were from guests of Alvis." Trent moved in beside me. "I checked with Rufus and I only followed the ones I believe were there earlier today. There are many scents in the hall once you get past the effects of the dead zone, but they're going back days."

"Did we find a place where Alvis kept a schedule?" I asked.

Casey finally looked up from his laptop. He'd been sitting at the back of the room ignoring all talks about toxicology and the science of soup. He was more comfortable around dead bodies, but he still didn't like talking about them. "He had an extensive online presence, and yes, I found a place where he kept his appointments and communicated with his mentees, as he called them."

"Are those like manatees?" Fen scratched behind his ear.

"No, babe. You're thinking of those big water creatures that sometimes get mistaken for mermaids by people who've never seen a real mermaid and don't know how slutty they can look," Evan replied primly. "Casey's talking about the fact that Alvis mentored young primals. He's the mentor. They're his mentees."

I was glad at least one of them had some interest in intellectual pursuits.

"Oh," Fen said, looking all dumb boy cute. "So by young you mean anyone under three hundred or so, 'cause the primals are old, if you know what I mean. And should we slut shame mermaids?"

"Yes," Evan and I both said at the same time.

Trent chuckled. "I think this is one of those things the ladies can say and we should stay far, far away from. Though I would like to point out that I prefer manatees. Perfectly friendly creatures and when you turn one down, they don't even try to rip your balls off."

Casey's lips had turned up slightly, but he got back to business. "Alvis kept meticulous records, and he used some high-tech ways to organize. For a vampire as old as he was, it's very modern. Henri still writes down all his notes in a leatherbound notebook. I tried to show him how to use an iPad and I swear his brain nearly exploded, but you know what wouldn't have happened if he'd used a damn tablet?"

"He wouldn't have lost all his notes when Myrddin took over the Council building," Trent finished, as though he'd heard the story more than once.

I needed to keep everyone on track. "So Alvis had appointments today?"

"Yes." Casey's eyes went back to his laptop screen. "But not until nine. He had nothing on his books before then. I can give you a list of who he's seen in the last few days."

"He has a lot of friends, though," Evan said. "All the times we've stayed here, I know Alvis often entertained."

"How does a primal entertain? I have to ask because most of the vampires I know are shitty hosts." I meant that in the nicest way possible. It wasn't their fault they couldn't eat food so they didn't think up elaborate dinner party menus.

"Probably like Dan used to," Nate added. "I love your dad, Evan, but when it was his night to host game night, snacks would be like a single bag of chips. Between like five of us, and one of us was a shifter."

Fen gasped like he couldn't think of anything worse.

"Well, he doesn't eat," Evan defended. "And I'm sure that was before he married Mom and Papa and inherited Albert. Albert would never allow someone to go hungry in his home. Even when we were on the run, somehow Albert and Eddie would find food and make sure everyone ate their fill. I often didn't ask what was in those tacos of Eddie's. Especially on the dinosaur plane."

"That was a good idea on your part," Trent assured her. "Though I have to admit, brontosaurus was pretty damn tasty. And nobody chide me about eating endangered creatures. I assure you those suckers weren't in any danger of going extinct there."

Well, of course my wolf would try all the weird meat. "I'd like a list of everyone Alvis met with regularly and we'll see if Trent recognizes their scents. I'd like to ID anyone he doesn't normally see, though I'll still need to talk to the people on that list."

Casey closed his laptop. "I think we should look into the witches down here. There are around twenty, and while each one passed all of Sasha's tests, we can't discount the idea that they could still be undercover agents for Myrddin. There are two in particular I'm interested in because I know they were in Alvis's circle."

"Relda and Jade aren't agents of Myrddin." Evan's shoulders squared, and I was starting to understand this was her "I mean business and I'm going to argue hard" stance. "They've been down here for years serving the citizens of the Under faithfully. Do you forget how they helped nurse Lee after he lost his eye?"

Casey stood. "No, I don't forget, but I also know that sometimes Myrddin can play a long game. He knows the king has returned, and that will move his timeline up. We've reached a dangerous time in this war. We can't trust anyone outside of the inner circle."

"Are you in the inner circle?" Evan challenged. "I don't see much of you so how would I know? Or perhaps I'm not considered inner circle. Should we have badges?"

"I'm an academic, Your Highness." Casey got somber quite fast. "One who has been working on this plane risking my life for twelve years while Trent and Sasha trained you. I'm not saying you haven't done your part. You were children and you needed to grow up, but I did my growing up here and I did it by wading through the blood of my friends and fighting people I still love. I work for the *Nex Apparatus*. Until she or your father dismisses me, I will be here and I will give my advice. I am not a *yes* man. I will give counsel as I see fit, and it will not be dependent on the whims of a princess."

A low growl came from Fenrir's throat, and I worried I was going to have to step between him and Casey—who I was kind of proud of for that speech.

Instead, Evan was the one who placed a hand on Fen's chest, and she softened her expression. "Stand down, Fen. I was being a brat because I'm still processing the fact that my parents are back and it didn't go the way I thought it would. I'm starting to understand that I had unrealistic expectations. Casey is right. He's been here for years longer than I have, and the academics have never faltered when it came to supporting my parents. Not once. Not even when they had stakes to their hearts." She turned back to Casey. "I apologize. And you know I don't go by a title."

Casey nodded, showing he accepted the apology. "But you do now. It's important that you acknowledge your royalty. Anything less is to say your father is not the king. You are Princess Evangeline of Vampire and Lady Evangeline of the High Fae. I know you have trouble with your Fae relatives, but you must acknowledge them now that your father is back. Devinshea might be able to bring them to our side."

"I don't like politics," Evan said with a frown. "I prefer being a fighter."

"You and me both, sister." I was on Evan's side in this. "I prefer to leave the politics to the men and kick a little ass."

"What Casey said is correct though." Trent's arms were crossed over that glorious chest of his. "We've all been in a holding pattern, and now the war will begin in earnest. That means we need to deal with the wolves."

"There is no *deal with the wolves*." Fenrir stepped back, and I could see he was emotional. It was there in the way his eyes darkened, how his hands clenched. "You know what they want from me, Father. I will not do it."

"I didn't say you needed to deal with them politically, son. I know what it means to have a mate. She is the one thing you can never sacrifice," Trent said.

"That's the problem. The wolves don't see me as a mate," Evan replied, her tone calm as though she knew she needed to keep Fen from losing his cool. "They see me as a crush their king has who will be easily forgotten once he's properly mated."

"Then they've never heard him call for you." Trent moved toward Fenrir, his focus going to our son. "Fenrir, you called to her when you were sixteen. We were on the wolf plane and the mountain troll attacked. You thought you were going to die, and you called to her in wolf form. That was a mating call, and it is only performed for one female in your whole life. Make no mistake. I will always support your relationship with Evan. I wouldn't ask you to give her up any more than I would give up your mother. When I say we deal with the wolves, we do it on our terms. You are a king. They will take you as you are or they will face your wrath."

I found him extremely sexy in that moment, but I did have a few questions. "Are you saying they'll bow before Fen or die? Because that seems pretty rough, babe."

"I didn't mean it that way," Trent hedged.

"He means they can accept me as their king with my mate at my side, choose to leave me alone, or I'll kill every one of the fuckers who come after her," Fen promised. "That's what he's talking about. There have been several attempts on her life, and they didn't come from Myrddin. Up until now I've been forced to negotiate to protect Evan. I won't do that a second more. I will kill anyone who thinks about harming my mate, and I will do it with the full force of the King of All Vampire behind me."

"And His Grace, the High Priest of Faery," Evan pointed out. "Papa might not like our relationship, but I assure you he'll like those wolves far less. Honestly, the one they should be afraid of is my mother."

"They should be afraid of me." I wasn't about to allow a bunch of wolves to harm my son or his mate. I wouldn't let them hurt anyone, but especially not two kids who kind of belonged to me.

Fen's gaze softened, as though my acceptance had calmed him in some way. "Yes, they should. My mother has killed far greater enemies. And she trusts Casey and the academics. Please forgive my lapse of control. I need a run."

"That's not what you need," Evan said under her breath.

He probably desperately needed his mate, but he'd made a deal with her brothers, and Fen seemed set on keeping his promises.

"Let's go," Trent offered. "I'll have Eddie take us back to the bayou. It's a full moon, and it's been a while since the townsfolk have had a werewolf sighting."

Fen shook his head. "It's your first night with Mom. I'll be fine."

"He needs to run since he won't do the other thing," Evan said firmly.

"Your dad and I are fine. We spent the whole afternoon together." I didn't want Trent to go but I had a few things to deal with here, and it was easy to see not running on the full moon was having an impact on Fen. The last thing I wanted was him out there alone. "Go and have a good time, and I'll see you tomorrow for breakfast. I'll catch you both up on everything we get done tonight."

Fen frowned. "Are you sure?"

I got into his space and brushed his hair back like I used to when he was a kid. "I am sure. Evan will help me with the investigation."

Evan gasped slightly. "I get to investigate? I usually get put on the sidelines."

"Uhm, not with me you won't. Or your mom. You should understand the chicks are back, and we're going to take control," I replied. The queen and I didn't sit on the sidelines. Our daughters wouldn't either.

Evan grinned and picked up the backpack again. "Excellent. Then I have questions about the book. I hope you don't mind I looked through it. I didn't get far because the words disappeared the minute Fen looked over my shoulder."

"The words disappeared?" Jamie asked.

Nate's eyes went wide. "I thought we needed that book. Should we be panicking?"

I waved off the fear. "Nah. She's just shy and she doesn't like men."

"That book is rude," Fen declared.

I hadn't even thought about the fact that Evan and I would be the only ones who could read the sucker. I'd worried about taking the queen's baby girl with us, but I now realized I totally needed her. "They'll come back. It can take a while though."

"Maybe it'll go faster if we do some feminine things around her," Evan suggested.

"I don't think doing mani pedis is going to help anything," Casey said with a sigh.

"I was thinking more along the lines of kicking the guys' asses. She might appreciate that," Evan offered. "I could use a sparring session. I don't get to work off my sexual tension in wolf form."

I liked the way that girl thought.

Both of my brothers put a single finger to their noses and said in harmony, "Not it."

Casey frowned. "Well, I'm not it."

"Spoilsports." Evan pulled the backpack into her hands and settled it on her back. "Come along, book. We'll follow Kelsey around and watch her baddassery and solve a crime while the boys play with microscopes and run around the woods. We have to find a murderer."

Yep. Woman's work.

Chapter Six

"So the book doesn't like men. You know you have a lot of men on your team," Evan pointed out as we walked down the hallway toward the apartment that was our first destination.

"Huh. I guess I never thought about it. I work with a bunch of vamps. They're pretty much all dudes." Vampirism was a gene that almost exclusively affected the Y chromosome. As with all things "gender," it's complicated, so there were a couple of female vamps out there, but I hadn't met them. "It was pretty much the academics and Liv."

"Yeah. Sorry about that. I had a friend go bad once," Evan said. "She got bitten by this bug that infects a part of your brain that affects moral choices, and she tried to murder me. But not before she slept with Lee. Everyone sleeps with Lee."

"There's a bug that takes away your morality?"

"It was another plane. Great baked goods, shitty insects," Evan replied. "I was fourteen, and she was the only friend I'd had in a long time. It hurt to lose her."

"Did you have to kill her?"

"No. Trent did it for me." Evan's boots barely made a sound despite the fact that we were walking on hardwood floors. "He was a good foster dad, you know. You should be proud to be his wife."

"I am." More and more every second. "I'm glad he took care of you."

"He took care of us and never let us forget who our parents were," Evan said. "He would tell us stories every night. He even told us about Fen's granddad, your real dad. I sometimes think those were his favorite stories. I know Lee loved them."

Probably because they were about him, about the him he'd been before. When my real father, Lee Owens, had died, he'd chosen to come back to earth and been reborn as Rhys's twin. "That doesn't surprise me. My dad had some adventures. How do you feel about Lee being a latent vampire?"

Evan sighed. "I'm relieved that when he dies he'll get another shot. You don't understand how much we all worry about Lee. He's a reckless asshole. I can't tell you how many times I thought he would die. Fen can run wild, but he has the power to back it up. Fen often had to run into danger because Lee got mouthy with some crazy, powerful creature who was about to take his head off. And I was the only girl. So I was the only sane one."

I could totally understand her position. "I'm sorry. You should have had a woman to help guide you. I know Sarah Day would have helped you if she could. I would have had I been here."

"Well, I wish you had because Trent trying to explain menstruation to me was all kinds of confusing," Evan admitted. "I wasn't sure if I was going to die or not. He said a lot of stuff about transformation, so I was worried I might turn into something, and not something good since he'd told the boys they should be careful around me during that time."

I snorted. "He grew up in a weird wolf cult. I don't think he got a lot of education on biology. I'm certain he never thought he would be raising a girl on his own."

"Well, he kind of wasn't. Sasha was off on a mission when it all went down," Evan explained. "When he came back, he found out I'd had my first period and he bought this book and sat down with me. In the beginning, some people thought I shouldn't go with my brothers because I was a companion and Sasha was a warrior. They thought I didn't hear, but I'm pretty good at listening in. Even the academics thought it would be ill-advised to leave me with Sasha. They wanted to take me to Faery and leave me with my grandmother. Trent wouldn't allow it. Sasha wouldn't leave me behind either. He's always been so gentle with me. Well, until he makes me practice fighting or archery, and then he's a harsh taskmaster. I think about that big vampire and how he sat patiently and read a book about my changing body and tried his hardest to explain things to me, and I know that even without my mom and dads I had this great gift of family."

"He had a daughter, you know," I said, thinking of everything Sasha had lost.

She nodded. "Natasha. We follow her on social media. She's in college. She seems happy. I'll show Sasha and he smiles, but I know there's an ache inside him. I wish he could find a companion he could love. I worry he's going to spend an eternity looking for his wife. He's sure we come across the same souls again and again. I would say he's overly romantic, but I know Lee's your father down deep."

"Do you remember that time?" My father had resurfaced for a couple of days after a spell had gone wrong. He'd proven that version of him was in the body of Lee Donovan-Quinn. Evan had been so young at the time.

She shook her head. "No. Not at all. I was four or five, I think. But Rhys remembers. Lee knows it deep down. I think Fenrir and I have been together before. Sometimes I think I was supposed to be a wolf and something got screwed up. Or Fen was supposed to be a vampire."

"His biological father is a vampire," I pointed out. "Have you thought about that?"

Her head shook. "It doesn't matter. He'll always be a wolf first, and I'll always be a companion. Someone pointed out that Fenrir will outlive me by at least a hundred years. I'll get old and die and he'll still be in his prime."

"Or you can take your father's blood," I countered. I rather thought I was being used as a sounding board for a conversation she needed to have with her mom. I was okay with that. "I know he sent some with you. I thought he was being careful, but it's more than that, isn't it?"

She stopped, turning to me in the middle of the hall. "Am I wrong to try to hold on to him? Am I going to be the reason he's miserable one day? If I walked away from him, would he be able to find a she-wolf and be happy?"

I turned to her, needing her to feel the full power of my will in this. "I have been on this plane for one day, Evan, and I already know that my son cannot be happy without you."

"Papa said it's young love and it always feels like this."

I was going to have a talk with Dev Quinn. I got that he didn't like the idea of his precious little girl in a serious relationship. I understood that in his mind she was still the five-year-old baby he'd left behind, but they were going to make a huge mistake if they tried to come between Fen and Evan. The last thing I needed was a Romeo and Juliet situation. Trent and I had talked about this earlier today, and he'd heard Fen's call. "Your papa isn't a wolf. We mate for life, and it doesn't matter when we find our true mates. Honestly, it doesn't happen for all wolves, but for those who find their mate, it's a connection we can't deny. Trent's soul speaks to mine. He can calm me with a touch. Like you can with Fenrir. I know it seems like the world is against you, and if that's too much, then that's too bad because this is fate, and I don't think there's a way around it."

Her green eyes shone with unshed tears, but her lips curved up. "I told myself if you didn't hesitate, I can stand up to my papa."

"You could always stand up to him." I'd already seen her strength. "You don't need anyone's permission to stand up for yourself or for your relationship. I will stand with you when it comes to the wolves but, sweet girl, you need to be practical and take your father's blood."

"But the very act of taking it points out that I'm not a proper mate for Fen."

"Or it's a gift you were given so you can stay with him for as long as you should." I knew how to turn this around. Strangely enough, Quinn had been the one to teach me how to turn what seemed like weaknesses into strength. "This soul of yours, that's the part that speaks to Fenrir, the part that has likely loved him before. That soul is housed in a companion body, and a companion with regular vampire blood can live a long time. As long as a wolf."

"I never thought about it that way. But it's true. Companions on vampire blood can live up to one hundred and fifty years," she mused. "Fenrir and I are almost the same age. My father's blood means we could have a whole supernatural life together."

"Your father's blood is a gift. Don't look at it like proof you're not a wolf. Look at it as proof that the universe will give you the tools you need if you're brave enough to use them." It was time to give her one more tool. "And the next time your papa says something, tell him that. Tell him the universe gave you everything you needed to fulfill your destiny."

"Okay, I'll bite. Why would I say that?" Evan asked.

"Because it's exactly the words he said to me when I didn't believe in myself."

Evan wiped away a single tear and smiled at me. "Excellent. It's good to know my papa believes in fate. He's going to have to believe in mine. I wanted to make sure you're okay with me and Fen. I would have understood if you were worried."

"Oh, I worry. I'll likely worry every day for the rest of my life, but *for* you, not *about* you, Evangeline," I assured the young woman who would someday be my daughter-in-law. "Now tell me what you know about the witches we're going to talk to."

She straightened up as though I'd said some magical words that turned her from lovestruck teen to soldier. "Relda is the older of the two. She's in her forties, I think. Jade is twenty-two. Relda led a coven in the Seattle area until she refused to swear fealty to Myrddin. He slaughtered half her coven, but she made it out."

"He's been killing witches?" I don't know why I was surprised, but I was. I suppose I thought he had some decency.

"Yes," Evan replied. "He kills anyone who gets in his way. He killed Jade's mother. They lived in the Council House in Dallas, and from what I understand her mom worked with Myrddin in the beginning. Until she saw what he was doing and started to fight back. Sasha says she fed the academics information for a while and then Myrddin caught her. She was burned at the stake. Jade was forced to watch, and then she was supposed to be 'reeducated,' as Myrddin calls it. My grandma got her out."

"The queen?" I thought the queen of the Seelie Fae had chosen to stay out of this war. I knew she'd refused my son entrance when they'd sought refuge. The Seelies had wanted Rhys and Evan, but they wouldn't allow Fenrir and Lee in. Or Sasha and Trent.

Evan's head shook. "My human grandmother. My grandfather's wife. You know my family isn't one of mere blood. Like you and Fen. Christine didn't need blood to be loyal to us. I'm hoping she can come home now. She's lived in the Council House for years."

I looked around to make sure no one was listening. "Evan, maybe we should…"

She reached into her pocket and pulled out a talisman. "Kelsey, I'm not a newbie. Lily makes sure we have a steady supply of these. No one can hear me talking unless I can physically see them. To normal people it would seem like I'm whispering and they can't quite catch what I say. They won't be able to hear you either. Unless I'm looking at them. Then they hear us quite well. Didn't you notice how Fenrir and I walked into the room and made eye contact with everyone? We wanted to make sure we didn't leave anyone out. I have to activate it. I wouldn't want it to suppress my voice all the time, but there are creatures here who have especially sensitive ears."

"How do you activate it?" I wanted one.

"Blood, of course." She slid the talisman back into her pocket. "Or tears. Like I just did before I talked about something I would never talk about in the open. I would never mention my grandma's name. Even here. But you're the *Nex Apparatus*. You're Kelsey. I trust you the way I would my own parents."

That got me a little teary, and I didn't even need tears to prime some talisman that made it so I could talk around potential enemies. "Well, thank you. I'm glad you're here with me. But if one witch knows about Christine Wharton, we have to worry that they all do."

"Oh, no. Grandma is way sneakier than that." Evan started walking again. "She smuggled Jade out, but not before giving her a whammy. Jade was languishing at the reconditioning school one day and in the back of a van the next, and she didn't know anything except that she trusted the people driving her. That was part of the whammy. Jade didn't know a lot about her powers until she came here. Relda taught her most of what she knows. Myrddin wouldn't allow her to be trained until she'd proven her loyalty."

"Were either of them close to Alvis?"

"Everyone knew him, but I'm not sure how close they were," Evan admitted. "I've stayed in Frelsi most of the time for the last two years. We've run raids from there. Since we started actively fucking with Myrddin, we've stayed away as much as we can."

"But Trent was here when we got back."

"Well," she began.

I knew the kids and the adults had a disagreement about when we would potentially return. They'd needed an enormous amount of magic to break into the Coven House, and storing it up had taken them years. They'd had three dates, and Sasha and Trent had agreed to expend all of their magic on one.

Not the one Rhys Donovan-Quinn had decided was the right one.

Sasha would have been easy to handle. He spent his days in a vampiric coma. It was Trent they had to deal with. If they waylaid Trent, Lee could easily steal what they needed, and Eddie would take them anywhere. Especially if they presented it to him as a life or death, no time to think scenario.

"How did you get rid of Trent?" I couldn't be mad at them. They'd been right. If Sasha and Trent had their way, we would probably be in a cage somewhere in Dallas being tortured by my old bestie. So my questions were strictly out of curiosity. There would be no lectures from me about respecting authority.

She stopped before we reached the end of the hallway. This section of the nest looked like I was walking into a soothing spa. There was a rock wall to our left, and water flowed down it, the sound rhythmic. Dark green ivy sprouted all around, and we walked on a carpet of perfectly kept grass.

"Rhys had the gnomes tell Rufus there was a serious problem. Sometimes the gnomes hear things from the grapevine."

"Grapevine?"

"Yes. It's not literally a grapevine, but it is a vine," she allowed. "It's how the gnomes communicate on this plane. All underground. Like an earth-friendly telephone. So the gnomes said they heard a rumor about Myrddin preparing a raid on one of the safe houses, but they wouldn't talk until Trent got there."

It was the oldest trick in the book. "He should have known."

"I can be convincing when I want to." Her eyes went wide and tears formed there. "Please, Trent. I have friends in safe houses. I could go instead. I could take care of it."

My hand drifted to my stomach, the reality of being a mom washing over me once again. "I'm going to have to be the authoritarian with this baby, aren't I?"

The tears were gone. "Absolutely. And I'm sure he's annoyed with us, but we took the chance that Rhys was right. He'd read the signs. I know the academics think they're good with prophecy, but give me a Green Man and a wriggly mystic pig any day of the week. Here we are."

We stood in front of an ornately carved wooden door. The arced double doors were adorned with a massive tree of life.

I'd seen that tree once when Gray and I had been transported to a place where all fates were possible, where the world was nothing but a seemingly endless string of prospective futures. It had been the place that imbued my demon husband with his dark prophet powers.

It was also the first time I'd thought of having children. Because I'd seen them in that space, seen their smiling faces and felt the love I had for them and their fathers.

Where the hell was Gray? What was I going to do about this boy's father?

"Kelsey? Are you okay?" Evan asked.

I wasn't but it didn't matter. I had a job to do. I steeled myself and nodded and Evan rang the bell.

* * * *

"I can't believe he's gone." Relda Tolk was a statuesque woman, the long gown she wore gliding over her slender limbs. She definitely had a hippie witch vibe, but then that would describe her whole domicile, as Eddie would put it. "Alvis has been a member of our community for as long as I can remember."

"Which isn't long compared to the life of a primal." Jade looked like a typical teen/young adult in her jeans and T-shirt, long curly hair in a pile on her head. She settled a tea set on the table that sat between them and Evan and I in their living room.

Though it seemed more like an art studio. There were several unfinished canvases around the room. I hadn't seen what the artist was painting. I'd had a glimpse of one black canvas with dots of light before we'd taken our place here on the comfy couch.

"Yes, it's true." Relda used an old-school handkerchief to dab at her eyes. "The breadth of knowledge and wisdom we've lost... Well, it hurts my heart."

Relda began to pour out cups of tea with a practiced hand.

"I was told he was quite popular down here." I wasn't sure I should drink that tea. "None for me. I'm trying to avoid caffeine."

"Oh, it's green tea, dear," Relda promised. "No caffeine for me either. I have to keep my system pure. It's the only way to truly mirror the goddess and what she wants for us. Clean body, strong spirit."

Jade snorted. "She's worried it's poisoned, Rel."

"No, she's not." Evan shook her head and obviously wanted to play the politician.

I'd tried polite. It never works. Best to be upfront. "Your friend is right. I don't know this place or the people down here, and while I adore Evan, I have to make my own decisions. I'm fairly certain poison was used to weaken Alvis to the point someone could kill him. The dude is probably still on my shoes. I'm not drinking anything my butler didn't make for me. No offense."

But it was obvious I had offended the witch.

Jade simply sat back. "I think that's a smart call for a woman whose job is to guard the supernatural world. You know if you hadn't been galivanting across the planes, we might not be in the shithole we're in."

Relda gasped. "Jade, you can't talk to people like that. And in front of the princess."

"Oh, the princess can curse up a storm, and Jade knows that." Evan reached into her seemingly never-ending pockets—I had to wonder if that jacket of hers wasn't enchanted—and pulled out a small package. She flipped it open and brought out a tiny dropper she used to extract some liquid from the cup she'd been given. She quickly dropped it on something in the package and then turned it my way. "See. Perfectly fine. This device is something Casey cooked up using one of those smart watches and some tech I don't understand. I only know it works on pretty much everything that can poison a chick. Even not actual poison. One time I tried it on the meat the trolls said was chicken. It was not. You gotta be careful with trolls. They do not mind eating a pet or two."

I wanted one of those. Like most academics, Casey's strongest talents were in one intellectual discipline. If I needed medical knowledge, Henri was my guy. Same with legal for Hugo. Casey had a talent for technology. He could fix machines he'd never used before, and he could gadget up a chick. "Excellent."

Relda frowned and continued pouring the tea. "It seems a bit rude to assume someone is going to poison you."

"Well, it happened to Evan's mom, and it was in tea," Jade said, sitting back. "Queen Zoey lost a child to that tea. I think the *Nex Apparatus* is smart to be on the lookout. She doesn't know us. We're witches. We're kind of the poster children for evil right now."

"We certainly are not," Relda insisted. "And now she knows my tea is perfectly fine and she can have some."

I frowned. See, politeness doesn't get you out of shit. "Well, it's still tea."

"Yes." Relda held it out for me.

Jade snorted. "I think she's saying it's tea. It tastes like wet leaves and sadness."

Tea was probably sad it wasn't beer.

"Tea is delicious." Evan accepted her cup, and I wondered who'd taught her manners because they were perfect. Someone had worked hard to teach her how to comport herself in society, and it wouldn't have been my husband. "And yours is well known to be superlative, Relda. Thank you for your hospitality. You'll have to forgive my friend. She's a wolf, and I would bet she's sad that tea isn't beer."

Hah. Truth. "I'm simply not a fan, and didn't that happen to Zoey...I mean the queen in Faery? I wasn't aware that was widely known on this plane."

I only knew because Marcus liked to gossip. I mean he called it writing shit down for historical purposes, but I say gossip is gossip.

Jade perked up. "Oh, everything about the queen is known. Did you know that when she was young she stole the Essence of Tor? Like right out from under the owner."

I liked the queen, but I didn't know her every move, and I definitely didn't want to hear about her stealing essences. That usually means some form of bodily fluid, and I'd had enough of that today. "Very cool."

"Jade has been working on a biography of my mother for the last couple of years," Evan explained.

"A biography?" I was wondering if the queen knew someone was writing about her.

I was also wondering how detailed it would get about her and the king and Quinn. Marcus would have written about the whole horny threesome-marriage part by saying something like "and then the king took a companion and the prince of Faery joined them." I was hoping for a little more elaboration when it came to the "joining" part. Because I would read that book.

"Oh, yes." Jade suddenly seemed way more interested in what was going on. "It's not the first, of course. That was done by Callum O'Dowd. He's an academic from Ireland. He wrote the first book about the king's political rise and how the queen aided him. *The King's Companion.* And then there's *The King's Man.* Now that was written by a Fae, and it way outsold the other one."

"It had a lot of sex in it." Evan's nose wrinkled. "Or so I've heard."

I was going to need to read that book. But only when Evan wasn't around.

Relda shook her head. "It was over-the-top graphic, and he couldn't possibly have known what happened between the king and the high priest."

Evan shrugged one shoulder. "I don't know. His cited source is a pixie, and they did tend to hang around my papa. They're also famous gossips. One could be around him often and he wouldn't have noticed."

Not even if he'd been having some raucous sex. Of course Quinn was Fae and a sex god, so he likely wouldn't have cared and would probably read the book and shrug it off. Or maybe offer to narrate the audio version. "So someone's writing a bunch of books about the royals?"

The quiet made me stop. All eyes were on me, and all those eyes had that look that told me they knew something I didn't. And I wouldn't like it.

"Just the royals, right? Like no one else." Horror was starting to creep along my spine. "I get it. The royals were gone, and they were really important to the resistance. You needed to keep that history alive. But just the royals. The rest of us don't need a book. Nope. Not at all."

"If it helps, Trent did not authorize it," Evan said with sympathy. "And it mostly doesn't talk about your sex life."

I was going to kill someone.

"And the play was excellent." Jade clapped her hands together. "I hope when I finish my bio that a group of roaming shifter actors adapt it to a three-hour musical."

"It was a musical?" I was not going to do what I wanted to do—run from the room screaming and murder anyone who'd had anything to do with this humiliation.

"'The Hunter is in Love' is my favorite song ever." Jade put a hand to her heart. "I'm serious. It's beautiful. And the wolf call at the end of act two. So romantic."

I would have to change that title to "The Hunter Tears Someone's Heart Out." Starting with whoever wrote that shit.

I needed to turn this convo around. Fast. So I could get back to Trent and ask him why he'd left out the part where my life had been turned into a fucking musical. He was supposed to protect me, and that included my dignity. Honestly, I could protect my body. I did need someone to guard that dignity thing, though.

"So do you know anyone who might want to harm Alvis?" I decided to get back on track. I would need to figure out who had written that damn book, and more importantly, who'd written the fucking songs.

"Never," Relda claimed.

Jade made a little sound. You know. That "eh" that really means "well, yes."

I turned to the young woman. "What do you know?"

She'd blushed slightly. "Look, it's been crazy here the last couple of days."

"Since my parents got back," Evan prompted.

"Everyone is excited," Relda promised.

Evan's head shook. "I don't need you to protect me. I understand the upheaval this will cause. It's better to know what we're facing than to be surprised by it. I assure you, my fathers have gone over every scenario possible and they're preparing for them all. They won't protect my mom from the truth, and while they might try to pretend they can put me back in a bubble, it popped long ago, and I prefer reality."

Relda seemed to come to a decision. "It's a complex situation, Princess."

"Yes, because we've been in a holding pattern for years, and there's some odd comfort in that," Evan allowed.

"You weren't in a holding pattern. You've had to fight to survive for years." Jade sat up straighter.

"And we've given her shelter when she needed it," Relda pointed out.

"But we didn't fight with her." Jade seemed determined to argue with her mentor.

I approved, but I needed to cut through the obvious tension between the two to get to the truth. "I understand that our reappearance upends what has been a somewhat peaceful time, but you have to know Myrddin's been plotting and planning. He intends to close the door to the Heaven plane and allow demons to run wild right here on the Earth plane."

Relda's eyes went wide. "But the humans would know."

"Yes. I think they'll notice when the doors to Hell open and billions of demons run out looking to party," I replied. "Myrddin doesn't care. Myrddin believes he'll be the king of the entire Earth plane then. There will be a war that will make any human war look like a tea party. The humans will likely employ every weapon they have, decimating the planet."

"But we can't live that way." Relda had paled. "We need our plants and herbs and… We need balance. There can be no balance with demons."

Had she genuinely thought Myrddin wouldn't blow it all up? I understood that many people would think that way, but she'd been living in the Under for years.

Maybe that was part of the problem. They were somewhat insulated here, having formed their own community since they couldn't pass in society the way other vampires and supernatural creatures could. They'd been forced underground, and for the most part the supernatural world left them alone.

They couldn't stay out of this war. "No. There will be no balance with demons, and I believe Myrddin is underestimating his control over them. They're using the wizard, and once they're in power, they'll get rid of him and his witches. So I need to know what's going on down here. I'm sure there's a faction that thinks it can stay neutral and survive, but that's not true. There will be no neutral positions in this war. Have you thought about the fact that you're physically close to one of the entrances to the Hell plane? Do you think they'll leave that door closed if you don't declare for the royals?"

"Why would they need to come here?" Relda's voice had gotten quiet, as though she was afraid to even ask the question.

"Because they'll conquer everything." I felt for her. No one wants war, but sometimes we don't get a choice. Sometimes it came no matter what we wanted or how much diplomacy we tried. "Myrddin is in a position where he cannot back down. He made a deal with the demons to back him as the head of the Council."

"The Council doesn't exist anymore," Relda argued.

"It does," Jade countered. "It simply isn't located in Dallas. It's being forced to operate on the run, and they've been weak for a decade. We've fallen back into old fights, but the king is here and he united us once. He can do it again. He must do it again. You've heard the rumors about what Myrddin wants to do."

Relda shook her head. "I did not think they were logical."

"He's not logical. He's power hungry, and that means his logic is off." I needed these witches on my side, and that meant sharing some information with them. I wasn't sharing anything that wasn't out there in the world, but I was confirming. "He's been apart from his grimoire for years."

Jade grinned. "Hah. I knew that was true. I heard the queen stole the grimoire and she intended to bury it somewhere in the outer planes where he can never find it again."

Well, I knew that was wrong, but I was only going to give them so much. "The grimoire is gone, and the loss is playing into Myrddin's desperation."

He needed that grimoire to close the door to Heaven. He also apparently needed my sword. Gladys wouldn't help him. Even if he could find her.

Relda seemed to come to a decision. "I've heard that some of the primals aren't as interested in helping the king as the rest are. They think aiding the king will turn Myrddin's eye toward our nest. They believe the king and the royals didn't do much for us."

Was Relda one of those? "What did the king need to do?"

A slim shoulder shrugged. "I wasn't here before. I lived with a coven in Seattle. I hate the wizard. He killed my sweet friends when they wouldn't do as he demanded."

I needed to know her story to determine how she would react to her world potentially shaking. "What did he demand?"

"Fealty, and proof of it." Relda's hands shook slightly as she put the cup and saucer down. "Each witch had to prove our mettle, as he put it. And that proof came in our willingness to torture and kill for him. He wanted us to kill his enemies and take our places at the Coven House or in the houses he approved of."

"You'll find the resistance has a list of all the coven houses Myrddin deems worthy. There are ten, and all of his witches must live and work within them," Evan explained. "They are watched by Myrddin's own counselors."

I was sure Liv was involved in that in some way. "And what do they do in these houses?"

"They train for battle," Jade replied. "They give Myrddin their power. They prepare to do his will."

She'd been in one of those houses before her mother died. She'd seen the horror of being held against her will when she was very young. "Do you think the Under community should stay out of the fight? I won't judge you for it. I'm simply trying to figure out the mood of the Under."

"I think we're turning a blind eye to the suffering of others, hoping if we don't look that way it won't happen to us." Jade's eyes shone with unshed tears. "I will not look away. It's not what the goddess commands us to do."

"As it harms none, do as thou wilt," Relda said quietly.

"But it is harm," Jade argued. "Sometimes doing nothing is harm, Relda." She turned back my way. "If you want to know who dissented with the primals, I'm sure Rufus has a list of the way the elders voted. If you want to know who dissented down here, Relda did, but she is incapable of harming anyone. All she wants is to paint and be left alone. I overheard Rose talking about wanting to stay out of it, but she's a companion. If she's forced to leave here, every vampire who works with Myrddin will take a shot at her. She's also recently adopted a kid, and she's worried about her."

"Rose wouldn't know how to poison someone," Relda said. "I'm the best candidate."

The best candidate didn't usually point herself out. "Do you have belladonna?"

"Of course," she said with a sigh as she stood. "I'm well stocked in all the herbs, both medicinal and for spells. Belladonna can be used in both, though, of course, one wouldn't suggest ingesting the root. Any part of it, truly. It takes a skilled hand to prepare such herbs. I can show you."

I stood and followed her down the hallway, taking the time to glance back at the paintings that seemed to dominate the living space. There were three, and the one I got a good look at made me stop and stare. "What are you trying to capture here?"

Relda stopped, glancing back. "It's a series I've had in my head for a little while. I've been working on them in my painting class. It's called the darkest night. It's going to be three moons on three nights. Summer, fall, and winter. I can't see spring yet. Perhaps it will come to me."

I was struck by the color. She'd painted the canvases all black, but the color was rich and deep, drawing the eye in. "Is there a magical component to the painting?"

"There always is." Jade and Evan had joined us. Jade gestured to the work closest to her. "We mix our own down here and often work in certain herbs the gnomes grow. It can give the paint magical properties."

"The gnomes keep a garden deep in the nest where they grow bioluminescent plants." Relda began walking again. "They aren't found here on the Earth plane, of course. They're from the Fae planes, but the gnomes found a way to grow them here in the Under and they are beautiful. I do believe some of those plants are in the paints, which gives them an otherworldly glow."

"Do the gnomes grow all the plants down here?" I might have to go visit the wee ones. Evan might come in handy there, too. I would bet the half-Fae princess knew how to talk to gnomes.

"Oh, not at all." Relda seemed much more comfortable now that the conversation had turned to herbs and paint instead of the war that would occur. "Jade and I have a garden in the sun space. The gnomes help, though. And the Green Man always walks through when he comes around, but those are normal plants that require our sun spells to grow. Here we are. This is our witches' cabinet. I managed to smuggle it out of our old coven house. It was my mother's and hers before. She had it carved from an oak tree from the old lands." Relda put a hand on the wood as though she gathered strength from it. "This is where we keep our dried and prepared herbs. I've spent the last year training Jade in how to handle our herbs and make our medicines."

"I've gotten pretty good at it," Jade replied. "I'm also learning how to use said herbs to help out. We don't get many doctors down here in the Under. Every now and then Dr. Jacobs comes, but it's mostly Relda, and Rose who runs the clinic. Evan's gotten good with first aid."

"Yeah, well my brothers needed a lot of it," Evan said under her breath. "I had to learn."

Relda opened the big cabinet and then stopped. "It's not here."

I had a big suspicion what she was talking about. "The belladonna?"

Relda looked toward me. "It was here just last night. I did an inventory." She went a deathly pale. "You must think... I didn't kill Alvis. I could..."

And then she fainted.

Yeah, I scared pretty much everyone. I looked to Jade, who was on her knees beside her mentor. "I'm going to need a list of everyone who can get in and out of your place."

"Uh, everyone down here." Jade reached for something, opening a vial. "We don't have locks or anything. Or security systems. Not inside the nest. Sorry, she actually faints a lot. I don't think she's eating enough. She's always on a cleanse."

I backed away. "I'll talk to her later. Please let her know I'm going to need to know everyone who would possibly know how to use the belladonna, and do not tell me everyone in the Under."

Jade gave me a weak smile. "I'm pretty sure Rose and her kid don't know. Or Chris. He's never been interested in the craft for some reason. Some of the primals."

So she could rule out mostly no one.

Fuck my life.

"Make me a list. I'll need to interview people tomorrow." Because tonight I had shit to do.

At least I'd figured out where the poison had come from.

Jade waved the vial under Relda's nose, and the witch started to come out of her stupor.

"Oh, Jade, my dear." She shook her head and started to sit up. "I had the worst dream. The *Nex Appa…*"

She caught sight of me. Her eyes widened, and she fainted dead away again.

Evan grinned, and I noticed she still had the backpack in hand, still protected *The Path*. "Does this happen a lot around you?"

"Relda, stop being such a drama llama." Jade was starting in with her vial again.

It was time to go. "Kind of comes with the job. Come on. We've still got things to do."

"Bye, Jade," Evan said.

We turned to go.

"Hey, *Nex Apparatus*." Jade was still cradling her mentor, but her attention was on me. "I want to talk to you before you leave. I was serious. I want to fight in this war. I want to join the king and his witches and take down that fucking wizard who killed my mother."

I nodded.

And hated myself because I would let her come. I would let her fight. I would turn girls into soldiers because it was their world to fight for, too.

Fuck that. I didn't hate myself. I didn't choose this world. Myrddin did.

And he would pay.

Chapter Seven

I stepped into our assigned apartment and breathed in the heavenly smell of whatever Eddie was cooking and wished that Trent and Fen weren't out scaring people on the bayou.

Evan set the backpack down on the big table in the middle of the living area. "So now we try to figure out who got into Relda's cabinet?"

"I'll have Fenrir and Trent take a smell when they get back." Luckily the witches wouldn't die with the dawn the way the vampires would. Talking to the primals would have to wait until tomorrow night since they were all in some mourning ritual now that I'd taken the samples I needed from Alvis's apartment. Most of the nest was busy with the rituals and rites that went with a couple-thousand-year-old vamp exploding, so my investigation was on pause. "Unless someone is covering their tracks with a spell. It's the only thing I can think of that would fool Trent's senses."

"There are a lot of ways to cover a scent, but what Fen was describing seemed more magical," Evan agreed. "There are herbs that I could use, but it would have the scent of the herb. Fen told me it was like nothing was there."

"Can he still do that?" I hadn't asked before, and the question struck me. "When Fen was a kid, Trent couldn't smell him. It unnerved him."

Evan shook her head. "Nah. He hit puberty and now pretty much everyone can smell him from a mile away. He scares the crap out of other wolves just by walking into a room. I've watched big-ass alphas avert their eyes when they catch his scent."

He'd gone through puberty. He'd grown up. I'd promised him I would be his mom and he'd grown up without me.

"Kelsey, it wasn't your fault," Evan said quietly. "He knows that."

"Am I being so obvious?" I had to take a deep breath and shove that emotion down because Trent wasn't here to soothe me and sometimes I get violent when I get emotional.

Although this didn't feel like anger. Or fear.

This felt like unimaginable loss.

Somewhere in this nest a group was mourning their friend.

I was mourning years. I was mourning potential. I was mourning for Liv and Gray and the whole world that had changed into something I didn't completely understand.

"Not as obvious as my mother," Evan replied. "But I don't think it's a huge leap to understand how much losing that time must have hurt. I was so young I barely remember you. My parents—I have some memories of them, but it's hard to remember exactly what it was like before. I was five. I remember how safe I felt. I remember they loved me. I wonder if they can still love me."

"Yes." I knew the answer to that one, and I didn't have to consult the queen. "They love you."

"They don't know me."

"It doesn't matter. They love you. Your mother is processing. It's what she does. Don't be surprised if she comes up with some plan to right this whole thing."

A brow rose over her hazel eyes, an expression I'd seen many times on her mother's face. "Like turn back time to when I'm five again?"

I could see the queen trying. It wouldn't work, but I could see her plotting. "She'll think about it, but in the end she'll understand that there are some things we can't undo."

"How are you so sure?"

"Because Gray saw this years ago, and he's never wrong. There was nothing in his prophecy that said we would get a mulligan on this one." I thought about the fact that in some ways, I'd seen it, too. "You know sometimes I have prophecy dreams. I hate them because they don't make sense to me until after things have happened."

"You have them because you were connected to Grayson Sloane when he transitioned, right?" Evan asked.

I'd been his balance that night, holding onto his kite strings so he didn't fly away. It had affected me mightily. It had been the first time I'd realized how much Trent would come to mean to me, and the first time I'd seen my children.

My demon boy and she-wolf.

"Yes. I sometimes dream, and one of the dreams I had a few months ago…it's been years for you." My heart hurt to think about it. For me it had been a few months since I'd gone into those woods with Casey and Liv and my guys. And little Lee. I'd gone into those woods and come out with my son, Fenrir. "We were in Wyoming."

"When you found Fen."

I nodded. "I had a dream about Lee and Fen. I saw your wedding, Evan. Your wedding to Fen."

A soft look came over the princess's face. "You did?"

"Yes. So don't worry about Fenrir. He will be there on the day, and he won't let anything stop him," I promised her. "And so will your parents. I saw them there, too." I didn't mention that only one of her dads had been giving her away. Zoey and Devinshea had been standing to the side. Huh. And now so much of that damn dream made sense. "I think that dream told me about Lee. Jacob, the heavenly prophet was there, and he kept going on and on about the new world beginning and how the crown is twofold. And then Lee stabbed himself with a sword and died."

Evan huffed. "That sounds like my brother. He will definitely try to upstage me at my own wedding."

"He was smiling when he did it, and I think I was supposed to figure out he's a latent vampire from that." Dreams are never plain old here's-what's-going-to-happen things. There's a lot of metaphor involved, and I'm not particularly good with those. "At one point Lee turned into my dad and he said something about how it was written in his DNA. I probably should have figured that out. I wonder if he's a king. I wonder if that's what Gray meant when he said don't believe the myth there can be only one."

Evan's eyes rolled. "I hope not. He would be insufferable."

But it kind of made sense. I would have to run that by the royals when we got back. "The crown being twofold seemed to talk about Fenrir and Lee. Gray warned me to not leave the king behind. At that moment I thought he was talking about your dad, but now I think it was Fenrir. Our world has never seen both a vampire king and a wolf king."

"Well, they have now since my dad is a king," Evan pointed out.

"But a vampire king and a wolf king who grew up as best friends could change the world." Vampires and wolves were often at each other's throats. What if their kings were as close as brothers? The simple fact that Fenrir was marrying Daniel Donovan's daughter would bring about a change in how the two groups worked together.

I could still remember how somber Jacob had been as he'd stared and told me to let the new world begin.

Evan pulled the book out of the backpack. "You've said this book contains a prophecy about the two beings who can kill Myrddin. Is it possible we've gotten it wrong and Fenrir is one of the two?"

I could at least put that worry aside. "No. It's clearly talking about Dean Malone. That book of prophecy is specifically about the outer planes where Dean grew up. Otherwise I doubt there would be anything about the situation at all."

Evan put the book down, her hand stroking across it as if she couldn't quite help herself. "So let me see if I understand. Myrddin spent time with the demon Nemcox after he healed my father's heart. During that time, he was given a vision of two creatures in all the planes who could kill him. One was your father, Lee Owens. One was a baby."

"Who wasn't born at the time. It's precisely why Myrddin chose to roam the earth for years. From what I understand, in the past the wizard had spent time with the king of the sword, mentoring him. Immediately after waking, he took his place at the king's side. But this time, he chose to leave the king to his own devices."

"Because he'd already planted the thrall stones in my dads, and he needed to find that child," Evan surmised. "So he finds Dean and instead of killing him, he sends his mother off plane where he grows up on a vampire plane and learns magic. Is he any good?"

"Dean?" From what I could tell he was still a baby witch. "He's very strong, but he needs to learn more. Are the words back yet?"

Evan unfolded the book, and I heard her sigh as though the act of opening *The Path* had brought her some sense of satisfaction. "They're here. Is it weird that it's in English?"

"I don't think it is," I replied. "I think it's in whatever language the reader recognizes."

"That's some cool magic. This one sounds like someone shouldn't drink her morning coffee." Evan's fingers moved on the page as she read. "Beware the darkest brew. Waves of sickness may overcome the unwary."

"Yeah, there's some pretty simple ones in there. The witches of Arete found a way to track every single prophecy that has ever come to one of their witches, not just the important ones. I was lucky I was able to find the one about Dean," I explained. "Or maybe not. I also think the book wants to be helpful. Go on. She knows which one we want to see. You can read it."

The pages turned immediately, without any help from Evan, and she was suddenly staring down at the prophecy I'd found, the one I'd lost years for.

The one that might save us all.

"The spawn will rule, using all his power to open one gate while closing another, locking the lower away. But one munition remains, one hidden from view. The two shall rise, saved from the schemes of the spawn by their mothers' touch. Two shall rise despite time turning. It is in the turn, in the wave he set off himself, that the hope of all the planes lay. Prime the light. The magic cannot flow without the two. Without the magic, the two are merely strong. With the magic, the two shall topple the wizard. One crown. One wand. One light. Seek her in the light. She left a map behind, the true gem saved by another mother's love. Only a combination of three can save three. The darkness, the earth, the light together or all will end." Evan was quiet for a moment. "Well, now I understand where the crown comes from." She wrinkled her nose. "Don't tell him until he needs to know. Like I said, he'll be insufferable."

I fully intended to tell Donovan I thought Lee might be a king when we returned to Frelsi. I certainly didn't want to get Lee's hopes up. "The light is a weapon."

"Do you think it refers to a companion? I don't know many companions who would be considered a weapon. Though my mom is often referred to as bringer of chaos. That's kind of a weapon. And

I'm handy with a bow. I could shoot Myrddin."

"I don't think it's about you, but I am interested in the word *light*. It can mean a lot of things though," I mused. "And the word *her*. What I get is that this is a magical weapon that requires priming. Dean's the one with magic. I'm not sure what Lee's supposed to do. Probably bleed on something since he's a vampire."

"How does three save three? You should understand that Lee will view this prophecy as a way to have a threesome, probably more than one," Evan explained. "He'll try to convince Dean to have as much sex with as many women in between them as possible."

It was so hard to think of that big, charming man as little Lee, the boy who claimed girls were gross. Now he was apparently the stud of choice to a whole lot of the supernatural world. While Fenrir and Rhys were saving themselves for the women they loved, Lee loved everyone. Lee's affections went past gender and species. Which might be a good thing because I'd seen the way Dean had looked at Lee, and it appeared he was very fluid as well, and totally interested in Lee.

"Dean told me he dreams about Lee. Has Lee ever mentioned dreaming about a man with silver hair?"

Evan snorted. "Lee mostly drinks himself to sleep these days. He wouldn't remember a dream if he had one. It's a good thing he's a vampire because he'll need a new liver soon." She sobered as she looked back down to the page. "I wish Alvis could have seen this. He was the best when it came to deciphering prophecy."

"Yes, so I've heard. What if someone doesn't want this prophecy deciphered?" I asked the question that had been running around my brain for hours.

"How would they know?" Evan asked. "You've barely been back for a day, and Sasha keeps things tight in Frelsi. So how would Myrddin know you have the book and that there's a prophecy?"

It was a good point.

"Kelsey, I think you're trying to take guilt on yourself," Evan said quietly. "You need to step back and view this as logically as possible. Right now you're looking at everything through the lens of the twelve years you had taken from you, the years you didn't give to Fenrir. Every problem he has you're going to wonder if they wouldn't have happened if you'd been here. Deep down, you know the answer."

I did, but guilt was hard to shake. "He might have had different problems. Easier problems."

"But he still would have had them. Support him now, and as soon as you can, dump the guilt. I've learned guilt does nothing but weigh us down. It's an insidious thing because it seems like something right and good to take on, like it will teach us to make better choices. But what it does is make us question every choice. It puts us in a corner where we can't choose properly at all because it's all we see. It coats our love and sticks to our souls. I am not saying we should thank Myrddin for the years he stole. I'm not doing some martyr, we're-better-for-our-pain thing. But we're here and we can't take it back, and guilt is one of the weapons he's trying to use against us now. Don't give in."

I studied her for a moment, in awe of her quiet wisdom. She was so heartbreakingly young, but somehow she'd figured things out that I hadn't. "How did you get so smart?"

Evan closed the book. "Many an awful experience. Rhys is still dealing with the guilt that came with Lee losing his eye. Hopefully now that he knows Lee will get it back he can chill a little."

"My mistresses." Eddie stood at the door that led to the kitchens. "I have created a luncheon for you. Since Mistress Kelsey has been on a far off Fae plane with none of her usual happy foods, I thought I would make pizza and brownies."

I loved Eddie so much.

Evan smiled the demon's way. "I'm looking forward to it. And maybe I can convince Kelsey to tell me the story of how she and my mother took back our Amazon sword. It's in the biography but they kind of gloss it over, and I think it's probably way cooler. Did you really shove a sword through my mom's heart?"

"Oh, it went totally through her body, but she was on your dad's blood, so she was cool." I could tell her a bunch of stories that would be old times to her and yesterday for me. Was that what getting old meant? I started to follow Evan into the dining room when another terrible thought struck me. "Hey, that didn't make the musical, did it?"

"Oh. Yes, but instead of blood when the actress playing you stabs my mom they throw glitter everywhere," Evan replied.

That was not how that particular night had gone down. "It was blood. Lots of blood."

"And Master Casey's song for that act was beautiful. When Kelsey sings to convince the archangel Raphael to give her another chance," Eddie began as he wiped a tear away, "there is such emotion."

There hadn't been emotion. There'd been fucking pain because I was pretty much gutted at that point, but I didn't care. "Casey? My super-mopey, thinks he can be an emo star Casey wrote the songs for the musical?"

Evan winced. "Yeah, we probably shouldn't have told you that."

"Oh, no my mistress. You must listen to them." Eddie held the door open for us. "The end when the whole cast sings of Kelsey's glory as she's carried to the Heaven plane by angels while Trent and Gray wave good-bye…heartbreaking."

Eddie started crying.

And I started wondering if Casey would explode like Alvis had.

* * * *

It was past three in the morning when I finally made my way to the bedroom. Evan and I had sat up for a while eating pizza and discussing the case.

I'd felt better when we'd been talking about the investigation. I could put my logic hat on but it was off now and I had to think about the events of the day from an emotional stand point.

My mind was a chaotic mess thinking about everything that could possibly go wrong. And all the things that already had.

My son was charming and loyal and loving, and a mess emotionally, and for a lot of reasons. I would chalk it up to horniness, but it was anxiety and fear, too.

My father's soul was about to become a vampire, and I wasn't sure simply turning immortal would fix Lee's problems. I was also responsible for Dean, who'd left a cushy existence on the Vampire plane where he'd had a family who loved him because I'd convinced him to save us all.

My bestie had given up her soul, and it was not a good look for her.

Her boss was trying to turn the plane into a demon orgy.

And my demon husband's new boss was Lucifer himself.

All in all, it did not make for restful sleep.

I needed Trent here. I needed to know Fenrir was safely inside this place, and Trent could put his arms around me.

I pushed through the doors of our bedroom and set the book down on the dresser, thinking I'd change into PJs and go wait for them to come back. I had no doubt there would be a comfy set of pajamas waiting for me because Eddie knew how to take care of things. There would be nothing I needed that Eddie hadn't provided for me. I might go hang with him and let him tell me stories about when the kids were young.

Stories I should have been a part of.

But hadn't I known I wouldn't? I couldn't help but think about the fact that I hadn't seen Fenrir in the vision I'd had about my children. I'd seen the boy I carried now and his she-wolf sister, but Fenrir hadn't been there.

Because it had been written in some fate that I wouldn't raise him?

The ache pierced my heart again, and I almost let out a cry when I realized I wasn't alone in the room. I hadn't turned on the light because my eyes are pretty good and I hadn't been planning on staying long, but now I could see red eyes staring at me from the darkness.

Something was in the corner of the room, something large and demonic. Those eyes were definitely demonic. They burned from the darkness.

"Gray?"

"I don't know if I should be here, but I can't seem to make myself leave." His voice sounded deeper than I'd remembered. "Please don't turn on the light."

There was a glow from the bathroom that gave me some illumination. We were deep underground, so if Eddie hadn't made sure there were nightlights around the place, we would be in pitch dark. My eyes are good, but not that good. Still, with the soft blue light coming from the crack in the door, I could start to make out Gray.

"Okay. I can do that." My heart hurt at the thought that so much had changed he didn't want me to see him. Or perhaps he didn't want to see me. "Why do you think you shouldn't be here? Is it because twelve years made you change your mind?"

"Change my mind?"

"About me. About us." I wasn't going to tell him about the baby. I would, but I didn't want a decision about me based on the fact that my womb worked. Honestly, if he didn't still want me, I doubted he would want the baby.

"I could never change my mind about you." The words came out aching and tortured.

Ah, but he could change his mind about us. He'd done that a dozen times over the course of our relationship. I wasn't sure I could handle this conversation again. "It's amazing that twelve years doesn't change a thing. Go away, Gray. I don't want to do this tonight. If you want a divorce… Do we have paperwork? I was going to tell you to send me the paperwork, but the Council doesn't exist anymore. Well, that makes things simpler. There. We're divorced. Carry on in your new job serving the Dark Lord."

I heard a low growl and knew he was going to be difficult. But then that had probably been the point of him coming here tonight. Gray was always difficult.

I wasn't ready to deal with difficult. My heart hurt. I was tired.

"You won't get rid of me so easily." The words came out as a silky threat.

I was sure for some women those deep, dark words would scare them, but not me. Those words held a promise coming from Gray. Anyone besides my husbands would get a swift kick in the ass for saying those words to me. From my husbands, those words made my panties drop.

Usually. Tonight I found them annoying because he didn't truly mean it. "You know you could have called and avoided the whole hiding in the corner thing."

I saw his shadow rise and realized he wasn't in his human form. His demonic form was at least a foot taller. When Gray went demonic he got these hot as hell horns, and he seemed to expand.

I'd been told by an archangel that there was nothing inherently wicked about demons. Like everyone on all the planes, they chose how to handle their souls. I'd never been able to get Gray to understand that there was nothing wrong with his demonic form. His demon had done nothing but love and protect me.

I thought his demon was sexy and beautiful, but he withheld this part of himself from me.

It was an old argument between us, a wall I was too tired to try to climb.

"You want to see what twelve fucking years without you has done to me, wife?"

"You could have avoided those twelve years by figuring out a way to tell me to not get close to that painting, Gray." I didn't want to be logical. I'd lost twelve years with my son, and Gray had known it would happen.

The light came on, though neither of us was close to the switch. It was a magical switch, of course, and apparently Gray was good at controlling it. That was a difference. He hadn't used to be able to do anything like that.

Of course he also hadn't had such magnificent horns. They were longer, curling around three times, and his eyes had taken on a red hue.

"Obviously made you even hotter." I gestured up and down that sexy bod of his. I had to tilt my head to look up. "Is this all you have to say, Gray? Because if so, you can go and I'll wait for Trent and our son. You know the one you apparently abandoned."

"I scared him." Gray practically roared the words.

"Dude, don't yell. Eddie brought brownie helpers with him, and you *will* scare them. As to scaring Fenrir, yeah, if you showed up like this when he was a kid, you probably scared him. Did you even try? Did you offer to give him a ride on your shoulders? He could have held on to your horns and had a fun time, and then he's not scared of his demon dad anymore. Did you, Gray? Or did you get your feelings hurt by a nine-year-old and run away like you always do?" I knew I was being a bitch, but he deserved it. He'd left Trent and Fen. Fen didn't even call him Dad.

"Fenrir was scared, and it wasn't merely about Gray's appearance. When he comes back from the Hell plane, he requires a period of decompression. We weren't ready for that the first time." Trent strode into the room, stopping in front of me and putting a hand on my hip as he leaned over. "Let me handle him."

"You handle him?" I was curious about that phrasing.

"Yeah, baby." He kissed my forehead. "I keep all of us calm. It's my job in life. Luckily I learned how to handle you first. Did I mention how well you've dealt with all of this? Twenty-four hours. You held it together for twenty-four hours. Your world fell apart and you didn't lose your shit. He hasn't figured it out yet, so go easy on him."

He was right. I hadn't even thought about the fact that my she-wolf had been relatively calm. A few months back I'd required sedation when I got super emotional. I'd managed to keep my shit together for a whole day. And even when I'd gotten to Trent our reunion hadn't been about him handling me. He'd held me and we'd mourned what we'd lost together, but there hadn't been a violent spark in my system.

Because it wouldn't have helped Fenrir. It wouldn't have helped the baby growing in my body.

Because honestly, it wouldn't have helped my husbands.

My wolf and I were on the same page. Our family was more important than our impulses. We had to temper ourselves to be good for our children, for the men who loved us.

I watched as Trent moved toward Gray.

"Did you get my message?" Trent was wearing the same jeans and T-shirt he'd worn all day, which told me the run had likely gone well. He hadn't had to quick change and had the time to dress after he and Fenrir had finished.

Gray frowned. "No. I...didn't check. I came here because I knew you were here and then I smelled her. I've been sitting in the dark trying to figure out if I should stay or leave."

Trent moved right into that big demon's space. "Why would you leave?"

"You know why. I can't... Trent, please. I hate her seeing me like this."

Trent put a hand on Gray's chest. When Gray was in demonic form, he towered over our wolf, but Trent seemed to be the one in control. "I don't know why. I would bet she thinks you're hot as hell. I don't actually have to bet. My nose works very well."

The old human me would have been horrified that Trent could always tell when I was aroused. I let my wolf lead in most of the sexy stuff because she didn't care as long as she got an orgasm out of it.

She thought it was sexy her mate could tell when she liked what she saw.

And she had. The wolf liked Gray, too.

There were times now when I didn't think about my she-wolf. She was simply me and I was her.

"She doesn't understand." Gray gasped when Trent's hand moved over his side. He pulled up the long tunic he wore. "Fucking touch me."

Okay. Now I was real interested.

What had they been doing? How had Trent been soothing Gray? I knew how Trent soothed me and it was mostly with his dick.

Twelve years was a long time and their relationship had naturally evolved. It would have to.

Had they moved on without me? I'd always known they would go there someday. Trent wouldn't fight it. Trent trusted his instincts, and he'd been attracted to Gray from the beginning. Gray would see it as one more proof that he wasn't normal.

But I didn't understand his hesitation. There was nothing more normal than loving our mates, than finding comfort in souls we'd meshed with. If our souls were connected, I didn't see why our bodies couldn't be.

Gray's eyes closed as Trent's hand disappeared up his shirt and he ran it over the tattoo that had marked Gray from puberty. It was a sign of ownership, proof that he'd been born a legacy, his soul given to Hell by his mother before birth. But that tat was a tricky thing. While it would have allowed Gray's father to force him to the Hell plane had his contract not been annulled, the tattoo was attached to Gray's soul and loved the people Gray loved. When I touched it, I could feel it hum and purr under my hand.

Once it had been a mighty dragon, a symbol of his father's house. When we married it transformed into a wolf.

I wanted to see if it was still a wolf. Still mine.

"What do you need, Gray?" Trent asked, his head tilted up. "Come back to us. She's back. She's here and she needs us no matter how well she handled things. She's still feeling the loss, and now she's worried about you. She doesn't understand what's gone on, and you have to know that she's going to fuck things up because she's Kelsey."

"Hey." I didn't like the sound of that.

Trent looked back, his hand not leaving Gray's side. "Baby, you were here for like five minutes before you started to tell me all the ways I did things wrong and how I should have done them."

"You're a fucking saint, Trent. I would have spanked her then and there." Gray sounded more like Gray now.

I was not opposed to that. I quite liked a nice spanking, and throw in some bondage and I can be a happy camper. "I wasn't trying to be a bitch."

Trent's lips curled up. "And yet..."

He was mean sometimes, but then the man had spent the last dozen years of his life taking care of our son and the royal kids, running a war, and apparently soothing Gray's inner beast. "I'm sorry, babe. But you know I'll probably do it again. And I already told Gray we're divorced."

Trent's hand came down, a look of outrage on his handsome face. "What?"

"He was being an asshole."

Gray growled again, his eyes going dark. "I was trying to protect you."

"For the one millionth time, I don't need to be protected. Are you going to tell me all the dark and dirty shit you want to do to me?" I'd heard this excuse so many times. "Because I like the kinky sex stuff."

"Kelsey," Trent began.

I ignored him. "I liked it when you used to spank me and tie me up and get super bossy during sex. I'm not some tender thing you have to take care of."

"Kelsey." Trent moved away from Gray.

"I like your horns and fangs, but what I would like even more is a guy who's fucking comfortable with himself," I complained.

That was when Gray roared and brought his fists down on the ground, making the whole room shake.

Trent moved in front of me. "Kelsey, when he gets back from Hell he can be violent until he's calm enough to take his human form. Stop arguing with him. Stop it right fucking now and let me handle him."

Gray picked up the nightstand and threw it across the room.

The door behind me burst open and suddenly a massive wolf was in front of me. Fenrir growled low from his throat, and his pitch black fur stood up.

Evan gasped behind me. "Kelsey, we should ease back. Don't make any quick moves. Fen, remember who he is and what he's done to protect all of us."

The growl from my son told me he didn't care.

"Fenrir, go back to your room right this second." Trent got between the hulking violent demon and the massive wolf who looked like he would kill to protect me. "He's not going to hurt me or your mother and you know it."

"He won't mean to. We know that." Evan seemed to speak for Fen when he was in wolf form. "But you can't blame him for trying to protect his mother or you."

Gray punched a hole through our nice wall, disrupting the magic and exposing the rock behind it. His fist started to bleed.

"I don't need protection," Trent replied. "I need privacy. Kelsey, if you can't stop…"

I'd done enough damage. "Fen, please leave us. He won't hurt me. Your dad would never let anyone hurt me."

Fen merely growled again.

"Kelsey, I think you have to come with us," Evan said. "I don't think Fen will leave."

Gray was staring at Fen, baring his fangs. Those big, hot as fuck fangs. I didn't have to kneel to look my child in the eyes. Fen's wolf was big enough I barely had to lower my head to make eye contact. "Fen, I'm about to do all sorts of weird sex stuff with your dads…"

My son turned as fast as he could and ran away.

Evan grinned. "I bet that'll work with my brothers, too. All righty then. Carry on, adults."

She closed the door on her way out.

Gray stood in the middle of the room, his eyes gone red. He breathed in and out as though trying his damnedest to hold on, to stay still.

To not hurt us.

What had Hell done to my demon?

"All right, babe. How do we handle him?" I was going to let Trent lead me. This was his world and had been for years. I was the newbie here, and I would wreck things as surely as Gray if I didn't stop and listen to Trent.

"He needs to be touched, to be reminded he's here and not there." Trent had a grim look on his face. "I'm not sure you should be here. He's too emotional around you."

"Well, that's sad because I *am* here and I'm not going anywhere." I would listen to him about anything except leaving. I couldn't do that. I knew Gray. If I lost him now, it would be weeks before I saw him again. I pulled my shirt over my head and tossed it aside before going to work on my bra.

Gray's head rotated, and suddenly his fangs weren't the only thing that were bigger than I remembered.

Trent took a step toward me and suddenly Gray moved, growling in that caveman-possessive tone of his that would have any other man getting out of the way. Not so Trent. He merely frowned. "Not even to calm you down will I give up my claim on her. If you want to do this the hard way, we can. We can stand here and fight it out. Or you can remember that she's our wife and I'm your partner in all things. Which way does that dark demon in you want? Blood or sex?"

I was hoping he wouldn't go for both. I can handle a lot of kink, and I can handle blood. I wasn't thrilled with a combo act.

Of course there was always the chance he chose neither and transported his hot ass out of here the same way he had gotten in. I moved around Trent. I needed to touch Gray. I needed to see if my touch still worked in any way after all this time. "I know what I vote for. I would like sex."

I moved in front of him, watching how his eyes went straight to my breasts. He started to reach out a hand and then seemed to realize his claws were out. I caught him before he brought it back. "You won't hurt me, Gray. Be gentle in this form and you won't hurt me."

"I don't know he's capable of being gentle in this form," Trent said softly.

"He will be for me." I brought his hand to my chest. "And when he's back in control, he won't have to be gentle at all. You know I love it when you fuck me hard. I've missed you, Grayson Sloane."

His eyes closed, and I felt a sigh go through him as he touched me. His hand was so big in this form that it practically covered both breasts. I felt the connection between him and I. This. This magnificent electricity was why I kept coming back for more. I knew what we could be if he gave us a chance. I thought we'd gotten past this, but he'd always warned me what would happen if he had to descend.

Trent moved to my back, his hands on my shoulders. "We've missed you so much, baby. You have no idea. We weren't complete without you." One hand shifted around me, going to Gray's arm and connecting my men to each other. "Like we couldn't be complete without you, Gray. Stay with us. Stay as long as you can."

He could stay forever. He didn't owe Hell anything as far as I was concerned.

The air around me shifted and suddenly Gray was his normal still very large self. The clothes he'd been wearing hung off him, and Trent immediately drew the tunic off his shoulders, tossing it away.

Gray put a hand on the back of his neck, stopping Trent from moving too far. "I'm sorry. I got lost down there. I forgot it was almost time for her to come home. Forgive me."

Trent's hand went right back to the tat, and sure enough it was still a wolf. "Always."

Gray turned my way. "You are a sight for sore eyes, Kelsey mine."

I moved between them—where I was always happiest. I went on my toes and brushed my lips over his. "I know it wasn't long for me, but I missed you. I missed you every second I was gone."

His hands found my hair, and he devoured my mouth.

His tongue swept inside and played with mine. Every inch of my skin lit up as they started to touch me. Trent palmed a breast from behind me while Gray's hand went straight to my pussy, easing past my jeans and finding the spot that was already soft and wet for him.

"I've dreamed about this every single night for years and years." He'd reverted to human form but his fangs were still larger than usual, and they dragged lightly across my neck. "I dreamed about when my wife would come home to me. When we could finally be together again. All of us."

He picked me up and carried me to the bed, dropping me there before undressing me with quick hands. Trent snuck in behind me, easing under my torso, my back against his chest. I could feel his erection against my spine, and his big hands cupped my breasts. I spread my legs wide for my demon husband, loving the fact that I was about to be in between them again.

It was where I longed to be, where I'd found my peace.

Gray joined us on the bed, pressing me down into the warmth of Trent behind me. He kissed me while his cock found its home and sank deep inside.

I held him and reveled in being together with my men.

Chapter Eight

I was cozy and warm the next afternoon when I finally woke up. Gray and Trent were in bed with me, cuddled on either side, and I thought seriously about indulging in more sex, but even for me the night before had been a lot. I was a bit sore, and we had a few things to talk through, things I'd let go the night before.

"So you want to explain the whole 'I work for Lucifer, Lord of the Hell plane' now?"

Gray groaned and let his head fall back to the pillow. "Not really." He turned on his side, propping his head up with his hand, and looked over me to Trent. "You didn't tell her about the whole protect her humans thing?"

Trent kissed my shoulder and cuddled close. We were calmer this afternoon, and Gray hadn't even lost his shit once. Not that he'd had time to. We'd pretty much fucked all night until I couldn't keep my eyes open a second longer.

I'd awakened to two pairs of hands on me and the joyous smell of bacon frying somewhere in our apartment. Eddie was hard at work, and I was going to enjoy having him spoil me again.

"Yes, that's what I explained, but you know she's not going to believe it until she hears it all from you," Trent prompted.

I could feel the new talisman he'd picked up brush against my skin. He and Fenrir had gone into town and had dinner after their run. Apparently there was a woman in the small town who ran a hair salon that also sold magical items. Trent said that while the woman's love potions were mostly sugar water with a hint of vodka, her talisman against demonic influence was solid. It had proven its worth the night before because Trent had been perfectly solid. I intended to make sure he wore that sucker all the time.

Gray sighed, and his eyes met mine. "Jacob saw what could happen to your brothers and mom if they were left without protection during these years."

Jacob was Gray's mentor and Heaven's prophet. "He told you what to do?"

"You know he can't do that," Gray replied. "He can merely give me the prophecy and I have to figure it out. Obviously I couldn't see it myself since I'm involved."

"But you saw me leaving the Earth plane for twelve years."

His head shook. "It wasn't like that. I didn't know exactly what was going to happen. That prophecy...it was important. I don't know I'll ever have a more important prophecy, certainly not one that touches my own world. I know you think I should have been able to spare you, but..."

I put a hand on his chest, loving the feel of his skin under my fingers. "I had to go because I had to find Dean. I had to go because I needed *The Path*."

"What was it?" Gray's eyes flared in obvious curiosity. "I know it wasn't an actual physical path."

This was why prophecy was so stinking annoying. He'd known the words weren't literal but he couldn't tell me. Like he'd probably known "summer" was actually Summer and a person not a season, but he couldn't fix my misinterpretation. It wasn't that he was good at following the rules set up in the prophet handbook. It was that he physically couldn't fix it, couldn't do anything about it beyond repeating the prophecy over and over. I'd heard a lot about a trick and a trap the last couple years. "It's a book of prophecy."

It would be interesting to see how the book reacted to Gray.

"Where is it?" Gray sat up. "I don't think you should leave it out in the open. That book is important."

I waved the worry off. "She doesn't want to be stolen. She's good."

His brow rose. "She? Like Gladys?"

I frowned his way. "Gladys didn't want to be stolen either, but she doesn't have pages that are made of magic and the ability to find her way where she needs to go. I don't think I could have left *The Path* behind even if I'd wanted to. That book was determined." Something tickled my memory. "Hey, if you can't help, how did you tell Albert to take the children?"

"The prophecy wasn't about the children," Gray insisted. "Look, sometimes I take a shot and sometimes I score. I think whatever it is that gave me these powers has rules they don't want messed with and ones that aren't so rigid. I try and if what I'm doing to help works, then I figure the powers that be are cool with it. I couldn't tell Albert anything more than to protect the kids if something went wrong. When you think about it, it could mean anything."

"Semantics," Trent argued. "When the dark prophet walks in and tells you to protect the kids, you know he's not talking about a scraped knee. The fact that it was Gray meant Albert would take him seriously."

"And the fact that it was Jacob speaking to me made me take the threats to your brothers and mother seriously," Gray said solemnly. "Back then there was no magical city to protect the resistance. There was chaos and the open targeting of anyone who might aid the royals should they ever return."

I didn't like the explanation, but I did accept it. "Okay, but why Lucifer? Couldn't you have offered to do another job?"

A brow rose over Gray's eyes, an amused expression. "Like what, baby? The satans didn't need a lunch lady. I don't think they needed my janitorial services. I'm a prophet. It was always going to be about prophecy."

"Okay, then why can't you just tell him a bunch of prophecies. I don't understand the focus thing." All I knew was some demons used other demons as focal points to… Yep, that was all I had.

"Lucifer has built up his own prophecy powers over the millennia." Gray's expression had shuttered, and I could see how hard this was for him to talk about. "He doesn't want the prophecies I can give him. He wants ones he learns on his own. He believes prophecy is built into the fabric of the universe, and all he needs is to find it. So he meditates and opens his inner eyes, and he discovers the secrets the planes whisper to him."

"The planes whisper?" I didn't get the metaphors Gray was

using.

"Yes."

Okay, maybe not a metaphor. "I don't understand how ground and trees whisper."

"Doesn't the wind whisper to you sometimes?" Trent asked. "Sometimes when you're still, you can sense what's about to happen. You might not understand it fully, but you know deep down something's coming."

That I could go with. "But that's instinct, not prophecy."

"Because that's how you perceive it," Gray countered. "You call it instinct. Lucifer experiences it as something else. He often talks about how he can find fate written into the fabric of the universe. Think of it like how Eddie creates this pocket world we're in."

Liv had explained it to me a couple of times. The magic came from being able to manipulate the natural world. "Eddie uses the space between atoms."

"Yes," Gray agreed. "He draws that space together and creates whole places. Lucifer does something similar except he's looking for clues there, for echoes of what happened in the past. What has happened in our future. We experience time as a through line, but it's not. What happened in the past is still happening, as what will occur 'til the end of time is occurring right now. Time is in layers all around us. It's how Myrddin tricked you. Up until the moment you walked through that painting, you were still living the same days as we were. The painting was basically a wormhole through time on the way back."

"So we should have found a way to get home without using the painting."

"No. It wouldn't have worked." Gray sighed and twisted his big body, sitting up. "It's what I'm trying to explain. What happened to you and the royals was an event that was written into the fabric of the universe. Not even the nexus point could have changed it."

"But I thought the queen's choices changed fate itself." Zoey Donovan-Quinn was a nexus point. It meant she was a being with no ascribed fate. Fate was apparently a real thing, and prophets and death gods could often see the fate, or the most likely fates, of those around them. Zoey's choices often changed the destinies of people she came into contact with.

"There are some events that are immutable, and nothing anyone does will change it. In all timelines, the trap is sprung," Gray replied. "It is from that moment, the moment of your return, that the roads diverge."

"Lucifer is looking into the different timelines? Into what happens in each?" Trent asked.

Gray nodded. "He wants to figure out why he is sometimes triumphant and why he fails so he can avoid the pitfalls."

"And he uses you to do that?" That seemed like something we would want to avoid. Lucifer taking over the planes was a bad thing. It was life lesson 101 in the supernatural handbook—Don't let the Hell lord take over.

"I am his focus. When I transitioned, my body changed. I am capable of seeing these different timelines. Most of the time I do not. Lucifer uses my unique chemistry to force the issue. Think of me as a prism. When he properly uses me, he filters the whole of the universe through my soul, parses it out and can select which plane or timeline he wants. He can study it through me."

"Maybe we shouldn't let him do that anymore." I kept my tone as gentle as possible because I wanted to avoid Gray hulking out again.

"He is not the kind of creature you say no to," Gray replied. "Especially after one signs a contract."

I felt my eyes narrow. "I just got you out of a fucking contract, Gray."

Trent moaned behind me. "Didn't we go over this?"

I forced myself to shove the anger down. We'd won the war against Gray's father, against his legacy status. He shouldn't have been forced to descend. "Fine. I'd like to read the contract."

"Eddie can explain it to you." Gray stood and walked to the dresser where he opened a drawer and pulled out a pair of sweats. "It's certainly not open ended. I owe Lucifer focal time for as long as you are gone plus six weeks Earth time. So if I don't reup the contract, we need to move your family to Frelsi as soon as possible."

My brothers would be thrilled with the forced relocation from the homes they'd built. I was sure their wives would love it, too. Not. My mom would likely get there and start explaining to the brownies why they all should have husbands or partners. My mom didn't care about sexual status, merely that all of the plane's creatures have mates and start producing babies for her to adore. "I don't think Jamie and Nate are going to want to go. They have jobs and homes and families here."

"Then I'll reup," Gray vowed.

Trent shook his head. "They'll be fine. They've already expressed an interest in coming with us and you know it. They can work for the king and the resistance. They've always wanted to be more involved than we've let them. Gray is not reupping that contract. You might have only six more weeks on this plane, but time is different on the Hell plane. You're spending months down there for every day you're gone. Maybe more. Lucifer controls the way time works on the Hell plane. He can fuck with you."

"How long do these sessions last?" I didn't like the idea that Lucifer could screw around with time and cost Gray years.

"I don't know." He pulled a T-shirt over his head. "I'm not necessarily all there during those sessions. And no, it's not painful, but being in Hell and in the presence of Lucifer...changes me. It takes Trent longer and longer to bring me back. This is why Fenrir and I are distant. He was around once when I returned from Hell and I didn't mean to, but I threw a boulder his way. If he hadn't been quick..."

"He knows you didn't mean to hurt him," Trent argued.

"He didn't seem to know that yesterday," Gray pronounced with gravity. "He looked perfectly prepared to defend his mother, and I happen to know you have told him time and time again how well Kelsey can defend herself."

"I think that was more about his brother," Trent said and then stopped. "Fuck. She hadn't told you yet."

Gray had gone...well, gray. I hadn't thought about it. I'd taken all the pleasure Gray and Trent could give me and then let myself rest. How could I have gone so long without telling him I was pregnant? "I'm sorry. It slipped my mind. I was wrapped up in seeing you again."

"You're pregnant." The words didn't come out joyous. Gray stared at me like something terrible could happen any minute.

My heart threatened to squeeze in my chest. "That's pretty much what happens when you perform a fertility ritual, babe." I was going to give him time to adjust, but we did need to talk about this. "Quinn says the baby's fine. What happened with the whole trick and a trap thing didn't affect him at all."

"You're pregnant." Gray's hands clenched.

"She's pregnant and she's fine." Trent slid out of bed and dragged his pants on. "There's no reason to worry. You were careful with the contract. Hugo read it over himself, and Eddie approved it. Your contract can't hurt me or Kelsey or any of our children. Fenrir was running on instinct last night. It wasn't about you. It was about any threat to his mother and brother. You knew she would likely be pregnant when she got back. There's nothing to worry about, and absolutely nothing to get upset over."

Gray was on the edge, and I'd put him there. We should have had this talk the minute I'd realized he was in the room. I'd let our past get in the way of our future. "You know I've seen this baby, Gray. He's happy and healthy and he loves both of his dads. Trent loves this kid already. The same way you're going to love Trent's daughter."

Gray took a long breath. "Okay. But if I ever…"

I shook my head. "You won't. Once you stop descending, you'll be normal again. But, babe, you have to make things right with Fenrir, and that means talking to him. He told me that over the years you've become a helpful authority figure to him. You have to be more."

"Fenrir might run on instinct," Trent said. "But he also fully understands pack dynamics. Start acting like a father and he'll treat you like one. You were afraid of hurting him so he was also afraid. You can start by being affectionate around him. Not with him. Not at first, but with Kelsey. You're cold when you're around the kids."

"I'm trying to maintain control," Gray admitted quietly. "I don't mean to be cold. I don't feel cold toward him. I feel regret that I wasn't what he needed me to be."

"You know you couldn't have come with us," Trent pointed out. "You have to be on the Earth plane. I think some of the unbalance you feel is from Lucifer fucking around and keeping you in Hell longer than you should be."

Gray had become a prophet here on the Earth plane. Despite what his father had warned, Gray needed to be on the Earth plane for his powers to work properly and for his own health. He wouldn't have been able to go running across the planes with Trent and Sasha when they'd fled with the kids. Gray had to stay behind and protect the people I loved here.

I needed to stop yelling at him and start understanding what was going on now. I definitely needed to repair the relationship between him and Fenrir since I had zero intention of having my family split. I slipped out of bed and put on a robe as there was a knock on the door.

Trent opened it. "Morning, Evan. Is everything okay?"

Evangeline Donovan-Quinn glanced around, her eyes lit with mirth. "I'm supposed to tell you breakfast is ready in the dining room, though Eddie said he'll bring it in here if you want."

"That would be..." Gray began and then stopped. "No. We should all sit down and eat together. Tell Eddie we'll be there in a few moments. Is Fenrir all right? Do you think he'll be okay sitting down to breakfast with me?"

Evan's grin kicked up a notch. "He was supposed to come with me, but he turned down this hall and stopped and then he noped out. It was so funny. I have to say I'm thrilled I don't have supersmell. I would love to have the other stuff, but being able to smell when my parents have sex is not a helpful power."

I felt myself go beet red. "Awesome. I'm taking a shower."

"I think that's a great idea," Evan agreed. "I'll make sure Fen doesn't eat all the bacon."

Embarrassment gone. My son was a walking gut, and he needed to remember that I was eating for two and so that made me two walking guts to his one. "Never mind the shower."

Trent laughed and suddenly there was an arm around my waist, hauling me back toward the bathroom. "Eddie will make more, baby. Let's get you cleaned up for the day. Fen's not the only one who can tell what we've been doing."

"But if Fen's grossed out by his mom and dads making perfectly normal kinky love, he'll eat less and that's more for me," I argued even as I knew I would lose this one.

"Tell Eddie we'll need half an hour at least," Gray said as he closed the door behind Evan. He pushed his sweats down and followed us. "We can get her dirty again before we clean her up."

"Hey, now wait," I protested.

But they proceeded to show me how fun dirty could be.

* * * *

"She's pregnant, you know," Fen said around a mouthful of cinnamon roll, his eyes narrowed. "You can't get her more pregnant than she already is."

Apparently my shower hadn't been enough. "Sex is about more than baby making."

"As my brother will tell anyone who's even slightly horny." Evan seemed thoroughly amused by the events occurring around her this morning.

"Lee's different. He's..." Fen seemed to realize what he'd been about to say, and suddenly his mouth was closed.

"He's what, baby boy?" I was working on my mom voice. From the way Fen went perfectly still, I would say it was getting good.

Fen shrugged. "I was only saying he's human and not picky about who he sleeps with, and you are extremely discerning. A woman of taste."

I snorted, barely managing to swallow the coffee I'd just sipped. "Your dads did not mention my tequila years, obviously. And I know you were going to say young. I'm not old. Neither are your dads. And you know even if we were, it would be good for us to still be having sex." I needed to get off this subject. "How was your run last night?"

Fen relaxed as though he'd managed to avoid a terrible fate. "Good. Had some gumbo but only after I caught a couple of rabbits. Downed a squirrel. There's some tasty snacks on the bayou."

Evan made a gagging sound. "Poor bunnies. You know you're the reason I can't have a pet."

"You totally could have had one of the dinosaurs. The little ones loved you," Fen replied with a frowned. "We can't have a dog because we're always on the run and we can't have a cat because... You get that I'm not ever going to be a cat person, right?"

"You're not a pixie person either," Evan countered with a frown of her own. "The only one who will get close to us is Dannan, and he's Lee's. I'm a literal faery princess and I should be surrounded by tiny creatures who adore me, but no, you have to eat the squirrels and pixies."

Oh, we were not doing that. "Fenrir Owens. Did you eat a pixie?"

Fen flushed. "Uh, I was very young and I didn't know what I was doing, and I was in wolf form at the time. And Trent made me spit the tiny dude back up."

Trent chuckled. "I had my hand halfway down that wolf's throat before I found the pixie. He's fine, but he and the others won't get close to Fen and that means they shy away from Evan, too. Also, he paid for that."

"I can still feel the fleas." Fen scratched behind his ear like they were there.

"They don't like me either." Gray hadn't eaten much. He'd sat down and allowed the brownies to serve him an omelet and bacon, but so far he'd mostly sipped his coffee. "Or your dad. But they adored your mom. Every now and then she would go in and talk to the queen and when she would walk out there would be all these pixies clinging to her hair."

"That's how I remember my mom." Evan grew obviously wistful. "When I think about her I see this beautiful woman with pixies fluttering around her. I guess it's why it hurts that they don't like me."

"They're afraid of Fen, and I will fix that," I vowed.

"Why do they like you?" Fen asked. "They should be able to smell the wolf on you. I know I can. Even when the wolf isn't my dad. You smell like a wolf to me, so I don't get why the pixies don't view you as a predator."

"Because your mother's prey is different from ours, son," Trent said solemnly. "She was born to protect our world. It's written into her DNA."

"Because she's a Hunter," Fen replied.

"And the *Nex Apparatus*," Evan added.

"I'm the *Nex Apparatus* because your dad is smart when it comes to politics." I wasn't about to use the words I should use. Donovan and Quinn were both ruthless bastards, and they'd made a bet on me that could have gone poorly. "Before I came around, the *Nex Apparatus* was always a vampire. He was an assassin. A Hunter isn't an assassin. She's a protector. So the king needed supernatural law enforcement and he found me. I didn't belong to a pack. I'm not a vamp. I owe no loyalties to any species, but I was born with the power to defend myself against almost all of them."

"Hunter is what we now call her, but once she was the Amazon's champion," Evan said quietly. "That's who we were. The companions were Amazons, and Hunters like Kelsey were our ultimate warriors. I think about that a lot. I think about how we banded together because we weren't the strongest. The very power we had attracted predators to us. We had to form our own army to protect ourselves because no one else would. The pixies love Kelsey because they understand that time and time again she's sacrificed her own comfort to stand up for creatures others consider lesser. They love Kelsey because while other people look away from atrocities happening, she walks in and does what she can to stop them. Everyone's happy that my parents are back and it's great, but if you ask the prey creatures and the companions and the wee Fae who they've been waiting for, it's Kelsey Owens."

She was going to make me cry, and I didn't like to do that. "That better not be from a song, Evan."

She chuckled. "Nope. All me and all true. And I will take you up on helping me out with the pixies. I really do find them fascinating, and Fen hasn't tried to eat a single one in years and years."

"You're settled in Frelsi now, right?" Gray asked.

"For now." Fen straightened up. "We'll likely move to New Zealand soon. We move between the two bases when the seasons change. We chase the winter for Sasha's sake. Longer nights means we have our general around more. The village there is as comfy as Frelsi. Only moving twice a year is a nice change."

"But you should be able to have a dog if you like. Dogs like you, Fen. They're attracted to you like wolves are," Gray pointed out. "Unlike cats. Evan could have a pet if she wanted one."

Evan sighed. "He's right about a dog, unfortunately. I'm afraid the Fae of the villages include trolls, and they are not great around sweet puppies. In Fae culture, dogs aren't viewed as pets. Not domesticated human plane dogs."

"How do you feel about a hellhound?" Gray asked and held up a hand. "Like most demonic beings, they're not all bad. If you raise one from a puppy, they can be quite lovely pets. I mean they will kill anyone who attacks their people, but I would think that's not a bad thing in your case. And I happen to know they won't have a problem with werewolves, especially one as strong as Fenrir. They enjoy being part of a pack, which is why it's sad that they're usually kept as solitary animals, but that's the Hell plane for you."

Evan's expression had gone soft. "Awww, they sound cute."

They weren't. They were big balls of what looked like rage and murder, but Gray was right. They could be loving pets. Hellhounds were a lot like most creatures. The more care you put into them at a young age, the more loving they tended to be.

"How do you know so much about hellhounds?" I had to ask because Gray had always actively avoided anything related to the Hell plane.

"I looked into it a couple of years back," he replied.

"He looked into hellhounds when Evan first started talking about wanting a pet," Trent corrected.

"You did that? For Evan?" Fen sounded surprised. I could have told him Gray Sloane would do almost anything for the people he loved.

"No. I did it for you. Even when you were young, you loved her," Gray said quietly. "If Evan was unhappy, you couldn't help but feel it, too. I had halfling friends growing up who kept a hellhound or two, and they were great."

"He talked to me about it when you were...fourteen or so." Trent reached for the plate of bacon. "We'd come back for a couple of months but before we could make it happen we had to leave again, and we didn't come back to the Earth plane for a couple of years."

"I can't leave the inner planes," Gray explained.

"I know that, but I guess I didn't think about it that way. You were there the first couple of years," Fen began.

"Yes, for a few years after I descended, I was still in control." Gray gave up all pretenses of eating. "I could still be near the children, but I would scare them sometimes when I prophesized."

"We would be playing a game and suddenly Gray was talking about the planes running red with blood." Evan took a sip of her coffee. "It could be disconcerting at times, and then he came to us when we were in Colorado with one of the big packs."

"He would show up somewhere close to where we were, and this particular time I was the only one around and he was still in his demonic form." Fen leaned in. "I changed. I did that a lot when I got scared back then. Gray didn't seem to recognize me, and he defended himself."

"I got there quickly and calmed the situation down, but Gray was shook," Trent explained.

Gray turned to Fen. "Fenrir, I know I don't deserve to have any kind of title with you, but I hope you'll let me earn back your trust and affection."

Fen sat back regarding Gray with serious eyes. "You never truly lost it, but I will admit I've felt the distance between us the last few years. I think Mom being back will help you. I know Dad tries his hardest to help center you, but I think Mom is important, too. And I think baby bro will be helpful."

"Yeah, I recently found out about that." Gray finally reached for the juice Eddie had placed before him. "But the fact that your mother is pregnant only makes me want to connect with you more. Trent has been your father all these years, but you should know I consider you a son. I know it sounds odd, but staying away, staying in control around you was the best way I could think of to protect you."

"Protecting people who are hyper supernaturally strong is one of Gray's favorite things." I couldn't help but needle him a little. "Especially from himself. He reads *Twilight* a lot."

"I don't..." Gray began and then a smile crossed his face and he laughed, the sound booming through the room. "I have never read *Twilight*."

I shrugged. "I don't know. You got that whole 'I'm so bad for you' vibe going."

The whole room suddenly seemed brighter. Evan was talking about how very Edward and Bella we seemed. Fenrir pointed out that I hadn't left our Jacob behind. Trent then made fun of Fenrir for knowing all of these things.

"I believe I did point out the similarities of *Hunter, the musical* to *Twilight*," Evan argued.

Oh, in all the sexy angst of the last twelve hours I'd completely forgotten about that fucking musical. I pointed Trent's way. "How did you let that happen?"

His lips kicked up in the sweetest smirk. "Baby, I wasn't on the plane when it was written, but you can bet I took the kiddos to see it as soon as I could. And then I wished that the supernatural world had a rating system."

Fen's head shook. "I mean it wasn't like a porn, but it was not not like it."

"It was not. The singing made it not porn," Evan argued.

"Of all the things I wished I could have seen coming," Gray said with a sigh. "I would probably have stopped that. Even over your mother falling into a painting and the world exploding. That musical…"

The door came open, and Casey walked in. He was looking spiffy this afternoon in slacks and a collared shirt. His eyes lit up when he realized we were all having fun. "Musical? Are you talking about my musical? You know I won a Shiftie for that."

I felt my face go red. "You admit freely that you wrote that musical?"

Casey went still as though he realized something was about to go very wrong. "Uh, just the songs. Okay, now Kelsey, you have to know I process my emotions through music."

I stood.

Casey turned and ran. "I regret nothing."

I started after him. "I will make you regret…"

"Mistress." Eddie stood in the hallway, a puzzled look on his face. "Murdering Master Casey will have to wait, though you should know he won a Shiftie for those songs."

Apparently that was the supernatural equivalent of a Tony or something, and I did not care. "I can murder him real quick."

Why exactly did he have to process his emotions about me? Was there a "my witchy girlfriend went bad and now serves the Earth plane's magical autocrat" musical? I thought not.

"It has to wait," Eddie insisted. "That book of yours, well, she's glowing."

I sighed. It would definitely have to wait.

I prayed the book wasn't about to explode or open up and let all the witches of Arete walk through and join their magical master.

Maybe the trick and the trap weren't through with me.

Chapter Nine

I strode behind Eddie out of the dining room and into the hallway that would lead us to the great room. I thought. This particular pocket world Eddie had added into the rooms we'd been given was circuitous, and I'd gotten turned around more than once. I would have noted the problem to Eddie, but I'd questioned too many males in my life in the last couple of days, and Eddie took criticism hard. And he was the dude who controlled the food, so I walked behind him.

By this point I'd picked up a tail, as Evan had come out to see what was going on, and Fenrir had followed Evan. Trent had wanted to make sure I didn't kill Casey, and Gray simply wanted to be a part of the fun. Or maybe he wanted to ensure I didn't murder anyone either.

He might change his mind on the murder thing because I wasn't completely sure we weren't about to be invaded.

"Do you have any idea how long she's been glowing?" I asked. In some cases, spells took time to prime. They were usually the ones that went the worst for whoever the spell was targeting.

This was the moment I remembered that Liv used to keep some of my hair around for protection and location spells. At the time it had seemed like a great idea, but then I never once suspected she would turn evil on me.

"I want to know how the book got out of my room." Evan had

some questions of her own. "I took her with me last night because I wanted to write down some of the prophecies so the men can read them. It was what I was doing when Fen decided to go all wolfy on us and save his mom. You know you're also a little Edward-like."

The decision to document the prophecies had been a good call on the princess's part. So far as an assistant she got an A plus from me. It was like I got all the smart parts of Lee as an assistant and none of the parts where he tried to kill himself and/or others. Thus far Evan had been cool under pressure and hadn't once gone rogue on me.

"I am not like Edward," Fen argued. "I didn't know if Gray would recognize Mom in his demon form. He's been gone a long time. I don't know how much of it was spent on the Hell plane. The longer he's gone, the worse he is when he comes back. Also, I knew Mom would probably start in on him the same way she did Dad."

So Trent talked.

"I didn't say that." Trent stopped at the door to the great room.

"You didn't specifically talk about the argument. You asked me all kinds of questions about my childhood and whether or not you did a good job," Fen explained. "It wasn't hard to figure out that Mom likely had some thoughts about how things had gone. I didn't think Gray would handle it well."

"Way to show some emotional depth, babe." Evan was liberal with the praise. She stopped as she got a look at the book. "Wow. She is glowing like crazy. Fen, maybe you should stay back. Do you think this could be some kind of defense mechanism? How many men have been around her today? Kelsey, you need more ladies in your group."

Well, I'd had a couple over the years, and one of them had betrayed us all and the other was currently working for a bigger, better Hell plane.

The book sat on the table in the middle of the room. Like a big old witchy coffee table book. A glow was coming from the pages, but the book itself was closed.

She wanted me to open her. I could feel that clearly. She wanted...something more.

"She wants to be open." Evan proved she was on the same wavelength as the book. "But she can open on her own. She can flip her own pages. Why would she need someone to open her?"

Sometimes spelled objects were tricky things. Like the painting

I'd fallen into couldn't simply suck me in from across the room. I'd had to get close. I'd had to allow myself to get caught in its trap. "I'm worried it's another trap. Or a trick, because if we open it, a horde of witches could come through. Myrddin is known through the planes."

He was known by many names. Myrddin Emrys. Merlin Satanspawn. I'd heard some other. I just called him asshole.

"She doesn't want you to open her." Gray moved into the room, and his eyes had changed from their glorious violet to what I liked to call midnight prophet. He loses his irises, and pure black takes over his eyes. "She's interested in me. She's talking to me. Trent and Fenrir, stay away."

Gray started to walk toward the book, but I had some reservations. "She doesn't like men. She sometimes goes blank when a man tries to open her. I kind of need her whole today. I don't think Evan's finished documenting what we need."

I didn't have Alvis anymore, but I was hoping someone else could help us. There was a whole library down here, and surely someone knew how to navigate it.

Gray smoothed back my hair with a soothing smile. "She's trained to hide her secrets around men, but we share powers. Our magic comes from the same well, so she'll...suffer me." He frowned toward the book. "You know that's quite rude. I'm nice most of the time."

Was my demon honey actually talking to the book? "Do you have some kind of psychic connection with her?"

"I do. It's similar to the one I have with Jacob," Gray explained. "She can't read my mind or anything, but she can let me know what she thinks. She can open herself to me and I to her."

"Icy, ask her if she wants to be more specific about where this weapon thing is." I was a woman willing to use my connections. If my honey had a direct line to something I needed, I would work that hard.

I would use any trick I could to get around the whole figure-it-out-yourself thing. I usually figured it out by some bad shit happening to me and going, oh yeah that's what it meant.

Gray turned those endless eyes on me, shifting from my husband to the dark prophet with an ease that took my breath away. "You know she can't do that."

"Well, apparently she can talk to you," I pointed out. "You know what she's never done with me? Opened up a line to my brain and said 'hey, girl, let's hang.'"

Gray's lips kicked up in a grin. "Yes, she's extremely amusing. She's my wife, you know."

Okay, that part was weird. It was probably how the queen felt when her faery prince hubby talked to the ancient god who lived inside him. I moved back and let Gray get close to *The Path*, worry still playing through me since I couldn't feel her intentions. I really wished I'd had Gladys. Gladys could try to kick the book's... She didn't have an ass, so we'd have to go for her spine or something if she did anything wrong. It could be an Earth plane sentient weapon versus a witch plane sentient weapon thing.

Two seemingly inanimate objects enter the ring. One leaves.

Gray turned his head my way. "She's not going to hurt anyone. She merely wants to share some magic, and she's been patient. She sensed me the moment I entered the Under, but she also felt I wasn't ready to be approached."

So she wasn't a cock blocker. Good for her. "And you are now?"

"Yes. I'm calmer and much more open to what she needs to tell me," Gray agreed. "From the information she's sending me, she's Arete's version of what we would call a true prophet. Instead of placing all the burden on one being, the witches spread the power around, and *The Path* collects prophecies for the plane. When you think about it, it's much kinder. She doesn't get headaches the way I do, and she does not try to figure out her own destiny. But she does give papercuts to beings she doesn't like. All in all, a pretty nice life for her."

"Can you ask her why she hates men?" Fen asked.

"Because the men of Arete were such barbarians, the only way the women could protect themselves was to develop their magic," Gray intoned in a voice that almost didn't seem to be his. "They killed and raped and tortured with glee. Men took women's sons from their arms moments after birth and taught them to do the same, to see women as objects. The women of Arete lived millennia in pain and fear, each generation learning a bit more until they were able to overthrow their captors and build a new world where their daughters could live freely."

"Okay. Well, I understand then." Fen took a step back. My wolfy son had gone pale. "The truth is I'm not much of a reader, so I won't bother you further. Sorry about the torture and stuff."

"She understands it's different on this plane, but she was created in a certain way and cannot break those bindings. Men on her plane are allowed no magic for fear that they would turn it on the women, and they are not allowed prophecy. The witches of Arete will not submit to the bonds of their slavery again." Gray turned back and placed a hand on the book. "I'm different because of the magic we share. I'm going to let her know she can trust me. I sent my wife to find you, you know."

The book pulsed, and the glow became a warm amber color that encased Gray fully.

I worried that he would freak out, but he simply took a long breath and his whole body seemed to relax.

"Are you okay, babe?"

"She's simply sharing her knowledge with me." Gray's eyes remained closed. "There is no reason to worry. We have the same goals. She recognizes me as kin, and while she wishes the inner planes had more female prophets, she won't keep us in ignorance. She likes the idea that the women of this plane are warriors in their own right, that they have the ability to choose magic or to find their own strengths. What we do here will affect all the planes, and her brethren's fear might lead all to ruin. So she will do what she needs to, including leave them behind for a little while."

There was a warmth to the glow that I could feel even from where I was standing. This was a friendly experience for my demon husband.

And hopefully an informative one for me. "She knows Dean Malone. You know Lee Donovan-Quinn. Can she confirm they're the two in the prophecy?"

It was a long shot, but a girl had to try.

"What she knows is irrelevant," Gray said from his bubble of golden light. "What you believe is more important."

"Why?" Fenrir asked the question from his safe distance. "I would think properly interpreting the prophecy is the important thing."

"Yeah. What if we get it wrong?" Evan agreed.

But he couldn't simply tell me if something was right or wrong. I was sure his rules didn't get put aside even if *The Path* was speaking through him.

He'd gotten better about finding ways around his rules.

"What I believe is important." I needed to make sure it wasn't some off-the-cuff remark.

His head turned, and his eyes held the amber glow of the book. "One crown. One wand. One light. Seek her in the light. She left a map behind, the true gem saved by another mother's love. Only a combination of three can save three. The darkness, the earth, the light together or all will end. The spawn doesn't understand what he is trying to do. He doesn't understand what his will may bring to all the planes."

"Her." I was caught on that word. "Is the weapon a person?"

The amber light faded, and Gray stood before me once more. "You know I can't answer that, but you should follow your instincts. Find the map. Like all good maps, there's a clear marker to guide you to the treasure."

"Okay, so is the map actually a map?" I knew all the tricks by now.

Gray's deep prophet eyes made an appearance again, and he stayed connected to the book. "*The Path* cannot see on the inner planes, but together we can give you warning. A hidden place. A sacred space. Familiar and yet changed forever. All will feel lost, but there are other ways to follow her. The weapon was hidden out of love, taken from this plane through one door, but you can find another. The planes are connected in more ways than you can imagine. She is a door. She does not know it, believes her only power is chaos and death, but it is transformation, it is a bridge to new life. She can take you there, but only if she can find her faith. Faith in spring. Faith in herself."

Fucking seasons. I'd just dealt with summer. Now he was talking about spring?

The power seemed sucked out of the room, and Gray was back to normal. He smiled down at *The Path*. "Thank you. You can trust my wife. She will not let you down, but she might curse you a bit." He chuckled.

"What?" Sometimes you can tell when the joke is about you.

He took his hand off the book and turned my way. "She says you can curse her all you like. You have no real magic. That's why you need your sword."

Yeah. Gladys was good at defending me, though I tended to need some of the queen's blood to prime her. Of course I would need to steal her back from fucking Myrddin first, but I'd heard the queen had plans to do exactly that.

Was that what this weapon would need? The blood of a companion?

"Kelsey mine, do you remember what I told you in the woods?" Gray moved closer to me, his hands going to my shoulders. "When we were in Wyoming, back when we first met Fenrir?"

He'd told me a lot of things, but I thought I knew what he was talking about. He was getting around his rules. "Something about Fenrir helping the two if he was raised with her love."

I thought he'd been talking about my love at the time. Now I knew it was Evan's that truly could make or break Fen.

Gray leaned over and kissed the top of my head. "Yes. Follow your instincts, my love. They will never lead you wrong. You knew to bring him back with us. Even without you he was raised with love. You were born to do this job. I know I annoy you with the protective thing, but never doubt that there is no one in all the planes of existence I would trust more than you with this job."

"Wait, but that means I'm like backup?" Fen asked with a frown. "I'm supposed to be a whole ass wolf king. Like the only one in the world. There are shit tons of vampires and witches. How am I the sidekick?"

"Don't you have enough to worry about with all the wolves?" Evan asked. "You don't need to be responsible for saving the planes. Though I also don't think my brother should be. Has Fate met my brother? Rhys is much more responsible. Now let's talk about repeating some of those... Where did the book go?"

I gasped, turning around. The table was completely empty. *The Path* had disappeared. Fuck.

"She's returned to Arete. She's done her job here and has gone to be with the witches," Gray explained. "Like Jacob and I, she feels best on her home plane. They need her there, and now that she has connected with me, she can go home. She's been gone a long time, and they need her."

"Okay. Evan, did you write down the important one? You know the one I kind of gave up twelve freaking years of my life to find?" I'd left a copy with the academics back in Frelsi, but I wanted one for myself.

"Of course, and Casey has a copy of it saved to his laptop," Evan promised. "But I wanted to study the book itself."

"She didn't want to be studied, but she liked you, too, Evan," Gray said. "She enjoyed the hours you spent together and said when the time comes, you'll know what to do. Don't hesitate, even though the situation might seem dire. The crown is twofold."

"No." I was not taking this. "We have been through this. The crown is twofold refers to Lee."

"Why would you think that?" Trent had moved into the room now that *The Path* was gone and all his hot masculine wolfiness wouldn't offend her. "Dean isn't a witch king, is he? Is there such thing as a witch king?"

"Not that I've ever heard of, and it would be Myrddin if there was." Casey stood in the doorway. He held a hand out. "Don't murder me. I was processing my grief, and it wasn't simply about losing Liv. You were...you were the sister I never had, the friend I always wanted. I missed you and you might think it's stupid, but I felt better after writing those songs." He sniffled and straightened up. "And I did write songs about Liv. You can find them all on streaming services around the globe. It's a whole album."

"It's so good," Evan encouraged. "'Her Magic is in My Heart' is one of my favorite songs."

Fen sighed but probably smartly didn't say a thing.

Okay, it was how he processed. I wasn't going to tear him up over it. But I was also banning all the songs about me from being played in a one-mile radius. I might listen to the ones about Liv, though. "So if it's not referring to Lee potentially being a vampire king, then what does it refer to?"

"I mean it still could," Casey hedged. "But it could also refer to the idea that there can be a vampire king and a wolf king at the same time. That the way to move forward is to have both kings work together. Or it could be talking about someone else entirely. I think there was something about mothers and fathers giving blood. It could mean Evan's a queen like her mother. You know you've left her out of all of this."

Evan crossed her arms over her chest and shook her head. "Which kind of seems rude. I personally would like a couple of prophecies about me. Fen has prophecies. Lee has prophecies. The Fae worship Rhys to the point they try to kidnap him. I'm sure there are prophecies about him on that plane. What about me? And what does the whole other door thing mean? Will we not find the first?" She sighed. "I'm feeling a white board extravaganza coming on."

"You know I love a good white boarding." Casey seemed excited at the prospect. "Did you write down the new prophecy? The one Gray just announced?"

"Oddly, I suspect I can give it to you again," Gray promised.

"Good. While Trent and I talk to some of the people who saw Alvis last, you can sit here like a good prophet and repeat stuff while Evan and Casey write on white boards," I explained.

"Oh, I should go with my mom and dad." Fen looked slightly horrified to be left behind with the brains of the outfit.

Evan frowned his way. "I thought you were going to spend time with your pops."

A brow rose over Gray's eyes. "Pops?" He shrugged. "I'm going with it. You know we can play some video games. Eddie's got a nice setup down here. I can do the prophecy thing in my sleep, much less while trashing my own kid in Halo."

Fen's lips curled up. He would obviously choose fun over any kind of actual work. "That sounds like a deal."

"And I will make some snacks." Eddie looked perfectly satisfied with how the afternoon was going.

That was the moment the walls started to shake and the world seemed like it would fall in around us.

* * * *

"Kelsey!" Trent shouted and started trying to get to me. He leapt over the sofa and fell to the side when it bounced up to hit him.

The ground beneath me shook, causing me to start to fall back on my ass. Before I could hit the ground, big arms went around me and I was cradled against Gray's chest.

"Keep your head down," Gray commanded.

I heard the sound of tearing fabric and then a loud *oof*. Gray turned as the rumbling sound got louder, and I saw Fen had changed into wolf form and was covering Evan's body with his own.

"I can't breathe," Evan managed to get out.

I couldn't see her at all. Fen's massive wolf had her totally protected from falling objects, though if the roof fell in and the whole metric shit ton of earth came down on our heads, I didn't think it would really help her much. He would just die on top of her.

Trent stayed in his own form and finally managed to cross the room to join us. He pressed against me, his arms coming up to cover me better. "Is it an earthquake?"

"There's never been an earthquake here," Eddie shouted. His tail was out and it flicked around, proof that he was shaken. "I don't think the Under has ever had one. It is magically fortified. I don't know what this is."

The mirrors and paintings on the walls shook but didn't fall. What they did was seem to fade in and out. One minute it looked like the pocket world Eddie had created and the next I could see the rockface. Like last night when Gray punched through the wall.

When the magic was challenged enough physically, it couldn't stay in the form it had been assigned and reverted to its natural state. Though the furniture seemed real enough. And the plates. I could hear them smashing to the floor in the other room.

"Master Trent, what should I do?" Eddie looked up at the ceiling, his horns tipping back. "It is too far to run. I cannot take everyone through this rock. I can manage a couple, but not everyone. It is why you were forced to walk in the first time."

"Get Kelsey out." Gray put me on my feet, and Eddie took my hand. "Take Kelsey and Evan and then come back for us if you can."

Another round shook the nest, and I could hear some screams.

"We have to get everyone out." I could help. There were too many for Eddie to take us all, but we could move to the exits and try to get as many out as we could. The witches could help stabilize the nest.

I wasn't even sure what we would do with the primals. They were sleeping. We couldn't move them out into the light. They would all die the minute the sun hit them. We couldn't lose all their knowledge. Could they survive long enough for us to dig them out?

What the hell was happening?

Fenrir moved off Evan but stayed in wolf form. He could handle a lot more damage in his big canine body than in his human one.

"No arguments. Eddie, do it now," Gray ordered as I started to stumble.

Eddie's hand found mine, and in a flash we were in the daylight, the brightness nearly blinding me. I fell to my knees because I'd been trying to stabilize myself before, but now the ground was solid beneath me. I tumbled to the ground beside Evan, who seemed to have the same problems I did.

Eddie gasped and moved toward us. "My mistress, I am so sorry. I should have thrown my body under yours and caught your fall."

Eddie could be a bit over the top when it came to his charges. It made him the best butler ever, but he could forget himself at times. "And then I would have been impaled by your horns. I'm good. Can you get back?"

Eddie nodded. "Yes, mistress. It is not difficult with a few. As I explained, my blood is in the nest magical system, so I can teleport around. I will get back to Master Trent and bring as many as I can to safety."

With a pop and the faintest hint of brimstone, he was gone.

"Now I'm covered in Fen hair." Evan sighed and started brushing the sleeves of her shirt. Dark hair came off. Even as a kid Fen shed everywhere. "What was that? An earthquake? If it was, it's over now."

I forced myself up, looking around. We were in some kind of natural area. I wouldn't have called it a forest, exactly, but there were trees and no signs of manmade buildings in my line of sight. "Where are we?"

"We're right outside one of the entranceways to a cave that connects with the nest." Evan pointed to a tall rockface. "Atlanta's about ten miles away. They only use this route if they don't want to come out onto city streets, but let me tell you, it's not fun. Some real small spaces in there. But it's considered a meet spot if anything goes wrong in the nest. Shouldn't Eddie be back by now?"

My stomach knotted because Eddie could move quickly when he needed to. "Maybe they're trying to get the brownies out, too. You know how the men can be until the women are safe. Or maybe they're trying to make sure the structure is solid enough for us to come back. I would like to know what the hell just happened."

Evan glanced around. "I don't know. It seems perfectly calm out here. The birds are chilling. I don't see anything that looks like it's been displaced. Shouldn't some of those rocks have fallen?"

She pointed at the precariously placed rocks up ahead. Yeah, they should be on the ground even in a minor quake.

But this part of the country wasn't known for the ground shaking. "Is it something that can only be felt underground?"

Evan shook her head. "I don't think so. We're down, but not that far down. I know there are levels that go much lower, but where our rooms are we're pretty close to the surface. I suppose it could have been a localized event. Maybe something exploded."

I didn't have my damn cell phone. Not that it likely would have worked. I hadn't exactly been prepared for anything but a tasty breakfast. Worry started to pulse through me. Eddie should have been back with the guys by now. Even if the guys were being all heroic and shit, Eddie should have come back with some more rescues.

"Something's wrong." Evan glanced around again. "Something was wrong with that quake. It's too normal out here. Animals don't go back to normal so quickly. They hide for a while. Those squirrels are acting like nothing happened at all."

"Well, that's because nothing happened to them, Princess," a dark voice said. "They're all perfectly happy and skittering around without a care in the world. You, on the other hand, shouldn't do that."

I moved fast to get Evan behind me as Liv stepped from behind a tree. She was dressed for a BDSM-themed party, or maybe some weird apocalyptic future where leather and spandex were the only fabrics left in existence. "What do you want?"

"Well, I was hoping we could have an in-person chat, bestie," Liv said. "But I was hoping to do it on my home turf this time. I've got some friends I'd like you to meet."

"I think I've met all your friends. I'm good with never seeing them again." I had to get Evan out of here. We didn't have any weapons, and Liv had all that magic.

Magic can do terrible things. Magic can curse and hurt and make you hurt others. Make you hurt yourself and smile while you're doing it.

"Hello, Princess Evangeline. Where's that wolf of yours?" Liv seemed intent to play with her prey.

"Somewhere trying to find me, I promise you," Evan vowed. "And if you harm me or his mom, he won't stop until he takes you down."

Liv snorted. "His mom? Like Kelsey is anyone's mom. She spent what? A couple of months with him? And then she was a dumbass who fell into a painting and left Trent holding the bag. I know it was Trent because your demon boy signed another contract as soon as he could. He always wanted to go home, Kelsey. He lied to you. Deep down he's a demon, and Hell is where he belongs."

This was Liv ripped down to her basest instincts. I actually didn't blame her. Everyone has a dark side. Everyone has moments where they're mean and pointedly cruel on the inside. Most good beings can keep those instincts under control. Liv's were off the leash because she'd lost the piece of her soul that controlled them. Had I thought mean stuff about her? Things I would never say to her face because I knew deep down they weren't true? Yes. I'd had them a lot. They were me projecting my own fears. So I wasn't going to be mad at her for saying some of my greatest fears out loud. "That's not what he says, but that's not meaningful now. Why do you want to take me to Myrddin?"

"Because he wants to talk to you." Liv moved closer but stopped when I took a step back. "He only wants to talk."

"Okay. Will you let Evan go if I come with you?" I couldn't let Liv get her hands on Evan. If she did, she would have immediate access to the royals because the king would offer his immortal life for his daughter no question.

"No." Evan tried to move from behind me. "I'm not going to let you take her. Myrddin will kill her."

"I promise he won't." Liv suddenly looked fairly reasonable. "He doesn't gain anything from Kelsey's death."

She was lying, or he gained something else by having me in custody. Probably access to the dark prophet. He wouldn't need anything from Trent. Despite what Liv had said, Fenrir had shown every indication that he considered me his mother. If I was pack to him, he wouldn't allow someone to take me. But I had to play this cool. "How did you find me?"

She crossed her arms over her chest like she knew I was trying to buy time, but she was willing to indulge me. For now. "I can always find you."

I was going to do a few things to make it harder. There were tats I could get. I'd never had to protect myself from her before because I'd kind of liked having a witchy LoJack on me given my profession, but Liv was making that impossible. "Can they all find me? Did you share a nice ball of my hair with your friends?"

"I don't have a ball of hair," Liv said with a sigh. "And I keep what I do have for myself. I used a lot of it up in the beginning, you know. I did look for you. I didn't understand that the Great One had to get rid of you. I thought you were gone, and I could find you."

Evan was still behind me, but I could practically hear her brain working. She was a soldier, and she wouldn't sit this one out. I had to pray that whatever Liv had done to keep us separated from Eddie would fail and that demon would show up with my hubbies who would likely want a word.

"I'm sorry. I didn't mean to leave you, and you have to know I didn't mean to make you feel alone because you never let me feel alone for a second." She'd been the best friend I'd ever had. I loved her. Sometimes in life you get these people who fill in spaces in your soul, and she'd been one of those for me. She was my sister in everything but blood. "Even when I was utterly unlovable, you never left me behind. Liv, I love you. I am so sorry for what happened. I need you to understand that no matter what you've done, I still love you. You are still my best friend."

I saw the moment I got to her. Her jaw tensed and her eyes went slightly misty.

Liv's magic required that a part of Liv was still there. Myrddin couldn't pull her soul completely out of her body because a witch's soul was the base of her magic. He could pull out most of her goodness, but not all of it, and I could appeal to that part.

She still felt for me, and that meant I could save her.

"And I can't wait to listen to Casey's album." Sarcasm had been a language for us.

Her eyes widened as though that had been the absolute last thing she'd expected from me. And then she laughed and for a second she was my Liv. "It was...I can't even. I can't believe he did that. He has a song called 'Liv and Let Love.' He's such a dork. I..."

She stopped as though she couldn't quite say what she'd been planning to say. Her expression hardened and her eyes closed.

That was when Evan threw a knife her way. I hadn't even known she'd had it on her, but it sailed past me and was about to sink itself into my bestie's chest when her eyes opened and a hardness hit her gaze. She brought her arm up and the knife stopped in midair.

If that had been the only thing that knife had done we would have been okay. Nope. It stopped and turned, the pointy end coming back our way.

"You should move, Hunter. I'm going to gut the princess and then maybe she'll learn how to play nicely," Liv growled. I didn't know Liv could growl.

The knife started for us, and I decided to take Liv's excellent advice. I moved. I turned, letting my every instinct flow, and wrapped an arm around Evan's waist, pulling her with me. I couldn't do what I wanted to which was tackle her. Being on the ground would leave us vulnerable, and I rather thought Liv was done playing around. I needed to get us out of here and fast. It was obvious she'd done something to make it so Eddie couldn't transport—whether that was an actual spell to keep him underground or so much chaos he was trying to fix it. It didn't matter. Getting the princess out safely was my job now.

"There are wards on the tunnels, right?" I whispered the question to Evan even as I felt the slight pulse in the air around me. I knew that feeling, though it was stronger than it had been before. It was Liv about to work some magic. The air around her slightly crackled, like the tiniest bit of static electricity hitting my skin. I usually had to be closer to her to sense the beginning of her spells, but now I was yards away and I felt it.

Losing that piece of her soul had gained her a whole lot of power.

"Yes, but I'm not leaving you," Evan replied.

So much for her being easier to deal with than Lee. I turned around, not willing to give Liv too much time behind my back. "Liv, you do not want to hurt the King of all Vampire's only daughter."

I didn't mention Evan was the only one for now. That side didn't need to know about all the pregnant chicks on our side, and that included me.

"Oh, but I do. That little bitch has taken out some of our best spell casters. There's a nice bounty on her head." Liv's body moved back and forth as though she was gathering something between her outstretched hands. Likely the energy she would need to send a magical bomb my way.

I wanted Gladys. Even though she couldn't cast a spell, she could often lead me in the way I needed to go. She could push or pull me this way or that, or when she was primed, she could draw on the energy and power she'd stored up over her long existence.

I didn't even have Evan's knife. The kid was better prepared than I was, and I was supposed to be the *Nex Apparatus*.

I was used to dealing with wolves and demons and things that tried to gut me. Liv wouldn't do damage with her claws and fangs. She would come at me with something completely different.

Her hands moved back and then forward, and I felt a rush of wind come my way.

I jumped again, hauling Evan with me, but fire burned against my side as I caught the edge of that spell.

Agony pierced through me. Agony along with a deep sense of dread.

I wasn't good enough.

I couldn't do this.

I would be the reason everything fell, and I would prove myself to be as weak as I'd always suspected.

I knew this spell. I'd felt it before. It was the same type of spell that had been used to pull my she-wolf off my soul. She wasn't trying that with this particular spell. It took way more time, and she'd have to knock me out to separate my she-wolf and I, but she could send doubt into me. She could shake my walls and set me off balance.

But my wolf was still there, and she wanted to fucking roar. When she felt doubt, she liked to take a chunk out of whoever caused it.

I ignored the pain in my side. I could literally smell my flesh burning where the spell had touched me. If that fucker had gotten Evan, it could have burned a hole through her and she would have died in agony and doubt.

That was not acceptable.

I started for my bestie.

Liv's expression turned fierce, and she started to whisper as her hands came up again.

Evan reached for my hand. "No, Kelsey. She's deadly. What about the baby?"

There was a gasp and then another fireball whizzed past, but this one didn't even come close.

Liv had pulled her shot.

She stood there, her eyes wide as she looked at me.

And then she was gone, popping away as quickly as she'd come.

Evan's eyes were filled with tears as she looked my way. "Oh, Kelsey, I'm so sorry. I wasn't thinking. I didn't want you to run her way. She's killed before. I've watched her. I couldn't..."

She couldn't be standing there when the love of her life's mother and brother died. She was a warrior but she was still seventeen years old, and she'd just gotten her parents back. I took a long breath and squeezed her hand. "It's okay."

But Liv knew, and that meant Myrddin would know that I was having that long-awaited child. The Hell plane had always been interested in a child from a Hunter and a royal demon dark prophet.

I had an even bigger target on my back than I'd had before.

Evan and I were safe for now, but I had to wonder if our situation wasn't even worse.

Chapter Ten

"Lie down, Ms. Owens. I can't tell if you're all right unless you stay still." The woman who stood over me had tawny brown hair in a messy bun that sent tendrils around her face. "I've sent for Relda. She's our healer. My skills are in first aid only, but I need to look at that burn on your side."

"Oh, mistress, please let Relda look at the injury." Eddie had tears in his big old demon eyes as he looked up at me. "I can't stand the thought that my mistress has been harmed and I could have prevented it."

Eddie had shown up two minutes after Liv had disappeared. I'd kind of fallen to my knees because that burn hella hurt. Eddie had found Evan and I there and quickly gotten us to this clinic in the Under.

"Everyone slow down. I need information before anything happens." I wasn't dying, though I wouldn't turn down some vamp blood at the moment. "What happened down here?"

The nurse leaned against the exam table, obviously giving up on getting me on it. "The whole of the Under shook, but it was a spell of some kind because there was no geological activity. We keep track of such things, and our scientists claim everything was calm according to their instruments."

"When I tried to take Master Trent and Fenrir through, I was unable, mistress," Eddie explained. "I was only able to transport myself out a few minutes ago. When I couldn't bring anyone else out, Master Grayson concluded something was wrong. Should I go and find him and tell him you were attacked? You were attacked, weren't you?"

Yes, by a witch, and that meant I had to wonder why that witch had been able to get through our witches' wards. "It was Liv. How would she affect the Under? I thought we were safe down here."

The nurse held her hands up. "I don't know any more than you do."

She was awake, which meant she couldn't be one of those vamps I talked about earlier. She seemed pretty human, but some witches were excellent at hiding their nature. "How long have you been down here? What's your name? You should understand that you're not going to touch me. I can take care of myself, so stay back until I figure out what's going on."

"Are we safe, Momma?" a soft voice asked from above. "You said it would be okay to have the Hunter here. You said she wouldn't want to hurt me. You don't hurt my momma."

I tipped my head up and felt my eyes widen. There was a kid hanging from a bar above my head, a tiny girl with raven dark hair and massive black eyes staring back at me. Long dark hair hung around her pale face like a waterfall cascading down. She couldn't be more than five or six.

"Luna, you're fine." Evan stood beside me. "She's not going to hurt you. A witch tried to kidnap her so she's cranky, but she's definitely not going to hurt your mom."

"Luna, you're supposed to be taking a nap." The nurse looked up, her hands on her hips and a definite mom frown on her face.

"I got scared." The little girl started to drop, and I tried to catch her. "Everything shook, and I could hear the uncles were worried. Did the Hunter lady make our nest shake?"

That's when I heard a popping sound and suddenly a bat was flying around the room trying to evade my hands. She flew up to a higher bar on the ceiling and wrapped her dark wings around her tiny body.

"That was a werebat." I was shocked and a little in awe. "I've never seen one before. I thought they stayed in their colony, far away from any kind of civilization."

The prey animal werecreatures were rare. Most had gone extinct long before due to predatory creatures finding them way tasty. But there were a few deer herds and a few droves of werepigs, and I'd heard there were some werehorses out there. The bats were rare, with only two known colonies, and they were found in rough terrain far from any city.

"Luna's colony was wiped out after Myrddin took over," the nurse explained. "King Daniel had placed protective status on all prey werecreatures, but Myrddin wanted help from a couple of weresnakes and he allowed them to hunt as much as they liked. They could easily live off normal bats, off what we call non-sentient creatures. But they liked the hunt."

Assholes. "Why don't you write those names down for me." I winced as I moved toward the center of the room. "Hey, Luna, sweetie. I know I look scary and stuff, but I don't hurt anyone but the bad guys. And I'm being irritable toward your mom because I got hit by a fireball. It sucked."

She dropped to the floor and looked up at me. Now I could see that unlike a lot of other werecreatures, Luna had a distinct look about her. Her nose was flatter and upturned and her ears were pointed. Even in her human form, Luna wouldn't be able to live in the human world. "A fireball?"

I nodded, dropping to one knee so she didn't have to stare up at me. "Yup. A big old fireball, and then she lobbed another one my way, but I was better at ducking that time. Singed my shirt." I held up an arm to show her.

I wasn't better at ducking. Liv had thrown off that shot or she'd been so shaken by the news Evan had delivered that she couldn't aim properly.

A part of me wanted to believe the former. I'd almost gotten to her. There was a part of Liv still there in her cast-iron breast armor. I had to find that part and bring her back to me. Or find a way to hold her down until I could locate that piece of her soul and shove it back in her body.

Luna slipped into a robe her mother held out for her. Mom obviously knew to keep one around for her tiny werebaby. The mom didn't look like a were to me. If I had to bet, I would say she was human or something close.

"I think that would hurt," Luna said. "That witch sounds mean. Our witches are nice."

I hoped so. I was worried because Liv had gotten deep enough into the wards to shake the ground beneath us.

"They are nice, and Relda can help with that burn of yours. It has to hurt." The nurse was dressed in comfy clothes and had a lovely British accent. She turned Evan's way. "Are you all right?"

"I'm good, Rose. Kelsey kind of threw her body in front of mine," Evan admitted.

The doors to the clinic flew open, and my massive wolf boy slid into the room on four feet, Trent and Gray running behind him. His big old paws hit the slick floor, and he did that all four paws went different directions thing that I always find hysterical.

"Thank the goddess," Trent said, moving toward me. "Eddie couldn't get to you and then he could but he didn't come back. Then Fen caught your scent."

We were levels down, and we'd walked around all yesterday. Fen's senses were far beyond even a normal alpha. He could track us through thick rock and a throng of other beings worried about what had happened.

"Don't you change. Luna's here and she doesn't need to..." Evan began.

But Fen didn't listen to her. He changed in between steps going from four to two feet with complete and effortless grace. "What happened? Are you okay?" He took a long breath. "I smell magic. Dark magic. And..." He turned my way. "Mom, you're hurt."

"What happened?" Gray asked, moving in, and then there were three big dudes crowding me.

I held my hands out, trying to get some space. "It was Liv. I suspect she's the one who made the nest shake, though I'd like to know how she did it. I think we should check the wards as soon as possible."

"Eddie, I need you to take me topside." Trent held out a hand.

Fen popped right back into wolf form and went to stand beside his dad.

"I don't think that's..." I began.

But Eddie had hands on them both and they were gone.

"Necessary." I sighed and looked to Gray. "Liv's gone. She's got a teleportation spell now. It would have been nice back in the old days when I had to drive everywhere."

"I think she paid dearly for that power." Gray touched my shirt, pulling it up to get a look at the wound. "Are you okay?"

"We can't possibly know because she won't sit long enough to allow me to examine her, and I'm fairly certain she's going to tell me not to let Relda try to heal her." The nurse had her daughter on her hip, the little were hanging on her while watching everything that went on.

"I put the king's blood my mom sent down here." Evan crossed to the refrigerator. There was a lock on it, and she pressed in the code. "It should work."

"That's for you," I replied.

Evan pulled out the thermos I'd seen Fenrir carrying the day we arrived. "It's way more than I need, and I happen to know that Relda's going to have a hard time with that wound. Rose, we were facing one of the Profane."

Rose set Luna down with a sigh. "She's right. The Profane use spells that resist magical healing. They resist regular healing. Vampire blood is the only thing that can heal it unless you can find an angel to touch you or you want to wait a couple of weeks before you can move comfortably again. Maybe months, the way that looks."

"Great. We have a ton of vampires down here," I pointed out. "If we can't find Casey, I'll wait until the primals are up."

Rose's head shook vigorously. "No. Oh, no. We don't use primal blood to heal. It often…changes the person being healed. It can go wrong sometimes."

There was a piece of trivia I'd never heard. "What do you mean *wrong*? They turn into primals?"

"Not exactly," Rose hedged. "Sometimes primal blood takes… I don't know how to put it but it takes root in a person and changes them. No one's tried it in many, many years. It's forbidden for a primal to share blood with a non-primal except in extreme cases when a life is truly in danger. The last person to take primal blood lost their hair and grew fangs that wouldn't recede. He also developed a…hunger for blood that couldn't be denied."

"That's what always happens?" I was curious.

"Not always. Sometimes it's smaller changes like talons that grow or a sensitivity to sunlight," Rose explained. "I read that once the change was nothing more than developing extremely sensitive hearing. But they cannot take the chance that they create a monster. I'm married to a primal, and I don't share blood with him. The academics are kind enough to send the companions blood so we can stay with our husbands as long as we can."

It was an exchange begun long ago when companions and vampires realized the way they fit together. Companions fed their vampire husbands, and the hubby paid her back with a much-elongated life through his blood. Anyone marrying a primal apparently would get the shaft if the academics weren't such a kind group of dudes.

"Okay, but we can wait for…" I was about to say Casey, but that was the moment when Gray's fingers barely skimmed across the wound, and I groaned because the pain went sky high. The pain had been sitting at a low hum of misery, but I kind of saw stars when anything touched my side.

"And she's going on the bed." Gray simply leaned over and picked me up, crossing to the bed, and I clamped my jaw down to keep from shouting out. "We're not waiting for Casey. That's a whole damn thermos of king's blood, and Evan's not going to be here for more than a couple of days. Evan, I take it your dad got back and realized he could slow down your aging process to match Fen's."

I winced as he laid me down on the bed.

Evan handed him the thermos. "Yes. It was pointed out that Fen will outlive me by a couple hundred years, and my dads put me on the every other day blood shot plan. I would rather wait until I'm like twenty-five or so, but they want me to have the healing properties, too. I tried to tell them we all take vamp blood before we go into battle, but my dads are super overbearing and protective."

"I would like to try to apply it topically," Rose said, setting her daughter down and crossing to wash her hands. "I worry since we're dealing with a wound given by one of the Profane that it will scar if we don't put it directly on the skin. How deep does it go?"

"It looks superficial, but she should be healing this," Gray said. "Aren't you supposed to be on king's blood?"

"Well, excuse me if I was on a Faery plane and the king turned all human on us. So I've been off the juice for a couple of days," I said. "I didn't think about it."

It was a routine at home. I was the Council's *Nex Apparatus*, and that meant a wee dose of king's blood in my morning coffee. While I'd been stuck on a weird Fae plane, I'd had neither coffee nor a functional vampire king. I'd gotten back and home had been taken over along with my refrigerator, so I was off track. And that fucking fireball hurt.

"So she's been off it for almost a week in her time," Gray said. "And she doesn't take the same dose the queen and Quinn take. Topical it is, then, and when she gets back she'll dose up again. I'll talk to Casey about a donation this afternoon."

Casey kind of owed me, and I wouldn't hate having some more protection for me and the baby. I wasn't worried about the vamp blood doing anything to my son. The queen had three healthy kiddos and she was always on the juice. Apparently it didn't cause any complications unless it was primal blood.

I gritted my teeth as the nurse examined the wound. "So Profane spells are worse than regular old witch spells. Do we know why?"

"The Profane share some power with the demons who work with Myrddin," Gray explained.

"Ah, hence the demonic power I can feel coming off her." My bestie was going to need some serious deprogramming and probably a hearty detox. "Ow."

It sizzled where the king's blood touched, but in a good way. Still a hurty way, but I could feel the skin closing.

"Wow, that's gross," Luna said from above.

She was a strong were because she had to have flown up again. She was popping in and out of her form, and like my son, didn't care about a robe.

"Sorry, kid." I laid back, letting Rose do her job. "Do you like it up there?"

She grinned and was heartbreakingly cute, like a lot of kids her age. "It's fun in here because I get to watch Momma work, but I like it better when I get to hang out with my dad." Her grin faded. "He was sad last night. Alvis died. I don't like the word *die*. It means I don't get to see people again."

Poor kid had already seen way too much death. "Sorry about that.

I'm going to find out what happened. I promise."

Her already big eyes widened, and she looked to her mom. "Momma, I hear a sound. Something's coming."

"It's probably Eddie," Rose said, finishing up my wound care. "He'll be bringing Trent and Fen back."

Luna's head shook. "It's from below."

Suddenly I was looking at a bat who wrapped herself up in her wings as though she could hide. So much trauma in her young life.

And then I smelled brimstone as a demon popped into existence right in front of me.

I'd thought my day was done, but I got ready for another fight.

"Don't, Kelsey." Gray stepped in front of me. "He's not here to cause trouble."

Evan moved closer to me. "They always cause trouble. They live for it."

The demon was a slender male dressed in an elegant suit. With the exception of his horns and red eyes, he looked perfectly human and well-heeled, with slicked back brown hair and male-model high cheekbones. He glanced around and offered a courtly bow. "Good afternoon, residents of the Under. I'm pleased to make your acquaintances."

"What the fuck are you doing here?" I wasn't playing around with the demons. "How the hell did you get through the wards, and what did you do to the nest?"

The demon frowned. "What happened to the nest?"

"Kelsey, he didn't do anything," Gray corrected.

"He's here." I wasn't going to avoid the evidence in front of me. "He's standing in a place that is supposed to be protected by a whole bunch of wards. Liv obviously couldn't get through them, hence the plan to ensure I was brought to the surface so she could light me up. So how did this asshole get through?"

The demon gasped and put a hand to his chest as though there were some pearls there he could clutch. "That is extremely rude, Lady Sloane."

I shook my head and slid off the table. "Oh, don't you dare call me that."

"It's your title," the demon insisted.

Gray stepped between us. "My wife doesn't ever intend to take her place in the House of Sloane, so her title is not necessary."

"You gave up your place in the House of Sloane when your contract was…" I should have asked more questions. He'd signed another contract, after all. "Did you agree to take on your house responsibilities again, Grayson Sloane?"

The House of Sloane was supposed to have fallen after what Gray's father had done to him. When his legacy contract had been declared void, his father had been dragged to the Hell plane and the house he headed had lost its lofty place. It certainly wasn't supposed to now be headed by the dark prophet.

I'd fixed this problem.

"The House of Sloane is a highly regarded house on the Hell plane," the demon assured me.

"Kelsey, it's not what you think. No one is torturing souls," Gray replied. "But it was necessary to revive the house in order for me to regularly descend. Your title is nothing more than a formality."

"Does Trent have one or does he get left up here when they find a way to drag us both down?" I wasn't feeling fair.

The demon waved a hand as though this was not an issue at all. "Lord Sloane's pet wolf will be welcome in his house, of course. I am ever ready to welcome Trent, as I am eager to serve My Lady."

"Pet?" I practically screamed the question, and I was done. I needed to talk to my husband because he should have told me he'd taken over his father's role when he'd become Lucifer's butt monkey. "Get the fuck out. You are never to come to the Under again. Ever. Do I make myself clear?"

The demon took a step back and look horrified. He turned to Gray as though he could save the demon from me. "I cannot believe Lady Sloane is so rude, My Lord."

Gray simply sighed. "That's because you've never met her. Why are you here, Tix?"

A look akin to sympathy hit the slender demon's face. "Our Great Lord Lucifer requests your presence given recent events."

"Ah, the king," Gray acknowledged. "I should have expected that he would want to contemplate Donovan and the queen's return to the plane. I'd hoped for a bit more time with my wife."

"He just got back," I complained. "He's not going to descend again. He's been topside for less than twenty-four hours. You can tell

Lucifer to fuck himself."

"Oh, I think that would be a bad idea, my lady," the demon said, going a bit pale. "He does not understand your comedy."

"It's not comedy. I want him to fuck himself with a sword or something," I shot back.

"Kelsey, little ears." Rose pointed to the ceiling.

I was scaring the children again, but I wasn't about to back down. I would, however, lower my voice. "Gray, tell him to leave."

My husband's expression turned grim. "I can't do that. I mean I could, but he won't leave without me."

"How is he even here? I was told the wards held against demons who aren't in the system. Are you telling me you allowed him in? You opened us up to this?" I was shocked at the thought.

"I can find My Lord wherever he is," the demon assured me. "What kind of a butler do you think I am, my lady?"

"We already have a butler." I did not like this guy one bit.

The demon snorted. "You have a freak. An outcast satan is not a real butler. You should understand that I run a proper household and look forward to welcoming any…"

Gray held up a hand. "I'll go. I'll be there soon, Tix. Give me a moment to talk to my wife and I will follow."

Gray turned to face me. "Kelsey, I have to go."

"No, you don't." He'd just gotten here, and I needed him. Fenrir needed him. "You should stay here and reconnect with your son. Gray, that demon was going to say he's ready to welcome any children we have. We're having a son in less than nine months. Did you even protect him?"

His eyes flared and went the slightest red. "You think I wouldn't protect our son? I made sure no one can touch you or Trent or Fenrir. I did it all to protect the three of you, and I took into account what happened on our wedding night. If things go wrong, I am the only one who will pay. As always."

"The only one who pays? Are you fucking kidding me? You know you have a martyr complex, Gray. If you're the only one who pays, it's because you won't allow anyone else to help you. You're doing what you've always done throughout our relationship. You're making decisions about my welfare without me."

"Well, I couldn't ask you because you were on another fucking plane of existence."

"I will tell Lord Lucifer you will be along shortly." Tix shook his head slightly as though shocked at what he was seeing.

He popped out of existence.

"You are not going anywhere." I wasn't about to let him go back to Hell. "I'm calling Hugo. Or I'll have Eddie look into your contract."

Our butler was a satan. He'd left behind his brethren, but he could still judge a contract. If anyone could find some wiggle room in a contract it was Eddie.

Gray took a long breath. "Baby, I know this is hard on you but there was no other way."

"Did you even try?" He often didn't. He saw the thing that would cost him the most and decide that was the only way. He was the Eeyore of the demonic world.

"I'm not having this argument with you right now. I have to go. I have to play this game for another six weeks, and then we'll be through. I'll talk to Jamie and Nate about moving to Frelsi," Gray promised. "We'll discuss this further when I get back."

"I won't be here when you get back." I might or I might not. I might have gone back to Frelsi, and I would bet if Gray's butler from Hell could pop in wherever he happened to be, he wasn't going to be welcome in the royals' home.

It was likely why he no longer had a relationship with our son. Why he was going to fuck it up again with this one.

It wasn't fair or right, but I couldn't help myself in that moment. I was pregnant and scared and unsure I would be able to find this weapon Lee and Dean would need to fulfill their destiny. For now, the fate of the plane was on my back, and I wanted Gray with me.

I needed him.

When I'd left before we'd been in such a good place. We'd been a family, and now it felt like we were on the edge again, like if I let go for a second we could fall apart.

All I knew how to do in these moments was to fight.

He stared at me as though he wasn't sure what to say.

"Stay with me." I did know.

"I love you, Kelsey mine."

And he was gone.

Again.

"Trent and Fen are coming back." Luna was on the ground again and putting on her pink and purple robe. She looked up at her mom. "Everything is busy today, Mama. It's loud here."

Sure enough, Eddie was back with Trent and a wolfy Fen.

Fenrir sniffed the air, and a low growl started in the back of his throat.

"Where's Gray?" Trent seemed to immediately know what had happened.

Luna stepped up to the massive wolf who should have terrified anyone in a room with him and put her small hands on either side of his face. "It's okay, Fen. The bad man went back down, but he took your other dad."

Fen's head hung, and Evan moved in beside Luna, putting a hand on his head and stroking down his back.

Trent pulled me into his arms. "I'm sorry, baby. He'll be back. I promise. He always comes back."

I held on to him and hoped he was right.

Chapter Eleven

"How are you feeling?"

I took a deep breath and fought the urge to scream. I'd been asked this question five hundred times since I'd been released from the clinic the day before. I'd been told to rest for the night and while I would have ignored that advice, Trent was suddenly interested in following the nurse's orders.

"I'm good, babe," I managed to say between clenched teeth and what I was absolutely certain was a forced smile.

Because I was the one forcing it.

Trent sat next to me in bed, wearing not a stitch of clothing. He stretched that magnificent body and yawned. "I'm glad to hear it. Eddie's been in the kitchen all morning."

I still wasn't entirely sure why I'd been forced to rest after my encounter with Liv. The vampire blood had done the trick and my wound had healed, but the nurse had mentioned my blood pressure was slightly high and then all the men had freaked out.

I'd had to send Evan to question several of the people I'd been scheduled to interview the night before because Trent had carried me down to our rooms and then watched over me like a damn hawk. "I didn't need to take the night off."

He leaned over and kiss my forehead. "Says the woman who slept for twelve hours."

I frowned. "Seriously? I've been asleep for twelve hours? What time is it?"

He kissed his way down to my nose. "Nine. Ish. In the morning. We can sleep far longer. No one is really awake down here until after noon. The primals have only been asleep for a few hours."

So I was going to throw my sleep schedule way off, but then it was crap anyway. Jet lag is a real thing, and when your jet lag comes from traveling through a time portal...well, it's bad. Throw in early pregnancy symptoms and it wasn't such a huge surprise that I'd slept.

Trent settled back down and cuddled me close. "Evan left notes from all of her interviews. I can't thank you enough for trusting her. Evan needs some way to contribute. It's been difficult to be the only girl. All of her role models were stories rather than people. I think watching you in action will be good for her."

"Well, all she could do last night was watch me sleep. She's going to think I'm a lazy *Nex Apparatus*." I knew I should get up and start in on those notes, but the truth was it felt good to lay in his arms. I only wished Gray was with us. I was used to him being gone. He was often working, but this was different. Now I had to think about where he was. "How long do you think he'll be gone?"

He was quiet for a moment, his hand stroking over my back. "Not long here. A long time for him. We could get lucky and have some crazy thing happen that he's supposed to witness. His prophecy instincts can break Lucifer's hold."

"What do you mean?"

"Sometimes Gray gets pulled to a place," Trent explained. "The first time it happened was roughly five years after you disappeared. We had recently established Frelsi. The kids, Sasha, and I at this point were still out on the planes, but we came back to Earth from time to time to meet with our allies and check on Gray. We were there at the time, but Gray wasn't in Frelsi and we didn't expect him. I'm fairly certain he was on the Hell plane when it happened."

"When what happened?"

"When a strange girl showed up outside the city," Trent continued. "She shouldn't have known where we were. No one should have. I can tell you her showing up the way she did caused many meetings. We were torn about what to do. We left her outside for days. The general consensus was that she was someone Myrddin had sent. And then suddenly Gray was beside me. He was in full-on prophet mode. I asked him why he was there and he told me he needed to witness something important."

"Was it Shahidi?" Evan had told me about the young woman who held her grandfather's soul. Shy came from a family of psychics. Myrddin had killed most of the well-known families with supernatural powers. Shy had been spared because she'd slept over at a friend's house the night Myrddin had killed her whole family. But without her mother and grandmother to guide her, when she'd come into her powers she couldn't handle them. At some point the queen's father had been killed and his spirit had found Shy. She'd given him a space in her soul and he'd guided her and taught her how to navigate out of the mental health facility she'd been kept in and into the supernatural world that should have been hers. "She can talk to the dead, right? Gray was there to see Harry Wharton reunite with his grandchildren?"

"I don't think so. I did in the beginning, but now I wonder. When Gray comes to witness a prophecy being fulfilled, he tends to disappear after what he's there to see happens. Gray didn't leave that day. He stayed until a moment that happened the next morning. Shy was scared when Harry wasn't in control. He had to rest at times. Shy hadn't seen the supernatural world. Not much of it. The Fae creatures kind of freaked her out until Rhys took her hand and promised to show her around. He made some flowers grow, and she smiled for the first time. And then Gray was gone."

"That was the important moment?" If that was important enough to pull Gray from Hell, it had to mean there was a prophecy about it.

"I suspect, though all he would be able to tell us was that yes it was important. Not why."

"So Shy is important. Not Harry. Shy and Rhys." My mind was playing around with everything I'd learned. Something tickled at the back of my mind. I hadn't spent much time with them. Less than a day, and I'd slept a lot of it. "She still holds Harry Wharton's soul, right?"

"Yes. I have no idea what we would have done without Harry the last few years. He's taught us all about how to steal stuff we need," Trent admitted. "More than that, he still has spectacular connections and knows who we can and can't trust. I'm glad he gets to see his daughter again, but you should know I don't think he'll be around for long."

That had me sitting up. "Why? I thought this was something that worked for both of them."

Trent seemed to think about how to explain. "I think he's been holding on until Zoey, Daniel, and Dev returned. In the beginning, he did bolster Shy. He found her in a mental hospital. He explained things to her that her mother would have handled had she lived."

"About her powers."

"Yes. Imagine being eight and you see your first ghost. Even if you've been told it will happen, it has to be terrifying. She was at the mercy of the human health system, and they did not understand how to help her. Harry did. And they've needed each other for years, but he thinks he's holding her back now."

"Holding her back from..." It hit me. "She and Rhys are a couple."

"They're quite bonded, but the inclusion of Harry makes things awkward. Harry thinks she's ready for a relationship now, so he's going to leave as soon as he knows his daughter is all right." Trent reached up and ran his fingers through my hair. "He says there's a light where he is, and it calls to him. I knew there was a Heaven plane. I guess I never thought it would be for us."

I couldn't even contemplate the idea that there was some sort of afterlife. I was too worried about this one. "So you think once Harry is gone, she'll turn to Rhys?"

"I think she turns to him now, but the romantic aspect will likely be more comfortable for them both. I worry about Rhys. He's a Green Man. He wasn't meant to be a virgin at his age, but he refuses to take any woman who is not Shy, and she hasn't been ready. He's patient, but we're all waiting for him to explode. Not literally."

I couldn't help but think about what Liv had said. "Magically. All that fertility power needs somewhere to go. Liv told me they have witches who look for big bursts of Fae magic because they want to use Rhys to locate the others."

"Frelsi is protected, and so is the Under," Trent assured me. "We also can take him to the Unseelie plane if he needs to let off some steam. I've spent the last couple of years balancing the sexual frustrations of teen supernaturals with trying to make sure Lee doesn't get an STI. I wish I'd known about the whole latent vampire thing. I might have had less anxiety."

I brushed my hand over his chest, loving the feel of his skin against mine, how warm he was. "You had a lot to deal with. You can't imagine how amazing I think you are, how comfortable I am having this baby with you. I love Gray but his life is complex, and knowing you're here…"

I let the words dangle because I didn't want to say anything harsh against Gray, but I needed Trent to know how I felt about him.

He rolled on top of me, pressing me into the mattress. "No matter what happens with Gray, I'm here for life. I love you, Kelsey. I love him. But Gray and I agreed a long time ago that you are always our highest priority. Our children will be too. I need you to know he won't allow our kids to descend. Ever."

"I don't know that we'll have a choice." I spread my legs so I could wrap them around Trent's lean waist. "You have to understand how long the House of Sloane has waited for this child. Do we know if Gray's father is still around?"

Trent lowered his head and kissed my neck, nuzzling me softly and starting a hum of arousal through my body. "I'm not sure. He won't talk about it. That tends to make me think his father *is* hanging around somewhere. Death wouldn't have been his punishment for what happened in Wyoming. Torture is something they take seriously on the Hell plane. And if he's hanging around, then we have to be careful. I promise I'll do anything for our kids."

I knew he would. I never doubted it. I wrapped my arms around him and let him kiss me over and over, his hands starting to move across my skin while the events of the previous days played through my head.

I had to find that weapon, and the sooner the better. I was starting to believe the weapon was a person and that The Path was a little on the kinky side.

"So I've got two young men who are the only two who can prime the weapon," I mused as Trent made his way down my body, licking and kissing and drawing my nipples into his mouth. I was feeling pretty primed for something, and I had to wonder if this wasn't what The Path had meant. "What if the weapon is a woman? We've got a lot of sexual tension in the younger group. It feels like a theme. And the prophecy specifically mentions a *her*. I have to wonder if it's Mia

Day."

Trent kissed his way down my belly. "I know her going missing has bothered Lee. I sometimes think he would be a different man if she was here. Now that we know he's a latent, it makes sense that those two were always together. They were drawn together from childhood."

Because even as a latent he would have been attracted to her light. He wouldn't have been able to see it, but something inside him would need to be around her. "When you think about it, it kind of makes sense. It takes three to save three. Three of them save the three inner planes."

"I've looked for the Days." Trent's mouth hovered over my pussy, his breath warming me. "Every plane we've been on, I've asked about them. I've never gotten even a thread to follow. All any of us know is the Days were in the Council building when Myrddin pulled his coup. No one saw them leave, and no one has seen them since. The most likely scenario is they died. That's what we all believe."

I shook my head. "If Myrddin killed Sarah Day, he would have paraded her head around. There's no chance that he killed her and she died in the Council building. I'm not saying they couldn't be dead, but it's highly unlikely Myrddin wouldn't have used her death in some way. Do we know where he holds prisoners?"

I felt something tickle across my arm and brushed it away.

I didn't think he would keep the fact that he had the Days locked away in prison quiet. Holding the queen's favorite witch hostage would be something that would make Myrddin look good. He might even try to turn her.

Out of the corner of my eye I caught sight of something moving. Trent was teasing me with his tongue, so I let it go.

I needed to talk to the witches again. I needed specifically to talk to someone who'd spent time in the houses where Myrddin sent his prisoners.

Mia Day would make an excellent soldier in Myrddin's army. If he could turn Mia Day, it would be a huge coup. She would be in her early twenties now, but she'd been a child that day twelve years ago. She was the daughter of a powerful witch and a fallen angel.

But why would he keep it a secret?

Unless he'd been waiting. Unless he'd been biding his time for that moment when he could spring his weapon on the royals, who would never think to question the daughter of some of their best friends.

Mia Day could be an excellent sleeper agent if Myrddin could turn her. If he could keep her identity secret, the royals wouldn't know what hit them.

And then a ladybug landed, a bright red spot on my arm.

How had a ladybug gotten this far down? I hadn't seen any bugs at all now that I thought about it. It was such an odd sight, that bit of sunshine down here.

And then I wasn't thinking at all because Trent held every bit of my attention. His tongue played at my core and I laid back and let everything else go.

* * * *

A couple of hours later, I wandered into what Evan told me she liked to call the "downtown" of the Under. It was a bit like an underground town square, complete with a magical sky overhead. I didn't worry about getting claustrophobic down here.

"It changes to moonlight at night. It's synched to the light outside to help the non-vampires who live here," Evan was saying.

I was right back to contemplating where Sarah, Felix, and Mia had gone. I couldn't help but consider how the prophecy was worded. *Her.* It called the weapon a *her* and spoke of her mother's gift.

"That's the diner. It's what we call it. Most people down here either eat at home or don't eat real food at all, but there are a bunch of us who stay in the Under who need a human diet and don't cook. I never learned because Albert and Eddie would have lost their minds at the thought of one of us cooking. So if I'm here without them, I hang at the diner a lot." She waved to the tall man who stood behind the counter. "Hey, Ben. How's it going?"

The man, who had the look of a shifter about him, went a little pasty. "Princess. If you're here…"

Evan quickly shook her head. "Eddie's here, too. You do not have to feed Fen."

The man named Ben breathed a sigh of relief. "Thank the

goddess. The last time he was here with only his father I ran out. Ran out. I had what should have been a month's worth of meat, and he ate it in three days and asked where the rest was. It's like the Goddess Circle. They can go through some wine, if you know what I mean. And the herbs. I don't know what worries me more—Fenrir's endless gut or whatever it is Jade burns as incense. I'm pretty sure you can get a contact high from it."

"No, you can't because it's not something that makes you high." Jade walked out of the back of the small diner, an apron around her waist. "If you didn't want to have to deal with perfectly normal smells, then you shouldn't have placed your business across from the social center." She looked me over. "Hey, *Nex Apparatus*. You here to eat?"

"Nex Apparatus?" Ben was back to pale again. "I didn't do anything."

"She's investigating Alvis's death," Jade pointed out.

Ben nodded. "Oh."

Evan gave the man a bright smile. "I don't suppose you know anything."

"I hadn't seen Alvis in a couple of days," Ben said. "Which is actually weird because he usually teaches this class over at the center."

Jade pointed toward the brightly colored doors across the square. "Alvis teaches a couple of classes, including a painting class. Relda attended regularly, but he canceled the last two weeks. I don't think he was feeling well. I probably should have mentioned that when you interrogated me."

"She interrogated you?" Ben's eyes had gone wide.

"I asked her some questions. It's not like I put a light in her eyes and threatened her." I felt the need to defend myself because it wasn't like I'd scared the young witch. I didn't want her scared. I wanted her talking about something she likely wouldn't want to talk about.

"She didn't need to," Jade replied. "She's the Hunter. There are songs about how fierce she is. She pulled out a duke of Hell's heart and then ate it."

"I did not eat it." What the hell? I'm sure Casey would call it "artistic interpretation," but I did not eat that wretchedly cold heart. I might be werewolf adjacent, but I only eat cooked food. Mostly. I do enjoy some sushi, but definitely not mean old man heart.

"But you did pull it out of his body." Evan had her notebook and a pen. She was getting into her role. "However, she was super nice to you, Jade. You shouldn't spread rumors about her being mean."

Jade had flushed a nice pink. "It was only for the street cred. Which doesn't mean a lot since we don't actually have streets in the Under. I can't wait to get back to a place with a real sun and moon." She stopped herself. "I mean I'm grateful. I'm very thankful."

She was also a twenty-something kid who'd been through a lot. And I didn't know what kind of magic she did. For witches, being in specific places could be comforting. If, say, Jade derived her magic from air or water, being down here could feel stifling to her. "It's okay. I was hoping we could talk. What's good here?"

"Ben's good with the fryer." Jade looked wary again. "I thought we talked the other night. Though now I realize I should have told you the other stuff."

"I got that from his calendar." I'd known about the missed classes, though he hadn't put a reason down, merely marked them off. I hadn't known Relda took the class. Still, I needed some other information from Jade, information she might not want to talk about with a large audience. "Ben, can I borrow her for a few minutes? It doesn't look too busy."

"It's never busy," Ben admitted. "Sure. I'll go and make some fries and bring you a couple of sodas."

"And a burger." Yes, I had recently eaten Eddie's lovely breakfast, but I was eating for two and I had to fight two wolves for my share of bacon. I glanced at his menu. "Some onion rings sound nice, too."

"You're Fenrir's mom." Ben shook his head like he hadn't expected that behavior from me. He should have. Casey should put a song in that musical called "Kelsey Eats the World." Ben simply turned and walked into his kitchen.

"Evan, could you go over to the center and see if anyone knows why Alvis canceled his classes?"

Evan looked at me and then Jade as though trying to figure out why I wanted her alone. She finally nodded. "Whatever you want, boss."

Evan strode across the square. I watched and noted the other "buildings" that surrounded us. There was a clothing store and a general store. There was something I suspected was a place for childcare.

"The stores don't actually charge," Jade said with a sigh. "It's something they set up for the non-primals so it feels more like we're in a real town and not a half-mile deep."

"It wasn't always like this?" I started for a booth in the back of the diner that looked like it had been plopped in from the fifties. There was a jukebox and a long bar where a couple of patrons sat sipping coffee and finishing up their late breakfasts.

Jade pulled her apron off and nodded to the other server, who gave her a salute that seemed to say she would take care of things. "By the time I got here everything was in place, but some of my friends came in a couple of years before me and they said it was very spare. Like the library was tight, you know. And there were conference rooms and stuff, but not a lot of fun. Which is weird because the primals aren't what you would think. They like fun. The first time I went to a social hour I walked in and there was this tall bat dude playing foosball with a little troll, and the dwarves were betting on the outcome, and I felt like I was finally in a place I could breathe. Because it was weird but there was happiness here. I hadn't seen happiness in a long time. You want me to talk about it, don't you? Being held by Myrddin's witches. I'm not sure I understand how it fits into Alvis's murder."

"It doesn't." She was a smart kid. "But I didn't come here to solve a murder initially. I came here to investigate a prophecy, and it might have something to do with that."

Jade settled in. "A prophecy? Like something the dark prophet said?"

"This particular prophecy comes from the outer planes." I needed to treat Jade like the badass she was. She'd survived a lot, and she didn't need hand holding, though if she did mine would be ready. I don't think needing comfort is an admission of weakness. It's strength. "It's about defeating Myrddin."

She straightened up, her gaze becoming serious. "What do you need to know?"

If she was acting, she was spectacular, but then she could have been trained. I didn't like being so suspicious. Over the last couple of years, I'd grown to be less cynical. I wasn't sure I could afford that now. Though I'd also learned to trust my instincts, and every one of them told me this girl was the real deal, that she was being genuine. "When you were in the…what did they call it?"

"An academy for young witches. That's what they called it." There wasn't much emotion in her tone. I could understand that. It made me hate having to put her through this again. "It was truly a conversion camp."

"Did he put all young witches in this camp?"

Her head shook. "There were several educational facilities. We all knew the academy I was assigned to was for what they called difficult ones. We were all either orphans or we'd done something our parents viewed as abnormal. That was only a few of us though. Most of us were older children of witches Myrddin had slaughtered. The younger ones were spelled to forget their moms and dads. It doesn't work when you had too many memories. I was ten when he killed my mom. I spent five years there."

"Was this place actually in the Council building…Coven House?"

"It was the Council building. I never would call it the Coven House, and no. The academy was in the country a few miles outside of a town called Rockwall. There was a place on a big lake that should have felt like a wide-open space, but somehow they made it small. The wards were there to keep us in and keep us quiet and docile."

"How many girls were there?"

"At any given time probably twenty to thirty of us."

"So you knew them all."

Jade nodded. "Of course. When you're in hell, you get to know your fellow prisoners. Of course sometimes they sent in people to spy on us, so you had to be careful. I had a friend who was almost out. She'd passed all the tests of loyalty and then she opened up to the wrong person and instead of graduation she faced the fire."

A chill went up my spine. "They actually burn witches?"

"Oh, yes." She sounded haunted now. "And they made us watch, made us listen as they pleaded for their lives as they promised to be good."

"You know it was never about being good."

"It was about being what they wanted us to be."

"What Myrddin wanted you to be."

Her head shook. "No, Kelsey. If there's one thing I can teach you it's that he isn't alone in this. You want there to be one bad guy. You want to be able to kick his ass and be done with it. But that's not what happened. He had witches who helped him, who killed vampires and weres and shifters and Fae on his command. They didn't have to. They weren't under his influence, or rather they allowed themselves to be. They chose this path when they could have fought. Like my mother fought. They chose to toss aside everything the goddess teaches us. We're to do no harm. That is all they do. If you don't think like them, they torture you until you do. Or at least you'll never speak against them again. No one man can do that. It takes a small but powerful group to do the dirty work, and it takes an army of the apathetic to turn their eyes and allow it to happen."

I reached out because her story was getting to me every bit as much as Casey's had. I had come home to a generation of young people forever marked by trauma, by loss. The mother in me ached for what they'd gone through and was also so damn proud that they were still pushing, still fighting. "I'm going to do everything I can to make this plane safe for you again."

"That's what they said," she replied quietly, but she didn't pull her hand away. "I know that we have hope now. I do believe you, but you should understand somewhere in their fucked-up brains, they convinced themselves they were right, that anyone who didn't believe the way they did was out to hurt the witches. A small group became convinced that they were oppressed and the only way to fix the situation was to oppress everyone else. They believe Myrddin can give them the plane, and once they kill or force the humans into bowing to them, they'll be safe."

He'd used their fears against them. "I assure you that's not how it's going to go. Once he opens that door, the demons will reign, and they will not care about what the witches want."

She sniffled and tears gleamed in her eyes. "Why won't the Heaven plane save us?"

I had asked that question a million times. "That's not how it works. From what I can tell, Heaven is for later. It's something we can't understand in the form we're in now. Or maybe it's the bargain.

Free will means responsibility. We have to fight, have to sacrifice, and we have to save ourselves. And we will, but I need help. I need to find Mia Day."

Jade's eyes widened and her mouth opened slightly, a sure sign of her surprise. She sat back. "Are you asking if I've seen her? If she was in the academy with me? No. I haven't seen Mia since the morning of the attack. We were in classes together. Not at the school. She was a grade ahead of me at school, but we were in the same magical training classes. She hung out with the royals, but she was super nice to everyone. None of the royals were in this particular class. It was strictly witches. It was an earth magic class. We were sitting there and she was helping me with a spell to grow flowers and herbs when her dad ran in."

This was what I needed. This was important. I had someone who had seen her on the day she disappeared. "Do you remember what he said?"

"Mr. Day talked to the teacher, and we all knew something was going wrong because she started to cry and then she told us we all had to go back to our homes. We had to find our parents, but mine was at work. So the teacher and Mr. Day moved us down to a more secure room. I remember how scared Mia was."

They'd been protected little girls who hadn't had to think about how scary the world could be, and then suddenly it was. "Did her father say anything about where they were going?"

She seemed to think for a moment. "He said they had to find her mom. It was complete chaos, but I got the impression that Mia's mom had something important to do and they were meeting her at their place. Mia was crying because she wanted to get to Lee, the king's son. He was her best friend. She was insistent on getting to the royal apartments because she didn't want to leave without Lee."

Poor Mia. By then Albert and Trent and Eddie had gotten the royal kids and were probably on their way to Venice. It had been the first stop on their long road, the stop that had brought Sasha into the group because he'd been staying there. "I don't think it would have been a good idea to go to the penthouse. The first thing Myrddin did was attempt to get control of the king's children."

"Mr. Day wouldn't let her go. He said her mom had a way out."

That was what I needed. "She had a physical way out of the

building?"

"That wasn't the impression I got. I think it was magical. He promised Mia they would come back and find Lee, but they had to go...what did he say? It was weird. He said they had to go visit family first, and that she shouldn't be afraid," Jade explained. "I thought it was weird that she would be afraid of her family."

But Mia Day's family included angels. Had Sarah Day found a way to contact her in-laws? Had they gotten her out?

"Here you go," Ben said, putting a big tray of food between us. The heavenly scent of burgers and fried food assailed my nose and proved that even when I was faced with a hell of a conundrum, I could still eat.

Because I was fairly certain I knew where the Days had fled.

The Heaven plane wasn't a place I could buy a ticket to. Well, not a physical one, and punching that particular ticket was usually one way unless one had brothers and sisters up there.

And Heaven was exactly the place Myrddin intended to close us off from. The only weapon that could take the fucker down might end up on the other side of that door.

I had to find a way to get to Heaven. I prayed Sarah Day had left a map behind.

"Hey, is that a ladybug?" Ben stared down at my arm.

Sure enough, my friend from before was there. "Yeah, I noticed it earlier. I guess it followed me." There was suspicion again. "I don't suppose it's real. Is it a spell? Is it tracking me?"

Jade frowned and reached over, putting her fingers out. The ladybug had been walking down my shirt sleeve and simply continued its walk onto Jade's hand. She brought her hand up, carefully inspecting it. "I don't sense any spell."

Ben sniffed the air. "Nah. That's natural. It's just a bug, but not one we have down this deep. It's the weirdest thing. The last couple of weeks we've had some odd visitors. I think someone's playing pranks."

"Visitors?" My instincts were flaring again. "What kind?"

"Animals," Jade said, still looking at the ladybug. "First it was a couple of butterflies. We made sure they were real. Then about a month ago it was a bunny. We would have tested it, too but, well, Fen ate it."

I was going to have such a talk with my son. "How would a rabbit get down here?"

The bugs I could understand. They could come in on a visitor's clothing or in their suitcases. A bunny would be hard to miss.

"Oh, there are lots of animals in the Under," Ben corrected. "The primals have to eat, after all. That particular rabbit wasn't the species we grow down here. We grow Flemish Giants. They get up to twenty pounds. It's easier that way or else the primal needs two or three smaller ones a night."

Okay, ick. But they did have to eat. "And this bunny wasn't one of those?"

"No. It was much smaller and white. The Flemish Giants are brown." Jade settled the ladybug on her shirt and picked up an onion ring. "This ladybug might be from the gnomes. They sometimes have helpful bugs brought in. Not sure about the rabbit, though. There should be records. The primals keep tons of records. I wouldn't worry about it."

But worrying was all part of the job.

I still ate those onion rings.

Chapter Twelve

"So all in all Alvis canceled four classes in the last two weeks."
Evan took a long sip of her juice. She'd gotten it from a shop that had
a bunch of green stuff in it. An older woman had mixed it up for her.

It looked super healthy.

There were more of the Under's citizens wandering around now
that it was late afternoon. Somehow even this far beneath the surface I
could feel dusk coming on.

When the primals were up, they would perform their rituals again
for Alvis. I still had a full day before I could sit down and question
them. But there was still plenty to be done. I'd already met with
Casey, and we'd talked about my thoughts on where Mia Day could
be. He was hitting the books this evening. He had two jobs. One was
figuring out how we could communicate with someone on the
Heavenly planes that didn't involve mere praying and hoping
someone was listening in.

The other was figuring out where Myrddin would keep that piece
of Liv's soul I needed to get back. Once he had a location, I would put
the queen on that one. She was a hell of a thief, and she would have
fun with it.

"Did he have other classes going on during those two weeks?" I
sat with Evan at one of the picnic tables. There was a park at the back
of the square. It was really more of a circle with hallways that led in

different directions, but it was easy to see this was the heart of the primals' nest and that they'd worked hard to adapt to the needs of those they sheltered.

To my right a small group of kids played on swings and slides, their parents or guardians indulgently watching them. I had to wonder if Fen had ever swung or thrown his body down the slide. Probably not. He'd been trying to survive.

Evan searched her notes. "Yes. During the same time period, he taught two other classes and held therapy sessions for survivors. He made all of those."

"Why would he cancel the painting classes? Did they run out of materials?" I asked.

Evan shrugged. "Not according to the records. I checked. He'd recently received a shipment from above, and he'd had an order filled for the supplies they get from the gnomes. The woman who coordinates told me Alvis was cagey about why he needed to cancel. He told her he didn't feel well enough to teach the first two classes and then he canceled without warning or explanation the second week. I didn't think primals got sick."

"They don't." They were like their other vampire brethren in this case. No virus could take them down. But there were ways to fuck with a vamp. "Have there been other reports of primals not feeling well? We could go by the clinic."

"Already did." Evan handed me a folder. "While you were having...do we call that second breakfast? First lunch?"

Snarky thing. "It was a snack."

"It was two burgers and what had to be a pound of onion rings," Evan countered. "It's cool. I'm used to it. Anyway, while you were snacking I went to the clinic. No primals have been in. Not like ever. Rose said she's never seen one get sick."

"And what does that tell us?" I liked playing the mentor to young detectives. It was fun. Made me feel good.

"Well, it tells us that if someone poisoned Alvis, he was the target since no one else has had a problem. Their food is all sourced from the same place, and if there's not an outbreak of primals exploding, he's the only one who took the poison. I thought about whether they tampered with his blood. That would be hard. They eat live rabbits. Well, live when they start in. Any poison that would kill

Alvis would also kill the rabbit, thereby rendering the rabbit ineligible as dinner."

Her logic was sound. "It could be the poison wasn't ingestible. I'm still intrigued by the idea of witches using belladonna in their rituals. So what we've got is poison, painting, and a dead primal. How do we connect these things? And now we have weird creatures showing up in the Under."

"Like the white rabbit Fen..." Evan shut her mouth.

"I know he ate it."

Evan gave me an apologetic smile. "If it helps, he was in wolf form. Lucky for us the sucker wasn't poisoned. When we asked about it, we were told it was probably from the gnomes. They keep creatures from time to time. We didn't, like, report it to them or anything. The gnomes already have problems with the werecreatures."

"So I've been told. Have you been down to the gardens?" It looked like I might need to meet those gnomes.

"Pretty much any time I come here with Rhys we end up in the gardens. He gets claustrophobic, but the gardens calm him."

"Are we talking about Rhys?" Fenrir slid into the booth beside Evan, leaning over to kiss her cheek. "Because dude's got problems, if you know what I mean."

It was so clear to see the affection between the two. Evan immediately shifted so she was slightly leaning against Fen. "Your mom was asking about the gnomes."

Fen frowned. "They don't let me in the gardens. I think it's rude."

Oh, I knew what had happened. "Well, you ate their rabbit, didn't you?"

Fen's cheeks flushed slightly. "I have predatory instincts. I can't help it."

"And yet you can," I chided.

A deep *V* formed over Fen's eyes. "Dang. I didn't realize how judgmental moms can be."

"What did you think a mom did?" I knew mine, and judgment was a big old part of her job. Oh, it was doled out with a hug, but it was there.

"I thought there would be more cookies," Fen admitted.

Evan snorted. "It wasn't just about the rabbit. The gnomes used to welcome Fen, but last year they brought in this new little guy and he's terrified of Fen. And Trent. He was nearly killed by werewolves, so he can't stand to be around them. It's not really Fen. Also, I looked into the rabbit at the time because it was weird that it got out, and all of the garden rabbits were accounted for. It definitely wasn't one of the primal rabbits."

"Nah," Fen said. "They're solid. Like this one was barely a snack."

I was going to have to teach my kid some manners.

"So where did that rabbit come from?" I was curious.

I went still because something tickled at the back of my mind. Fen talked about his predatory instinct. This was the opposite. I could feel someone watching.

"I've always worried it was someone's pet," Evan explained. "Like some kid snuck a bunny in and Fen ate Snowball."

Fen sighed. "It was a full moon night, and I wasn't allowed out of the Under because there were witches seen in the area. I came right here, to this park, and I ran as much as I could. Mostly I ran in circles and Rhys tossed beef jerky in the air so I could catch it. And then there was a rabbit. I swear it hadn't been there before. I'm good at picking up on a scent, if you know what..."

I did know what he meant, and suddenly his eyes had gone dark.

"Are there new wolves in the Under?" Fen's voice had deepened.

Evan sat up straight. "I didn't ask. I'm sure Rufus would have mentioned it."

Rufus had his hands full. The male was distracted, so he could have forgotten, but it shouldn't have been a problem. Wolves were normally welcoming of other wolves. I turned and realized where that sensation of being watched had come from. A man stood around fifty feet away from us, his eyes locked not on Fenrir but on Evan.

Some wolves could be distinctly mean to those who weren't considered pack.

I wasn't going to let the man sit there and stare at her. I stood, calling out across the yard to him. "Hi, do you have a problem, buddy?"

I'm not a "hope things go away" kind of girl. I'm more of a "bash the problem until it goes away or dies" kind of girl.

The man moved my way. "We all have a problem with that…woman."

Fenrir growled, a sound that had the hair on the back of my neck standing straight up, and I was his mother.

"Do you know what you're costing every single wolf?" The were was a big man, had probably been either the alpha of his pack or one of the betas.

Evan had a hand on Fenrir as though she could hold him back. Her jaw had tightened, and she didn't respond.

Did she have to put up with this shit all the time? "She is not your business."

The were looked me up and down as though considering whether he could take me. I could have told him. He couldn't. "She is every wolf's business since she is the reason the king hasn't taken control. The packs were decimated under his watch."

Fenrir growled again, but I was going to take charge of this. I pointed a finger his way. "You stay in your human form and listen to what I'm about to say because you need to hear this, too." I turned back to the werewolf who really needed to think about the damn timeline. "He doesn't have a watch. He was nine when this war started. Nine. He was a baby, and he was forced to go on the run."

The wolf's brow furrowed, eyes shining in the light. "He should have been turned over to a proper werewolf family."

"My dad is a werewolf. He's a powerful were, and he could take out you and your entire pack." Fen seemed determined to defend his father.

"Trent Wilcox licks the boots of vampires, and he sold you to them. He sold our king to the vampires." That fucker seemed equally determined to get his ass kicked.

"Stay calm, Fen." I stared down the were. "I need you to understand what I'm about to say to you. My name is Kelsey Owens and I am Fenrir's mother. You are talking about my husband, and you need to shut your mouth because you will not be dealing with Fen or Trent. You'll be dealing with me."

Luckily my reputation preceded me.

"You're the *Nex Apparatus*."

"I am."

"You're gone," he said with a frown.

It looked like not everyone kept up with current events. "I'm back and so are her parents. You want to say this shit to the King of all Vampire? Because he can be here very quickly, and he'd love to discuss this with you."

"He doesn't care about the packs. He only ever used us to bring himself into power and then he allowed Myrddin to fuck the world over." My new friend seemed to be fueled with anger.

A woman ran onto the scene, her long, dark hair flowing back. "Billy? What are you doing?" She stood in front of him, looking to Fenrir. "He didn't mean anything. We've just gone through something terrible, and he doesn't mean anything he's said."

"I think he means it." Fenrir stood, his shoulders straightening. He turned quickly, realizing someone was walking up from behind him. "And I bet you mean it, too."

Two other males were making their way toward us, and I had to believe they were wolves as well. One wore a trucker hat, the other a stately looking cowboy hat. He was bigger than either of the others and wore jeans and a button-down shirt, a bolo tie around his neck. There was something in his eyes that let me know of the wolves gathered here, he would be the top dog, the alpha the others would defer to.

"Hello, Fenrir," Cowboy Hat said. "I was hoping we could talk."

"Evan, sweetie, maybe you should go and find Trent for me." I would feel better if she was out of the equation. This suddenly felt like a trap. We were surrounded. Had they been following my son?

Evan stood and suddenly there was a massive knife in her hands. "Oh, I think Trent will figure it out. You should understand—I don't run from a fight."

"Don't bother, Mom," Fen said. "I've tried everything to get her to hide when these bastards come around and she won't. She's absolutely as fierce as any alpha bitch. As Jered should know. Mom, meet the recently installed alpha of the American packs."

Jered's gaze found mine, his eyes narrowing. "Then it's true. The Hunter has returned."

"Yes, I'm back, and you better know that I'm going to protect my son." Beyond hunting demons, I was also pretty good at keeping overly ambitious wolves in check.

He frowned my way. "I didn't come here to harm Fenrir." He

gestured across the table toward the wolf couple. "I came to escort some of my people back to Colorado. It's where we've gathered, those of us who survived Myrddin's assaults. This is Billy Gibson and his wife, Lora. They were trying to stay in their own home, but the witches are good at picking off wolves who don't belong to a pack."

"I belonged to a pack," Billy insisted. "They killed us. They didn't even have to get close. They stood outside our homes and lit us up from within."

I got that he was in pain, but I wasn't about to let him blame Evan. "And I'm sorry for that. The king is even now working with our allies. He will put a stop to it."

Billy pointed Fenrir's way. "My king is sitting right there. He's not helping his people. He's mooning over vampire property."

Evan's middle finger made an appearance.

"Billy, stand down," Jered ordered. The wolf at his side had gone tight, though he didn't say a word. It was obvious Jered had an enforcer. "You and your mate should go and get your things. We're leaving for Colorado shortly after sundown. I hope you've been kinder to our primal hosts."

"I've hated every single second I've been in this extravagant palace. They live like kings while my people are on the run. They surround themselves with magic when magic is exactly what killed my brothers," Billy spat. "Anyone who uses magic should be killed. We should be executing these people not making bargains with them, and it should start with her. She's put our king under a spell. We should kill her and release him."

I was done with Billy.

My hand had shifted, going to the nearly impenetrable demon skin I got when there was a battle to be fought. I got my taloned hand around Billy's neck and squeezed barely enough to let him know I could pop his neck like a grape if I wanted to. "You are going to leave this nest now and you will not come back. If I ever see you around those kids again, I will take your head off so fast you won't realize you're dying. Go to Colorado and stick your head in the sand and pray I don't see you again. Do I make myself clear?"

I felt him swallow under my hand. Apparently he could sense the wolf inside and his own responded to my authority. "Yes. Yes, I'll take my wife and go join the pack. I don't want to be here anyway."

I released him, and he grabbed his wife's hand and disappeared down the nearest hallway.

Evan's eyes were wide as she moved close to Fen. "Remind me not to piss off your mom."

Fen grinned. "Nah, you can make her mad all you like. Those eyes won't ever be for you."

I've been told when I'm really angry my eyes change, become all kinds of predatory. I'm never looking in a mirror at the time. I should try because I think it would be pretty cool.

"Hunter, I'm not here to fight." Even Jered seemed to respond to whatever the hell was in my eyes in that moment. "I promise I haven't lied. I truly am here to pick up the new members of our pack."

"You're the alpha." It didn't make sense for him to come all this way. "You don't run these errands yourself. Unless they mean something to you."

Jered glanced at his guard and nodded. The massive were took a big step back, obviously obeying some silent command. "All members of the packs mean something. They have to because we've suffered such massive losses over the last twelve years. But no, I didn't merely come here to personally pick them up. I heard a rumor you were here. I wanted to talk to you, to see if you can be more reasonable than your son."

"I would say no," Fen said under his breath. He picked up Evan's drink and brought the straw to his mouth.

"Definitely." Evan seemed to relax, sitting back down, and the knife was no longer on display.

Fen took a drink and then coughed. "Baby, that's terrible."

Evan's eyes rolled. "I don't have a wolf metabolism. I have to eat healthy."

They were chill, and that let me know the possibility of violence had ratcheted down. I wanted to tell this Jered person to fuck off, but in this case I had to think about the bigger picture. In this case, I had to consider my place as the *Nex Apparatus*, and that meant opening a dialogue with the head of a group who could be our allies. I'd been told Donovan was planning on meeting with some of the European packs as soon as possible. I could at least tell him what I learned about the American wolves. Beyond they were kind of dicks. "I got a hot minute."

I settled on the bench beside Evan, leaving the other side of the table to the alpha.

He gracefully slid on the bench, though it was almost too small for him. "I appreciate the time, Mrs…Ms. Owens."

Smart man. "That's my name."

One thing I could tell the king was that the alpha was politic and had obviously done a study on me. Most people immediately assumed I took my husband's last name.

"I represent the largest pack in North America," he explained as he took his hat off and placed it on the table. "I'm sure your husband and Sasha Federov have already put a bunch of reports in front of the king, but it's going to be all numbers to him. I need you to hear me. Over the last twelve years Myrddin's army has taken out sixty-two percent of all wolves on the North American continent."

That was a kick in my gut. I hadn't read those reports yet. I'd been more concerned about seeing my family, the loss of those precious years, and there was nothing wrong with that. It was utterly normal for me to need to see my husbands and son. But I had to face the new reality. "I'm so sorry to hear that. Are you well protected now?"

"The majority of the remaining wolves are concentrated in Colorado. I estimate there are still nine hundred wolves in hiding around the country. They worry our compound is ripe for an attack," Jered explained. "But as Billy has seen, there is some safety in numbers. We've survived the last couple of years because we've left Myrddin alone and he's been satisfied with it, but we can only protect wolves who live in our compound. He considers us properly caged."

The last was said on a low growl that let me know even the thought angered the wolf.

"And you believe that the royals' return will change all of that." It was a common theme lately.

"Of course it will. Unless Donovan no longer wants the throne. There's little chance of that, since he's already reached out to the Scottish wolves. Myrddin will hear of that, you know. He has his spies as well. I believe there are spies even here in this nest."

I was sure there were, and one of them had probably killed Alvis. "I'm sure I'll be tasked with finding them. What does this have to do with my son? I assume this is about Fenrir since my husband is a perfectly reasonable man. He would have done anything he could to help you."

"Anything but the one thing that could make a difference."

I had an inkling, but he was going to have to say it. "And that would be?"

Jered's eyes went steely. "He is the wolf king. There is no doubt. Do you know how long our people have waited for a wolf king? So long that the last one is nothing but a myth."

"He's also young. He's not ready to lead."

"He would be if he'd taken his proper place in a pack."

Now I couldn't help but roll my eyes. "Sure, because a regular old pack would have taken in a wolf king. I've already had to save him from wolves who thought he was an abomination."

"Lupus Solum does not speak for the wolf world. They are fringe lunatics," Jered insisted.

They were. Lupus Solum was basically a cult, and Trent had grown up in it. Their entire existence had been centered on bring about the Lupus Rex. They did it in fun ways like forced breeding and oppression. We'd taken out most of one group, but I couldn't imagine they were all gone.

"Are they fringe at this point?" Evan asked. "Because all my intelligence points to them recruiting. There's a compound in Maine that's almost as large as yours, and the word is they're angling to make a deal with Myrddin. The enemy of my enemy is my friend and all that."

"None of which would be happening if Fenrir would take his place at the head of the packs." Jered's hands were on the table, but they fisted now.

Fenrir growled low in his throat and those hands loosened.

I needed to understand if there was a political way out of this. If Fen could take over the great pack, that was absolutely to our advantage. "What would be involved in him taking his crown?"

"Mom," Fen said.

I shook my head. "I want him to say it. I know he's said it to you and to your father, but he knows I represent the royal family and I want him to say it to me so that I can officially inform your godfather, the King of all Vampire."

We hadn't had a ceremony or anything, but I like to think on my feet. I'd done enough service for the Donovan-Quinns that he wouldn't hesitate to take the position.

Jered's jaw tightened. "He cannot have a human mate. He must take a she-wolf. Even the king will understand. He has a companion. The vampires would never have accepted a human wife. I'm willing to negotiate. The king should understand this. He has his proper companion and his lover."

Evan groaned. "And I've told you it wasn't a political thing. My parents love each other. All three of them. My dad and mom did not marry to cover up his relationship with my papa. So tossing some rando she-wolf in for political expediency isn't going to work. And before you plead with me to do the right thing and push Fen aside for the sake of all of wolf kind, you should understand I tried that. He didn't go away."

"She is my mate, and I will accept no crown that doesn't include her. She is not some dirty secret to be kept hidden. She will be at my side always. No matter where I am," Fenrir said quietly.

"Fenrir, would you be willing to accept the crown and your place among the wolves if they conceded that Evan is your true mate?" I wanted to see how far he was willing to go.

"Yes," he said grimly. "I do understand that I'm needed, but I'm unwilling to sacrifice her."

"Then you are not a true king," Jered replied.

"Excellent. Then you don't need to bother me anymore," Fen said with venom. "I am fine with that outcome, too."

"You have to see the position you are putting us all in." Jered's gaze moved between Evan and Fenrir.

"And you don't see the position you're putting me in at all." Fen slid off the bench, holding his hand out to help Evan do the same. "You insist that I'm a king, that I give up my life to serve a bunch of wolves who would never have accepted me when I was a child. You can lie all you like, but I remember my father having to kill wolves who wanted to execute me for being an abomination. I agree to do this service to my species with one request—that I have what all wolves want. My mate."

"She is not..." Jered began.

Fenrir's fist came down on the table, cracking it in two. "Do not tell me my mate is not proper. She is mine. I don't care that you do not understand, that you see her and think my soul can't possibly be mated to hers. You don't walk in my body. You haven't heard my call to her. I will no more give up my mate than you would yours."

"Mine is a wolf."

I stood. "Then the wolf world hasn't changed in the time I've been gone. You are still rigid and unaccepting of any who don't meet your strict criteria. My son is unique in all the world. You call him a king and then you won't negotiate with him. What you want is his strength, his power, and for him to win this war for you, and then I suspect you won't need a wolf king anymore. You tell me that my husband ruined him. I'm going to tell you the truth. My husband saved you. Not him. When Fenrir came into our lives, I was told by the dark prophet that I could raise him in love or cast him out. One way led to peace and strength. The other to utter destruction."

Jered nodded. "Yes, and we're on the path to destruction."

"Oh, no. If I had left Fenrir to be raised by wolves, he would be an entirely different kind of king. Have you pondered why he hasn't killed you? He could take his throne by rite of strength. All he has to do is kill every alpha and the wolf world would fall in line."

"I seriously doubt..." Jered sighed as though giving up the argument. "And then we would lose a generation of strength and leadership."

"And that is what his father taught him." I was glad I could make my point. "Trent taught him how to be a real king. You are the one being stubborn. My son has pointed out what it will take to get him to accept the crown. Give it to him or leave them alone. He'll still be fighting for all of us in the war to come."

"Even if we win, we have problems. We are fractured," Jered said, his deep voice tortured.

"I've found it's easier to bend than break." I felt for the guy, but the wolves had made their bed. It was up to them whether they lay in it or wake the fuck up. I wasn't putting that on my twenty-one-year-old son. I didn't care that his DNA pointed to a particular fate. I was here and I would fight for him. "You're in this position because you cling to old prejudices. If someone like Evan isn't worthy for the simple fact that she isn't a wolf, then go and join Lupus Solum because you're not any better than they are. You believe the same. You just want to pretend you have a place in the modern world. You enjoy its conveniences but not its obligations. You want to keep all the power in the hands of the same wolves who've had it for millennia, and that's where you'll go wrong with Fenrir. My son won't allow a kingdom he rules to stay that way. He'll change things, and in the end you won't like him for it. You want a weapon you can put a crown on. So go away. That's not happening to my son."

"Then maybe we'll tell the King of all Vampire we'll stay out of this war. Or perhaps we should look for new leadership," Jered warned.

"Then be prepared to die or live as demonic pets. You don't have any leverage in this, Alpha. You can fight beside the king or let the demons in."

"I've heard that rumor. It's ridiculous," Jered scoffed.

"Are you willing to bet your existence on it?" It was time to move along. "Stay away from my son and from Evan. If you want to talk, you talk to me or his dad or the king. And let everyone know that if they come after Evangeline again, I will be the one who hunts them down and ends them. Do I make myself clear?"

Jered stood, squaring off with me. "As crystal, Ms. Owens." He nodded to someone behind me. "Evening, Wilcox."

I turned, and sure enough Trent was there, and I wondered how long he'd used those exquisite senses of his to listen in. He didn't move to join me, merely stood there letting me know he had my back. He nodded the alpha's way and put a hand on Fen's shoulder when he got close. Evan and Fen joined Trent, showing everyone they were together. They were a family.

The son in my womb would get that no matter what happened with Gray. He would have Trent to guide him through life, and it wouldn't matter that they didn't share any DNA. "You have the chance to change things. You can let our world remain broken or you can offer to bend. It's your choice."

"That's naïve of you, Owens," Jered said with a frown. "I didn't expect that from you."

"You'll find I can be very surprising from time to time. Do you know who's naïve? Those kids over there. They think they should be able to love each other without reservation, without some old dude who has no idea what their lives are like interfering. You're clinging to the old world. He's the new, and yes, he's naïve enough to think the world should be fair, should be without hate and prejudice."

"It's not prejudice to want our traditions upheld," Jered insisted.

"Then close off your society and don't bother us anymore," I explained. "Those are your options. Good luck with what's to come. I hope you make it."

I turned and walked back to my family and left the wolf behind.

Chapter Thirteen

Hours later I stepped into the apartment that once belonged to the primal known as Alvis. The last time I'd walked in here it had been covered in the remnants of Alvis's murder, but now I could see all the mementos of his long life.

"They did a great job." Trent took a deep whiff of the air around us. "I can't even smell the cleaning products. It must be some kind of spell. All I'm getting is the jasmine."

Alvis had grown night-blooming jasmine in pretty pots around his place. I had briefly noticed them during the initial investigation, but the gloom of murder had dulled how lively his space was. Now it had been cleaned and sorted and made to shine for this gathering.

I glanced around the room. There were thirty or forty beings milling about. Some had wine glasses in their hands, while the primals were all in somber robes. Grim expressions would sometimes turn to bright smiles as a story about the deceased was obviously shared.

This was a wake for a male who had walked the Earth plane for thousands of years. Who'd been born a human and devolved into what many would call a monster, and yet he'd been part of a gentle, intelligent society. One of the walls of his inner office was covered in pictures of people who had to be his friends and students. Some were black and white and obviously taken at the dawn of photography, and some were Polaroids. Some were printed copies of cell phone pics.

He'd witnessed the plane go from feudalism to modern times, watching from the shadows.

Now he was the one who would have to be remembered, and I had to ask myself if one of these people hadn't killed him.

"How do you really feel about the new alpha?" I brought the lemonade I'd been offered in lieu of wine to my lips as I studied the wall of pictures. We hadn't talked much about my meeting with Jered Armstrong beyond Trent asking me if I was okay.

I wasn't. I didn't like thinking about what Fen and Evan had been forced to go through. Being confronted with their ongoing struggle had placed their situation in the back of my mind all day.

"I have notes on him. A whole file," Trent said blandly.

I turned his way, keeping my voice low. Soft music was playing through the rooms, provided by a well-dressed small troll playing a baby grand piano. "I don't want notes. I want to know how you feel."

Trent seemed to think about how to reply. "I feel like he would likely be an excellent leader in another time. He's good at staying calm and he knows how to compromise."

I stared at him, willing him to see the problem with that statement.

He sighed. "You know how rigid the wolf world can be. He's in a vulnerable position. He has to balance the needs of the ever-shrinking pack with the traditions so many of them follow. I want you to understand that if I thought for a second he was the one behind the attempts on Evan's life, I would kill him myself. Those came from rogue packs. There are a few of them. They're more extreme than Armstrong's, but they don't agree with Lupus Solum. The rogue packs want Fen at the head of the wolf world, but they want their own daughters at his side."

"And Lupus Solum wants him dead because he had a primal father." That summed up the situation neatly.

"I think Fen prefers the death threats to what the rogue groups want from him," Trent said with a chuckle. "You know they tried to offer him three mates, a daughter from the three most powerful families. That's not saying much though. There's not a lot of power among the wolves these days."

"Three wives? How old was he when they suggested that

scenario?"

"He was fifteen and horrified," Trent explained. "I'm afraid he's far more used to the idea of having another man involved in a marriage than multiple women. Not that he would have considered any offer. When we turned them down, that was when the assassination attempts started. The truth of the matter is I don't think they would stop even if Fen agreed to take a she-wolf mate. As long as Evan is in his life, they will come after her."

"Have you thought about how to change that?" We moved down the hall, and here the photographs changed to paintings. I stopped in front of the first one. It was a beautiful seascape with brilliant light seeming to illuminate the canvas from within.

"Of course." His hands skimmed over my shoulders as he stood behind me. "I've kept up with the heads of the rogue packs. I've thought seriously about assassinating them to send a message, but it's been fairly quiet lately. I suspect now that Evan's fathers have returned they'll think twice."

"Or they'll get desperate." I had to wonder what Donovan would be walking into. I moved to the next painting. This one was a portrait. It showed a lovely young woman in old-time clothing. I wasn't a student of history, but she looked like she could have walked out of a Jane Austen novel, so I was betting that was the time she was from.

"We're all desperate these days," Trent whispered. "Now that you're back, they will try something. They will go on the offensive because if they don't the king will shut them down. They have to come after us. We have to be ready."

I wasn't sure we could be totally ready for them. I'd read the intelligence. I'd spent much of the afternoon in the library reading through everything the primals had on Myrddin and what he was capable of. Throwing in a couple of rogue wolf packs who wanted to kill the princess was one more problem I didn't know if we could handle.

How many wakes would I have to go to? How many friends would I lose?

"She was a companion," a deep voice said. "Her name was Marie."

I turned and there were two primals and the woman who'd seen to my wounds yesterday. Rufus was taller than the new guy, but

Christopher Miller was built on slightly bulkier lines. I recognized the primal as the male who nearly killed us all in Wyoming months... Yep, that was years ago. This whole time thing was hard on me.

Rose stood with Christopher, her hand tucked away in his. "Alvis said she loved to sing. She's why he always has a piano. Had a piano."

I'd been meaning to sit down and talk with Christopher and Rose but hadn't found the time yet. Rose worked in the clinic all afternoon, and Christopher's time had been spent contemplating Alvis's death as part of the primal funeral rituals. I glanced back at the portrait they were looking at. Again there was a glow that seemed to come from the painting. "She was beautiful. Was she Alvis's companion?"

"Not in a technical sense, of course," Rufus said. "But she did abide with him for the majority of her life. She was a bit like our Rose."

"How so? If it's not rude to ask." I hadn't questioned her while she'd been working, but I was curious about how she'd come to live with the primals.

Rose started to reply when a little whirlwind rushed into our space. Luna was cute as a button in her jeans and a pink T-shirt, her mass of hair barely held back with a sparkly tie. "Mama, they have grapes. Can I have some grapes? Luthor is hungry, too."

Rose smiled down at her adopted daughter. "Of course. You'll have to ask Luthor's father though."

"Hector will not mind," Christopher assured them. He put a hand on Luna's head, a gesture of obvious affection. "Go back and play, sweetheart. I saw some butter cookies on the buffet, too. You can have one and so may Luthor."

She grinned and ran back out.

"Luthor is another orphan. He's a year younger than Luna," Rose explained. "He was taken in by another member of our community. The non-vampires watch him when his adoptive father cannot. It helps Luna to have another werebat around. It can be hard to be the only one. I should know. I was the only human for years."

"You lived in Council headquarters, love," Rufus corrected. "There were always companions in Paris, from what I understand. Most of the Council members kept a companion."

Christopher snorted, an oddly human sound. It was the sound that let another person know they'd stepped in something.

Sure enough Rose's expression turned distinctly salty. "I assure you those companions weren't really human. They were walking visions of pure snobbery who were only looking to climb that particular social ladder."

Oh, I liked a girl who didn't mind telling it like it was. "So you were the companion to a Council member?"

"She was married to the head of the Council before the king took over," Rufus explained, his voice going grim.

I felt my eyes widen because according to Marcus that had been one bad dude, but there was a problem with that. "I thought the queen was forced to marry him."

"Yes, I was the castoff companion." Rose took a long breath, obviously steadying herself. "When Zoey was kidnapped, I was to be sold, but she told me to run if I had the chance. I did."

Trent's head shook. "You didn't run. You escaped and made your way to the king and offered your blood to keep him strong. Don't ever say you ran. You are not a coward, Rose. Never."

Rose had been around during the first war. Well, the first in my lifetime. She'd been around for the war that brought Daniel Donovan to the throne. "I'm sorry to hear that. What were you doing before Myrddin took over? Were you still a part of the supernatural world?"

She shook her head. "No. I took advantage of the protected person status the king's Council offered. I returned to my home in London and I lived with my mother and the man who protected me like a father when I was in the Council stronghold. His name was Robert, and he was from a slave family. The humans who work for vampires were often from families whose service went back generations. Daniel freed them, and Robert chose to come with me. The day he married my mum was the happiest of my life. Taking care of them both was something I was happy to do. Robert went first. He had a heart attack. My mum had cancer. I can't tell you how much I wanted to ask a vampire to save her. We'd lost so much time, but I'd promised I wouldn't be a part of that world again, wouldn't invite it in. She wouldn't hear of it. I meant to live as a human for the rest of my life. And then Myrddin upended the world. I was contacted by the primals and offered sanctuary here. I was so scared when I walked into the nest for the first time."

"And that was the moment my life began again." Christopher leaned over and brushed his thin lips over her hair. He seemed to breathe her in for a moment, and I wouldn't have to make sure he'd forced her to marry him. They fit together somehow. All the tension in Rose had dissolved the minute he'd hugged her. "I will be forever grateful to the dark prophet for giving us his warning."

"I assure you my partner was happy to help," Trent replied. "We appreciate you allowing Gray to come and go as he must."

"Were you aware Gray's…" I wasn't sure what to call him. He wasn't our butler no matter what he said. "Were you aware the emissary from the Hell plane can get through the wards?"

"They knew," Trent said. "Before I came here the first time I let them know that there are no wards on the Earth plane that can keep Tix away from Gray. But it's only Tix, and he cannot bring anyone else nor can he bring any kind of weapon."

Tix was a demon. He *was* a weapon.

I hated that he was bonded to Gray, that he could find Gray no matter where he went. There was no hiding from a bonded servant.

"We allow the dark prophet to come and go as he pleases," Rose explained. "He and the heavenly prophet have been helpful to the primals from time to time. It was their warning that allowed the primals to be ready for refugees when Myrddin first took over. They had a network set up to bring in any companion or friendly witch who wanted protection."

"How exactly did Gray help?" As far as I knew, all Gray could do was say his prophecy and move on. And then let Lucifer use his soul as a focal point.

I was still bitter.

Rufus took that one. "He gave his prophecy and the primal council considered it. We have protocols concerning prophecy. We are given the prophecy and take time to reflect upon it. We study and then come together to reach a consensus on how to proceed given the knowledge they've been gifted. When a prophet shows up in the Under, we all take it seriously. In this case, we didn't understand that Myrddin would take over, only that a tragedy would occur and we should be ready to aid the unfortunate."

"Like me and Luna and Luthor." Rose's smile softened to something bittersweet.

"We were the lucky ones," Christopher insisted.

"Yes." Rufus agreed with his friend. "Having a vibrant community filled with beings like Rose and Luna is a blessing to us. We have always opened our home to those who needed help, and we were blessed with their unique friendships. Like Marie. She had a similar story to Rose, though her vampire was not a Council member. Still, she sought refuge here and found a kindred soul in Alvis. They abided together many years. It was Marie who taught Alvis to paint. I believe when he practiced his art, he felt her presence and was warmed."

"Do you have any idea why he canceled his classes the last two weeks?" I had to ask since Alvis had given the people I'd spoken to no real reason.

Though Rufus had no eyebrows, the skin above his eyes cocked up, giving him a quizzical expression. "I was unaware he'd canceled. Teaching was everything to Alvis. He filled his nights with classes and sessions."

"He didn't cancel them all," Trent explained. "Only the painting classes."

"Curious." Rufus frowned. "Were you able to find his notes? He would have kept meticulous notes concerning his classes and therapy sessions."

Any kind of planner or journal was important to my case. I'd done a thorough search of the apartment on the night of the murder. I'd only found Alvis's laptop. "My brothers went through Alvis's computer, but they didn't find anything like a personal journal. He kept his mentoring notes and class notes, but nothing that would tell me why he canceled."

"I will make some inquiries," Rufus said with a grim resolve.

A gentle chiming went through the domicile, and every primal's head turned as though they were a flock called in from the fields.

Christopher nodded and held his wife's hands in his. "It's time. I will see you before morning. Tell our Luna I love her and to stay out of trouble."

Apparently the chiming called the primals to their funeral rituals. Those rituals were kind of killing my investigation. Luckily there was only one more day of them and then the primals would be available during their waking hours. Unlike most vampires, primal sleep was not tied to sunrise and sunset. Primals required more sleep than their warrior or academic counterparts. Combine that with hours of silent contemplation, and I hadn't been able to get much done.

"I will seek you out tomorrow, Hunter," Rufus offered. "You shall have my full attention after this evening. Until then, feel free to poke around as much as needed. Alvis's apartment will remain open until morning. There is food and drink, and I hope everyone here will be willing to speak with you."

I gave him a nod, and he and Christopher joined the other primals in taking their leave. "Where will they go? Do you have any idea what's involved in this session?"

I had asked Evan earlier, but she hadn't known. She knew the most about primals from what I could tell, but even she was in the dark about their mourning rituals. Likely because there hadn't been a primal death in decades. Many of the non-primals in this nest had never experienced one.

Rose began to walk back to the large living area. "I can only tell you what I've read or how Christopher explains it. These rituals are only for primals. From what I understand, the primals will take no sustenance for the next forty-eight hours and they will gather together at rise and rest to contemplate their fallen member and discuss a path forward without Alvis's gifts. It's their version of a wake." She gestured around the nicely decorated space. "This is for the non-primals, a way to make them feel welcome."

"Hospitality is important to the primals." Trent reached for a beer.

Across the room I saw Fen devouring a sandwich while watching over Evan, who seemed to be happily chatting with a couple of gnomes. They didn't seem particularly worried to be near my werewolf son. "Has Fen had trouble down here?"

"Fenrir?" Rose selected a glass of wine. "Not at all. Did he have trouble with the werewolves today? I know there was a family using the Under as a shelter until they could get to Colorado. They were told to stay away from the princess."

I could see Rose was getting upset. "It was all words. No one tried anything."

"Words can hurt," Rose said with a frown.

"He mentioned he's not allowed in the gardens anymore," I

began as I watched Trent amble over to Fenrir.

"Yes, but I've talked to him about that. It's not personal," Rose said quietly. "There's a gnome who is still affected by an attack that occurred before he came to the Under. As you can see, Shamus and Murtagh get along quite well with him. It is only Elrin who needs distance, and I've been told his therapy is coming along. Although he'll need to be assigned a new partner."

"Alvis treated the gnome?" I had seen the name *Elrin* on his schedule, but I hadn't read through the notes since they were private. I could if I needed to, but so far I'd tried to respect the patient confidentiality of a therapist. I might not have that luxury.

"Yes, they had therapy sessions twice a week. I don't know exactly what was happening, but I knew Alvis was pleased with the progress. Being around other gnomes and staying in the gardens seemed to help Elrin immensely," Rose explained.

"So he was attacked by wolves?"

Rose nodded. "He was brought here by some trolls who found him."

"Why here? Why not take him to one of the *sitheins* connected to the Earth plane? There's a door fairly close. From what I understand, all Fae creatures heal better in a *sithein*."

"He wanted to come here. I don't know exactly why Elrin didn't leave the Earth plane when the veil closed, but he preferred to stay here. We accept all creatures who come to us with need. I helped heal him in those first days. It was terrible. His wounds, that is. I feared he wouldn't survive. The attack was vicious, and he's not over it mentally. It's why he fears Fenrir and the wolves who come and go. I hope Fen doesn't take it poorly. It's truly not about him."

I glanced over to where my young wolf king was scratching behind his ear and grinning like the weirdo, barely twenty-something, supernatural kid he was. "I think Fen's fine."

He wasn't. No one could go through what he'd been through and be fine, but he was doing all right. I could let go of that piece of guilt. My son was whole and healthy and had good guidance.

"Do you think he'll be afraid of me?" I was going to have to talk to the gnomes eventually, and Elrin in particular since he had close contact with the deceased.

She seemed to consider the question for a moment. "I'm not sure.

You don't have a particularly wolfish look, and I believe it was male wolves who harmed Elrin. He might worry about you being the *Nex Apparatus*, but I'll have the primals talk to him. Would you like me to set up an interview with him tomorrow?"

"That would be good." I would prefer to simply show up and not give anyone time to think about what they would say to me, but I had to honor what the primals would want. "If I could talk to him tomorrow afternoon, I would appreciate it. I take it he's like other gnomes and he's awake during the daylight hours."

"Yes, even here in the Under, they follow their own internal clocks. Rather like my daughter," Rose said with a nod. "I'm going to check on her. Please let me know if there's anything else I can help you with. You should know that Christopher believes you saved him and Fenrir. He believes you're the only reason he still has a connection to Fenrir, and while his heart aches sometimes, he's so happy Fen had you."

Wow. There was the guilt I'd tried to shove away. "He didn't have me."

"But he did." Rose smiled, and when she did she glowed a bit like one of Alvis's paintings. "I know this, Kelsey. I was a child when the vampires took me. I spent years without my mum, but she was there. You imprinted on him at an important time. When the rest of the world was hunting him, you reached out a hand and gave him a family. Do not doubt Fenrir's love for you or his deep belief that you will accept him as he is."

"How did you manage to get over it? I ask because I met another companion, one who let what happened destroy her." She'd been the reason we'd almost died in Wyoming. When I think about it, she was the reason Liv and I were on opposite sides of this war. Meredith had been through the same thing Rose and the queen had gone through, but she'd reacted so differently. Rose had gotten out. She'd built her life, and it had been wrecked again by supernatural forces. "How did you manage to fall in love with another vampire?"

"Oh, I never loved the first at all," Rose replied. "Well, that might be a lie. At first, Louis was somewhat kind to me. I suppose I saw a beautiful face and tried to adapt. It's what we do as humans. We adapt to our surroundings. I was so young then. My view of life, my personality, my sexuality were all molded by that abuse, but I had the grounding of my mum's love, and I know that's what saved me. Being able to be with her again…well, it gave me the fuel to survive this time. I don't think I would have given Christopher a chance if he'd been beautiful like Louis. I know they look frightening, but I understand more than many that beauty can hide evil, and what seems like a ruined body can house the sweetest of souls. You never truly get over the kind of crime that was done to me, but at some point you must decide if you're going to live or not. I thought about the not option. I thought about joining my mum and Robert, wherever they went. But something whispered to me. Something pushed me to come here, to see if I could help. I thought a lot about the fact that Zoey could have ignored me. She was in a bad place, and she chose to be kind. I had ignored the supernatural world for over a decade, and it was getting bad again. Women and girls like me would be hurt. I had knowledge and experience. I had a degree in nursing. I could make it easy on myself or I could perhaps make it easier on someone like me, someone who desperately needed me. So I chose to live, and I was rewarded with the family I never thought I would have. I opened my heart because I wanted more than to merely survive. I might get that chance now that you're back. I don't have incredible powers, but I will fight this time. I will stand and hold the line. I will die if I have to because oddly enough, I've figured out that this life is worth it."

"I'm going to do my best to make sure your Luna has a safe place to grow up," I vowed.

"I believe you." Rose stepped away. "And tell Zoey that I'm back and want to be involved when the time comes. I can work with the academics to ensure we have adequate medical care in all our bases."

She walked toward the hallway, and I was left alone listening to the hum of conversation around me.

"He would have liked this. Alvis always loved a party," someone was saying.

I let the conversation flow around me, but I didn't hear anything interesting. I found myself wandering toward the back of the apartment. I'd been in Alvis's studio the night of his murder, but I'd only done a cursory search. I slipped inside, feeling like an intruder.

His private studio was bigger than any room in this place, with the exception of his great room. There was a magical window that no one had shut down. In the next few days I was sure one of the witches would come through and snuff out the magics, or perhaps they would simply repurpose the space. For now it felt like a peek into the male's soul. Soft light infused the room like some spell had managed to capture the perfect morning illumination. Out the window I could see a pastoral scene that gave me the impression of a warm spring day, and for some reason it felt like another time. Perhaps the 1800s. This might be a memory from an old lover's mind, something that connected them and made him feel like a piece of her was still here with him.

I was getting thoughtful in my old age, or maybe it was pregnancy, but I felt for Alvis as I stood there in his studio. I hoped that there was some heavenly plane where souls were reunited. The idea of eternal peace didn't make sense to me, but if it did to Alvis and his Marie, then I wished it for them.

There were no notebooks or journals here. Only paints and brushes and canvases. He had one on an easel, the painting half covered with a cloth. A familiar darkness peeked out from beneath, the cloth slung in a haphazard fashion, which was odd to me. Everything else in the room was perfect, as though Alvis was almost pathologically neat. But the canvas cloth was only halfway on.

I pushed the cloth aside, and I was right about the familiarity. The whole canvas was dark as night, painted with the same almost glowing-from-the-inside paint Relda had been using. He'd used the dark paint as the background and had started working in stars at the top of the canvas.

"I don't like that one."

I turned, surprised someone could sneak up on me, but then Luna was pretty small.

And sometimes small creatures knew big things.

"What don't you like about it, sweetie?"

She had a banana in her hand and cocked her head slightly. "It hums most of the time. Sometimes I think it screams so loud I can hear it in my mama's clinic."

Oh, I was interested in that bit of information. I didn't question what she was saying, didn't shove it to the side or write it off as childish imagination. Nope. Luna was a werecreature—a bat. I wouldn't question her ears any more than a wolf's nose. "Is it humming right now?"

She shook her head. "No. It's like someone turned it off." She walked further in the room and stared at it for a moment. "But sometimes when I walk by, I can hear it humming."

"And sometimes it screams?"

She nodded solemnly.

"Do you remember the last time you heard it scream?"

Another nod.

"Was it the day Alvis died?"

One more nod.

I gently placed the cloth back on the canvas, making sure it was completely covered this time.

I had one more piece of the puzzle, and I knew who I needed to talk to next.

Chapter Fourteen

"What is it supposed to mean? The painting screams?" Fenrir hurried to keep up with me. He still had a sandwich in his hand. When I'd explained I was going to speak with Relda again, Fen had given me a nod like he would happily see me later.

"It means Luna hears something the rest of us can't." Evan had not been as easily left behind. She'd immediately stood and said good-bye to her friends. Including Fen, who had looked longingly at the buffet and finally begrudgingly grabbed some sandwiches as he hustled to follow Evan.

"She can hear the painting?" Trent hadn't wanted to leave either, but both wolves seemed to understand when it was time to follow the women in their lives. He'd stuffed a couple of shrimp down his throat as we'd walked out. "I can't hear anything. I've got excellent hearing. How about you, Fen?"

"I don't hear anything at all. Not that I would say sounds particularly like a painting," Fen managed around a mouthful of tea sandwich. They were tiny, so Fen had eaten a lot of them. "But I wouldn't know what a painting sounds like. I skipped art class. Have we considered that Luna is like what? Four?"

"She's five. She turned five a couple of weeks ago," Evan

pointed out as we started down the stairs that would lead us to the residential levels for non-primals.

I had instructed Casey to secure the painting and to have Luna point out any others that bothered her. "I don't care about her age. I care about her hearing."

"How is her hearing better than mine?" Fen asked, a bit of arrogance in his tone.

I stopped on the stairs and turned his way. "Are you serious?"

Trent winced. "He skipped biology class, too. Pretty much all of the classes. And werebats are rare. Until he came down here, he'd never seen one. He knows more about fighting than anything else."

"But I'm really good at that," Fen insisted.

"Echolocation," Evan said with a sigh. "I didn't have classes either, but I did read. Luna can hear frequencies up to 200 kHz. A normal wolf can hear 80. You can hear maybe 100 since you're the wolf king. She can literally hear twice what you can, and you're considered one of the most powerful creatures in the supernatural world."

"Huh. That's pretty cool." Fen polished off his last sandwich. "We should use her when we want to listen in on Rhys and Lee plotting pranks."

"Or we could use her to try to figure out what the hell is happening with that painting." I started back down the stairs. "It seems to me it all comes down to that class. From what I was told, Alvis was working on the night sky painting for the class he'd been teaching."

"And that tells us what?" Fen asked.

I shrugged. "I don't know, but I think I should find out."

"Okay, but isn't this that…what did Sasha call it?" Fen jogged down in front of me to get to the door first. "Sasha taught us a lot about investigating things, and one of the most important things we learned is that just because something seems to connect, doesn't mean it's connected."

"But we can't know it's not connected if we don't investigate," Evan argued.

"But we're investigating something on the word of an imaginative kiddo." Fen opened the door, allowing us to pass through. "The last time I was here Luna told me she talks to owls. She talked about being the only bat allowed in the Secret Owl Society."

Evan shook her head. "She has a bunch of stuffed owls."

"See, she talks to stuffed animals and has whole conversations with them. Maybe it's the same with paintings," Fen argued.

Trent patted our son on the shoulder as he walked by. "Your mom knows what she's doing, and one of the things Sasha taught you was to follow your gut. Your mom's gut is pretty smart."

I stopped just inside the hallway and turned to Fen. "I've learned when a supernatural creature with crazy good senses tells you something is wrong, it's usually wrong. And even if I don't see the connection right away, it's usually there and waiting to bite me in the ass. So I give in to instinct and see where it takes me. Relda's paintings look a lot like the one in Alvis's studio. She was taking Alvis's class. I need to know way more about what was happening in that class. I've talked to three of the students, and none of them were working at the same level as Relda. She's my connection. I want to talk to her and take one of those paintings she's been working on back to our apartment so I can compare them. Casey is moving Alvis's even as we speak. I'm going to study it and break down the paint that was used."

"And we can bring Luna in to see if Relda's paintings scream at her, too," Evan added.

The princess had a whole lot of detective vibes going on. I approved. "That is my plan. Rose is going to bring her by before they go to bed. Now I have to hope that Relda is going to cooperate."

"Well, if she doesn't we'll simply take what you need and handle the situation," a deep voice said.

I practically jumped out of my skin because no one had let me know someone was approaching. I'm not easy to sneak up on, and then my jaw dropped when I realized who was standing behind me.

Tix stood there looking dapper and all too human in his three-piece suit, dark hair slicked back. He wore what looked like a pair of expensive loafers, but they'd made no sound at all on the hardwood floors.

Trent stepped beside me, his hand coming around my waist to touch my hip as though he needed to keep a hand on me to hold me back. Or to protect me. But probably the first. "Tix, is Gray back, then?"

Tix moved closer, his hands going into his pockets. "Not at all. He's in session, but you should understand that things are going well. However, I cannot interrupt Master Gray and the Dark Lord, and I need guidance. There is a problem in the household, and I'm not sure how to handle it."

"Sorry about that. You can talk to Eddie, I suppose." I wasn't sure what it had to do with me, and if Trent regularly helped demons with their cleaning problems, I would be heartily surprised. I started to turn to get back to my investigation.

"Oh, my mistress, Eddie has never worked in a demonic household. I'm sure he's excellent at solving the variety of domestic issues that arise between the gentle Fae creatures he employs, but I must deal with demons. Their issues tend to be a bit more…serious." Tix hurried to keep up with me.

Fenrir growled and I stopped. I turned back to Fen. "I can handle one demon."

Tix frowned, putting an open hand to his chest. "Handle? Me? Why on all the planes would you need to handle me?"

"Because you are a demon. You demon. Me Hunter." I wasn't going to play around with Tix.

"Mistress, you do know I am bound by blood oath to never harm you, right?" Tix asked. "And I am bound by my oath to do your will."

I looked to Trent. "He has to do what we say?"

Trent's head shook. "You, baby. Not me. On the Hell plane I am merely a treat for his master to enjoy."

"And a delicious treat you are, Trent," Tix crooned. "I completely understand why the master keeps you close to his side, and you should know that if you choose to come visit our manse, I will ensure your every comfort as I would with all of Master Grayson's lovers."

Fen made a gagging sound. "I do not need to hear that."

"I'm going with him on this one," Evan admitted. "That word is super weird when it comes to parental units. So you have to obey Gray and Kelsey but not Trent. That feels rude and very old fashioned of you. I suppose you're one of those 'marriage is between one man and one woman' kind of guys."

"Not at all. I think a man should be able to marry as many beautiful creatures as he can safely force to submit, though I would advise against more than, say, two or three. Once a demonic head of household married four female demons and they were all succubae. In his defense he did have three penises. I think he thought that would save him. He was a husk within a week. Luckily our Trent is a werewolf and shan't have his sexual desires sucking the life out of the master. I assume that the mistress is also free of any sexual superpowers. I mean above her obvious charms, which are many."

"Then why don't you have to obey my dad?" Fenrir asked, his brow in a deep furrow. "Or me, for that matter. I'm Gray's son."

"And you are welcome, and I shall do everything I can to ensure your happiness, Fenrir," Tix vowed. "I am more than pleased to view you as a part of the family."

"But you don't have to obey me." Fen seemed to have picked up on the important part.

"I am not bound to obey you, no," Tix replied. "But I am also certain you would never ask anything of me that I could not in good conscience do. I don't actually have much of a conscience, so that won't be a problem. Do you need assistance, Fenrir? I heard the alpha of the North American packs was here. I could kill him for you."

"He's not looking for an assassin," Evan insisted.

"I think my son can handle his own problems." Trent was studying Tix. "But I find some of your wording interesting. I assume you don't have to obey me because Hell doesn't recognize my marriage."

"I'm afraid Hell is a bit traditional when it comes to its heads of state. In the House of Sloane, only his lordship and ladyship are recognized, and therefore the servants are only oathed to those with the blood of the line," Tix explained. "So now that we have that out of the way, mistress, it appears that our finest chef has been having an affair with a chaos demon, and it is affecting our home. His very presence within our walls has caused whole rooms of the manse to go missing. At least I hope they're only missing. There were twenty servants in that wing. What should I do? I would execute the chef, but he makes the most delicious barhovka. It's the traditional stew of our lands. Can't get it anywhere else. So delicious. So you can see it might be worth a bit of chaos to keep it."

He spoke quickly, and none of that was my problem. "Good. Then keep him."

"But what if the chaos demon causes me to lose Lord Sloane?" Tix asked.

"You're not going to lose the dark prophet," I returned. "He can't be lost. Apparently now he thinks where he wants to go and there he is. No wards can hold him. That's precisely why your ass can get in here."

"But Kelsey, he can't lose whole wings of the house. That would cost the family." Evan seemed to actually consider the problem. "Are they in love? Or is it a sex thing?"

"Can a chaos demon truly be in love with anything but chaos?" Tix asked.

Evan nodded as though she'd thought that would be the case. "Then you need to break them up. Start a rumor about the chaos demon. Ooo, or you could seduce the chaos demon and make sure the chef catches you."

Tix gasped. "Princess. Oh, you are a clever one, and a little mean. I like it. Though I certainly won't do the deed myself." He shuddered. "This particular demon is covered in a pus I can't stand. It's yellow and I prefer green. I can, however, force one of my underlings to do the deed. The chef is prone to jealousy. You've given me much to think about, Princess."

"Uh, wouldn't the chef quit? I wouldn't work for someone who slept with my girlfriend," Fen argued.

Evan shook her head. "Household staff on the Hell plane are enslaved to the houses. He can't go anywhere."

Tix bowed his head. "The princess's knowledge lightens my heart. So few on the Earth plane truly know our customs. You have been properly educated."

And I hadn't. Something tickled at the back of my head, but I really wanted to ignore it. I had problems of my own, and I didn't need to deal with the Hell plane and temperamental chefs with problematic lovers. "Excellent. Go forth and break up the happy couple."

"Tell Gray to come back to us if you see him. Tell him he's welcome here," Trent said. "Always."

Tix's expression turned distinctly…disappointed. I don't know that was the right word. He looked almost lonely. "And you are welcome in House Sloane, Trent. You were always welcome."

He stood there like he wanted to come with us.

Which he probably did. He probably had some awful plan, and those big old anime sad eyes of his didn't move me a single bit. He wasn't Eddie. He didn't have a sad-sack story that would touch my heart. He ran one of the thirteen houses of Hell. He wasn't an outcast.

"Thanks." Trent seemed the slightest bit awkward. "Well, we should continue on our way."

"I could help you," Tix offered. "It sounds like you're worried this Relda person won't cooperate. I'm excellent at gaining cooperation from those who would rather not."

Somehow I thought the primals would disapprove of me setting a demon on Relda. A demon who shouldn't be here.

Yes. There it was. That thing I hadn't wanted to acknowledge. "How are you here?"

Trent sighed as though things hadn't gone the way he'd wanted.

I turned to him. "What do I not know?"

"Likely any number of things," Tix began. "But I am a repository of knowledge. Ask me anything. I am bound to answer."

It looked like he would be the better bet. I got the feeling Trent was covering something, likely something that would make his partner look bad.

"Kelsey, maybe we should talk about this in private. We can go back to our apartment and let the kids grab Relda's paintings." Trent started to reach for my hand.

That wasn't happening. "Tix, I was under the assumption that you could follow Gray wherever he goes."

A brilliant smile lit Tix's face. A weirdly menacing smile. "Yes. You have properly deduced that fact, mistress."

"Gray's not here, Tix."

That smile widened, like he was proud of a particularly smart toddler. "No, he is not. Again, you are correct."

"So the wards should have kept you out."

"Well, they would have if you weren't here," he replied.

Yep. That's what I'd been afraid of. "You made no blood oath to me, demon. I wasn't married on the Hell plane. What did Gray do?"

"He didn't do anything, baby," Trent said quickly, as though trying to head this thing off at the pass.

"You don't have to have been married on the Hell plane. The

truth is the Hell plane doesn't actually have marriage ceremonies you would recognize. Mostly it's the higher demon deciding to take what he or she wants," Tix explained. "And then everyone either falls in line or they get their souls consumed by the most powerful among them."

"It's like the bloodiest oligarchy ever," Evan added. "And it's mostly men. Don't let them tell you otherwise. Sure there are a couple of powerful demonesses, but they are still a strong patriarchy."

"That's right, babe. Don't let them spread that propaganda." Fen winked her way.

"Change is slow on the Hell plane," Tix acknowledged. "But you should understand that I consider myself a feminist. I think females can eviscerate as well as any male, and they should have the same opportunities to torture souls as their masculine counterparts. Girls get it done, I say."

I did not need an update on how progressive Hell could be. "You have no way to follow me, Tix. I'm not a tourist when it comes to this. There's no mystical connection between me and Gray that you can pick up on. So you would have to have secured some of my DNA. I would like to know who gave it to you."

"Oh, I can't follow your DNA at all, mistress. And you are correct that I never took a blood oath to you, but I did to the Sloane line. I can follow all who are of the blood, and I am bound to obey. As to a connection between you and Lord Sloane, of course there is. I can feel him even now."

My son. Fuck. He was talking about the fact that I was pregnant, and he could follow my son, who was of the Sloane bloodline. The horror of it dawned on me. He hadn't needed me to agree. He'd secured Gray's permission when Gray had taken over the House Sloane, and now my son was connected to it for all of time.

"Mom, are you okay?" Fenrir was suddenly at my side.

"You went pale." Trent was there, too.

I turned to him. "Did you know?"

Trent was the one who paled now. "I suspected, but I wasn't sure."

"He'll always be able to find my son." I put a hand on my belly.

"Of course." Tix had a confused expression on his face, as though he wasn't seeing the problem. "How else would I be able to serve the youngling? I'm already preparing a nursery and training our staff. Do you know how long it's been since we have had a child to raise? Everyone is thrilled. It's precisely why I have to get rid of that chaos demon. They shouldn't be around fragile halflings. Not that our boy will truly be fragile."

"Not yours." I backed away. "Never yours. This child is mine and Trent's, and he won't be Gray's if I find out he understood what he was doing."

He'd promised me. He'd promised that Hell wouldn't be able to touch our child, that our son would be protected.

It was the only reason I'd been willing to have a child with him at all. No amount of sweet visions of children would have tempted me if I'd known they could be dragged to Hell at any moment.

"I cannot harm the child." Tix was back to looking vulnerable. "I serve the child as I serve you and your husband. I don't understand. You have a demonic butler on this plane. Why wouldn't you have one in your true home?"

"I will never allow my son to descend," I vowed. "And you let your master know that. Now, is it true that you must obey me because I'm carrying your master's child?"

Tix blinked, studying me. "Yes, mistress. You have to understand that demonic pregnancies slightly change the DNA of the mother to allow her to carry the child. That change is permanent. All of my instincts and senses view you as a member of the House of Sloane. Not by marriage but by right of blood."

No one had mentioned that to me either, though I did know that sometimes pregnancy could make minute but permanent changes to maternal DNA.

Betrayal washed over me. I was pregnant, and now all of Hell would view me as property. I'd known that would happen, but I hadn't known I was accepting a demonic tracker so they could always bring me back to their master.

I was in shock, and there wasn't a lot I could do about it. I would have to talk to Hugo. Hugo could help solve this. He could find a legal way out of this, but Hugo was back in Iceland and I was stuck here.

Actually, there was something I could do. "Leave."

That hand came back to Tix's chest. "Me? You wish me to leave?

But I only just got here. I was hoping you would go over the nursery plans with me."

It was too much. "Get out. Get out now. If what you say is true, you must obey…"

I was left with the smell of brimstone and no demon in the hallway.

"Kelsey…" Trent began.

"Did he know?"

"Mom, I don't think it's all about the baby." Fenrir stared down at me. "Tix is a tricky fellow, and as nice as he can seem, you have to remember they all like to sow discord. Not Eddie, of course, but that's part of his nature. Satans seek organization and a version of justice. Tix is a regular old demon, and no matter how reasonable they seem if they can cause harm they will. Don't forget your arm."

"Baby, the fact that you get demonic skin and claws when you fight proves that your DNA was already changed," Trent said quietly. "I don't know if it occurred to Gray that Tix would be able to find you because of that. He didn't grow up in a demonic home. He grew up here."

"Oh, but it would have been in the contracts." There were always contracts. Always. Even if it's not on paper, there's a contract when it comes to a demon, and Gray did know that. When Trent tried to say something else, I held up a hand. "No more. We still have a job to do."

Trent sighed as though infinitely weary.

I hated that I was the one making him that way. I moved to stand in front of him, wanting to stave off his worries. "I don't blame you. I don't blame the baby. Hell, the truth of the matter is I'm sure I won't blame Gray at the end, but you have to know I'm going to find a way out of this. I'm not going to let them have a connection to my child."

"Our child," Trent corrected. "And we're already working on it."

I had to be content with that for now. "How long will he stay away?"

"As long as you command, but you didn't exactly give him a timeline," Evan pointed out. "And you should know that his connection to Gray holds sway over everything else. You could tell him to do one thing and Gray another and he'll do what Gray wants. Even telling him to stay away from you won't keep him from Gray."

So at least I knew the rules. I had to hope that Gray would keep our son safe. I would still study up on all the laws that bound a demon like Tix, but I had to let it go for now. For now I still had a mystery to solve, and being worried about the future wasn't going to help me. Tomorrow the primals would be finished with their death rituals and we could focus on the prophecy I'd brought back. I needed to figure out who'd murdered Alvis and what those paintings had to do with it so I could focus on the fact that Myrddin wanted to gift the Earth plane to a bunch of demons and then nothing would matter.

I brushed my lips against Trent's to let him know we were okay. I wasn't sure what I would do with Gray, but Trent and I were cool. Then I turned and strode down the hallway toward the apartment that housed Relda and Jade.

"I'll contact Hugo tomorrow and get him started on the problem with Tix." Evan rushed to stay at my side.

"I would appreciate that." The princess was infinitely helpful. "You should also call your parents."

"I already did," Evan promised. "They were being mysterious about something big going down tomorrow. Mom was hedgy, but I can tell something's going on. Have they contacted you?"

"No, but I don't expect them to." It mostly worked the other way. I called the royals to let them know what was happening. In this case I was more of a trusted employee. They would tell me what I needed to know when I needed to know it. "And don't be surprised if they don't talk freely even over secure lines. There are always ears listening."

"I think they're leaving Frelsi," Evan said quietly.

"Uhm, they're totally leaving Frelsi," Fen replied. "They're going to Dallas tomorrow or probably now, given the time thing. Lee's excited. He's going to steal something. Oh, and it turns out Myrddin is Dean's dad. That was a piece of hot gos."

"What?" No one had told me.

Evan nodded. "Yeah, apparently Myrddin showed up and figured out that his son was back. Also Mom kicked our uncle in the gnads, and something's up with Rhys and Shy. It's a lot to take in."

Trent growled a little. "You talked to Lee on an open line?"

"No, we're on a secure text. Come on. You know we keep in touch," Fen argued. "It's always been like this."

"But things have changed." Trent never stopped walking. "The royals are back, and now things are infinitely more dangerous. We have to have new protocols, and that means being far more careful. There's a reason we've used the mirror system sparingly. If the queen has something she needs to steal, we should be quiet about it."

I knew exactly what she would be going for. My mind was still whirling about the news that Dean was Myrddin's son, but I shoved it to the background for now. We needed to concentrate on getting back our weapons. "She left some magical bag in her apartment at the Council building."

"She's going after Myrddin's grimoire," Evan said.

A thrill of hope went through me because there was more than a magical book in that bag according to the queen. "And Gladys."

I might get my sword back, and I couldn't wait. It felt wrong to be on this plane without her.

I rounded the corner with renewed vigor because I trusted the queen. If she thought this was the right time to steal the bag, then I would have Gladys back as soon as I returned to Frelsi. One more reason to get this job done as soon as I could.

A hand reached out to stop me. Fen had his nose up. "I smell blood."

"Me, too," Trent agreed.

I jogged down the hallway, praying they were wrong.

"Evan, wait," Fen called out.

Trent knew better. He simply kept up with me. He was by my side when we got to the open door and realized things had taken another turn.

Jade was on her knees in the foyer, Relda's body in her arms and a knife at her side. Tears flowed down her cheeks, and she registered shock as she realized we were standing there. "I didn't...I didn't do this."

But it certainly looked like she had, and I had another problem to solve.

Chapter Fifteen

I forced down a piece of toast as my brother stood in the middle of the bedroom and gave me the distinctly bad news. "Really? You didn't find anything?"

Eddie had popped over to Dallas to bring back Nate. Jamie was apparently on call with the royals being in Dallas. They were both preparing to make the move to Frelsi in the next few days. My mother was currently packing way too much and fully intended to "help" me through my pregnancy.

That had been conveyed to me with an almost vicious glee. I was way more afraid of her than I was of Tix. The thought of my mom moving seriously close to me and not having any kind of a job except mom and grandma was terrifying, but I had to move the morning along.

"Yes, I found all the stab wounds," Nate replied with a yawn. "She was stabbed. And with what looks like a kitchen knife. Not even a ceremonial one. It's kind of sad. If you're a witch and you've got to go out, one would think it should be with a ceremonial knife."

"Could you be serious for five minutes?"

"I'm too tired to be serious," Nate quipped, reaching for the mug of coffee Eddie had brought him. "I know you want me to connect this to Alvis's death, and it's probably true, but I can't tell because there wasn't a lot left of Alvis. He could have been stabbed but a knife wouldn't kill him. I can tell you that the witch died from a butcher knife to the heart, and not a particularly clean one since I found some trace elements of herbs in the wound and on the knife. It looked like she'd been using it in the kitchen and then someone killed her."

"But she wasn't found in the kitchen. My question is why was her body found in the foyer?"

"Because she was killed there and the other witch was found with the knife because she was the one who did the killing," Nate summed up. "Sometimes these things are easy, and what we see is really what happened. Most of the time, actually." He looked down at his watch. "I wrote it all up in my report. I've got some samples to take back for further testing, and I'll send that to you as soon as I have it, but I don't think that's going to change the outcome of this investigation. I know you like the girl, but sometimes people disappoint us."

People disappointed me all the time. It wasn't like I was Suzy Sunshine. There were times in my life when I was Nihilistic Nancy. I was now trying for Reasonably Suspicious Ruth, with a pinch of Optimistic Opal. My brother was seriously annoying me. "I'll find Eddie for you."

"Don't get mad at me because I don't give you the answer you want." Nate softened slightly and sat on the bed beside me. "Are you feeling better?"

I'd had a morning. After trying to talk to Jade and getting mostly hysterical tears, I'd finally gone to bed and gotten some sleep. I'd had dreams of Tix throwing me a baby shower that ended with him locking me up so I would be forced to deliver my son on the Hell plane. I'd woken up and promptly had one of those amazing experiences where I throw up a lot and generally feel miserable for about thirty minutes before Nate had come in to deliver my not-so-great news.

"I guess so." I wasn't sure because my appetite hadn't returned, and that made me worry. I liked my appetite.

"Jeanie had a rough first trimester." He chuckled. "It's hard to believe I use words like 'trimester' now, and I know what a cervix is and that it dilates. Yesterday I was concerned with our next D&D night."

No matter how irritated I was with him, he was still my brother and I adored him. I shifted so I was sitting next to him and I could wrap my arm around him. "I know. I'm still surprised you know what sex is."

That got me a hearty laugh, and he leaned against me. "I am, too. Sometimes I look at this life and I'm so in awe of how we get to live." He took a long breath, sobering. "And then sometimes I'm terrified that this kid is going to come out and be so disappointed to have a human for a father. What if she can't change? What if she hates me for taking that chance from her?"

"First of all, I don't think that's going to happen. Those shifter genes run pretty strong, and second, if it does, she'll have plenty of human relatives. She won't be the only one. She'll have Jamie and Nicole's kids, and there are humans in Frelsi. She'll grow up surrounded by lots of creatures who don't have superpowers. Most of the Fae creatures' powers aren't cool things like being able to change forms. The brownies have super cleaning skills. The companions are all glowy, but ninety-nine percent of us can't see it. If she can't change, she'll find her badass in another way. Look at Evan."

"When the hell did you become the voice of reason?" Nate asked with a smile.

I had no idea. I had been the fucked-up one, the one my brothers worried about. The one they'd almost lost. Well, I guess when I thought about it, I did know. "I found my place in the world."

"Because you found your superpowers."

"But that's where you're wrong. I always had the power. It was always part of me, but until I found a peace inside myself, it was a dangerous thing. The real power is in believing in myself. That's what I've come to learn. In accepting who I am and what I can contribute and not being jealous of what other people get to do. It's in finding some contentment that I'm here and I'm necessary, even if other people don't see it. And you need to find that before this kid gets here."

"That's in, like, a couple of days, sister. That's a lot to unpack in a couple of days."

"Is it?" I mused. "Haven't you already done most of the work? You decided you loved this woman and adapted to live in her world. You're necessary to her. You and Jamie are necessary to me. Don't doubt your place here because you're human. That's what I love about the Under. The primals are such powerful beings and yet they open their home to everyone. Their place could have been the superpredators of the supernatural world, but instead they chose to help. I could have become something destructive. Instead I think I'm pretty helpful. I think I was supposed to be here. Any other investigator would take what you've said and stop looking. I, on the other hand, will likely toss out all of your thoughts and try to find the real killer."

Because it wasn't Jade.

Nate groaned, but his arm slid around my shoulders. "Fine. Ignore the forensics specialist. I'm betting you're going to ignore me when I give you another bit of advice."

I wasn't sure I needed more advice, but I was going with it. "Hit me."

He turned, forcing me to face him so I could see how serious he was. "Kill Liv."

I felt my whole soul sag. "I can't. I mean I won't let her kill me, but I don't know if I can kill her."

"Kelsey, she's so powerful, and that sword of yours won't help because she won't let you get close enough. She doesn't have to be close. She can kill you from afar."

"So why hasn't she? She's had the chance." I'd thought about this very little because I knew the answer. "She doesn't want to kill me. There's a part of Liv that still loves me."

"And that's the part of herself she wants to destroy." Nate stood and started to pace.

I glanced over and saw that Trent had come in. He wore a pair of pajama pants and had a mug of coffee in his hand. He leaned against the door jamb as though simply letting me know he was there. I cocked a brow to let him know I wouldn't hate his opinion.

One broad shoulder shrugged. "He's not necessarily wrong. Nate, you have to know how hard it is for her to give up on anyone she cares about."

"I know and I love her for it, but she's got to understand the rules of engagement are different now," Nate argued. "Liv is different now. If she doesn't kill you it's because Myrddin wants you alive. She's doing his bidding, and if he tells her to kill you, she will. I know I'm supposed to stay out of it, but Jamie and I have been keeping track of things."

Trent huffed. "What?"

"We live in Dallas. You can't expect us to completely stay away. Our families are at stake." Nate's spine straightened, his expression turning stubborn. "And we've stayed as careful as possible, but I know some things. I have friends who are willing to get me information. I didn't contact anyone because I knew we weren't at a point where you could use it, and I knew you would freak out if you found out we had a couple of spies. One of Jeanie's closest friends is another shifter who specializes in small creatures. I mean really small."

"We've tried sending shifters in." Trent moved into the room now, joining the conversation that I suspected would turn into a lecture for my brother. "Myrddin's cat killed two of them. We couldn't ask more to risk their lives."

"Because you sent in mice or rats or birds," Nate replied. "But Alecia can shift into a fly."

Trent's eyes widened. "Are you serious?"

The shifter body can do some remarkable things. Many shifters can move into bodies that were much smaller than their human ones, hence the rodent spies Trent and Sasha had used. However, Myrddin had a familiar, and according to our intelligence, the cat had been trained to kill any small creature who entered his master's home. But a fly might go unnoticed. A fly might sit high on a windowsill, listening in at all hours of the day.

But I had some questions. "I thought they had wards."

"That's the brilliant part," Nate remarked. "They've found that unlike werecreatures, who they can ward against with a single spell, shifters are different. Each family is unique and requires special wards, and the wards that would normally keep out humans don't work when a shifter is in his or her form."

"How long have you had this spy in the building?" Trent asked shortly.

I knew all of that wolf's tells and he was pissed, but he was also going to use whatever my brother had done to better our position.

"Alecia's only been in a couple of times over the last few months. We didn't want to overuse her. She's got a life outside of the spying she does for us," Nate explained. "I know she's risking her life every time she goes in, so all she's done so far is some surveillance. She's been documenting who lives where in the building. I'm going to be honest. I was going to use it to prove to you a group of shifters who can small shift will work as frontline spies."

"I'd like to see everything she's done so far. Can she listen in while she's in fly form?" Trent asked.

"In certain forms. Most flies don't have the ability to hear, but a few parasitic ones do. Alecia had to get the right form down but now she hears quite well," Nate replied.

"So we could potentially put her in one of their meetings." Trent seemed to be warming to the idea.

"Once she's had some more training," Nate allowed. "But she's already overheard some interesting things. She went in yesterday and Myrddin is worried about the queen. He knows she stole his grimoire and believes she also took the sword. He's looked everywhere for them. Done every kind of locator spell."

"We knew that. He's not a fool. When one of the world's best thieves pretty much loathes you and your precious goes missing, it was probably her." I didn't doubt Myrddin would know who to blame, but I'd been assured no locator spell would be able to find that bag. However we had other problems. "I think the queen might be going for the bag today."

"Myrddin knows she'll come for it at some point, but he thinks his wards will hold," Nate replied. "This is the important part, and it might not mean anything at all for now since we don't have the sword."

"You found out something about Gladys?" I sat up straighter. My brain went straight to the worst-case scenario. "Please tell me he hasn't figured out how to unleash her power on his own."

"No, but he does have some theories on how she stores power and that she doesn't have to use it all the minute she fights. He believes Kelsey can choose which power she uses."

"Absolutely. When I fought Jude in the arena, it was almost like there was a file I could flip through. I had access to all of the power, but I chose which one to use." I could still remember how it felt to have all that power at my fingertips, but I'd been afraid Gladys had been drained.

"According to Myrddin the power is still there. He believes the sword has sentience and can make choices of its own," Nate continued. "Which is why he feels like he's going to need you to wield it and the queen to power it. He thinks he might be able to use Evan, but he definitely needs you to convince the sword to do what he wants."

"Good luck with that." I wasn't about to tell Gladys to help out the evil wizard.

"Kelsey, he can use the people you love to force you," Trent pointed out. "This is why I need you to be careful. He can use Fenrir or me. And you have to know what I would want."

I moved into my guy's space. "You would want me to save you."

"I would want you to do what's right for our family and the plane." His hands came up to brush back my hair. "I would want you to know when it was time to make the sacrifice."

I wasn't going to sacrifice him at all, but I simply hugged him and agreed because it wouldn't do to argue with him.

"She's lying," Nate said with a snort.

Trent sighed and held me close. "I know. She's stubborn when she wants something."

"Always has been." Nate started to move for the door. "And one more thing. Alecia thought this was interesting. I'm not sure how it would work."

"How what would work?" Trent asked.

"She says she overheard Myrddin talking about the fact that there's another reason he doesn't want the sword falling back into Kelsey's hands," Nate began. "Apparently back when he was studying the sword, he cut himself on it."

Oh, that was news I wanted to hear. "Are you kidding me? Like he bled on Gladys?"

"Yes." Nate made it to the door with a yawn. "He cut himself, and that means his power is stored inside her, too. But his power is magical. Wouldn't it take a person who can wield magic?"

I would have to think on that. I might be taking some classes. "I would love to find out."

"I would, too, but we have to be careful. Of course none of it matters if we can't find the sword." Trent moved to my side. "I'd like to be informed when your spy goes in again. Is there any way she could be there today? With the royals being in Dallas it might help to have another spy in the building."

"Another? Please tell me you're not talking about Jack the Ripper." I'd been informed Alexander Sharpe was playing both sides. I didn't trust him at all. I certainly didn't like the idea of the queen being forced to rely on him.

"No, we're talking about someone else. Someone who will help Zoey and Lee," Nate replied. "She's been in the building for years. And unfortunately Alecia can only pull off the fly thing about once a month. It's so small. She's training to handle it more often, but it would be dangerous today. If I'd known the queen was planning a heist, I would have held her back."

But then we might not know about Myrddin's power being contained in the sword. "The queen knows what she's doing. Can we contact her?"

"They're in lockdown," Nate explained. "I can contact the king if I need to, but the queen can't go into the building with a cell."

I would like to have had a talk with her before she'd gone on that mission. I knew she was looking for the sword, but if she could find this map that Sarah Day might have left behind, it would be helpful. I would likely have to plan my own foray into enemy territory. At least I knew I would have a little friend who could help me out. When Alecia was ready, I would send her in to look for anything even vaguely resembling a map.

But for now my brother had to get back to his wife, and I had to figure out who'd killed Relda because I was sure it wasn't Jade.

I hugged my brother and noticed that Evan was sitting awfully close to the bedroom door, a book in her hand.

I frowned her way, and she gave me a sort of apologetic smile as though to say *what did you expect me to do.*

I had to face the fact that all the kids were trained spies, and they felt the need to listen in. Because they'd learned information was the only thing that could save them sometimes. I looked down at the queen's daughter. "I'm getting dressed and then we'll go and talk to Jade. If you have any questions about what you heard, you can talk to me then."

I wasn't going to punish or shame her for something that had been bred into her by the men who raised her. Besides, if Fenrir had wanted to hear the conversation, he could have from several rooms away. Same with Trent or most of the people in Evan's life.

"I'm sorry. I shouldn't have listened in," Evan admitted. "I only heard what was said after Trent walked in."

"Because he would have caught you before?"

She shrugged.

"Well, you missed a talk with my brother about how he's afraid of being a dad to a shifter and he thinks it was Jade." I brought the princess up to date.

"It wasn't Jade." Evan got to her feet. "Kelsey, I know her."

"Then let's prove it."

Evan nodded. "Let's prove it."

And we would. After breakfast because my appetite was back.

Chapter Sixteen

Jade's eyes were red and swollen as I entered her room, and I realized Eddie should never be a warden or a prison guard because the room was filled with cookies and tiny cakes and mini sandwiches as though high tea had exploded across it. There were also soft blankets and pillows, and I noted a folded set of pajamas that Jade hadn't used. All in all, it was a solid prison cell if one could call a high-class hotel suite a prison.

And someone had put in a big screen TV and an Xbox that her "guard" was currently using to save the universe from whatever the universe needed saving from.

Fen sat on the sofa, a controller in his hand and a bottle of soda on the table in front of him. I marveled at the fact that there were still sandwiches left, which made me wonder how many Eddie had made.

"You know she could have knocked you out and run by now." I felt the need to point out the flaws in my son's protocols.

He didn't even look up. "I don't think so. I've got a pretty thick skull. Also, she promised she wouldn't run."

"I won't." Jade had started crying again. "I don't...I don't have anywhere else to go."

I turned to the young girl who had to be terrified. "You don't have to go anywhere, Jade. I promise I'm going to figure this out. I was joking about how lackadaisical Fen is being."

"First, I don't know what that means, but it's probably lazy, and I'm not. I can do two things at once," Fen assured me. He grinned up at Evan. "Hey, babe. Can you hand me those snickerdoodles?"

I merely shook my head and gestured for Jade to sit down at the table with me. "How are you feeling?"

She sniffled. "I feel like this has to be a dream and Relda's not really dead."

I could understand that. "I'm sorry, sweetie. She's dead, and we need to figure out what happened. When was the last time you saw Relda alive? Was she still alive when you found her body?"

Jade's head shook. "No. She was dead, but I didn't know that. I tried a couple of spells to help her, but they don't work on dead people."

There was a hollowness to her tone that got to me. I needed to move this along and not let her sit too long with her grief. "Walk me through last night."

"I went to the party for Alvis for about an hour," she began.

"She did. I saw her there." Evan slid into the seat next to Jade. "She left around midnight."

"I told Evan I was meeting up with friends, but I wasn't. I was in the meditation room at the community center." She bit her bottom lip. "It's quiet, and no one will come in. I needed privacy because I've been working on a spell."

"A spell for what?" I shouldn't be surprised. "Please tell me it wasn't for something that's not allowed."

The rules were clear in the Under. Spellcraft was carefully guarded, and only certain spells were considered permissible since the use of magic could open up the entire group to Myrddin's influence. Wards and protective magic were fine, but no dark magic was to be worked in the Under.

She frowned. "It's not dark."

"Okay, then what is it?"

Tears dripped from her eyes. "It's a rite. It's our rite."

Fuck. There were several longtime witch families who performed rites of passage. They weren't necessarily dark magic. Witches who specialized in air magic had a ritual first flight performed on the first full moon after the witch's thirteenth birthday. Water specialists proved their power over the waves. Others had different methods of proving they were ready to join fully with their covens.

Centuries of tradition were behind these rites, and I couldn't imagine how hard it was to let go of something that should have been a part of her life. She'd had her family stripped from her. Shouldn't she be able to have this one thing?

I understood that, but I had to know how bad it was. "Jade, what kind of magic do you practice?"

"Earth magic," she replied quietly.

Evan frowned. "Jade."

A stubborn expression covered Jade's face. "Well, it's mostly earth magic. My mom's family traditionally practiced earth magic, but my dad came from a line of witches who worked with blood magic. It's not as scary as it sounds. I know blood magic can be used in violent ways, but so can wind and water."

"Blood magic can also call demons," I pointed out.

She paled visibly. "I wasn't doing that. I wouldn't do that. Never."

"Then what were you doing?"

"It's a rite of passage and it didn't work. It's called The Seeing. It allows us to get in touch with our lost family members. I wanted to see my mom again," Jade admitted. "But it didn't work and now I think I might have... What if what I did caused Relda's death?"

I had to hope she hadn't. "I need to understand how this ritual works."

She went silent.

I sighed because I could bet why. "Does it involve belladonna?"

"The ritual uses belladonna to put the witch in a trancelike state where she can reach out into the ether to try to find her ancestors." The words came rapid fire out of Jade's mouth, as though she needed to say them quickly or she might not say them at all. "I was trying to find my mom. I just wanted to see her, to talk to her. I wanted to know if she's still out there somewhere. I didn't mean to hurt anyone. I don't see how it could have hurt anyone since it didn't work."

"Explain the ritual to me."

She looked so tired, and I would bet she hadn't had a moment's sleep. "I made the witch's ointment."

"You're the one who stole the belladonna." I needed to get that on the record.

"I didn't steal it. I only used it. I was going to replace it before Relda found out, but then Alvis was killed," she explained. "I know I should have told you the truth, but I thought it would make me look guilty."

"It totally makes you look guilty," Fen said from his spot on the couch.

Jade's tears amped up again. "I didn't kill Relda. I swear. I was coming home from the ritual—which again did not work. I didn't see anything close to my mom. I saw…terrible things. It wasn't anything like I thought it would be."

"That's what happens with psychedelics," Fen added helpfully. "You never know if you're going to get a fun trip to happy town or if a horror movie's going to play out in your head." He stopped, his head turning and eyes wide. "Not that I would know. That's what Lee tells me, Mom."

Sure he did. I ignored my son. "How long were you in the meditation room? Did you wander out?"

She shook her head. "No. I had a spell in place to keep me inside until I was coherent enough to leave."

"Do you have any idea how dangerous that was?" I understood she'd taken some precautions, but it wasn't enough. She should never have tried spell casting at that level without someone to help her.

"You should have asked me to watch you," Evan told her with a frown. "Look, I don't think you should have tried it in the first place, but if you have to, you need someone to watch over you. I wouldn't have told anyone."

I wanted to be the strict mom here, but Evan was right. "What you should have done was talked to the primal council and explained why you wanted to do the ritual. They're reasonable. If you absolutely couldn't force yourself to come clean to them, then yes, you should have found a dumbass loyal friend who wouldn't let you be in it alone. Anything could have happened to you. You opened yourself up to magical forces. Some witches use rituals like that to access portals."

"We have wards against those." She sat back. "Of course we do. I'm so dumb. That's why it didn't work. Essentially I was trying to open a window into the ether, and it can't work down here because we have too many wards. I would have to go to the surface. I'm so stupid. If I hadn't been doing that ritual, I would have been there for Relda."

"What do you remember about finding her? Do you remember what time it was?"

She clasped her hands in front of her. "It was late. I had to come down, and that took a while. Two hours at least. I think the party was still going on. I know I saw Casey walking through the hallway carrying something."

That would have been around two thirty, when we left the party. Casey had been packing the painting up as we left. That meant if Tix hadn't waylaid us, we would have been there before Jade and could have avoided that particular trauma. "Did Casey see you?"

She nodded. "He said hi and everything."

"Good. My brother should have a time of death soon and if it's earlier, then that should help to clear you. What happened when you got home?"

"I opened the door and she was lying there and the knife was in her chest. I don't know what I was thinking. All I could think about was my mom. It was like I was ten again and it was that awful day when they came for her. I don't even remember pulling the knife out of Relda's heart. I just remember that I had to try to save her."

"Had you seen her earlier in the day?"

"Of course. She made breakfast and we talked about the party for Alvis."

"Relda didn't go," Evan pointed out. "At least I didn't see her there."

"She was too sad to go. She wanted to spend the evening in what she called 'quiet contemplation,'" Jade explained. "It was precisely why I decided to try the ritual last night. I'd been planning it for a while, but I didn't want her to know about it. I was going to replace the belladonna. She uses it so rarely."

"How were you going to replace it?"

"Well, Relda wasn't really telling the truth when it came to the gnomes. They do grow a bit of it, though they're not supposed to grow poisons or anything that can be used against someone. They used to grow some wolfsbane, and one night a werewolf who shall remain nameless got into it and it was awful."

"I didn't mean to," Fen said, putting down his controller and turning my way. "I was fourteen. I'd never seen it before. It looked pretty, and Evan's favorite color was purple."

Evan smiled, a bright expression. "He picked it for me. It was so sweet, and then I had to take care of him for two days. I thought he would never stop scratching. Rhys and Lee laughed for the longest time."

Every story they told me about their childhood had a bittersweet bite to it, but now wasn't the time to get all angsty. I focused in on the important part. "So the gnomes are growing things that are not allowed?"

Jade winced. "I don't want to get them in trouble, and the belladonna is being grown in a safe way. Only Relda has it. Had it. She wanted to keep it around for medicinal purposes."

"Is there any way Relda was involved in what happened to Alvis?" I had to ask the question. If she threw Relda under the bus now, I would have some information. I liked Jade but I also wasn't going to be naïve.

Her head shook. "No. She loved Alvis. She adored him, said he'd saved her. She would never, ever have harmed Alvis. She wanted to find out who killed him." Jade's face flushed slightly. "She wasn't sure you would do it."

"Solve the crime?" I asked, curious.

"She thought you would be too busy with your prophecy to care about Alvis."

"Well, I can't really get anything done with the prophecy until all the mourning rituals are over," I pointed out. "If someone wanted to put me off the prophecy stuff, this would be a good way to do it. But I don't think that's what's happening here. Too many things are leading me to think this is a problem that's been going on for a while."

"But Alvis would have been the primal most likely to solve the prophecy," Evan countered. "I think this is about you."

I didn't. I was going with instinct on this one. "Nah. They can only slow me down for a day or two, and there are many primals well versed in prophecy. No. Alvis found something out, and I would bet Relda did, too. It has something to do with those paintings. What do you know about the latest class?"

"I know Relda was a bit obsessed with it," Jade admitted. "She was super sad when Alvis canceled the last couple of classes and told her to stop working on the paintings."

"He told her to stop?" There it was—that one seemingly random fact that could start me down the right path.

"Yeah, he said he wanted everyone to stay on the same pace, and that meant taking a break," she explained. "At least that's what Relda told me."

"But she didn't stop, did she?"

"No. She said she felt compelled to follow where the muse led her. She was kind of weird about the painting stuff," Jade replied. "She started about two years ago when Alvis invited her to join the group he teaches. She found it soothing back then, but she wasn't, like, crazy obsessed with it the way she has been the last couple of weeks."

"What changed?"

One slim shoulder shrugged. "I don't know. They started a new series."

I remembered how those canvases had been sitting around her apartment, ghostly and silvery. "The nighttime series. She had three canvases, right?"

"Yes, and she never seemed to be done with them. Like they would look great and I would think she was done, and the next day she would be there at the canvas adding on to it. She said they weren't perfect, and then she would spend hours staring at them. I know that sounds weird, but it was kind of who Relda was. She would really get into whatever she was doing, whether it was spellcasting or knitting, and she could focus."

"You never tried?"

Jade chuckled. "Oh, I tried. I'm like the anti-artist. I can't draw more than stick figures, and I flunked finger painting in preschool. I took one class and knew it wasn't for me. Now I wish I'd kept going, if only because Relda wanted me there." Her tears were back. "I treated her like an overly pushy mom, but that's what she was and now she's gone."

Evan reached out as Jade broke down again, and I realized that was probably all I was going to get out of her.

"I'm going to go check on some things. Evan's going to stay here with you. I'll take Fen with me." I pushed back from the table.

"I thought Fen was supposed to make sure I don't run," Jade said between sobs.

"I'm not really worried about you running," I admitted. "But if you tried, I assure you Evan could stop you."

"I won't." She turned and cried into Evan's shoulder. "I don't want to go anywhere."

Evan glanced up, mouthing the words *I'll watch her*.

I walked out of the room, frustrated but knowing what I needed to do next. I started down the hall, feeling Fen moving behind me.

"Thanks, Mom. I don't know what to do with crying chicks. Evan is so much better at that stuff," Fen said with clear gratitude.

"How long have you been kept out of the gardens?" It was time to go talk to some gnomes, after I put in a request with my brother.

Casey stood in the living room where the paintings now sat side by side. Four of them. He was staring at them as though trying to find the differences. He turned when he heard me enter. "Hey, Kelsey. I brought all four of the paintings in here. I think you can see they're all pretty similar. Also, I don't think it could have been Jade. I saw her last night. Do we have the time of death yet?"

"It wasn't Jade." Jade had no reason to kill her guardian. She was a dumbass kid who was messed up and traumatized, and she'd made a mistake. "I want you to take samples of the paint and have Eddie pop you to my brother's. Don't come back until you know what's in that paint and you have a clear time of death. There's something in it, and those gnomes know. I want an accounting of where their little asses were last night and the night of Alvis's death. Now Fen, when did they start refusing entry to wolves?"

A lot of things were coming together in my head.

"Last year." Fen smoothed a hand over his head, pushing back his thick, dark hair. "I always got along with the gnomes. They're cool. The new dude is scared, though."

"Because he was attacked by wolves," I prompted.

"Yes. According to the primals, Elrin requested asylum roughly a year ago. He was brought to the nest to recover from his wounds," Casey explained. "I could pull up the report. There's always a report."

"I need you to figure out what's in the paint. According to Relda and Jade, there was something bioluminescent in the paint that came from plants in the gnomes' gardens." I stared at the paintings. They were quite similar, as though they were painting from the same instructions. The moons in the paintings seemed to glow from within. "I'm worried there's something more than bioluminescent plants in that paint."

Casey had already pulled a plastic bag and a small knife out of the kit he'd brought with him. He moved to the first of the paintings, scraping off a bit of the paint on the edge of the moon. "What are you looking for?"

"Belladonna. Henbane. Mandragora. I want you to look for anything that could be in a witch's ointment."

Fen's eyes had gone wide. "So you really think it was Jade? Damn. Like I knew I could stop her if I wanted to, but if I really thought she was a killer I probably wouldn't have played so much Xbox. Or offered her a beer."

He shouldn't be offering anyone a beer. That was a lecture for another day. "No, I don't think it's Jade, but I think someone knew she was making witch's ointment and knew why she was doing it. Or they could have put the idea in her head. The point is someone wanted her to make that ointment. They knew about its hallucinogenic properties."

"So they wanted Relda to hallucinate?" Fen asked.

"I think they wanted her open to suggestion." I wasn't a scientist and I wasn't a witch, and this was where it would have helped to have Liv on the team. Instead I had to wonder if Liv was the one out there pulling strings. I was pretty sure I needed to make sure those strings got cut and fast, but I had to know what was going on. "Jade said Relda seemed obsessed with the painting. She kept coming back to it. What if there's something in the paint that calls to these painters? She would stare at it for long periods of time and say she was contemplating what she wanted to do next. What if someone was whispering to her through the paint? What if that's what Luna's hearing? She can hear something coming through the painting but she's never touched the paint so she can't hear the exact words. It's at such a high frequency that Relda and the others didn't realize it was coming through and influencing them at all."

Casey's head came up. "Are you thinking sleeper agents?"

Fen suddenly got real serious. He might not know the word *lackadaisical*, but he damn straight understood what a sleeper agent was. "I should go and get Dad."

"That's fine. You should update him, and this evening you should take the chance and call Sasha. But first off we need surveillance on anyone who was taking that class." I wanted to see if anyone else had been affected by whatever that paint was doing. I wanted someone watching every single one of them to make sure they hadn't been convinced to commit some kind of sabotage. "And we need to collect all the paintings."

My mind was working overtime. There was a ton of sabotage that would work in the Under. They were uniquely vulnerable to someone poisoning the ventilation system. Fires could wipe out whole sections before people could evacuate. There were any number of horrors that could be brought down on the primals and all the knowledge stored here.

"We need to lock down the library." I wasn't sure what was going on, but I knew when you had something as precious as ancient knowledge, someone better protect it.

Casey nodded. "I agree. I'll let the head of security know before I go to Texas. They keep the part of the library that houses the oldest books and artifacts locked during daylight hours, but I'll put a guard on it, too. Hopefully I'll have some answers for you in an hour or two. I can help Nate run the tests."

Because he was a smarty pants when it came to anything technical. I was so lucky to have Casey with me. "You do that. I'm going to talk to that gnome. I'll have Evan run down those reports. Fenrir, I need you to go and find Rose. I'd like to have Luna tell me if all the paintings hum for her. I want to know how many paintings we're dealing with and how many I'll need to destroy."

After I figured out what was really going on.

"I want to help." Jade stood in the hallway with Evan at her side. "I'll stay with Evan. I promise. But I want to help you. You can even put some wards on me so I can't hurt anyone. Relda crafted some for the security team. I'll go right now and let them spell me."

I wasn't going to put her through that. I looked to Evan. "Can you handle her?"

Evan nodded. "I assure you I'm far better at physical combat, and I genuinely believe her. Kelsey, I've known Jade since we were kids. She didn't do this, but she might be able to figure out what's going on. It almost certainly involves witchcraft. She's not the strongest caster because she's never really been able to practice, but she knows the theories and academics behind witchcraft."

"All right. Go to the town hall and get me any records you can surrounding how Elrin came to the Under. I need the list of students from Alvis's class you got yesterday," I ordered.

"Sure," Evan agreed.

Jade wiped the tears from her eyes. "I know the woman who runs the records room. She'll give us anything we need."

Casey had collected all of his samples. "I'll go by the security office and have them lock down the library, and then I'll have Eddie take me to Dallas. I'll be back as soon as I have the information we need."

Then we had everything in place. I nodded Casey's way and he left. Before I could send the kids on their way, though, there was the sound of wind and the world seemed to twist around a single spot in the living room.

"It's Gray," Fen said when I started to get into a defensive stance.

Suddenly my hot demon hubby was standing in the middle of the living room wearing a beautifully fitting suit and carrying a bouquet of gorgeous flowers in one hand. There was a big box at his feet.

Trent chuckled as he walked in from the bedroom. He was grinning as he crossed to me while his eyes were on Gray. "You do not usually look this good when you come home."

Gray's lips tugged up slightly. "You don't usually care how I look. I was hoping she would."

"I do care," Trent corrected. "I care when you look tired and heartsick, neither of which you look today. I meant what I said. You look good."

Now Gray smiled in a way I rarely saw. Bright. Open. Happy. "I took some time to get ready. How long have I been gone?"

"Two days," I said, and yes there was accusation in those words because I wasn't ready to forgive him simply because he looked like sex in a suit.

Gray sighed, a relieved sound. "Excellent. I was worried it had been longer. I brought presents."

Now his eyes were on me, and I felt the pressure of everyone in my family staring my way. But I was still mad at him, and some flowers weren't going to fix it. "And I had a delightful conversation with your butler yesterday. Do you know how he found me? He tracked our unborn child. He's assured me he'll always be able to find our son."

"Yeah, she was pissed about that, Pops," Fenrir said, but he was sniffing the air. "Is that what I think it is?"

Gray's happy expression went right back to grim. "I'll order him to not ever contact you again, and I can assure you I can get him to stay away from our son."

"But he'll always have a connection," I pointed out.

"He's bound to the House of Sloane."

"I bet I could unbind him really fucking fast," I countered.

Trent sighed. "Tix is immortal, and if you somehow found a way to off him, Hell would simply grow a new one. There's always a keeper of the house as there is always a head of the house. And before you accuse Gray, if he steps down, he opens up the head of household spot for one of his relatives, and none of it will sever the connection to our son. It simply means Gray doesn't have any control."

I didn't care in that moment. "Which he should have told me before he decided to knock me up."

"I didn't really understand how it worked because I never thought to ask. I knew any child of ours couldn't be forced into Hell. I didn't grow up in the house and didn't go there as an adult, so I didn't understand that the keeper of the house could track me." Gray held out the flowers. "I got them for you. I thought you would like them."

I took them. They were beautiful. Black and purple and midnight blue blooms that seemed to shimmer. "They're lovely."

"They're grown in the gardens surrounding the palace," he admitted quietly. "I know you're mad, but I'm trying, Kelsey mine. Can we talk?"

"I need to work."

Fenrir groaned. "Come on, Pops. I can smell it. Do you know how long it's been since I had some?"

"I have to admit, I missed it, too," Trent said.

Gray leaned over and brushed his lips across my forehead. "Wolves." He stepped back and reached into his pocket. He pulled out a bag and what looked like a small piece of beef jerky. "Here you go, buddy. I told the kitchens to make sure they have a steady supply."

Gray tossed it into the air and Fenrir easily caught it. In his mouth. Like it was a frisbee except he ate it.

Thankfully Gray simply handed Trent the bag.

"Damn that smells good." Trent downed one, too, before offering me the bag. "You want to try one, baby?"

Evan cleared her throat and looked at me with wide eyes that told me I should ask questions.

"What is that made of, Gray?"

"Meat," came the reply. "Like all jerky. It's a snack the kitchens came up with."

"The kitchens on the Hell plane," I pointed out with deep suspicion.

"In Demonish the name for it is *zyll a ill pora*." Evan seemed to know way more than I did.

"And in English?"

"The Meat of My Enemies," she replied.

"Are you feeding my son treats made from the flesh of your enemies, Grayson Sloane?"

"They taste great," Fen assured me. "This is both nutritious and delicious. Hit me, Dad."

"Don't you dare, Trent." I pointed his way, but he seemed to have half the bag down his throat.

Fen groaned.

"It's just a name. It's actually made from cattle found on the Hell plane," Gray replied. "But I would like to point out that you're the one who wants me to be comfortable with my demonic side."

"I meant for sex stuff not for slaughtering your enemies and making them into treats. Why is that box moving? Please tell me that's not something else for Fen to eat," I complained as I pointed to the twitchy box. "He will get a tummy ache and we have a million things to do tonight."

Yes, I was the fun mom.

"Oh, this is a present for Evan," Gray said, dropping to one knee.

Two paws and a head popped up over the side of the box, and the goofiest, ugliest, most adorable thing I'd ever seen was suddenly drooling up at me.

Evan gasped. "Is that what I think it is? Is that a hellhound puppy?"

"You said you always wanted one, and he was the runt of a litter born on our estate. They were going to feed him to the others," Gray explained. "Come and hold him. He'll bond to you if you keep him close and feed him. He's small and impressionable. Hellhounds have to learn to be violent and aggressive, and he's so young he hasn't started training yet. He's barely twenty-four hours old."

Evan dropped to her knees and picked up the chubby puppy. "Hi, boy. You are the sweetest thing. Look at you."

Pitch black eyes stared at her with obvious worship, and his purplish tongue lolled out from between sharp fangs. His body wriggled as though he wanted to be close to her.

It was cute and sweet and completely the wrong time. I turned to my husband, who might have been trying to make some amends to the kids and me, but he was also causing trouble. "Is that dog even house trained? Do we even know if the primals allow hellhounds in the Under?"

Gray frowned. "He's only a puppy. And we're going back to Frelsi soon, right?"

We? That was the first time I'd heard him use the word *we* when he was talking about the future. "I don't know if the king is going to want Tix popping in and out of Frelsi."

"I love him so much." Evan held the puppy close. "Kelsey, I'll take care of him. I'll get him a crate and a leash, and I'll walk him and train him. Oh, please don't make him go back. They'll kill him. He's so sweet. Look at him."

She held the hound out, showing me how cute and wriggly he was, and then he burped and a little jet of fire flew out of his mouth.

"Okay, so we're pretty sure there's some dragon in his background," Gray admitted. "He'll get control of that very quickly."

"He burps fire, Gray."

Fenrir was laughing. "He farts it, too. A tiny bit came out of his butt. That's awesome, Pop. I mean that is the best. We should call him the Mighty Fire Farter."

Evan held her new baby close, as though protecting him from Fen. "No, we will not. His name is Puff the Magic Hellhound, and you are not going to make him feel bad about farting. None of you boys should ever do that. Hypocrites."

"I wasn't making fun of him. I think it's cool," Fen tried.

Chaos. That was what Gray had brought. Pure chaos. I had a

murder to solve, and Gray had brought me a fire tooter.

"Where is he going to sleep, Gray? Does he have a crate? Does he have a water bowl? Does he drink water or should I pour out the blood of his enemies?" I started.

"He doesn't have enemies," Evan argued.

"Well, I mean they were going to feed him to the others," Fen pointed out.

"I don't know. I think anyone who smells his farts might disagree." Trent sniffed and then shook his head. "We're going to need to find a proper diet for the little guy."

"Oh, I have a spell for that." Jade was finally smiling, petting Puff's wouldn't-be-little-for-long head. "I'm probably not good at it though. I bet someone in Frelsi could do it. Or the gnomes have some herbs that erase scent."

"Did you stop at a pet store?" I continued because this was a terrible plan that Gray had not thought out in the least.

"There's not a Petco on the Hell plane." Gray seemed every bit as frustrated as me. "But I can certainly go now. I kind of thought Eddie would do it. I knew you would be upset if I sent Tix, though he would do just the same as Eddie."

"Except he would buy evil things." I didn't even care how stupid the words coming out of my mouth sounded.

"No, he would buy what I tell him to buy," Gray countered.

"Guys, let's bring down the heat." Trent got in between us, putting a hand on both of us. "Let's go back to our room and talk this out. Gray was trying to reconnect with Fenrir."

"He did a good job, too. His enemies taste great," Fen announced. "And the little guy is supercute."

"I hope you think so when you are picking up his poop." I wasn't letting anyone get out of this easy.

Gray had left us and he would leave us again. And no matter how well-meaning he'd been, he'd placed our son in a terrible position.

He'd placed all of us in a terrible position.

"I'm not really good at that," Fen said with a shake of his head. "I have a sensitive nose… I will get over it and hey, maybe we can train him to burn off his own poop. Problem solved. Please don't make me choose between my mom and Pop. I know I should choose Mom because of the whole staring down the alpha thing, but I really missed that jerky, and I don't think Evan is going to give up the hellhound."

The hellhound was currently trying to lick Evan to death, and I prayed she was fireproof, and what had Jade said?

"I'm going with Casey." Trent stepped back with a sigh. "I'm not going to play referee for you two again. I'll go to Dallas and help Nate with anything he needs. I sincerely hope you two can get it together before I get back."

I knew I should be more upset about that. Trent was practically a saint and I'd managed to drive him off, but I was stuck on what Jade had said as Trent walked away.

"What do you mean the gnomes have herbs that negate bad smells?"

Jade's eyes widened as she realized somehow in all of this drama she'd become the center of attention. "Well, they do. All smells, really, though we don't normally use them."

"Well, that explains how Fenrir couldn't track anyone from Alvis's apartment." I needed to regain control of this situation. There were a whole bunch of moving parts, and they all threatened to go off the rails. "Evan, you're on dog duty. The first thing you teach that dog is to not eat the brownies, and you better warn them about his fire breathing from both ends."

"I thought I was getting the reports." Evan held Puff, who had now fallen asleep against her shoulder.

"Nope. You now have a baby and you have to take care of the baby, who can't leave this apartment because we're not sure your baby is allowed to be here."

"I could..." Gray began.

I turned on him. "If the next words out of your mouth are anything about Tix coming to watch the dog for a while, you should rethink them."

"I could stay with the dog," Gray offered in a way that let me know I'd been right about what he'd meant to say.

"No, I should stay with him," Evan admitted. "He needs to bond with me. Fen can take Jade to get the reports, and that way Gray can back you up, Kelsey."

"That is an excellent idea. I'll go change into something more appropriate." Gray walked off toward the bedroom.

Evan looked at me with wide, innocent eyes, but I knew when I'd been manipulated into a situation.

A tiny burst of flame accompanied the puppy's bout of gas.

"Oww." Evan frowned. "I need to figure out how to keep this baby's tummy settled. What do you think he eats?"

Fen shoved another piece of jerky in his mouth as though he knew where his girlfriend would go next.

It was a good move because Evan was ruthless.

"There are some herbs I can blend up to help with that," Jade offered. "Maybe Kelsey can grab them when she goes down to talk to the gnomes."

I was pretty sure the gnomes wouldn't be friendly after they figured out I was going to accuse them of murder.

I should probably get those herbs first.

Chapter Seventeen

It took almost an hour to get everyone settled and off on their individual errands, and it was getting close to sunset by the time Gray and I started for the gardens. He'd changed from that superhot suit to jeans and a T-shirt and he was still sexy as hell, and I was still somewhat irritated.

"I didn't mean to cause trouble," Gray said quietly as he moved alongside me. "I really was trying to reconnect with Fenrir. And I do promise the jerky isn't someone who pissed me off. It's made from cattle."

"Demonic cattle." Even I could hear the stubbornness in my tone.

"I won't do it…" He sighed, a heavy sound, and stopped. "No. I'm not going to tell you I won't do it again because Fen enjoys it and there's nothing wrong with him having a snack he likes. It's not going to turn him into something. It doesn't control anyone's mind. It's just tasty. Kelsey, I'm confused, and I need you to tell me what I'm doing wrong. Not about signing the contract in order to protect your family. You won't convince me there was another way. I'm talking about now. I'm genuinely trying to be okay with my demonic side. Being around Lucifer is unsettling, but I'm going to be honest, I gather some strength and energy from being at the house my ancestors built. I think I know why my father didn't want me to go there until I was older. I think I would have been more powerful had I spent any time at all in that house."

"Are you planning on taking this child to Hell?" I couldn't help the fact that my hand drifted to my belly.

His jaw tightened. "I would never do anything you would be uncomfortable with, but he will have a demonic side. Are you planning on pretending he's human?"

"He might be human." You never could tell. Lee had a human mother and a Fae father and…he was somehow a latent vampire.

"He won't be and you know it. He'll be part demon, part Hunter—whatever that means in a boy—and none of us knows what to expect yet. What I do know is he'll be very much like his mother, and that means he'll be stubborn and he'll want answers. He'll be part me, and that means feeling an enormous amount of shame when it comes to being part demon. You're the one who made me see that I didn't have to be ashamed. You showed me I could embrace the good part that comes from the circumstances of my birth."

"I meant I thought you should be okay being kinky when we have sex, Gray. I did not mean for you to become one of the thirteen princes of Hell," I shot back.

He growled, a low sound that came from the back of his throat, and his eyes went the slightest bit red.

And I was not afraid of him at all. "That demon can track our child, Gray. You are the one who taught me never to trust a full-breed demon."

"I'm not a damn full breed and don't trust Tix with secrets, but I think he can probably handle shopping for a dog crate," Gray replied. "And you seemed okay with the idea of me getting Evan a hellhound puppy the last time we were together."

"Yes. That was sometime in the future when the queen could handle everything. Not in the middle of my murder investigation."

"Well, I wasn't sure how long it had been, and I wasn't even totally sure where I was going to show up," Gray admitted. "I thought I might be going to Frelsi."

"You didn't know where you were going?" I wasn't sure how this new power of his worked. When I'd left the Earth plane, he'd been like the rest of us. He'd either caught an airplane, drove a car, or walked on his own two feet.

"I track you and Trent in a similar fashion to Tix, though for different reasons. My wolf can find...well, my wolves. And if you think it's a nasty demonic..."

I moved close, letting my hand find the side where that magnificent, sentient tattoo lived. There was nothing wrong with that tat. It was proof that Gray did belong to a demonic royal house, but that tat wasn't good or evil. It was a piece of Gray's soul, and it could find the ones he loved. "I wish you'd been able to track me through time."

His expression softened, and he brushed back my hair. "Who says I didn't? I felt it when you were coming back. When you were coming through the painting again, I knew when you would be here. But you have to understand I couldn't interfere."

"You couldn't tell Trent what day it would be." I did understand that. It was frustrating to be Gray sometimes. He had all the knowledge and no way to act on it.

"Technically I'm not allowed to interfere in anything having to do with my prophecies or with the coming war between the royals and Myrddin," he explained. "But I didn't see a problem borrowing Arkan Sonney from the Unseelie and perhaps releasing him in a place that a certain Fae prince might see him and decide it was a sign that he should go and pick up his parents."

Rhys Donovan-Quinn had disobeyed orders because he'd seen a small white pig viewed as a sign of good fortune by the Fae. If he hadn't, we would have been trapped in the Council building with no way out. "You stole a pig?"

"I borrowed a pig who is really a hedgehog but who looks like a pig when the little guy becomes a portent of good fortune for superstitious Fae. That society is weird." One side of his mouth curled up in the sexiest smirk. "And then I politely took him back to his *sithein*. Then I was called into session with Lucifer and I missed you coming home altogether." His hands held my shoulders, squeezing lightly. "Kelsey, I've only got six more weeks of service to him and then my contract is over and we'll be out. If you don't want me to descend again, I won't. I'll give the house title to whoever is next in line after our son and we'll be through."

But we wouldn't. We would never be through. I'd been fooling myself. "Who's next in line?"

His jaw tightened, and I knew what was about to come out of his mouth. "Well, I could have handed it to my brother if he wasn't dead."

That was a fight I was so over. "Sure. It would be better for me to be dead because that would have been the outcome of Trent not acting."

He groaned and turned away from me. "Damn it. All I'm saying is I wouldn't have to hand it over to my father if Nemcox was still alive. I know you hated him, but he would have left us alone. I can't say the same for my father. He's been working his way back up, and I think if I have to step down at this point, they would hand it over to him. The House of Sloane produces a lot of the food eaten on the Hell plane."

"Yes, like Meat of My Enemies jerky."

"We have agriculture." Gray paced along the stone path that led down to the gardens, his hands on his hips. "What are you going to tell our son when he wants to understand that part of his nature? Are you going to tell him what people told me? Are you going to tell him the part I gave him is corrupt and vile and he should pretend it doesn't exist?"

That knocked the wind out of my sails. I wasn't about to be the one to make my son feel shame over something he couldn't control. "I don't know what I'll tell him. I never thought about him being part demon. I thought about him being part you."

His hand came up, touching his chest. "I am part demon, Kelsey mine, and you've always known that. I don't have the perfect connection you and Trent have. He and your wolf have something I can't even understand. I call to the human part of you—the messy, complicated, confused, and yet arrogant part of you. We're never going to have that perfect peace you have with Trent, and once I would have walked away because I would have thought that was all you need. But damn it, I'm part of this too."

"Then you shouldn't have left them."

He stopped, his eyes finding mine. "I thought I was doing the right thing. I wasn't out partying. I was trying to help our family, trying to keep the people we love safe. I love you, Kelsey, but the way you look at me right now I don't know that you feel the same way. I might have made mistakes, but I meant well. I might still be fucked up, and maybe that's the problem. Maybe you're too together for me now."

"Together? You think I'm together? I'm barely holding on because I lost twelve years, Gray." The emotion was welling up inside me again. I'd hoped I'd purged it all that afternoon with Trent, but here it was, a river of anger and grief pressing against the dam I'd erected so I could function. "Twelve years. The little boy I fell in love with is a young man, and he's struggled so much. I had to explain to the alpha of the North American packs that I would kill him if he tried to force our son to do something he didn't want to do."

"I know," Gray said grimly. "I've tried to deal with them. Trent's tried to handle the situation. They're desperate, and no threat is going to stop them. One group wants to make him their king and the other wants him dead. I have spies in both camps, and don't think I don't walk through from time to time to remind them who the fuck they're dealing with."

"You've talked to them?" Somehow I'd gotten the impression that he'd become a watcher of sorts. It was what the heavenly prophet did. He watched and sometimes moved chess pieces around, but he didn't fight for either side.

"Of course. When I'm not working with Lucifer or fulfilling my prophet duties, I watch over them. Since they came back to the Earth plane, I've tried to stay close even if the kids didn't know I was there. You should know I killed a wolf who tried to murder Evan."

"Good."

"You don't want the whole story?"

"I don't need it. You took care of the situation and I thank you for it and hope you'll do it again if you have to," I explained. Knowing he'd been watching out for the kids even from a distance brought me some peace. When he'd described it, I'd somehow gotten it in my head that he forgotten about them, that he'd walked away and let Trent handle everything.

He stopped and sat on the stone wall that ran parallel to the path. "I couldn't follow them off plane, and you can't know how much that twisted me up. I suppose in those early days I reacted to being useless to the kids and Trent by consolidating power where I could. Have you considered that I now have a seat on the demonic council? That I have a say in what happens down there? That I have access to information that can help protect us all?"

"But you're not allowed to use it." I couldn't imagine they truly trusted Gray, even with all the contractual obligations they had him under.

"I can find a way. I always do," he said quietly. "I won't let our family down, but I think you need to decide if you still want to be with me. I thought being able to work through my shame and be okay with my demonic side would make you happy. I thought the fact that Trent and I have become comfortable with being in a relationship would make you happy. Now I have to wonder."

He was so beautiful and so frustrating, and he was wrong about this. I moved into his space, putting my hands on either side of that glorious face. "I hope you and Trent had all kinds of dirty, filthy, gorgeous sex while I was gone. More than that I hope you found comfort from each other. That's what I've always wanted for the three of us. The world is upside down for me. I'm coming to realize that I'm not ready for this baby, but then I never would have been. There's no way to be really ready for this. I thought I would be raising this baby in peace, and now he's going to know war. He's going to be born into a war I have to pray we can win. I'm catching up, and I don't think I'm doing a great job of it."

"We need some time together." Gray's hands found my waist. "I'm going to try to stay in Frelsi as much as I can. I've already made arrangements to move your family there. They'll be in Frelsi next week, and they have guards watching over them until that time."

"I appreciate that. I hope you can come with me when I go looking for the Days. My brother has a spy who I think will be able to help." It was so much nicer to talk about the future with him. I was still processing all the history that had happened while I was gone, and I suspected that wouldn't be over any time soon. "We need to figure out where Mia Day is, and I have some theories."

"I can try to help find Mia. I can go anywhere I like, but I need a reason. I'll think about it, but I'm sure I can find a way to help. I'll also contact Jacob. He's been quiet for years. I think he's been ordered not to interfere. You should know there are factions on the Hell plane who oppose Myrddin's plans. We can use those, too."

I was starting to see that having some power in the enemy camp might not be the worst thing in the world. "All right. How about you hang around as long as you can and we'll talk these things through." I leaned over and kissed him because no matter how irritated I was, I couldn't let him think I didn't love him. I did. I loved him so deeply, but he was right. It was a harder relationship than the one I had with Trent—who was now irritated with me. "Hey and if you can put a good word in with Trent, I would appreciate it."

He chuckled and drew me in closer. "I think all you have to do is give Trent some attention and he'll get over it pretty fast. I'll do the same. We have to go easy on him. We're rough to live with on occasion. I want nothing more than to get to be your husband for a while, to take care of you, to watch our baby grow and be with Fenrir. I want us to be a family. I want it so badly I dream of it at night. Stupid, ordinary dreams about sitting down to dinner and watching movies together."

He'd always wanted a normal life, and he'd ended up with me. "We can have some of that."

"While you save the world." His mouth found mine and he kissed me sweetly.

"And you reign over a portion of Hell." I wasn't the only one with a stressful job.

"A tiny portion," he said between kisses. "Practically minute."

I bet it wasn't, but I was done arguing with him. I let him kiss me over and over until I remembered we were here to do a job.

I stepped back. "Come on. Let's talk to these gnomes and figure this whole thing out so we can have a break before the next crisis."

He stood and then his eyes went pure black.

I knew what that meant. "Don't you dare. I do not need another fucking prophecy."

He frowned, his whole body tightening. "Not another prophecy. The fulfillment of an important one, one begun long, long ago. Kelsey mine, I have to go."

"No, you don't." He couldn't leave me again. "Grayson Slone, you said…"

And he was gone.

I was left standing alone. I would have to do this job all by myself, and yes, it was only a couple of gnomes, but I liked having backup. Especially since everyone—even small Fae creatures—get pissed when you accuse one of them of murder.

It had been a shitty day, and now both my husbands were gone and I had to deal with gnomes and weird paintings and figure out how to housetrain a hellhound puppy.

My frustration was pretty much at a peak.

"Kelsey!"

I turned as I heard a woman shouting my name. I jogged back up the path and found Rose clutching Luna, who was crying and holding her ears.

"What's happening?" I moved as quickly as I could because Luna was in obvious distress and Rose was crying.

"It's screaming. They're all screaming," Luna said between sobs.

"I think she's talking about the paintings," Rose explained, her arms tightening around her daughter. "A couple of minutes ago, she woke up and started crying. I don't know what to do. Christopher won't be awake for hours."

We wouldn't have the strength of the primals with us until long after dark.

It would be a perfect time to strike.

How would they use the paintings to strike? It was what I couldn't wrap my mind around.

How was it connected? Was everything connected? Luna could hear the paintings hum. Weird creatures were getting into the Under with no reason for them to be here. Someone killed two of the painters. The gnomes were growing everything they needed for witch's ointment.

Witch's ointment, which Jade had used to try to contact her mom because she believed with the right magic she could find the ether.

She'd wanted to open a portal to another dimension.

Luna had been able to hear Tix travel.

An idea started to form in my head. A horrible, wicked, nasty idea that I prayed I was wrong about.

"Luna, does this sound like when the prophet travels down to the Under? Or his servant?" I asked, praying the answer would be no.

Luna was crying as she nodded.

And I knew what the paintings had been for.

An invasion.

"Rose, I need you to hide. Tell everyone you can that they need to take cover because Myrddin is invading the Under. He's using the paintings to open a portal and get around the wards," I said. "The gnomes are in on it. At least I would bet the newest one is. He's a plant. You have to hide Luna, and find a way to protect the primals if you can."

Rose had gone pale. "I will. I'll hide Luna and let security know what's happening."

I took off running because four of those fucking paintings were now in my apartment, and as far as I knew Evan was alone because Eddie had taken Casey and Trent to my brother and wouldn't be back until they were done. Fen and Jade were running the errand I'd sent them on. It could be hours before they were finished.

I ran as fast as I could, my heart racing and dread flowing through me.

I ran and hit the door to my apartment with a thud just in time to see a boot coming through the moon on the largest of the paintings.

Liv stepped through, emerging from wherever she'd come from to stand in my living room, and she wasn't alone.

"Hey, bestie." Liv's dark eyes shown in the twilight coming from the magical lights. "Missed me?"

I was about to explain exactly how little I'd missed this version of her when I realized someone was behind me. I turned and another witch hit me with a spell that made me fall to my knees.

"Maybe you should take a nap, Kelsey." Liv stood over me, staring down with pitch black eyes, the veins reaching up through her neck, proof she'd had another dose of demon blood. She was at the peak of her power, and I didn't even have my sword.

She winked down at me and light flashed from her hands.

And the world went dark.

Chapter Eighteen

The awful smell of brimstone was the first reminder that I wasn't taking a nap. That and the warm feel of a tongue on my cheek.

I opened my eyes, hoping it was all a terrible dream and I would wake up and Trent was kissing me.

The goofiest puppy face grinned at me and a dark tongue lolled out of his mouth, slightly crooked fangs on full display.

"What the hell?"

"Yes, that was my question, too," a familiar voice said.

My hands were behind my back, tied in a harsh fashion, and my ankles were bound tight as well.

"Don't struggle or it will get worse," Liv said with a sigh. "That particular spell is nasty when you try to fight it. Simply relax and it won't tighten up."

I tried to take a deep breath so I could figure out where the fuck I was. A soft mattress was beneath me, and I quickly realized I was in the bedroom of our apartment in the Under. Liv was behind me and Puff was currently rolling on his back trying to get never-going-to-happen-because-my-hands-were-tied-behind-my-back belly rubs.

"He's awfully cute. Where did you pick up a runty hellhound?" Liv rounded the corner and came into view. She was dressed in what I now thought of as her comic book chic uniform. Lots of leather, and she seemed to think her boobs would distract her enemies. "Oh, is

Gray back? Did he bring you a present? Were you surprised to find out how high he ranks in the hierarchy of the Hell plane? I wish I'd been able to listen in on that conversation."

She reached out and picked up Puff.

"Hey, come on. Don't hurt him." I couldn't stand to watch her squeeze the life out of that puppy.

Liv managed to look hurt. "I'm not a monster. I told you. He's cute, and he could be very helpful one day. Get a hellhound this young and you can train him properly. I could use a familiar, though we usually bind to cats. Canines can be so dumb at times. Since when do you think I go around kicking puppies?"

"Since when did you knock out your best friend and tie her up?"

"Fair," Liv agreed, and put the puppy down with a pat. "I'm not going to kill you if that's what you're worried about. I've got a job to do down here and then we'll leave and you'll be alive, though you should know this isn't about you. You're simply the cherry on top."

"Sure. I'm just a side project," I said, trying to figure out how I could get out of these bindings if they tightened every time I moved.

"I haven't spent months getting these morons to create several complex portals because I wanted to catch you. I didn't even know you would be here when I started this."

"I thought the primals were off limits."

She glanced down at her watch. "Not really, but I don't want to bring them in. I've got about an hour before the fuckers are awake. The fact that they sleep longer than regular vampires makes this so much easier. The witch's ointment functions best at three a.m., but a turning hour works, too."

"Sunset," I surmised. If the primals had been normal vampires they would be awake, but Liv had more time because of their unique needs. "So you worked with the gnomes? Obviously you couldn't send someone in with the ingredients you needed."

Liv knelt down so we were roughly at eye level. "I've found Fae creatures can be very practical. Oh, not the little brownies. I didn't kill them either, by the way, but they will have some hella headaches when they wake up. Where's that demon of yours? I expected to have to deal with him."

"Wouldn't you like to know." I had no idea where Gray was. He would be helpful right now. So would Trent. Or my wolf king son.

She frowned. "I would, actually. You know this is a two-way street. I give you information. You give me information."

If she was really willing to talk, I would tell her what she'd likely already figured out. "He's not in the Under. He's investigating something for me. I was trying to prove the gnomes were responsible for the two murders we've had, but now I know it was really you."

"I certainly didn't tell Elrin to murder anyone. All he was supposed to do was grow the plants I needed, make the witch's ointment, and put it in the paint. I knew that moronic primal taught classes. Like the underworld needs a *Parks and Rec.* At some point they would paint suns or big-ass flowers. Something round that could serve as a focal point for the portal."

"And you've been practicing. That's how the ladybugs and butterflies got in. Did you know the bunny would be okay when you sent it through?"

She shrugged. "I thought it would. Well, until someone ate it. But it wasn't like I was going to test it on myself. We started with small things and when the bunny survived, we were pretty sure it would work on us. I sent Shera through first. I figured if she didn't get chopped in half, I would probably be okay."

"You've grown so thoughtful over the years I've been gone." I rolled my eyes because she really had turned nasty.

I always went through first. I would never put my crew in danger that I wasn't willing to accept myself, but Liv seemed to have forgotten what I'd taught her.

"No. I've learned to value myself and my talents," she replied with a primness that didn't match her actions.

"All right. So what is the plan if you're not going to murder me." I needed to keep her talking because Eddie would show back up at some time and he would either figure out a way to deal with the magical bonds or pick me up like a piece of luggage and teleport me straight out of here to someone who could.

Fenrir wouldn't have been in the apartment when Liv showed up, and he was seasoned enough to not freak out and come running in. Evan had been here, and Puff was proof.

But Evan was smart, too. She would know to hide and bide her time.

"Well, I thought you would tell me where that princess is and we can get out of here." Every word Liv said gave me life.

She couldn't find Evan. She'd likely come in with the most powerful locator spell she had, and Evan couldn't be found because she was well protected. Evan carried charms and talisman and magical gems with her at all times. "I thought she was here. I'm surprised she's not. I guess she and Fenrir went out for lunch since Eddie's not here."

"From what I can tell, Trent isn't either." Liv reached out and gave the puppy a scratch behind his ears. If it weren't for the weird eyes and hair and the fact that I was tied up, it could have been any Saturday afternoon girl chat we'd ever had. "I'm surprised they left you all alone."

Since she seemed willing to talk, I was going to ask her some questions. "What do you want with Evan?"

One slender shoulder shrugged. "I don't want her at all. Myrddin does. I think he thinks she'll work as well as her mom when it comes to activating your sword."

"The sword he intends to use to close us off from the Heavenly planes?" I needed her to hear those words spoken out loud.

She stood, staring down at me. "The sword he intends to use to free us from the shackles of the Heavenly planes."

"Shackles? You know they tend to stay out of what happens on this plane. It's the demons who try to fuck things up here," I pointed out and groaned because those bindings tightened as I moved to try to flip over.

"You see things from the wrong point of view. You've been indoctrinated by the king and his minions," she said primly.

"From what I understand you don't have the sword, so I'm not sure how the princess will help you." I tried to stay still now. The bindings were cutting off circulation in my wrists.

"We'll have it soon. I assure you my master is working on the problem," she promised. "Then we'll have the sword and the princess. I'll be rewarded, and I intend to use it to my advantage."

"Good luck with that. As far as I can tell, all Myrddin's done for you is steal a piece of your soul." I hated how cold she looked.

"It wasn't a piece I needed, and I gave it to him. He didn't have to steal anything from me. I have to go and look for the princess," she said, glancing around as though trying to make sure Evan wasn't here.

She looked back down, her expression going as soft as I'd seen her since her transformation. "I've changed my mind about leaving you behind. I'm taking you with me but not to hurt you. I want you to see how thoroughly the king has lied to you. Myrddin isn't bad. He's just doing what he has to."

This was what it felt like when a friend joined a cult. "He has to deliver the Earth plane to demons?"

"He has to elevate his people so that the vampires and wolves never subjugate us again," she said with the surety of a believer. She leaned over and pressed a kiss to my forehead. "When we get to the Coven House, I can't let him know how much I still love you. Not until he's taken care of your doubts. You might not believe this but it's what I meant to do with Casey that day. My plan wasn't to kill him. I meant to bring him back with me so he could see the beauty of Myrddin's ideas. Once you've spent time with my master, you'll see, and we'll get Casey and we'll all be happy together."

"Only if he manages to take control of my brain, sister," I replied.

She smiled down like I'd said something that pleased her. "Yes. Then we'll be happy."

There was a knock on the door, and I heard someone remind Liv of the time and she sighed.

"I'm coming. The Hunter is secure," Liv said as she walked past me. "Her only protector is a runt of a hellhound. We'll take him with us once we've found the princess. I know she's here. She's using magic, but it won't get her out of this apartment. I've locked us in tightly. The only way in or out right now is through those paintings. Did I thank you for moving them all in here? I thought we would have to sneak around."

I growled her way.

She laughed as she walked out the door. "We'll leave soon. Try to go in with an open mind and all will be well. It's only a matter of time before we find the little bitch."

They were still talking as they walked out and closed the door behind them.

Puff started licking my face again.

"Is she gone?" a soft voice asked.

Fuck. Evan was really here, and we were totally in trouble because I didn't think Liv was lying about locking the place down. "I don't know. Don't you dare come out of hiding."

Puff was up, two paws on my hip, sniffing the air and whining as he looked for a mom he couldn't see.

"Sorry, buddy," Evan was saying. "I tried to get him in my arms when I realized what was happening, but he was fast. Now I'm worried if I pick him up, I could screw up the charm. He can't smell me or see me. Poor baby. He's confused."

"Do not pick him up. She's not going to hurt him." I didn't need for Evan to get caught because her puppy wanted attention. "How are you invisible?"

"It's a charm, but she's right. It's not going to work forever, and they've taken control of the whole apartment." Evan's voice came from somewhere to my right. "They have wards up to keep Fenrir from getting to us, and Eddie can't get back into the Under at all which means that neither can Trent. Where's Gray? Did he get away?"

I growled at the thought of my husband leaving at such an inopportune time. "He's witnessing something. Asshole."

"Witnessing?" Evan asked, and I could feel her weight on the bed behind me. "Oh, like a prophecy being fulfilled. I wonder what's happening."

I didn't care. I cared about the fact that I was alone with a competent but still fragile princess who Myrddin would use to unlock my sword, but likely only after he shoved a thrall stone in my head and I joined his drooling sycophants. "I only care about what's happening here. Do you have a charm that might get me out of these bindings?"

"No. I'm pretty sure we're going to need a serious witch to get you out of those, and we don't even have Jade," Evan admitted. "By now Fen's got to know something's going wrong, and he'll stash Jade before he tries to figure out how to get in here."

"How many witches are we facing?"

"The whole of the Profane are in here, but I suspect there are many more up top. That's how they're keeping Eddie out," she explained. "From what I overheard, they've been planning this for a long time. They want to use me to unlock the sword. They aren't sure the sword will respond to Myrddin, so they want you as a backup. Basically they'll kill me and then either Myrddin or you will use the angelic power stored from your fight with Jude to close the doors to the Heaven plane. Whatever angels here will be stuck on Earth and vulnerable to the demons. The new gnome has been working with them. That's how they knew I was here in the Under. I overheard them talking and they faked the whole werewolf attack thing to ensure they could keep Fen and Trent away from the gardens. Either one of them would have been able to smell the secret grove where he grew the belladonna and other forbidden plants."

"Well, he's getting his ass evicted." If I could get out.

"They're worried about Fen. The witches think if they can find me and get us all out of here before the primals wake up, they'll be in the clear," Evan's voice said. "But Fen will come for us. He's out there right now, and he's coming up with some crazy plan to rescue us."

There was another scenario she wasn't thinking of. "Or he's stuck in the records room with Jade trying to find all the information I sent them after. If no one looks for them and tells them what's happening, he won't know. I have to hope Rose tells someone who finds him, but I doubt it. Security won't know where he is, and Eddie can't bring Trent back. We have to pray the primals wake up."

I heard a sniffling. "Or I could go with them."

The last thing I needed was a martyr. "Or you could get me out of these bonds."

"I can't. I don't have any magic, Kelsey. All I've got are a bunch of helpful charms. If you were held with actual rope, I could deal with that," Evan replied, and I could see where she was walking, her weight moving across the carpet. "If Eddie was here, he could probably handle it. Demon servants are excellent with magic, but the new wards will keep him out."

Eddie couldn't follow me anywhere because he was an everyday, normal butler who wasn't forced by contract to do his employer's bidding. Eddie might call me Mistress, but he wasn't a bound servant and could leave at any time. That was the way it should be, but it also meant Eddie wasn't magically bound to me.

Like someone else was.

I couldn't call out to Gray and expect him to race through time and space to find me, but there was someone else. At least I thought he could as long as I was incubating the heir to the House of Sloane.

"Evan, I need you to find a place to hide and be perfectly still. I'm calling in someone who might be able to help us, but I don't trust him at all," I explained.

I didn't want to call him, but I didn't see a way around it. Not if I wanted to get out of this apartment before Liv managed to knock me out again. The truth of the matter was my strength meant nothing against these magical bonds of hers. She'd gotten far stronger than she'd ever been when she had a whole soul, and I wasn't sure I could take her in a fight. I needed to get Evan out of here and regroup. I needed to triple up on charms and wards and talismans because I was going to need them against Liv.

But first I had to get out of here.

"Tix, I need you." I said the words grudgingly, but there was a thrill that went through me when the well-dressed demon was suddenly standing right there.

He looked down at me, big dark eyes widening, and then to Puff, who was jumping and dancing and trying to get the newcomer's attention. "Mistress, I am confused. You did not wish for me to track you and now here you are saying my name so nicely. I suppose I shouldn't have answered, but I am a true and proper servant to my family. You should understand that I did not teach that pup how to tie up his mistress. That must have been the master, and I can't go against his wishes. Not even to save you."

He was going to be troublesome. "The dog didn't tie me up, Tix."

"Oh, then it was the King of all Vampire's daughter." He frowned at the wall. "Don't think you can hide from me, Princess. What is going on? Are the royals moving on my house? I certainly can take care of that and quickly, young lady."

"He can see me." Evan sounded slightly panicked. "I don't think this charm lasts as long as I hoped. It was for emergency use only."

"Well, in the charm's defense, you're still a bit see-through," Tix admitted. "But my master will be cross with you if you've kidnapped his wife and unborn child. And I must ask, where is Trent? He's supposed to be guarding you vigilantly while Lord Sloane does his important work. Fenrir should be here as well. I expected more out of those wolves."

"I wasn't tied up by the dog or Evan. It was the Profane. They're here and they want to drag me and the princess to Myrddin, where they intend to force me into his service."

A hand came up, covering Tix's heart. If he had one. "Oh, that won't do. That won't do at all. Lord Sloane comes down firmly on the side of not allowing demons to take over the Earth plane, and I heartily agree. Do you know what a marketplace looks like in Hell? Well, it's not as nice as a luxury mall here, and demons like to screw everything up. I like Starbucks the way it is, and if I can't get a decent Cronut, I get quite cross. Humans can be clever when they're not being tortured, but honestly, they're useless once you've flayed them open. Can't get any work out of the buggers at all."

"Tix." He was an awfully talky demon. "Magical bonds. Can you get rid of them?"

He tsked and walked around where I could no longer see him. Puff used me as a boost to follow the newcomer.

"Well, that is excellent work," Tix said. "The Profane truly do know what they're doing. And you obviously played straight into their plans because you struggled and now your hands are a bit blue."

"Damn it, Tix. Can you get me out?" He was starting to annoy me again.

My hands and feet were suddenly free, and I could take a full breath.

"Of course I can. What kind of acolyte do you think I am? I know you're used to that little satan, but I'm a true servant of a great house. I'm incredibly powerful, but that power is only used in service of my family. And that includes not allowing the mistress to look quite silly for being captured by a witch. I expected more from the mighty Hunter."

I got to my feet, rolling my hands to get the circulation back. "Well, I was a bit panicked at the time, and I don't exactly have my sword. Not that it would work if I did. I mean it would if I could get close enough to her, but I don't think she's going to let that happen."

I could totally take Liv in any kind of a physical fight, but she could attack me with her damn mind, and from afar.

"Why on all the planes wouldn't the Sword of Light help you kill the witches and protect you from magic? Did you have a fight with her?" Tix gasped as though he'd thought of something terrible. "Is she not doing her job? Who can we talk to about this? I will put in a complaint immediately."

He was awfully prim sounding for a guy with horns poking out from his dark hair.

"You know that only works if I have the queen around," I replied.

"She'll take any companion blood if the situation is dangerous enough," Tix said offhandedly, gesturing toward Evan, who was weirdly opaque at this point. Puff had figured out the new love of his life was somewhat corporeal again, and he'd started wagging and jumping, trying to get to her. "The sword almost certainly has some kind of magical power stored up. Ah, Lord Sloane. So nice of you to join us. I hope you had a lovely visit with whoever you were seeing at the Coven House. Hopefully you weren't breaking your contract."

I turned to see my husband standing at the end of the bed, a bag in his hand. He frowned at Tix. "Why the hell are you here, Tix? I thought we talked about you leaving my wife alone."

I held out a hand to stop the argument. We needed to get out of here. "I called him. Baby, I'm so glad you're here. You have impeccable timing. Liv and her new friends are planning on taking me and Evan to their leader. We could use a ride out."

Gray moved close, wrapping big arms around me. "I can't teleport anyone but myself, Kelsey mine. But I can fight with you. I'm so sorry. It's a compulsion when something important happens. I would have tried to ignore it if I'd known you were in danger. Where's Fenrir?"

I hugged him tight, feeling better than I had since that terrible moment when I'd realized what was happening. I wasn't alone. Gray's demon version was a badass, and between the two of us we had a much better chance. "As far as I know he's down in the records room and he doesn't even know what's happening. I don't think he can get in. They've got wards up. They used the paintings to get around the Under's security systems, and now they've locked down the apartment. The only reason we're not already on our way to the Coven House is they can't find Evan."

Gray pointed. "But she's right there."

Evan's charm had run out of magic. She stood in the sitting area of the big suite, Puff in one hand. "I've been hidden by a charm I carry, but something drained it. It should have worked for another hour or so. I suspect the witches know I'm using some kind of magic, and they're going to find me soon."

Which meant the fight would start.

"I need a weapon." There were no guns allowed in the Under, and they kind of frowned on weapons of any kind, but I was banking on the kiddos having some.

"Ah, I can help you with that. I have Gladys," Gray said, offering me the bag he held.

"Mom found it." Evan moved in, her eyes going wide as she took in the sight. "You've seen my mom. She broke into the Coven House."

Gray's expression softened as he looked at Evan. "She's fine. She got into a fight, but she's fine. You should know your brother has gone through his turn."

My heart threatened to stop. Lee had turned? Lee had died? "What happened?"

"Well, Lee was killed, apparently by Alexander Sharpe," Gray explained.

I knew that son of a bitch was evil. "I will murder him. I will feed that asshole his own balls."

"Did Mom get him?" Evan was far calmer than I was.

"She did. He's gone, and Lee has become what I saw all those years ago," Gray said with pure satisfaction in his tone.

"He's okay?" Lee was a latent vampire. His mother was a companion. Vampires always killed when they rose, and boy would they drain a companion if they could. He wouldn't have meant to. He wouldn't have been able to help himself. "How many people did he kill? How did Zoey get away from him?"

Gray's lips quirked up. "She didn't have to. Kings are not led by impulse."

"I am never going to hear the end of this," Evan said with a shake of her head. "He'll be impossible to live with now."

Lee was a king. I remembered the words Gray had said so long ago. *Don't believe the myth that there can be only one.* At the time I'd thought he was talking about Fenrir being a wolf king, but now I could see how important Lee would be. A vampire king and the son of Myrddin Emrys himself. Lee and Dean both had powerful parents.

I believed now more than ever that Mia Day—daughter of a brilliant witch and a fallen angel—was the weapon I was looking for. Fate or the universe or that elusive God who'd set things in motion liked balance, and this was balance. Heaven and Hell and Earth were represented in those children. Well, they weren't children anymore. They were the keys to defeating the greatest threat the inner planes had ever known, and one of them was missing.

And I wouldn't find her if I was stuck under Myrddin's spell.

"Your brother is fine, as is your mother, and I'm sure at this point they've reunited with your dads," Gray continued. "Zoey lost the grimoire, but she brought us this gift."

I reached into the bag that did not look like it should be able to hold Gladys, but when I opened it, there she was. Something that had been tight inside me eased as I felt her weight in my hand, brought her out of the darkness she'd been left in all these years. "Hello, friend."

"That is a bag of holding. They're very rare," Tix was saying. "But of course the sword is much rarer. I can feel the power coming off her. She does have magic. She has his magic. I can feel it. Why would she have Myrddin's magic?"

"According to my brother, the gossip is Myrddin nicked his fingers on her when he was experimenting before the royals were lost. King Daniel allowed Myrddin to study the sword. When the queen decided to steal the grimoire, she took Gladys, too. How can you feel it?" I didn't like Tix knowing so much about Gladys.

"I'm descended from the same line of angels that created her," Tix explained. "I'm a cousin of the prophet Jacob, though I was born in Hell, my mother descending long, long ago. So I can hear some of her whisperings. She can defend you, Lady Sloane. She can use Myrddin's own magic to fight the witch. All you need is to prime her."

"I can handle it without priming Gladys. Unless you want to pop over to Dallas and bring the queen and king back, since she pretty much has to die in order to prime Gladys." I wasn't about to shove a sword through Evan.

"*We* can handle it," Gray corrected. "Evan, you should hide and don't come out until either Kelsey or I come for you. Do you want me to pop over to Trent and see if Eddie can bring him back?"

"I've been promised all teleporters are locked out for the time being," I explained. "You really can't bring anyone with you?"

"I'm sorry. I could bring Jacob if he needed a lift for some reason, but I've tried on others and it doesn't work," Gray explained.

"Tix could teleport you, but we would have to leave Evan behind. He can only teleport those who belong to the house he serves."

"I can stay behind." Evan's chin had come up in a stubborn expression. "If they manage to catch me, you have to know they won't kill me. They need me alive when they get the sword back. Kelsey can take the sword with her and then we're safe. That way Kelsey and the baby get out okay, and my parents have some time to come up with a plan to free me. Could someone take Puff?"

"Of course," Tix assured her.

"No," I said at the same time. Evan wasn't thinking. No, they wouldn't kill Evan, but they could torture her in ways she couldn't imagine. Her body would be alive, but they could take her soul, and that wasn't happening on my watch. I wouldn't be able to look the queen in the eye again if I lost her daughter.

Tix turned to Gray. "Lord Sloane, I think it best that we leave here. You have a contract, and I believe attacking Myrddin's favorite witches would be deemed in violation of that contract."

"I'm not attacking. I'm defending my wife," Gray growled, and I could see he was already getting into battle mode. His horns had started to poke through his hair, his eyes going dark purple. In a moment they would be pure black.

"I don't think the satans will see it that way," Tix said with a tsking sound. "Would you like me to evacuate Lady Sloane?"

"Don't you lay a hand on her, Tix," Gray ordered.

"As you wish." Tix then moved to Gray and put a hand on him. "But you know I must protect the house. I cannot allow you to break the contract."

I heard Gray shout and then he was gone.

"What the actual fuck?" I hissed, shocked to find myself alone with Evan again.

Evan held Puff close and seemed to be readying herself for what was to come. "He can override Gray if Gray's in danger. His highest purpose is to protect the House of Sloane and its lord. Gray won't be able to come back. We're on our own, which is why you should have let Tix take you, too. You can call him but Gray gave him an order not to touch you, and he won't disobey Gray."

"Except when it comes to allowing Gray to fight beside his wife." The words came out bitter, but there was a certain irony to Gray's predicament. There had absolutely been a time when he would have carted me off if he could. Now he knew how annoying it was to have an overly protective boyfriend. Who I might murder.

"Kelsey, we can't let them take us both," Evan said, her tone soft. "Do you understand that if they take the two of us and Gladys back to the Coven House, Myrddin has everything he needs. He has someone who can wield the sword and someone who can prime it."

"We don't know that you can prime it," I whispered back.

"I can. I know it," Evan said with a surety that made my hands tremble. "As Lee is my dad's son and Rhys has as much power as Papa, I am my mother's daughter. I can prime that sword and Myrddin knows it."

"Then we're going to get out." I wasn't sure how, but I was going to make it happen. "So hide. The longer it takes for them to find you, the better shot we have at the primals waking and saving us. Rose knows what's going on. She'll do her best to wake them, and some of the strongest should be able to. Any minute now they'll breach our doors, and we won't be alone in this. I assure you those primals might prefer a nonviolent life, but they can fight when they need to. I'm going to have a talk with my bestie. You do whatever you have to to stay out of their hands."

I turned to the door, but it was already opening.

A witch stepped through, her hands already crackling with magic. I braced myself.

The battle was about to begin.

Chapter Nineteen

Energy cracked out of the witch's hands, coming for me with the force of a lightning strike.

Gladys seemed to move against my palms, bringing them up above my chest so she caught the hit, absorbing the energy. I had to stand firm or the blowback would have knocked me off my feet.

Something had happened to my sword since the last time I'd held her. She was more powerful than before.

I couldn't hear her speaking with words in my head, but she was absolutely communicating. I could feel her more strongly than I'd ever before. Her needs seemed to pulse out of her hilt and straight into my brain. She wanted to be primed. She wanted blood so she could unleash hell on our enemies. Magic was something she was normally defenseless against, but she knew she could fight back now and she wanted to.

I shifted again, letting her take the lead so we repelled another lightning strike.

A horrible crashing sound shook the place even as I realized if I hit the next strike just the right way, I could blow it back to her. A howling rendered the air around me, but I focused on my opponent.

The next time she sent a bolt my way, Gladys and I moved as one and shot that fucker right back her way.

The witch screamed as her own magic hit her, blowing her back out into the hall.

"Fen's here." Evan put the hellhound down and he jumped at her feet, little bursts of fire puffing from his mouth. Evan had grabbed a small lamp, fashioning a club out of it. "We need to get to him. He's not great against magic. I doubt he has even a single talisman on him. We're supposed to be safe here."

They were supposed to be barely out of high schoolers out in the world starting their lives. Yes, they were supposed to be safe, but they'd lost that chance when they'd lost their parents, and I had to start making things right for the next generation.

And yes, I could hear that Fen had made his way inside from the strangled screams coming from the front rooms. I could also smell the brimstone that came with certain dark magic and knew the most powerful witches in the world were turning that magic on my son. Fen could likely tear his way through an army of wolves, but I didn't know what he could do against pure dark magic. I needed to get out there to help him. "Stay behind me."

I started to move out into the hallway. This was the very back of the apartment. No one could come up behind us, but once we passed the secondary bedrooms, I had to worry.

Of course first I had to worry about my front because the witch I'd blown away from me was on her feet again and trying something new. Out of pure instinct I glanced back to ensure I was covering Evan and a spell hit me, sending a wave of agony through my system. My spine went rigid, and I nearly lost my grip on Gladys. Every muscle seemed like it was on fire, and I had the sudden aching terror that this was happening to my baby, too.

Oh, goddess, I prayed my child couldn't feel this awful pain.

This was the horror I'd been waiting for. I wasn't the only one I put in danger's way, but I had no choice, and I didn't think I could have made another one even if I had. I couldn't have ever run and left Evan and Fenrir here alone.

I had to fight to save us all.

The next spell was coming my way, and I could see the gleam in the witch's eyes. She was enjoying this. She wanted to inflict pain.

I knew I wouldn't move in time. My body was slowed by the last spell she'd attacked with. My muscles were coming back online, but I wouldn't be fast enough.

Evan slammed into me and then ducked, the crackling ball of energy barely missing her as it crashed into the wall behind us.

Up ahead I could hear Liv screaming commands and Fenrir's roar. The witch in the hallway was already getting to her feet, but Evan was faster. Evan leapt onto the witch, punching out with deadly aim. She caught the other female with a hard uppercut, and I heard the crunch of bones cracking, but the witch had a hand on Evan's throat.

I could smell the beginnings of flesh burning, and I forced myself to my feet even as the witch started to gain the upper hand. She was beginning to turn Evan over when Puff jumped onto the back of her neck and set those needle-sharp puppy fangs on the witch's neck.

She screamed, letting Evan go, and when she turned I struck. I rushed forward, catching her in the chest with Gladys and giving my sword even more magical power.

I don't like to kill. I know that sounds wrong for a person who has to do it as much as I do, but it's true. I don't like it, but I'm forced to at times. I wished I could have saved her. I remembered her from the coffee shop. She'd been a smiling woman who made excellent banana bread and could brew a latte that would knock your socks off. If I'd had the time and resources, I would have captured her and figured out a way to reverse whatever she'd managed to do to herself because like Liv, she was covered in black veins. The demon blood would be somewhat like a drug. She would be addicted to it at this point. Like Liv.

But I had to save these kids. I had to save the one inside me. Evan's throat was red, but she pushed herself off the ground and gave her puppy a pat.

"You did good, bud." Evan's voice was deeper than usual.

"Are you okay?" My pain had receded. "Can you breathe?"

She nodded. "Nothing a little vampire blood can't fix. Kelsey, my dad sent blood. It can fix any injuries we take."

"Yes, but that blood is in the medical lab." I wasn't about to leave it in our fridge. The medical lab's fridge had a backup generator in case we lost power. "We need to move this fight out of the apartment and into the public spaces. Rose will have told security. They should be coming to help. When we get through this, I promise you'll have all the blood you need."

I jogged to the end of the hallway and saw that security was already here. Somehow Fenrir had gotten the door open, and it was a bloodbath.

Unfortunately, that blood was coming from both sides. I counted several of the Under's security team on the floor and feared they wouldn't rise again. But Rose had done her job and now we had a chance.

Liv stood on the big table in the dining room, sending out her spells in a way I'd never seen her do before. Bursts of energy came out of her, rolling through her arms like they were simply a part of her. She was graceful and moved with purpose as she took out her enemies.

Fenrir was a massive presence. Even in the majestic, palace-like apartment he looked oversized. He was just outside the great area we were in where the living room and dining room met and the hallways flowed to other parts of the apartment. He batted his big paws against some invisible barrier.

Liv had found a way to keep Fen out of this fight, and I needed him in it. He backed up and tried to jump over the barrier, his body leaping almost to the high ceiling, but he bounced right off whatever spell Liv had set.

"It won't hold him forever, Calliope." Liv jumped off the table, her stilettoed boots hitting the hardwood floors. "Find the fucking princess. We need to get out of here. Where is Talia?"

I suspected Talia was dead in the hallway, and I kind of thought I'd seen Puff peeing on her. We might need to worry about training the pup not to mark everywhere.

"Evan, I need you to hide until…" I turned and Evan was nowhere to be seen. Which would have been great if I'd thought for a second she'd decided to hide, but I knew better.

These kids didn't sit on the sidelines, and it had been a long time since they'd been given a ton of parental advice when it came to battle. They wouldn't hide and hope to be saved. They would take insane chances because in their world no one came to save them. In this world, they were the heroes and I was a newcomer they couldn't trust completely yet.

"Why don't you ask your friend." Calliope pointed my way with a snarky expression on her face. "I thought you said you used *liga inimicos meos*. Guess you're losing your touch."

Liv turned, a fierce frown on her face. "What the hell? How did you…" She shook her head as though it didn't matter. She held her hands up and started in on the Latin.

I wasn't about to take that a second time. I charged her and knocked her off balance. I twisted, trying to bring Gladys's hilt down on her head but she kicked out, catching me in the knee and proving that she'd taken some combat classes.

When we were a team, she'd always let me handle the physical stuff.

Pain flared through me, but I was used to ignoring pain. The problem was I didn't want to kill her. I wanted to incapacitate her. My bestie needed to spend some time in magical rehab, and today was intervention day.

A thick book came right for my head, but I managed to duck it along with a couple of knives. Liv was far better at telekinesis than she had been. She'd been studying up on everything except how to be a good person and not an evil one.

I did not manage to duck whatever piece of fire Liv sent my way. It singed my shoulder, burning the shirt I wore and singeing my skin. I hissed against the pain but kept moving.

Three more witches entered the scene, and it looked like they'd called in the cavalry.

If they surrounded me they could take me apart, could literally pull me limb from limb without ever laying a hand on me.

I could feel the tingles of someone trying to get in my head.

I slammed the wall down and a petite witch cried out.

"Don't try that with her," Liv warned. "Her head is too thick to get into. Concentrate on keeping that fucking wolf out of here and off my back."

Fenrir seemed to hear her and bounced against some invisible wall, trying to get to his prey.

"You can't win this one, Kelsey," Liv said, her dark eyes glowing. "I know you're good with that sword, but I have the master's power. We all have demonic magic, and you're nothing more than muscle with a shiny sword at this point."

I lunged her way, wanting to show her exactly how good I could be with a sword, but that was the moment she shimmered in and out, losing her corporeal body for just long enough to avoid the pointy end of Gladys.

Frustration welled. We were in close quarters and I still couldn't physically overpower her. That would change soon, though. "When Fenrir gets through that wall, you're all going to be in trouble."

It looked like Fen had already taken out a couple of the witches. There were a few bodies in the living room and a shit ton of blood Eddie was going to spend days cleaning. Maybe Tix had some tips on how to get witch blood out of Victorian era rugs.

"You should go back through those paintings again before he breaks down that wall of yours." I didn't want to let her go, but I did want to keep the body count down.

A snarl brought Liv's lip up. "Do you think I'm doing this for me? I rather thought I was being a good friend and not killing your son. But hey, I like to do what you want."

She brought her hand up and suddenly there was a popping sound and Fen was through. He charged toward the dining room, his mouth coming open and fangs showing.

"Make him hurt, ladies," Liv ordered.

Fen was in mid leap when they caught him. Three witches had managed to triangulate around him, and their magic trapped him midair, making his body twist in obvious agony.

My heart damn near stopped. She was trying to hurt my baby. My best friend was trying to hurt my son.

"We can kill him, my lady," one of the witches proclaimed.

"No, not yet," Liv said quickly. "I think we'll take him with us. I'm sure the master would be interested in him."

Fen's jaw was open, caught in a soundless scream.

I raised my sword, ready to kill them all. I held Gladys at the perfect height to skewer the nearest one right through the heart.

And that was when I realized I was stuck. I couldn't move. I could barely breathe. My son was being tortured right in front of me. He was trapped in a bubble of pain, and none of his strength could help him. He was the king of his kind, but three witches could take his life so easily.

I was a Hunter, but I couldn't fucking save my own son.

"I'm not going to kill him." Liv had moved in behind me, whispering in my ear. "I'll find a way to let him get away, but not until you agree to come with me. And tell me where the princess is.

Thanks for bringing the sword, by the way. I wasn't counting on that. I thought I would give my master a third of what he needed, but now I get to hand him his dream on a silver platter."

"Fuck you," I managed to grit between clenched jaws.

I could feel her hands on my shoulders. "Don't be so stubborn. You'll see when I get you back to the Coven House. You'll see how good it can be. We'll be a family again. You have to see that you can't win. We have all the magic of the Hell plane in our corner."

An arrow flew by my eyes, thudding and landing right in the heart of the witch to my left. Her hand came up, but she was already falling to the ground. Well, at least I knew what Evan had been doing. She'd been going for the weapons she'd been forbidden to bring.

I was so happy that kid was a rebel.

The spell holding Fenrir up failed and he hit the floor, turning immediately and howling.

Another arrow went flying, taking out a second witch, but chaos had already begun.

Liv headed toward Fenrir, her hands out.

I still couldn't move. The spell still had me, and I couldn't counter it. I felt tears pierce my eyes because I knew the reason. I'd neglected learning any kind of magic because until a week ago, I'd never needed it. She'd been there. I'd counted on Liv. I'd had my team behind me and I trusted every one of them with all of my soul, and now she was the reason I couldn't save my son.

"We need reinforcements," Liv shouted as she somehow managed to blow Fen back. I watched as his massive body slammed into the wall behind him. "And someone catch that princess or heads are going to roll."

An arrow shot straight for Liv but she held out a hand and it bounced off some invisible shield. She hadn't even looked back, couldn't have seen it coming, but Liv had known. Evan tried again but with the same results.

A swooshing sound marked the appearance of even more witches. They climbed out of the paintings, legs sliding through first and then the sleek glide of arms, pulling themselves through. Gladys pulsed in my hand, insistent and wanting. She wanted in this fight, wanted to unleash the energy she had stored up, and I'd made her impotent. It was the first time I'd felt her anger.

We had the power to wipe them all from the Earth plane, and we would use their master's magic to do it. She loved the delicious irony of it all. I could feel all those emotions flowing through me. Something had changed. She'd taken in Myrddin's blood and somehow converted a portion of it to give her more power, more communication with the woman who wielded her. Me.

She wanted me to kill them all, but she was stuck in my hand as I watched a group of witches surround Fenrir.

Tears leaked from my eyes, but I couldn't brush them away. Liv had told them not to kill Fen, but would they listen to her? Would Liv decide to punish me for fighting her?

I struggled to move, fought with every cell of my being, and I couldn't. Panic surged through me. We were being completely overrun, and they were holding Fenrir down with their spells. He howled out in pain.

"I have her!"

I watched in horror as a dark-haired witch dragged Evan into my field of vision. She had her hands wrapped around Evan's arms, and I could see where the princess had started to bleed.

"Thank the goddess." Liv turned, her relief obvious. "Take her through. The rest of us will follow. We need to clean up here and make sure all our people are out of the Under."

Evan looked over at me, tears in her eyes. "Kelsey, it's the only way. Can't let Fen die."

I tried to shake my head, tried to force the words out, but this spell seemed to work like the bindings Liv had placed on me earlier. They tightened when I struggled, and I felt pressure at my throat like an invisible hand choking the life out of me. If I didn't stop moving, it would cut off my oxygen supply and make it super easy for Liv to get me through her portal.

Fucking painting. I hate art now. You really can't trust it. One minute it's a nice little scene, something to brighten up the place, and the next it's a fucking portal to Hell.

We were about to be dragged through, and I didn't know what would happen.

I'd lost twelve years, and now I would lose the rest.

"We should kill the wolf," a dark voice said. "It's what the master would want. We kill the fucking dog and bring his pelt back."

Liv held a hand up. "No. We're not... Why would we kill him when we can sell him to the wolves who want him? He's a valuable bargaining chip."

Evan turned her head to look Fen's way, and then her whole body stiffened as though getting ready for something. Likely steeling herself for what happened next.

I wanted to tell her to survive, to stay alive because her parents would do anything to get her back.

Including trading their lives for hers.

I'd never felt so utterly and completely useless as I did in that moment when I realized I was going to lose them all. I hadn't meant to leave them in this world, hadn't meant for them to grow up in a place I couldn't even recognize, but they had, and I was failing them again.

"Hey!" The witch who held Evan kicked back, but I could see Puff defending Evan, sinking those fangs into the witch's ankle.

Evan took the opportunity to pull away.

Run. Run as fast as you can. I tried to yell the words but they wouldn't come out. I wanted her to run and not look back, to get out as fast as she could. She had a whole life in front of her. She was supposed to be the one I protected.

Instead I stood there unable to move as the witch who'd held her started trying to kill Puff, Liv argued about whether they should murder my son or sell him for profit, and Evan looked at me. So fucking young. So brave.

"It's the only way," she said.

And ran forward, impaling herself on Gladys.

I watched in complete horror as she reached up, taking the blade in her hands and forcing herself further on. The blade slid deep, and Evan began to bleed.

"Tell Fenrir I loved him," she whispered and then her head fell back.

And all the power in the world seemed to flow through my veins.

Chapter Twenty

The world seemed to recede around me, and there was zero doubt that this would work. Evan was as much a queen as her mother, and Gladys approved of her blood.

The first time the queen and I had worked this magic, Gladys had shown us our history, flashing us images of when we had been warriors, Amazons on the banks of the Thermodon. Gold magic had flowed through me, and I'd been suffused with a sense of joy.

Not so this time. This time the horror at what Evan had done was shoved back as a silvery cloud rushed over my brain and time seemed to still. Evan and I were caught in whatever her blood had unleashed, and I felt icy fingers move over my brain.

Myrddin. He was here. A piece of him, some echo that lived in his blood, now existed inside Gladys.

"Can you see her?" Evan's voice reached out through the fog we found ourselves in. She was here with me because she was connected to Gladys. Because Gladys was lodged in her chest.

At first I thought Evan was talking about Gladys, and then I realized I wasn't where I'd been before. I was standing in the Council House, the way it had been before I'd fallen through the painting.

Evan stepped back and she was healthy and whole, though I suspected that was an illusion, too.

Gladys soaked up power. I'd known that, but now I realized she could soak up memories, too, and she wanted us to see this one.

I was fairly certain we hadn't been transported anywhere, that this was all taking place in my head or somewhere safe Gladys could take us to. A place where Evan wasn't impaled on her. Where she wasn't dying, and I was safe. I could feel we were protected here.

But someone wasn't. Screams filled the hallway and the floor beneath me shook.

"This is the floor Mia lived on." In this place Evan stood beside me and she was whole and healthy. She looked up and down the hallway. "Did we go back in time?"

I shook my head. "We didn't go anywhere at all. We're still in the Under, but Gladys wants us to see something. When this happened with your mother, she sent visions to us, visions of our history going back to the beginnings of the companions. It wasn't like this though. It was like a movie playing through my head. This feels real. I suspect she wants to show us more recent history this time."

"This is the day, isn't it?" Evan asked with a grim certainty.

I nodded, not needing her to clarify. There was only one day this could be. "Yes. You're somewhere up in the penthouse. Or perhaps you've already left for Italy at this point. I'm not sure about the timing." I could feel something was coming, what she wanted us to see, but I had to face the elephant in the room. "Evan, what you did... I'm not sure you can survive that. I think you hit your heart."

My gut twisted at the thought of losing Evan. I had to find a way to save her.

Her eyes stayed on the hallway. "They were going to kill Fen."

"I don't think Liv would have let that happen." Liv seemed determined to keep him alive. "She knows I'll never forgive her if she takes my son's life."

"Well, the other witches don't care. They weren't listening to her," she said quietly. "Fen is uniquely vulnerable to magic. He can't get the same tattoos we can that fight the influence. He loses them every time he changes, and his body even clears the ones with silver in the ink. We've tried everything. Fen being surrounded by witches is one of my nightmares. And Fen can be fast. He can get to dad's blood. I can hold on. I don't think it's fully in my heart, but I'm having a hard time breathing. It's odd to be outside my body but to still feel it. And I meant what I said. There was no other way."

I wasn't sure about that, but the door at the end of the hallway opened and suddenly a familiar man ran toward us, a blonde child clinging to him as he held her.

Felix and Mia Day.

"Can they see us? How can Gladys know what happened this day?" Evan asked.

Another thing I wasn't sure about, and then I was.

"Dr. Day," a deep voice said.

I turned and Myrddin stepped from behind us, proving beyond all doubt that we were purely in memory now. He completely ignored us, stepping in front of the door to the Day's apartment and blocking them from safety.

Felix stopped on a dime, his blue eyes going wide as his arms tightened around his daughter. He stopped and tried to turn, but there was another witch behind him. I didn't recognize her but her hand sparked with electricity.

"Stay back," Felix ordered, but I wasn't sure what kind of power he could put behind his will. He'd given up all his power when he'd opted for a mortal life.

"I'd like to know where the children are." Myrddin wore plain black slacks and a dark shirt. He looked to be in the prime of his life, and perhaps when you're immortal you always are. "Something's happened to King Daniel, and I need to ensure the children are protected. Why is your daughter crying? Mia, dear, this is a good day. This is the day our kind has waited for centuries to see."

"I want Lee, Daddy. I want to see Lee." Mia buried her face in her father's neck. "And Mommy."

"Stay away from her," Felix ordered, and I could see the rush of panic on his face. He was feet away from safety. His home was right there, and I was absolutely certain Sarah Day had turned that place into a fortress. But he hadn't quite made it.

He'd used some of his precious time to ensure Jade was all right. He'd taken the time he'd had and gifted that child with her life. He'd been every bit the guardian angel he'd once been.

He'd given up that life, fallen in love, and then simply fallen. He'd had everything he'd ever wanted. A family. Friends. Love. A human life, and now he would have to know human tragedy.

"Why should I stay away from a witch with such potential?"

Myrddin asked the question casually, as though he wasn't threatening to take a daughter from her father. "I can feel her strength. She will far outreach her mother. She has her mother's dark power but also her father's light. I can kill that light for her and then she can own the darkness. She can be a queen." He stared for a moment. "She can be my queen one day."

"She's eleven. You stay away from my daughter," Felix said with ferocity.

"I can be reasonable." Myrddin pressed closer, and I had the deepest desire to get in between them, to defend these people I cared about.

But they were ghosts who moved right through me.

The hallway was filling up with witches and one… At first I thought he was a child. He stood at the end of the hallway, roughly four feet tall, wearing what looked like almost medieval armor, though I quickly realized it was only a breastplate. Was that an axe in his hand? The weapon was almost as tall as the…he wasn't a child at all.

He wasn't supposed to be here. Like we weren't supposed to be here.

"Felix!" Sarah Day rounded the corner. She completely ignored the what had to be a Fae creature with the axe at his side. But she didn't ignore the witches in front of her.

"She has mom's bag of holding," Evan said on a gasp.

And she had her own rage to guide her. Sarah held up her free hand and I saw her lips move a bare second before the witches who'd been behind her husband disintegrated, turning to ash and falling to the floor. Sarah's eyes had gone black, and I noticed she was bleeding heavily from her right side. She'd been in a fight, and she hadn't come out untouched.

"Get behind me, Felix," she ordered, moving around him.

"You're hurt." The words were said with a gasp.

Myrddin's eyes had gone dark, too. His face had lost the smooth lines of the politician he usually employed. The ferocious look on his face was exactly why his last name was Satanspawn. "You have my grimoire, bitch. You think I don't know what's in that bag? The queen stole it from me. Give it to me and I might let your child live."

Sarah forced herself in front of Felix, her hand coming up. "I will never let you take my child. I will die first."

"You're going to die either way." Myrddin's shoulders went back, and the air cracked around us.

Sarah muttered a spell under her breath, and Myrddin seemed to go stiff for a moment. He snarled and suddenly I felt a gush of wind blow past me as he started to move again.

"You're weak," he snarled and held a hand out.

Sarah dropped the bag and her hands went to her throat as though trying to touch the invisible fingers choking the life out of her. Her feet left the floor.

"Oh, goddess," Evan breathed. "How do I tell my mother Sarah's dead? They're all dead, aren't they?"

"Oh, Princess, you should have a little faith."

I gasped as I realized the small dude who'd been at the end of the hall was suddenly beside us. I'd thought he was Fae. Wondered if he might be a gnome. Yes, I was looking at an axe-wielding gnome. I frowned and stared down at him, giving him my most ferocious glare. "Are you here to fuck me over like your friends in the Under did? What the hell is this?"

If he was offended, he didn't show it. His lips quirked up, and he had a strong Scottish-sounding accent that told me he was likely Unseelie. "It was only Elrin who fucked you over, Hunter. The others of my kind remain true to the Under. They'll be quite devastated when they realize one of their own killed Alvis and Relda. They're doing all right, by the way. You should let Jade know Relda is fine and wants her to know she loved her like a daughter and blames her for nothing."

I realized the visions around us had stopped. Like someone had hit pause. No one moved except the three of us.

Gladys hadn't done that. It wasn't the way she worked.

And that was the moment I realized I wasn't truly dealing with a gnome. The hair on the back of my neck stood up because there was only one creature I truly feared. "You're an angel."

"One of the newest," he agreed.

Evan frowned. "Seriously? I thought they were all blonde and looked like Felix."

The gnome angel snorted. "You humans like to think all the planes of the universe were built for you. Or maybe you think we're all separate, but you, Hunter, should have learned that the planes with all their vast species are connected. We might look different, but we come from the same place."

I had learned that. I'd learned it when Summer took her throne as the queen of the outer planes. Her magic powered them, but her magic was fueled by something too. By the Goddess. By what some humans called God. Of course an angel was incredibly powerful. "You can look like anything you want, can't you? The Days came to Zoey and the others in a form they would feel most comfortable with."

He grinned. "Aye, they did, but you're different, Hunter, and you, Princess Evangeline. I rather thought you could see me for who I was during my life here on the planes. You could understand better if I told you I was a warrior once in an Unseelie kingdom. When I died, I was given the choice all souls are. I could try again, move to a different form, join my soul with the divine, or I could have the job I'd always wanted. I could protect the people I loved. Turns out on this side it's easy to love a lot of souls. It's easy to look past all the imperfections of life to see the soul underneath."

I could feel a familiar sensation pulse off the gnome…angel.

I'd done my best. I hadn't meant to leave the kids, and they knew it. They loved me, and it was all going to be okay because I was strong enough to save them. I didn't have to worry about the child in my womb because I would love him and do everything I could to support him. The same way I did for all I loved. For all of my flaws, I was perfect because I didn't give up.

"You're the new Faith," I said quietly. Angels, I'd discovered, came in threes and they were the embodiments of ideals. In this case—Love, Justice, Faith.

I'd killed the last Faith in the arena.

"Aye, and I'm sorry for what my brother put you through all those years ago," he replied with such sincerity. "It might be hard for you to believe in me after what he did. That's why I wanted you to see me as I was in my prior life. Jude had never walked the planes. He was a child in many ways. I am not, Hunter. I know what it means to love and to lose. I know what it means to be abandoned and what it means to be found again. Perhaps that's why I was chosen. Or maybe I was chosen because only a gnome who was foolish enough to think he could be a warrior would be willing to do what I am now."

"What are you doing? And how are you doing it?" Panic was back in my head. "Please tell me I'm not standing here in some 3D history class while they're tearing my son apart."

Evan gasped.

The angel held up a hand. "Of course not. We're in a place the Sword of Light can create. She's letting me use her to show you a few things. The Heaven plane understands what could happen if Myrddin follows through on his plan. We're of two minds as to how to deal with it. Three, really. A small group would prefer to use this as an excuse to wipe all the lower planes clean and start over again."

"Okay, that seems extreme." I should have known there would be angels who would rather wipe us all out.

"The rest of us are stuck between helping and staying back and watching," the angel explained. "I am on the side of helping. My brother and sister are with me, though they could not be here today because of circumstances you'll understand soon."

"Aren't you not supposed to directly impact your charges' lives?" Evan asked.

"We're not allowed to sit down and have a chat, to tell you what you should do, but what I'm doing is diving right into a gray area," he explained. "And we're protected from the other angels' sight by the sword. As for the goddess, well, she will do as she will. She can stop this from happening if she likes."

"She?" I asked. "The other guy talked about his father. Are you an angel for the Fae goddess?"

"Why would you think they would be different?" he asked. "If an angel would come to you in the form most likely to give you comfort, why would you think the goddess would be different? That's what I never understood. In the end we see what we want to see. Our eyes can't be trusted. It's our souls we should let do this work, the work of faith. It's comforting to believe we know exactly who created us and that he or she or they work in a way we can understand. But that's not faith. Faith is the knowledge that we cannot know what fabric the universe is made of, but we trust that it can warm us anyway."

So God had a lot of names. Got it. I didn't have time to contemplate the metaphysical.

"Is Sarah dead?" I prayed this wasn't where the sneak peek ended because I wasn't sure I could go on not knowing. "Are they all dead?"

"Perhaps you should watch. We can't stay for too long, but my siblings would very much like for you to understand what happened and that there is a way forward. What is lost does not have to remain lost." He stepped back and suddenly the world started to move once more.

Sarah was held feet off the floor, her throat in Myrddin's invisible hand. The bag had dropped, and Felix had placed Mia on the floor, trying to bring his wife back down. The scene in front of me was pure horror, and I couldn't imagine the trauma being done to this lovely family and all for one man's ambition.

"I can't watch it." Evan had tears running down her cheeks.

"Just a moment more, Princess," the angel advised.

Something rolled by my feet, a small crystal ball of some kind. It rolled to where Myrddin stood and then flashed, sending light everywhere. Myrddin gasped and then he was gone, disappearing in an instant.

Sarah fell to the ground, her husband dropping to his knees.

He put a hand on her and his head tipped back. "Oliver! Felicity! Please. Please."

"He calls to his brother and sister." The gnome got misty eyed. "Most of us aren't truly siblings in the way others are, but Felicity and Felix were made from the same clay."

"We have to get inside," Sarah was saying, her voice tortured.

"I'll help you, Momma." Mia held the bag of holding. "I'll take it inside and we can hide it for the queen."

Sarah nodded, allowing Felix to help her up. She limped toward her door, her husband at her side. "He'll be back. He's likely making his way back right now."

"What was that?" Felix leaned over and picked his wife up.

"A *sphaera motus*," she replied. "It's a transportation spell. It took him somewhere. Who sent it?"

"I don't know. It doesn't matter. Mia, get inside." Felix managed to get the door open. He looked back but the hallway seemed empty. The door closed and we were alone again.

"Who saved her?" Evan asked. "Was it one of the academics? Why didn't they come here and talk to Sarah? They could have gotten the Days out of the building."

I stared down the hall. Whoever had sent that sphere had likely stood where the hallway turned toward the outer stairs. They'd popped out and then run. They hadn't wanted to be seen.

She hadn't wanted anyone to know that she was helping.

"You can go look," the angel offered. "She might still be trying to get to the stairs."

Tears flooded my eyes. "Why would she save them?"

"Liv?" Evan started for the end of the hall.

I didn't have to. The actual embodiment of faith stood staring up at me with his kind eyes. Whatever else he'd wanted me to see, he'd also wanted me to see this. To know it in my soul.

Liv was redeemable.

"She hadn't lost that piece of her soul yet," he said. "This is who she is with her whole soul intact. She was scared and got caught up in something terrible and couldn't find a way out. You are her only hope. I want you to understand that it is not your responsibility to save her."

"Like fuck it isn't," I said through my tears.

"There's my Hunter," he said with a fierce smile. "You're mine, you know. You were Jude's and now you're mine, and I won't let you down. Not ever, lass."

Evan jogged back, a shocked expression on her face. "That was Liv. Liv saved Sarah. Why would she do that?"

That was a complex question. Liv had been filled with fear. I needed to view it that way because it's easy to forget that almost all bad behavior has its roots in fear. She'd lost her power. She'd loved the life she'd led, and that life was impossible without her magic. It was too dangerous to keep her on the team, and she feared she would lose not only the ability to protect herself and her friends, but she could lose those friends altogether.

She'd been afraid, and it led her down this path.

Could I lead her back?

I did what I should have done in the beginning. I gave the angelic gnome the respect he deserved. I got to one knee so I could look him in the eyes. "Is that all you want us to see, Faith? I will follow you if I need to see more."

"Only one more thing." He snapped his fingers and we were suddenly inside the Days' apartment.

Everything looked perfectly normal. I could even smell coffee and caught a glimpse of the table laid out with pancakes. It looked like the Days had been enjoying a breakfast for two before the attack had occurred. They had likely sent their daughter off to school and wanted to enjoy a quiet morning before Felix's appointments began.

It was nice and normal. Except now it was all ruined.

Sarah lay on the couch, her skin pale. Felix held her hand, smoothing back her hair.

"I love you." Tears streaked down his face. "I love you so much."

"You have to get Mia out of here," Sarah whispered.

Mia's head shook. "No. I'm not leaving Momma."

"We're safe here," Felix insisted. "No one can get in. Zoey will come for us. I know we're not sure where she is, but I have faith that she's alive and she'll come to help us. We just have to stay alive. I can get to the clinic."

Felix's voice was as hoarse as his wife's. I knew what he would want from the clinic. What we would need. Vampire blood. Daniel's blood was kept in the clinic for emergencies.

Sarah's normally perfect hair was matted with blood on one side, the muddy color contrasting with the seafoam green of the rest of her long bob. She grimaced as she forced herself to sit up. "No. You can't leave this apartment. He's already outside the door. I can feel him trying to find a way in."

Sure enough, I heard whisperings behind the door.

"We can't stay inside here forever," Felix whispered as though he didn't want Mia to hear.

She did, of course. "Lee's mom and dads won't leave us here. They won't."

Sarah reached out a hand to her daughter, the strain of movement obvious. "Baby, they're not here or none of this would be happening. I don't know where Myrddin managed to send them, and I pray to the goddess they're still alive, but they can't save us this time. Kelsey is gone, too, and I suspect their children have been taken somewhere safe. I saw Gray coming out of the penthouse, and he'd left Trent up there. I think he did what he could to save the kids."

"Uncle Neil…" Mia insisted.

"If he's done what we planned, he's already working to get as many of us as he can out through the tunnels we built," Sarah said with a cough that rattled her chest.

"We have tunnels?" I hadn't known we had tunnels.

"Uncle Neil and Aunt Sarah built them years ago," Evan explained. "They didn't trust the hold Myrddin had over my dads. They built the tunnels as an emergency option if they ever got caught and needed a way out. Like this day. Not everyone has an Eddie. She looks so bad. How do I tell my mom?"

A light shone and suddenly Oliver and Felicity Day were in the room.

I breathed a sigh of relief. "I don't think you have to."

Felicity quickly moved around the couch. She was everything I viewed an angel should be. Delicate. Beautiful.

But now I could see that our gnome angel was right. Angels would be as different as the charges they protected, and it should be that way.

I glanced down at the gnome. "You aren't here?"

He shook his head. "I'd only just joined them at this point. I stayed behind to ensure they didn't get caught. We were told by the archangels not to be involved, but they couldn't leave their brother's family behind. So we made a plan."

Felicity sank to her knees before Sarah while Oliver moved in to put a hand on Felix's shoulder.

"You came," Felix said, his voice unsteady.

"You are and will always be my brother," Oliver replied solemnly. "I will do anything I can to help you, but you have to know we've been told not to interfere."

Felix's shoulders dropped. "Then there's nothing you can do."

"They can take Mia." Sarah clutched at Felicity's arms. "Please save Mia."

Oliver's eyes rolled as though he thought all the drama was a bit much. "As if Michael's edicts can stop me. Felicity, if you please."

Felicity held a hand up and pure white light pulsed from it and into Sarah's body. She was whole again in seconds, the color coming back to her face. Felicity even got rid of the blood, and Sarah looked like she'd recently gotten dressed and was ready for work.

Felix dragged his wife into his arms, holding her tight. "Thank you. Thank you, brother. Thank you, sister."

"She's not entirely out of the woods." Felicity reached down to hold Mia's hand, bringing it up to her heart. "Sweetie, I need you to go and pack a bag of your favorite things. We're going on an adventure. You have to be quick. Don't worry about clothes. You'll find some there, but I want you to bring your favorite toys and books and pictures. Okay?"

Mia nodded and ran off.

"Where are we going? What's wrong with Sarah?" Felix asked.

Felicity's lovely face looked grim. "She seems to have been hit with a spell that's affected her heart."

"He tried to pull it out of my body," Sarah admitted. "Myrddin and I fought earlier. I managed to get away, but he knew where I would go. He wants my heart's blood. I warded the whole building with it. He can get into all of the public spaces and there are some rooms he can easily fight the wards off, but some places like this apartment, he will never get through. Only Neil or Zoey can get in here outside my family."

Felicity nodded. "That would do it. I can't fix this here. But where I'm taking you, your body should heal over time."

"We can't leave," Felix said with a shake of his head. "Our friends are out there dying. They are our family."

"And you've done right by them." Oliver pointed to the bag of holding. "You rescued the grimoire and the Sword of Light. Had they been left where the queen put them, Myrddin would eventually have found them. The grimoire would call to him. By leaving the bag here in this apartment, it is protected by Sarah's heart's blood. At some point in the future we believe the queen will return for it. It needs to remain on this plane, but you cannot."

"Because of Sarah's heart?" Felix asked.

Felicity nodded. "Yes. We were going to take you there anyway, but for a different reason. While we are willing to go against the archangel's decree, we cannot flaunt our disobedience or we risk that faction taking action. We have consulted with our new brother and he believes if we are discreet, the archangels will view this as nothing more than two siblings helping their beloved brother. They do not see the patterns that are emerging."

"Patterns?" Sarah asked.

"Mia is going to be extraordinarily powerful one day," Oliver explained. "She must not fall into the wrong hands. Her upbringing is very important. She needs to stay on the side of the light. If she ever fell into Myrddin's hands… The things he could make her do would break this plane."

Sarah's expression went from grave to bright, though I could see the strain in her eyes as Mia ran back in. The girl had a backpack around her shoulders and a big stuffed bunny in her arms. "Hey, you ready?"

"Can we see Lee?" Mia asked.

Felicity got to one knee. "One day. I promise. One day you will find each other again and you'll be ready. He will need you so much. But for now it must be this way so your mother can heal."

Tears pierced Mia's eyes, but she nodded.

"We cannot take you. Again, that would be too much interference," Oliver was saying to Felix. "But we can show you the way and promise there is a village waiting to take you in. It's a Heavenly plane."

"One of the minor planes that the archangels don't care about, I suspect." Felix had relaxed.

"Yes. It's very beautiful and peaceful, and they will welcome your wife and daughter," Felicity promised. "They are eager to learn from you all and to share their knowledge with you. Mia can grow and learn without the trauma she would certainly experience on this plane."

"It would have been nice if they could have taken all the kids," I said with no small bitterness because my child had gotten a full dose of that trauma. So had the young woman beside me.

"Some heroes need peace to balance their souls," the gnome said. "Some could turn if twisted the wrong way, as you have seen with your friend. And some are so solid they can wash themselves in the darkness and never once lose the light." He turned Evangeline's way. "You, Princess, are a light. Don't forget. You are literally made of light, and no amount of darkness can take you if you don't let it."

Evan went still. "That sounds like a threat."

I shook my head. "It sounds like he knows something we don't, and we should probably listen to him."

I was brought out of my revelations by Sarah taking a long breath. "If you can't take us, then I should get ready. I suspect opening a door to one of the Heavenly planes is going to take a bit of magic. I also want to write a letter to Zoey. I need her to look for us."

"Well, if we had time, I would hunt down one of the doors and send you through," Oliver explained as they walked toward the back of the apartment. "There are a couple, but they're well hidden. The Fae are good at hiding doors and piercing veils, aren't they?"

"Leave the queen a letter, but you have to let her know Myrddin cannot be allowed to access the portal. If he could gain access to one of the Heavenly planes, the damage he could do would be terrible," Felicity said. "And we must hurry. Our window is closing. You can't stay another full day here. Be quick with your note and even quicker with your magic. Leave the queen a map she can follow so one day she can release you."

The door shut, and I knew we'd seen what we'd had to see. The angels were playing fast and loose with their rules and regulations and all to help us. We had allies, and I intended to follow their sage advice.

I was going to have to go into the belly of the beast. I would have to get into that apartment and find a way to follow the Days to their refuge.

It looked like I would have to go to a place I'd never thought to see. Heaven.

"I will seek Mia Day as soon as I can," I vowed. "I think I know a couple of young men she needs to meet." I frowned as I thought about the whole "priming" situation. "Does Heaven take a stand on the whole one man, one woman thing?"

The gnome laughed, a surprisingly booming sound that filled the sad place with joy. "Ah, no, lass, and thank the goddess for it. That's a human thing. On the plane I spent my mortal life on, it was quite normal to form triads. My own brothers shared a wife." His smile became bittersweet. "I only wanted one woman. The most beautiful woman in all the lands. I get to watch over her though, and she's happy. So no, don't think there's some punishment for loving more than one person. I have to go. The Sword of Light is ready for her fight. She's angry about being touched by Myrddin, enraged about what he planned to do with her. But don't forget—you count, too, Hunter. She does nothing without your good hand to guide her."

I wasn't sure what he meant by that, but I was ready to fight. "She'll show me how to counter Liv's spells?"

His lips kicked up. "All you have to do is follow her lead. You've got Myrddin's power, and she's been soaked in it. She's figured out a thing or two and is ready to show off." He turned Evan's way and went somber. "Don't forget what I said, Princess. Your light cannot be dimmed by anyone but you. Remember. This was the only way. When the consequences come, you can find joy in them or allow them to turn you bitter."

"Consequences?" Evan asked.

"Aye." He hefted his axe, leaning it on his shoulder. "There are always consequences. Some seem hard, but when they're accepted we can find beauty in them. Are you ready?"

I steeled myself. "Yes."

"No," Evan said at the same time.

I turned to her, raising my brows.

She shrugged. "Well, you're not the one bisected by a sentient sword and about to face some kind of weird consequences."

There was truth to that. "It's going to be okay."

"That it will, Hunter. Remember that when you want to kill the queen," he said with a grin and turned.

Wow. I wanted to ask about that but I got the feeling I would only get one more question, and I had to know. "Hey, what can I call you? Did you take Jude's name?"

He turned and the lamp behind him made the sweetest halo around his helmet. "Bah, as though I would take that name. No. I like the one me mum gave me all those years ago. You can call me Duffy. And I'll be around, Hunter."

He lifted the axe and brought it back down, tapping the floor, and then we were back in the real world once more.

Chapter Twenty-One

The world came back and I knew what I had to do. The thought of the pain I was about to cause made me sick, but she'd been right. Now that I was here and Gladys was pulsing insistently against my palm, I knew Evan had been right. This was the only way. I pulled the sword from Evan's chest, her eyes going wide. She stepped back and then her body started to fall to the floor.

The world seemed to have gone oddly quiet. All the witches had turned, watching the daughter of the royal house sacrifice her life rather than allow herself to be taken.

"Stupid girl," Liv hissed.

Evangeline Donovan-Quinn wasn't stupid. She knew what they were capable of. She'd lived her whole life in utter terror of being caught by them. Used by them. She'd known what these women would do. They would kill her, but not before they'd used her to torture her parents. They had no souls.

"Evan?" Fen was suddenly in his human form, his eyes on the love of his life as she lay bleeding on the floor.

He started running toward her, completely heedless of the fact that he was surrounded by witches.

They did not forget him.

I watched as one of the witches held out her hands and started to send a spell toward Fenrir.

It was odd, but I didn't feel a sense of panic, not even a fear that my son could be hurt. That emotion seemed a distant thing now. I knew I could save him, but the revelation was an academic thing. It was there in the cool sensation that came off Gladys and fed through my skin and into my veins.

This was the moment when I would normally grow a handy demon arm and throw myself into battle.

That's not how it would go this day. I wasn't putting my body into this fight. It was my soul that would win this day, and it meshed with Gladys.

Now I understood what Duffy had meant. Gladys was angry. She didn't want to be used by the wizard. She wanted to wipe the wizard off the face of the Earth plane, to banish his soul forever for laying a single finger on her.

She'd been roiling in rage for over a decade with nowhere to put it. Now we knew where it belonged.

The human part of me understood that frustration. I'd been this angry, this wrathful, with nowhere to put it. I'd sat up late at night and wondered if it would go away if only I found someone I hated and watched the light die in their eyes, watched them plead and beg and find no mercy from me.

Except I really hadn't, but in this place Gladys had taken me to it felt like truth. I was protecting Fenrir because I was supposed to. He was part of the team. I wasn't feeling the maternal love I usually felt when I was near him, and it kind of felt good. I was cold, and that definitely felt good.

Before whatever the witch was sending my son's way could traverse space and time to inject him with the poison of her magic, I directed Gladys's blade her way and sent my will through.

A flare of blue light sparked from my sword and slashed through the witch.

Like really slashed through her. In an arc that split her in two. Pure satisfaction ran through me, and I knew I'd found the place for all my rage to go. It could go into her, into all of them.

Fenrir hit the ground as I waved Gladys again. The words she wanted me to say whispered along my skin, firing my blood and granting me the will I needed to make the words real.

"*Scutum praesidium.*" Then I heard a whooshing sound that let me know I'd gotten what I wanted—a shield around Evan and Fenrir.

My sword's rage pulsed through me, mixing with my own in a volcanic cocktail, and I couldn't hear what Fen was saying over the pounding through my head. Blood. I wanted it. Or she wanted it. It didn't matter in that moment. Fen and Evan didn't matter in the moment. What mattered was destroying every single one of these witches who wanted to use us to destroy the world. They thought they could use us to unleash Hell and make slaves of everyone we loved? We would show them.

Vaguely I understood that other things were going on around me, but my vision had narrowed to what Gladys wanted me to see—our enemies.

Every witch in the room had turned my way. They exchanged glances as though silently deciding how they would go about destroying the new threat.

A broad-shouldered witch hunched over as though gathering her strength.

I wanted to see what she would send my way. It was kind of like a cat playing with a mouse because I knew she couldn't hurt me. In that moment I was a magical god who could touch the powers of both Heaven and Hell through the energy Gladys had stored.

It was heady. It was intoxicating. It was fucking dangerous as hell.

The witch came up, throwing a massive ball of flames my way. I could feel the heat and wondered just how much strength she'd given up in her effort to prove she could take me out.

I simply held up a hand, whispering the words Gladys sent through my mouth, and it dissolved.

The witch's eyes went wide and I moved in on her, touching a single finger to her chest. "Bad girl. *Duratus*."

She froze where she stood, her whole body going to ice.

That was when the others seemed to realize I wasn't going down easy. Or at all.

They surrounded me and I let them since out of the corner of my vision I could see Rose had awakened her husband and they were working their way around, trying to stay out of the witches' sights.

They would help Fen and Evan. The shield I'd erected around my son and Evan would allow those of good will inside and keep everyone else out. I didn't have to watch over them. I could do what I wanted to. I could fight and kill so many of them. I could kill them all.

I let all thoughts of the people who should have been my priority drift right out of my head. The fact that I wasn't thinking of Fen and Evan should have been enough to warn me, but honestly, the rage felt good. I'd let my sorrow flow, allowed Trent and Gray to wring it out of me, but the anger was still a tidal wave waiting to be unleashed.

I did that now—let my fury unfurl in a slamming wave of death and pain and blood.

Twelve fucking years. They'd taken twelve years from me. They'd remade the world I'd fought to make safe, remade it into something completely unrecognizable. These bitches had forced the children I loved to run, to fight, to grow up far too soon.

So I cut them down. Every time they sent pain my way, Gladys and I gave it back to them threefold.

They took my life so I fucking took theirs.

Invincible. That was how I felt in that moment. I didn't need to be anything but vengeance. There was no softness in the magic that Gladys sent through me. There was rage and power and the absolute certainty that we would never be violated again. We would not be used. We would not be tricked.

I slaughtered them as they would have surely slaughtered me. I moved through, Gladys guiding my hand. When they tried to sneak back through the paintings, I sliced through anything that was left hanging out and reveled in the gasps of horror I could hear from the other side.

My gift to the witches—half-alive, soon-dead parts of their sisters. It was like prophecy. The witches at the Coven House would know this is what would happen to them eventually. They could run, but I would find them. I would stay in my cold fortress of rage until I'd killed them all.

I ran through them until only one remained.

Olivia.

She stood among the bodies, hands at her sides and eyes bled to black as we faced each other.

I could feel a fierce smile cross my face. "Hey, friend. You thinking of running?"

Liv's shoulders were back, her body tense, and I could have

sworn she was afraid of me.

I liked it.

"I don't know. You thinking of following me? You considering going to the Coven House and starting this war now?" Liv asked. "How long will that power of yours last? As far as I know, the sword can't keep this up forever. I take it my master bled on her during his experiments. It's the only thing that makes sense. You don't have a lick of magic in you but here you are whispering Latin words you couldn't pronounce before."

"I think she'll last long enough." I really wanted this fight. Of all the people who'd disappointed us, Liv was the worst. She knew how to twist our love, how to use it against us. "Just long enough to burn the Coven House to the ground with all of you in it. You want to see Hell so bad, Liv, I'll send you there and I'll send Myrddin with you. You can worship him all you like down there and then I'll lock the door so you can't ever get out."

"You would do the same thing Myrddin wants to do?" Liv asked, tension ratcheting up as she obviously built up power. She was stalling, but I was confident. "You would close off Hell from the Earth plane? It's okay if you do it, right?"

"I think I'll follow Gladys's lead on this one," I vowed.

"You can't win, Kelsey," Liv said with a shaky laugh. "If you do what the sword tells you to, you lose yourself. Just like I did. We destroy each other, and while you might stay standing, you won't ever forgive yourself. You're caught in her web, but when you come down and realize what you've done, you'll be broken. And that's the best I could hope for now."

Her hands came up, and she unleashed pain on me. Everything she had, and I waved it away. I could feel the power in her onslaught, and I simply brushed past her.

Poor Olivia. She'd given up her soul for that power and I was going to kill her like she was a bug I was stepping on. She was as insignificant as her sisters. Only Myrddin mattered, and she was a stone I would step on to get to him.

"Mom! Mom, please!"

I saw the fear hit Liv's eyes as she tried one last time, sending out weak sparks. She hit her knees, skin pale and hands shaking, and her defeat was…nothing because she wasn't the one I truly wanted to kill.

I wanted Myrddin's throat in my hands, squeezing the life out of him.

One more kill and then I would go through one of the portals and I would slaughter everyone in that Coven House. Myrddin would be the last. I would make him suffer before I sent him to Hell.

I drew Gladys back as Liv looked up at me, resignation in her eyes.

"I always knew you would be the reason I died," she said with a snarl.

The impulse to shove Gladys through her chest had my hand raised before I could breathe.

"Mom! I don't know what to do. Please help me." Fen's tortured voice clawed through the comfortable fog of arrogance and rage I found myself cloaked in. I'd drawn it around me because it felt so much fucking better than horror and guilt and fear. "Please."

But my son was begging me.

"Do it, Kelsey. You know you've always wanted to," Liv taunted.

I had. I'd always known she would turn on me. And she was right. I could feel the power starting to wane. Not too much, but enough that Gladys was worried we wouldn't be able to finish them all off if we waited too long.

Or I could use that power to open the portal and follow the Days to their Heavenly hidey-hole.

Or you could kill the wizard and then the Days can stay wherever they fucking want. They deserved it. They ran.

That wasn't my voice. It sounded like mine, but it was Gladys, and not the one I knew. This Gladys had spent twelve plus years stewing with Myrddin's blood working on her, influencing her the way he did with every creature he came in contact with.

But don't forget—you count, too, Hunter. She does nothing without your good hand to guide her.

Duffy had told me that she was angry, that I had to temper her.

What if what I felt wasn't Gladys? What if it was something else? She couldn't resist the call of that darkness, but maybe I could.

I could go one of two ways. I could kill Liv, slice her through and give Gladys more power, then we could absolutely challenge Myrddin. But the prophecy had told me this wasn't my fight.

Or I could have faith.

Duffy had shown me Liv wasn't irredeemable. He'd shown me I could save her if I only saw past the rage that flooded me.

I'd killed a dozen witches and the rage wasn't gone. No. It had fed off the violence, and it would need more. That rage was toxic. It was a drug that could consume my life, my soul. When I ran out of victims who "deserved" it, the rage would still want more, still push me to greater and greater evil because rage could not be dissipated by violence.

It had to be fought with something more. Love. Faith. Compassion.

My son needed me.

I felt the moment Gladys realized I wasn't giving in. I swear that sword huffed in my hand and gave up one last spell.

"*Somnum*," I said.

Liv's eyes flared before she fell over in a deep sleep.

I wouldn't have to worry about her for a while, but I did have a problem. Fenrir was crying as he held Evan, her skin a sickly pale, something dark and oily coating her lips.

Goddess how I wished for the cold because my love came rushing back and along with it the desperation for this girl to live.

"I didn't know... I didn't know what else to do," Fen said.

I looked over and Christopher's sleeve was rolled up, that oily substance on his wrist.

"You gave her your blood," I whispered.

Black tears pooled in Christopher's eyes. "I couldn't see another way. She was dying. I sent Rose for the king's blood but Evangeline's heart stopped. I had seconds. Fenrir... I couldn't let Fenrir lose her."

Consequences. Duffy had warned us. There was a reason primals never shared blood.

"I have it." Rose ran in, carrying the thermos Daniel had sent with us. She stopped when she saw her husband. "What have you done?"

"Give me the blood, Rose. We'll get it in her and see if her father's blood can counter whatever primal blood is going to do to her." I took the blood from Rose and handed her Gladys. She was a companion. Gladys liked companions. I didn't think she would go psychotic on me for letting Rose hold her. I dropped to my knees and opened the thermos. "Is she alive?"

I had to ask because Evan really didn't look alive.

"I can hear her heartbeat but it's slow," Fenrir said, his hands clutching her as though he could physically keep her soul here.

I tipped the thermos and managed to get some blood into Evan's mouth.

She immediately started drinking, and I breathed a shallow sigh of relief because she would live.

And we would face the consequences.

"Kelsey," a deep voice said. "What the fuck happened? Are you all right?"

"My mistress!"

Trent and Eddie stood among the throng of bodies, Casey beside them.

He turned and saw Liv. "Oh, god. Oh, god, no."

He dropped to his knees, and I could feel his heart break.

"She's alive." I wasn't sure which tragedy to deal with first. Now that I didn't have Gladys's power running through me I was back to being overwhelmed, back to caring about everything.

Not caring had been so tempting. Power with one purpose and none of the horrible human emotions involved.

That was Myrddin Emrys. That ruthless will—devoid of love and vulnerability—was what we were up against.

I'd felt his utterly addictive power, and I would have to pull it out of Liv.

Evan coughed and sat up, pushing the thermos aside. "What happened?"

Trent rushed over to me, panic in his gaze as he took me by the shoulders and looked me up and down. "Are you all right? We couldn't get back. Eddie tried and tried but we couldn't get through until now."

"I guess I killed enough of them to break the wards." I let him hold me and breathed him in, letting his closeness soothe me.

"I was on the sword and then I was here," Evan was saying.

Fen pressed the thermos to her lips again. "Take more."

She pushed it away. "No. Eww. I don't need it. I feel fine."

"What has happened to the princess's hair?" Eddie stood beside me, looking to Evan.

Sure enough, a big portion of her auburn hair had gone a pitch black, and I would have sworn she was far paler than normal.

"It doesn't matter," Fen swore. "You're fine. You're alive. And hey, you always said you wanted to color it."

Evan was staring at a long strand of midnight hair. "Yeah. It's fine. I'm fine. I'm sure taking Dad's blood stopped whatever transformation was going to take place. I feel fine. I do. Christopher, thank you."

Fen stood and picked Evan up, not caring a bit that he was naked. "Yes, thank you. She wouldn't be here without you, Father. I will never be able to repay you."

Christopher shook his head, and it was easy to see he was torn. "I hope you still feel that way over time. Evan...well, I pray the king's blood works as you hope it will."

We all did.

"Why is there a hellhound here, mistress?" Eddie frowned.

"His name is Puff," Evan said as Fen started taking her back to their rooms. "Come on, Puff! Eww, don't lick that. We don't know where that's been."

Sure enough, Puff was reveling in the chaos. He was running through the bodies like they were a field of daisies.

Eddie took off after Puff, vowing to clean him and the room up and swearing that his sweet brownie staff was going to require therapy.

And probably some whisky-soaked cream.

"Kelsey? What the actual hell? I'm going to kill Tix." Gray stood in the middle of the bodies, his hands fisted on his hips. "Puff, don't you eat that witch."

Eddie finally managed to scoop the puppy up. "I will handle the situation, Lord Sloane. Should I find a bed for Olivia?"

I moved to join Gray, Trent following me. "Nope. We need two crates. One for the hell beast and one for the puppy. You should make sure Liv's dampens magic. And that it's totally uncomfortable. It's cool. You've got probably until morning before she wakes up. I hit her with a hell of a spell."

"You worked magic?" Gray asked.

I shrugged and went on my toes to kiss him. "It was more like Gladys soaked up some Myrddin and spat it all back out through me. It was a lot. Weirdly, I feel better. Less murdery than usual."

"Well, probably because you killed an entire coven," he replied, shaking his head at all the chaos.

"She spared Liv." Trent moved in behind me. "Apparently we have a lot to talk about over dinner. I don't guess you need the reports Nate sent."

"Nope. I know who did it and why." A thought suddenly occurred to me. "We should probably destroy those paintings."

That was when every painting in the room seemed to explode. There was a cracking sound and then gray smoke came through, followed by what seemed like a hundred little projectiles. Casey covered Liv with his body and the boys closed ranks around me.

I got ready to fight again, but when I looked the paintings were burned out, holes in the middle of all of them.

I glanced around at the fallout.

"Did they blow them up from the other side?" Trent asked. "This looks like part of a kitchen cabinet. I used to have these in my apartment at the Council building. How weird is that?"

Someone's curtains had blown in, too.

"Yeah, that's weird, but we're burning them anyway. I guess they really didn't want me to come through." That had to be the explanation.

"I'm going to wait for Rufus to awaken." Christopher had taken his wife's hand. "I must explain why I have broken our highest law."

Gray moved to him, sidestepping a couple of bodies. "You have been forced to feed the princess?"

Well, I should have known the prophet would have seen that. It meant those consequences likely weren't over and would have far-reaching effects.

Christopher nodded.

"I will speak to Rufus," Gray promised. "There will be no punishment. This event was always going to come to pass. He will listen to me." He glanced back at Trent and me. "Take her out and feed her. I want her ready for tonight. She got to take all her anxiety out. I don't have a handy coven to kill so I'll take it out a different way. And Kelsey, I'll need the full story."

"Will do."

It was a good thing I got to eat first because this was going to be a long one.

Chapter Twenty-Two

"**Y**ou did what?"

I practically screamed the words. And I probably shouldn't have because I was talking to the Queen of all Vampire, but she'd shocked the holy fuck out of me.

And explained why Eddie had to clean up a variety of household objects along with all those witches.

Zoey frowned, obviously surprised at my reaction to her news. "Well, I thought you would enjoy the irony. I blew up the fucker's house on my way out. He might have gotten that grimoire back, but he's going to be digging it out of the rubble for days."

"Baby, maybe you should remember how you killed two thirds of the Profane and a whole bunch of other witches," Trent pointed out. "I believe you called it great stress relief. I think the queen was pissed Myrddin's spy had killed her son."

It was four days later, and we'd finally made our way back to Frelsi after doing a little research and ensuring the Under was safe again. Evan seemed normal with the exception of her hair being streaked with black and her skin being paler than normal. She'd been trying to train her hellhound. She'd been quiet and withdrawn, insisting nothing was wrong.

I hoped she would talk to her mother.

Lee grinned from his place on the couch, showing off his newly earned fangs. "I'm happy to say my murder didn't take. Although I would highly recommend not getting driven through by a sword."

Evan huffed and rolled her eyes. "Such a baby. I impaled myself, and I'm not a latent vampire."

She sat opposite her brother, Fen lying back with his head on her lap and Puff half asleep on his chest. Evan stroked a hand over both her pets' heads, keeping them calm. Fenrir had been even more overly protective than normal since he'd held her as she'd died.

"I think I had it worse," Lee complained. "It was really terrible, and then when I woke up Mom was all kinds of dramatic. She was all crying and offering to let me eat her." He shuddered. "It was awful. But then I ate like ten witches and I felt better."

"You did not have it worse," Evan countered. "I had to shove my body on a sword. All you had to do was stand there and let the dude murder you."

"Yes, Evan," her papa said with a frown. "Lee was murdered. You did it to yourself."

"See, Papa understands." Evan stroked Puff's back.

"Nope." Fen didn't open his eyes. "He's horrified, and so are the rest of us."

"I would have hoped someone would think it was brave," Evan replied with a long-suffering sigh. "I bet if Rhys had done it everyone would be praising him for his sacrifice."

Rhys touched his chest as though he couldn't even consider it. "I would never do such a thing. I would have found another way. Of course I would have known that it was probably one of the gnomes the minute I walked into the gardens. I would have recognized the plants associated with the witches' ointment. I should have gone."

"Sure, kid. Next time you can go and solve the murder," I offered. I was feeling for Evan. "And your sister was incredibly brave. We were surrounded and had no way out. Without Evan, we would have been taken into custody." I looked over to the queen. "Have you thought about that? We were supposed to be in that building when you blew it up. If Liv had been successful, we would be dead."

The queen gasped, paling. "No. No. I hadn't thought of that."

The king finally added his two cents. He stood near his partner, listening to everything that was said. "Kelsey, come on. You were never going to let Liv take you through one of those portals. Stop trying to make Z feel bad. If you had the knowledge and the tools, you would have done the same thing."

Probably, but he was ignoring an important point. "Sarah left a map. How are we supposed to get to her if Zoey blew up the damn portal she left behind?"

Evan and I had been planning to give the royals and their general, Sasha Federov, a full debrief concerning everything Duffy had shown us in the vision. I'd planned on a whole professional presentation in whatever passed for a conference room in Frelsi. Instead, the queen had greeted us with a lovely buffet and a gleeful recounting of how she'd blown the shit out of the only way to find Mia Day.

Lee's expression had lost its devil-may-care look, and he sat up straight. "You're telling me Mia is out there and we no longer have a way to get to her."

I took a long breath and caught control of my temper because this was beyond serious for Lee Donovan-Quinn. Lee and Mia had been connected since they were children. They'd been the best of friends, and I'd thought they might find that affection turning to romantic love as they'd grown. Now I knew it absolutely would have because Lee was a vampire and Mia a companion. The fact that his companion was out there and he couldn't get to her would make the vampire in Lee crazy.

"I'm going to find a way," I vowed.

"You really think Mia is the weapon the prophecy talked about?" Daniel asked.

We'd spent the last few days in the Under going over the prophecy with the primals. We'd all come to the same conclusion. "Mia Day is absolutely necessary to any battle Lee and Dean will have with Myrddin."

"He wants to force her to marry him," Evan said.

A low growl came from Lee's throat, and his fangs weren't just for show.

Fen sighed. "Baby, I told you we should ease him into that information."

"He should know." Evan's expression had gone stubborn, and she moved her shoulders as if she was uncomfortable, but she made no move to force Fen and Puff off. "I was there. Duffy showed us that for a reason. He wanted us to know Myrddin thinks Mia will be powerful enough to be his queen. He wants her magic."

"He won't have it." Lee stood, his hands in fists. "I will never allow him to touch her."

Daniel was at his son's side very quickly. "Take a deep breath. I know how you feel, son. Let's go and hunt before you take this out on the furniture."

Lee nodded and they moved to the door that would lead them out into the city.

Rhys watched the door close with a sigh. "He was always obsessed with Mia. We should have known he was a latent. I'm not sure how he's going to handle the fact that now we know she's alive and out there. Especially if she waited for him. We all know he didn't wait for her."

Hopefully Mia had been living it up in some tiny village on a minor Heavenly plane so Lee wouldn't feel the guilt that would come with knowing he hadn't been faithful. Personally I don't care much about virginity, but I know how I would have felt if Trent or Gray had started a relationship with someone, or a whole bunch of non-relationships with many, many people. Many.

"I didn't know those weird scorch marks were supposed to be a map." Zoey paced, tears in her eyes. "Obviously I would never have blown up our only shot at finding Sarah and Felix and Mia. I was only thinking about hurting Myrddin."

"Baby, we'll find a way." Devinshea put an arm around his wife. "I promise. We always find a way."

Evan tilted her head up, brows rising. "Are you going to put her out of her misery?"

Trent brought me a plate of Albert's mini cookies. "You really should, or you don't deserve these cookies. If the queen is too upset, we'll have to go back to our place, and Eddie's spent so much time puppy proofing the house that he hasn't been able to cook. You'll be eating peanut butter and jelly sandwiches."

It wasn't like I hated PB&Js, but Albert had made a bunch of tasty stuff and I wanted to try it all. "Fine. There might be another way. I'm pretty sure that's the real reason Duffy wanted me to see what he showed me. Sneaky little angel."

"He was a gnome and he was an angel?" Rhys asked.

"He was a warrior gnome," Evan said with a grin. "He's Kelsey's guardian angel, and his axe is almost as tall as he is. I liked him."

"And you believed him?" Rhys asked. "I'm sorry. I'm only asking because I've never seen a Fae creature become an angel."

"You've never seen an angel at all," his mother chided. "If your sister says she met one, I believe her. What did he say? Does he know the Days?"

"He's one of them," I explained. "He took Jude's place. He's now the embodiment of faith, and he's a good one. I feel comfortable with him on my side. He's sneaky, too. I've thought a lot about this and come to the conclusion that he didn't need us to see what had happened with the Days. He already knew you were going to blow up the building. He told me not to kill you."

Zoey's lips pursed. "Well, that's a bit over the top."

At least she trusted me. "So if he knew, then he wanted to show me two things. One, he wanted me to see Liv before she lost a piece of her soul."

Dev nodded. "She saved Sarah and Felix and Mia. She risked her own life and place in the coven to give them a chance. Have you talked to her about it?"

I winced at the thought. "Uhm, she's pretty much only using four letter words with me right now, and I don't mean the word *love*."

Liv was pissed. She'd woken up in a magical prison and not liked it one bit. My bestie and I had some things to work out, but I knew I couldn't leave her like this. I had to find that bit of her soul and shove that sucker back in because I did not like this Liv. She was difficult and had a big old potty mouth.

And she was mean to Casey, but he seemed to have turned a corner. When she threw bile his way, he simply sat and took it and told her he loved her no matter what.

"Okay, so the angel thinks we should save Liv," Dev said as though trying to process it. "You think it's okay to keep one of the Profane here in Frelsi? I'm sure someone has pointed out what an awful idea that is, right?"

I'd solved that problem, so I waved him off. "Oh, I have a new jailer for her. We're taking her there when Gray gets back. She's going to be hanging out at the House of Sloane where I've been assured as one of Hell's finest ladies, everyone will follow my orders or Tix will roast them. Literally. They make their enemies into jerky."

Fen groaned. "It's not the same."

I disagreed, and I wasn't trying it. "So Liv will be hanging out in Hell and I have a lead on where Myrddin keeps the souls he steals. Unfortunately that's also on the Hell plane, so we're going to descend while you guys handle the whole finding the door to the Heaven plane part."

Zoey's brows rose. "Well, that seems odd. You're going to need a thief. I'm your best bet."

This was the hard part since I knew some of Dev's relatives had been poorly behaved while we'd been gone. "The door is somewhere in the Fae lands. Oliver Day specifically said there was another way in. That was the other thing Duffy wanted to show me. When Oliver was helping get the Days to their sanctuary, he said something about the Fae being good at hiding doors and opening veils. Given the fact that the Fae *sitheins* attached to the Earth plane are the only inner plane Fae lands, therefore the only ones with a possible connection to the Heaven plane..."

Dev's head fell back on a groan. "I have to see my mother."

"And your brother," Zoey added. "Well, that's going to be fun."

I wouldn't bet on it.

But then Gray was in the room, and he flashed us a megawatt smile. "Hey, Kelsey mine. Everything is set. I'll take our guest to her new accommodations tonight and then we'll descend in a couple of days. But I want some time with you here."

"I'm going with you guys," Evan announced.

"Evan," Dev said with a hurt expression. "You just got back. And you were injured."

"And now I'm fine. Fen won't let his mom go alone, and I go with Fen," Evan said. "Besides, she's going to need a thief, and Mom's not available. That means Lee's going downstairs, too."

"I was actually going to suggest that." Rhys stood. "I don't think Lee should go to Faery. It went poorly last time, and the minute he thinks someone is holding out on him he'll lose control because this is about Mia. Sasha can come with us to Faery. You know how Grandmother loves an attractive vampire."

"Ewww," Evan said. "See, Hell will be so much nicer."

I doubted that.

But now we had a plan. And I had my guys. Gray got into my space. He reached out to bring Trent into the circle. "You two eat yet?"

"No," Trent said, but his lips curled up. "She's been too busy yelling at the queen."

"Ah, yeah, the blow-up thing," Gray agreed. "Well, we're doing takeout because I mean to spend tonight with the two of you. It's time to get serious about taking care of our woman."

"I agree." Trent winked my way.

At least my night was looking up.

Liv, Kelsey, and the rest of the gang, will return in *The Rebel Witch*, coming 2023.

Author's Note

I'm often asked by generous readers how they can help get the word out about a book they enjoyed. There are so many ways to help an author you like. Leave a review. If your e-reader allows you to lend a book to a friend, please share it. Go to Goodreads and connect with others. Recommend the books you love because stories are meant to be shared. Thank you so much for reading this book and for supporting all the authors you love!

Discover the Faery Story Trilogy
By Lexi Blake
Now available

Bound
Book 1

A stranger in a strange land

Megan Starke has given up believing in knights in shining armor. With an unrewarding job and a failed marriage, no one would confuse her life with a fairy tale. No one is coming to save the day or carry her off to a romantic fantasy. So when she wakes up in a magical world and discovers she is to be the grand prize in a fierce and bloody tournament, she isn't sure if she's having a sexy dream or a horrible nightmare.

Two kings without a kingdom

Beckett and Cian were raised to be the saviors of their people. Prepared all their lives to lead the Seelie Fae, prophecy proclaimed they would find a bondmate whose love would complete them and unleash their magical powers. But the thrust of a traitor's blade stole that future and now it threatens to take their lives. Struggling in exile, their glorious destiny has become a curse. Unless they can find the perfect woman to save them, they will descend into madness and ruin. When all hope seems lost, Beck sees Meg and knows she's the key to their salvation.

An epic battle begins

In a world filled with dethroned kings, upwardly mobile vampires, and dangerous, feline-loving hags, Meg will need all her strength to survive. Finding herself caught between Beck and Cian, she's willing to do whatever it takes to claim her happily ever after.

* * * *

Beast
Book 2

A playboy who needs to grow up

Fresh from his latest tabloid scandal, vampire playboy Dante Dellacourt has been given an ultimatum. Either he takes a consort and settles down, or his family will disown him. Unwilling to lose everything he has, he reluctantly agrees to find a wife. Marriage is just another kind of contract, after all. No one said anything about love being a part of the bargain.

An outcast who has only known hardship

Exiled by her pack, Kaja is a werewolf without a home. Her life was never easy in the frozen tundra she grew up in, but it was familiar. Waking up in a foreign landscape, surrounded by bright lights, loud noises, and far too many people has left her overwhelmed. Frightened and with no one to trust, she savagely fights to get free of this strange new world.

A passion strong enough to change them both

Called to defend the gnomes of the marketplace, Dante is almost blinded by the radiant light coming off the fierce werewolf. Kaja glows like no consort he has ever seen. Gorgeous and wild, she calls to him in ways he had not dreamed possible. For Kaja, she finds in Dante a man unlike any she has ever known. They could not be more different, but she finds him irresistible.

In order to claim his werewolf bride, Dante must first discover how to overcome their differences. Will he tame his ferocious beauty, or will she unleash his inner beast?

* * * *

Beauty
Book 3

The princess in the tower

In one horrifying night, Bronwyn Finn lost her family, her kingdom, and the princes who had haunted her dreams for years. Left alone, years pass as she fights for survival and craves revenge against the uncle who took everything from her. But she's never forgotten her Dark Ones. Now she hides along with her guardian, but the war rages ever closer.

Two dark princes

A tragedy marred Lach and Shim's lives. The future kings of the Unseelie Fae are obsessed with finding their promised wife— Bronwyn. Lach and Shim have never stopped believing that Bronwyn is their mate. She is the bond that connects the halves of their shared soul.

A destiny that will change a kingdom

With the blessing of the renegade kings, Beck and Cian Finn, Lach and Shim begin a dangerous quest to find their bride before Torin and his hags take her life.

Across two planes, a war will rage. Lives will be lost. Love will be found. And the Seelie Fae will welcome their true kings home.

The Dom Who Came in from the Cold

Masters and Mercenaries: Reloaded, Book 5
By Lexi Blake
Coming February 21, 2023

Kyle Hawthorne once believed his future would be a job in the private sector—a simple, normal life. Fate had other plans and he wound up in the military. Some newly discovered talents caught the eye of the CIA, and in no time he was working with a covert team. He found himself in a relationship with fellow operative, Julia—until she turned out to be the enemy. When her betrayal was uncovered, things got bloody and Kyle returned home broken, searching for a chance to walk the road not taken.

MaeBe Vaughan has never been interested in normal. Her happy place is a dark corner of the Internet, where she disrupts all the bad guys. She has a great circle of friends and a full life. She doesn't need a man. Until Kyle Hawthorne walked into her life. He's all wrong for her. Surly. Damaged. His uncle is her boss. But she couldn't help getting close to him. When his past threatened her safety, Kyle walked out without saying good-bye.

Kyle will do anything to keep MaeBe safe. He faked his death, hid in the middle of nowhere, and watched over her from afar. But when Julia resurfaces, he knows that to protect MaeBe, he'll have to get close. So close that if they manage to survive, he will never let her go.

About Lexi Blake

New York Times bestselling author Lexi Blake lives in North Texas with her husband and three kids. Since starting her publishing journey in 2010, she's sold over three million copies of her books. She began writing at a young age, concentrating on plays and journalism. It wasn't until she started writing romance that she found success. She likes to find humor in the strangest places and believes in happy endings.

Connect with Lexi online:

Facebook: Lexi Blake
Twitter: authorlexiblake
Website: www.LexiBlake.net
Instagram: www.instagram.com

www.ingramcontent.com/pod-product-compliance
Lightning Source LLC
Chambersburg PA
CBHW020224260626
47156CB00002B/531